Million

SUSAN MEIER
MICHELLE DOUGLAS
DIANNE DRAKE

MILLS
BOON

First Published in Great Britain 2017
By Mills & Boon, an imprint of HarperCollins*Publishers*
1 London Bridge Street, London, SE1 9GF

MOTHERS IN A MILLION © 2017 Harlequin Books S. A.

A Father For Her Triplets, *First Comes Baby...* and *A Child To Heal Their Hearts* were first published in Great Britain by Harlequin (UK) Limited.

A Father For Her Triplets © 2013 Linda Susan Meier
First Comes Baby... © 2013 Michelle Douglas
A Child To Heal Their Hearts © 2013 Dianne Despain

ISBN: 978-0-263-92960-7

05-0417

Printed and bound in Spain
by CPI, Barcelona

A FATHER FOR HER TRIPLETS

BY
SUSAN MEIER

Susan Meier spent most of her twenties thinking she was a job-hopper—until she began to write and realised everything that had come before was only research! One of eleven children, with twenty-four nieces and nephews and three kids of her own, Susan has had plenty of real-life experience watching romance blossom in unexpected ways. She lives in western Pennsylvania with her wonderful husband, Mike, three children and two over-fed, well-cuddled cats, Sophie and Fluffy. you can visit Susan's website at: www.susanmeier.com.

For the real Owen, Helaina and Claire...Thanks for being so adorable I had to write about you.

CHAPTER ONE

THE BEST PART OF BEING rich was, of course, the toys. There wasn't anything Wyatt McKenzie wanted that he didn't have.

Gliding along the winding road that led to Newland, Maryland, on a warm April morning, he revved the engine of his big black motorcycle and grinned. He loved the toys.

The second best thing about being rich was the power. Not that he could start a war, or control the lives of the people who depended upon him for work and incomes. The power he loved was the power he had over his own schedule.

Take right now, for instance. His grandmother had died the month before, and it was time to clear out her house for sale. The family could have hired someone, but Grandma McKenzie had a habit of squirreling away cash and hiding jewelry. When none of her family heirloom jewelry was found in her Florida town house, Wyatt's mother believed it was still in her house in Maryland. And Wyatt had volunteered to make the thousand-mile trip back "home" to search her house.

His mother could have come. She'd actually know more about what she was looking for. But his divorce had become final the week before. After four years fighting over money, his now ex-wife had agreed to settle for thirty per-cent interest in his company.

His company. She'd cheated on him. Lied to him. Tried to undermine his authority. And she got thirty percent of everything *he'd* worked for? It wasn't right.

But it also hurt. They'd been married for four years before the trouble started. He'd thought she was happy.

He needed some time to get over his anger with her and the hurt, so he could get on with the rest of his life. Look-ing for jewelry a thousand miles away was as good an ex-cuse as any to take a break, relax and forget about the past.

So he'd given himself an entire month vacation simply by telling his assistant he was leaving and wouldn't be back for four weeks. He didn't have to remind Arnie that his gram had died. He didn't have to say his divorce was final. He didn't have to make any excuse or give any rea-son at all. He just said, "I'm going. See you next month."

He revved the engine again as he swung the bike off the highway and onto the exit ramp for Newland, the town he'd grown up in. After buying the company that published his graphic novels, he'd moved his whole family to Florida to enjoy life in the sun. His parents had made trips home. Gram had spent entire summers here. But Wyatt hadn't even been home for a visit in fifteen long years. Now, he was back. A changed man. A *rich* man. Not the geeky kid everybody "liked" but sort of made fun of. Not the skinny nerd who never got picked for the team in gym class. But a six-foot-one, two-hundred-pound guy who not only worked out, he'd also turned his geekiness into a fortune.

He laughed. He could only imagine the reception he was about to get.

Two sweeping turns took him to Main Street, then one final turn took him to his grandmother's street. He saw the aging Cape Cod immediately. Gables and blue shutters accented the white siding. A row of overgrown hedges bordered the driveway, giving a measure of privacy from the almost identical Cape Cod next door. The setup was cute. Simple. But that was the way everybody in Newland lived. Simply. They had nice, quiet lives. Not like the hustle and bustle of work and entertainment—cocktail parties and picnics, Jet Skis and fund-raisers—he and his family lived with on the Gulf Coast.

He roared into the driveway and cut the engine. After tucking his helmet under his arm, he rummaged in his shirt pocket for his sunglasses. He slid them on, walked to the old-fashioned wooden garage door and yanked it open with a grunt. No lock or automatic garage door for his grandmother. Newland was safe as well as quiet. Another thing very different from where he currently lived. The safety of a small town. Knowing your neighbors. Liking your neighbors.

He missed that.

The stale scent of a closed-up garage wafted out to him, and he waved it away as he strode back to his bike.

"Hey, Mithter."

He stopped, glanced around. Not seeing anybody, he headed to his bike again.

"Hey, Mithter."

This time the voice was louder. When he stopped, he followed the sound of the little-boy lisp and found himself looking into the big brown eyes of a kid who couldn't have been more than four years old. Standing in a small gap in the hedges, he grinned up at Wyatt.

"Hi."

"Hey, kid."

"Is that your bike?"

"Yeah." Wyatt took the two steps over to the little boy and pulled back the hedge so he could see him. His light brown hair was cut short and spiked out in a few directions. Smudges of dirt stained his T-shirt. His pants hung on skinny hips.

He craned his head back and blinked up at Wyatt. "Can I have a wide?"

"A wide?"

He pointed at the bike. "A wide."

"Oh, you mean *ride*." He looked at his motorcycle. "Um." He'd never taken a kid on his bike. Hell, he was barely ever around kids—except the children of his staff when they had company outings.

"O-wen…"

The lyrical voice floated over to Wyatt and his breath stalled.

Missy. Missy Johnson. Prettiest girl in his high school. Granddaughter of his gram's next-door neighbor. The girl he'd coached through remedial algebra just for the chance to sit close to her.

"Owen! Honey? Where are you?"

Soft and melodious, her sweet voice went through Wyatt like the first breeze of spring.

He glanced down at the kid. "I take it you're Owen."

The little boy grinned up at him.

The hedge shuffled a bit and suddenly there she stood, her long yellow hair caught in a ponytail.

In the past fifteen years, he'd changed everything about himself, while she looked to have been frozen in time. Her blue-gray eyes sparkled beneath thick black lashes. Her full lips bowed upward as naturally as breathing. Her peaches and cream complexion glowed like a teenager's even though she was thirty-three. A blue T-shirt and jeans shorts accented her small waist and round hips. The legs below her shorts were as perfect as they'd been when she was cheering for the Newland High football team.

Memories made his blood rush hot through his veins. They'd gotten to know each other because their grandmothers were next-door neighbors. And though she was prom queen, homecoming queen, snowball queen and head cheerleader and he was the king of the geeks, he'd wanted to kiss her from the time he was twelve.

Man, he'd had a crush on her.

She gave him a dubious look. "Can I help you?"

She didn't know who he was?

He grinned. That was priceless. Perfect.

"You don't remember me?"

"Should I?"

"Well, I was the reason you passed remedial algebra."

Her eyes narrowed. She pondered for a second. Then she gasped. "Wyatt?"

He rocked back on his heels with a chuckle. "In the flesh."

Her gaze fell to his black leather jacket and jeans, as well as the black helmet he held under his arm.

She frowned, as if unable to reconcile the sexy rebel he now dressed like with the geek she knew in high school. "Wyatt?"

Taking off his sunglasses so she could get a better look at his face, he laughed. "I've sort of changed."

She gave him another quick once-over and everything inside of Wyatt responded. As if he were still the teenager with the monster crush on her, his gut tightened. His rushing blood heated to boiling. His natural instinct to pounce flared.

Then he glanced down at the little boy.

And back at Missy. "Yours?"

She ruffled Owen's spiky hair. "Yep."

"Mom! Mom!" A little blond girl ran over. Tapping on Missy's knee, she whined, "Lainie hit me."

A dark-haired little girl raced up behind her. "Did not!"

Wyatt's eyebrows rose. *Three kids?*

Missy met his gaze. "These are my kids, Owen, Helaina and Claire." She tapped each child's head affectionately. "They're triplets."

Had he been chewing gum, he would have swallowed it. "Triplets?"

She ruffled Owen's hair fondly. "Yep."

Oh, man.

"You and your husband must be so…" *terrified, overworked, tired* "…proud."

Missy Johnson Brooks turned all three kids in the direction of the house. "Go inside. I'll be in in a second to make lunch." Then she faced the tall, gorgeous guy across the hedge.

Wyatt McKenzie was about the best looking man she'd ever seen in real life. With his supershort black hair cut so close it looked more like a shadow on his head than hair, plus his broad shoulders and watchful brown eyes, he literally rivaled the men in movies.

Her heart rattled in her chest as she tried to pull herself together. It wasn't just weird to see Wyatt McKenzie all grown up and sexy. He brought back some memories she would have preferred stay locked away.

Shielding her eyes from the noonday sun, she said, "My husband and I are divorced."

"Oh, I'm sorry."

She shrugged. "That's okay. How about you?"

His face twisted. "Divorced, too."

His formerly squeaky voice was low and deep, so sexy that her breathing stuttered and heat coiled through her middle.

She stifled the urge to gasp. Surely she wasn't going

to let herself be attracted to him? She'd already gone that route with a man. Starry-eyed and trusting, she'd married a gorgeous guy who made her pulse race, and a few years later found herself deserted with three kids. Oh, yeah. She'd learned that lesson and didn't care to repeat it.

She cleared her throat. "I heard a rumor that you got superrich once you left here."

"I did. I write comic books."

"And you make that much money drawing?"

"Well, drawing, writing scripts..." His sexy smile grew. "And owning the company."

She gaped at him, but inside she couldn't stop a swoon. If he'd smiled at her like that in high school she probably would have fainted. Thank God she was older and wiser and knew how to resist a perfect smile. "You *own* a company?"

"And here I thought the gossip mill in Newland was incredibly efficient."

"It probably is. In the past few years I haven't had time to pay much attention."

He glanced at the kids. One by one they'd ambled back to the hedge and over to her, where they currently hung around her knees. "I can see that."

Slowly, carefully, she raised her gaze to meet his. He wasn't the only one who had changed since high school. She might not be rich but she had done some things. She wasn't just raising triplets; she also had some big-time money possibilities. "I own a company, too."

His grin returned. Her face heated. Her heart did something that felt like a somersault.

"Really?"

She looked away. She couldn't believe she was so attracted to him. Then she remembered that Wyatt was somebody special. Deep down inside he had been a nice guy, and maybe he still was underneath all that leather. But that only heightened her unease. If he wasn't, she didn't want her memories of the one honest, sweet guy in her life tainted by this sexy stranger. Worse, she didn't want him discovering too much about her past. Bragging about her company might cause him to ask questions that would bring up memories she didn't want to share.

She reined in her enthusiasm about her fledgling business. "It's a small company."

"Everybody starts small."

She nodded.

He smiled again, but looked at the triplets and motioned toward his motorcycle. "Well, I guess I better get my bike in the garage."

She took a step back, not surprised he wanted to leave. What sexy, gorgeous, bike-riding, company-owning guy wanted to be around a woman with kids? *Three* kids. Three superlovable kids who had a tendency to look needy.

Though she was grateful he was racing away, memories tripped over themselves in her brain. Him helping her with her algebra, and stumbling over asking her out. And her being unable to keep that date.

The urge to apologize for standing him up almost moved her tongue. But she couldn't say anything. Not without telling him things that would mortally embarrass her. "It was nice to see you."

He flashed that lethal grin. "It was nice to see you, too."

He let go of the hedge he'd been holding back. It sprang into place and he disappeared.

With the threat of the newcomer gone, the trips scrambled to the kitchen door and raced inside. She followed them, except she didn't stop in the kitchen. She strode through the house to the living room, where she fell to the sofa.

Realizing she was shaking, she picked up a pillow, put it on her knees and pressed her face to it. She should have known seeing someone she hadn't seen since graduation would take her back to the worst day in her life.

Her special day, graduation... Her dad had stopped at the bar on the way home from the ceremony. Drunk, he'd beaten her mom, ruined the graduation dress Missy had bought with her own money by tossing bleach on it, and slapped Althea, knocking her into a wall, breaking her arm.

Her baby sister, the little girl her mom had called a miracle baby and her dad had called a mistake, had been hit so hard that Missy had taken her to the hospital. Once they'd fixed up her arm, a social worker had peered into their emergency room cubicle.

"Where's your mom?"

"She's out for the night. I'm eighteen. I'm babysitting."

The social worker had given Missy a look of disbelief, so she'd produced her driver's license.

When the social worker was gone, Althea had glared at her. She wanted to tell the truth.

Missy had turned on her sister. "Do you want to end up in foster care? Or worse, have him beat Mom until she dies? Well, I don't."

And the secret had continued....

Her breath stuttered out. Her mom was dead now. Althea had left home. She'd enrolled in a university thousands of miles away, in California. She'd driven out of town and never looked back.

And their dad?

Well, he was "gone," too. Just not forgotten. He still ran the diner, but he spent every spare cent he had on alcohol and gambling. If he wasn't drunk, he was in Atlantic City. The only time Missy saw him was when he needed money.

A little hand fell to her shoulder. "What's wong, Mommy?"

Owen. With his little lisp and his big heart.

She pulled her face out of the pillow. "Nothing's wrong." She smiled, ruffled his short brown hair. "Mommy is fine."

She *was* fine, because after her divorce she'd figured out that she wasn't going to find a knight on a white horse who would rescue her. She had to save herself. Save her kids. Raise her kids in a home where they were never afraid or hungry.

After her ex drained their savings account and left her with three babies and no money, well, she'd learned that the men in her life didn't really care if kids were frightened and/or hungry. And the only person with the power to fix that was her.

So she had.

But she would never, ever trust a man again.

Not even sweet Wyatt.

Wyatt walked through the back door of his gram's house, totally confused.

Somehow in his memory he'd kept Missy an eighteen-year-old beauty queen. She might still look like an eighteen-year-old beauty queen, but she'd grown up. Moved on. Become a wife and mom.

He couldn't figure out why that confused him so much. He'd moved on. Gotten married. Gotten divorced. Just as she had. Why did it feel so odd that she'd done the same things he had?

His cell phone rang. He grabbed it from the pocket of his jeans. Seeing the caller ID of his assistant, he said, "Yeah, Arnie, What's up?"

"Nothing cxcept that the Wizard Awards were announced this morning and three of your stories are in!"

"Oh." He expected a thrill to shoot through him, but didn't get one. His mind was stuck on Missy. Something about her nagged at him.

"I thought you'd be happier."

Realizing he was standing there like a goof, not even talking to the assistant who'd called him, he said, "I am happy with the nominations. They're great."

"Well, that's because your books are great."

He grinned. His work *was* great. Not that he was vain, but a person had to have some confidence—

He stopped himself. Now he knew what was bothering him about Missy. *She'd stood him up.* They'd had a date graduation night and she'd never showed. In fact, she hadn't even come to his grandmother's house that whole summer. He hadn't seen her on the street. He'd spent June, July and August wondering, then left for college never knowing why she'd agreed to meet him at a party, but never showed.

He said, "Arnie, thanks for calling," then hung up the phone.

She owed him an explanation. Fifteen years ago, even if he'd seen her that summer, he would have been too embarrassed to confront her, ask her why she'd blown him off.

At thirty-three, rich, talented and successful, he found nothing was too difficult for him to confront. He might have lost one-third of his company to his ex-wife, but in the end he'd come to realize that their divorce had been nothing but business.

This was personal.

And he wanted to know.

CHAPTER TWO

THE NEXT MORNING Wyatt woke with a hangover. After he'd hung up on Arnie, he'd gone to the 7-Eleven for milk, bread, cheese and a case of beer. Deciding he wanted something to celebrate his award nominations, he'd added a bottle of cheap champagne. Apparently cheap champagne and beer weren't a good mix because his head felt like a rock. This was what he got for breaking his own hard-and-fast rule of moderation in all things.

Shrugging into a clean T-shirt and his jeans from the day before, he made a pot of coffee, filled a cup and walked out to the back porch for some fresh air.

From his vantage point, he could see above the hedge. Missy stood in her backyard, hanging clothes on a line strung between two poles beside a swing set. The night before he'd decided he didn't need to ask her why she'd stood him up. It was pointless. Stupid. What did he care about something that happened fifteen years ago?

Still, he remained on his porch, watching her. She didn't notice him. Busy fluffing out little T-shirts and pinning them to the line, she hadn't even heard him come outside.

In the silence of a small town at ten o'clock on a Tuesday morning in late April, when kids were in school and adults at work, he studied her pretty legs. The way her bottom rounded when she bent. The swing of her ponytail. It was hard to believe she was thirty-three, let alone the mother of triplets.

"Hey, Mithter."

His gaze tumbled down to the sidewalk at the bottom of the five porch steps. There stood Owen.

"Hey, kid."

"Wanna watch TV?"

"I don't have TV. My mom canceled the cable." He laughed and ambled down the steps. "Besides, don't you think your mom will be worried if you're gone?"

He nodded.

"So you should go home."

He shook his head.

Wyatt chuckled and finished his coffee. The kid certainly knew his mind. He glanced at the hedge, but from ground level he couldn't see Missy anymore. It seemed weird to yell for her to come get her son, but...

No buts about it. It *was* weird. And made it appear as if he was afraid to talk to her...or maybe becoming an introvert because one woman robbed him blind in a divorce settlement. He wasn't afraid of Missy. And he might not ever marry again, but he wasn't going to be an emotional cripple because of a divorce.

Reaching down, he took Owen's hand. "Come on." He walked him to the hedge, held it back so Owen could step through, then followed him into the next yard.

Little shirts and shorts billowed in the breeze, but the laundry basket and Missy were gone.

He could just leave the kid in the yard, explaining to Owen that he shouldn't come to his house anymore. But the little boy blinked up at him, with long black lashes over sad, puppy-dog eyes.

Wyatt's heart melted. "Okay. I'll take you inside."

Happy, Owen dropped his hand and raced ahead.

Climbing up the stairs, he yelled, "Hey, Mom! That man is here again."

Wyatt winced. Was it just him or did that make him sound like a stalker?

Missy opened the door. Owen scooted inside. Wyatt strolled over. He stopped at the bottom of the steps.

"Sorry about this." He looked up at her. His gaze cruised from her long legs, past her jeans shorts, to her short pink T-shirt and full breasts to her smiling face. Attraction rumbled through him. Though he would have liked to take a few minutes to enjoy the pure, unadulterated swell of desire, he squelched it. Not only was she a mom, but he was still in the confusing postdivorce stage. He didn't want a relationship, he wanted sex. He wasn't someone who should be trifling with a nice woman.

"Owen just sort of appeared at the bottom of my steps so I figured I'd better bring him home."

She frowned. "That's weird. He's never been a runner before."

"A runner?"

"A kid who just trots off. Usually he clings to my legs. But we've never had a man next door either." She smiled and nodded at his coffee cup. "Why don't you come up and I'll refill that."

The offer was sweet and polite. Plus, she wasn't looking at him as if he was intruding or crazy. Maybe it was smart to get back to having normal conversations with someone of the opposite sex. Even if it was just a friendly chat over a cup of coffee.

He walked up the steps. "Thanks. I could use a refill."

She led him into her kitchen. Her two little girls sat at the table coloring. The crowded countertop held bowls and spoons and ingredients he didn't recognize, as if Missy was cooking something. And Owen stood in the center of the kitchen, the lone male, looking totally out of place.

Missy motioned toward the table. "Have a seat."

Wyatt pulled a chair away from the table. The two little girls peeked up from their coloring books and grinned, but went back to their work without saying anything. Missy walked over with the coffeepot and filled his cup.

"So what are you cooking?"

"Gum paste."

That didn't sound very appetizing. "Gum paste?"

Taking the coffeepot back to the counter, she said, "To make flowers to decorate a cake."

"That's right. You used to bake cakes for the diner."

"That's how I could afford my clothes."

He sniffed. "Oh, come on. Your dad owns the diner. Everybody knew you guys were rolling in money."

She turned away. Her voice chilled as she said, "My dad still made me work for what I wanted." But when she faced him again, she was smiling.

Confused, but not about to get into something that might ruin their nice conversation, Wyatt motioned to the counter. "So who is this cake for?"

"It's a wedding cake. Bride's from Frederick. It's a big fancy, splashy wedding, so the cake has to be exactly what she wants. Simple. Elegant."

Suddenly the pieces fell into place. "And that's your business?"

"Brides are willing to pay a lot to get the exact cake that suits their wedding. Which means a job a month supports us." She glanced around. "Of course, I inherited this house and our expenses are small, so selling one cake a month is enough."

"What do you do in the winter?"

"The winter?"

"When fewer people get married?"

"Oh. Well, that's why I have to do more than one cake a month in wedding season. I have a cake the last two weeks of April, every weekend in May, June and July, and two in August, so I can put some money back for the months when I don't have orders."

"Makes sense." He drank his coffee. "I guess I better get going."

She smiled slightly. "You never said what brings you home."

Not sure if she was trying to keep him here with mindless conversation or genuinely curious, he shrugged. "The family jewels."

Missy laughed.

"Apparently my grandmother had some necklaces or brooches or something that *her* grandmother brought over from Scotland."

"Oh. I'll bet they're beautiful."

"Yeah, well. I've yet to find them."

"Didn't she have a jewelry box?"

"Yes, and last night I sent my mom pictures of everything in it and none of the pieces are the Scotland things."

"So you're here until you find them?"

"I'm here till I find them. Or four weeks. I can get away when I want, but I can't stay away indefinitely."

"Maybe one of these nights I could grill chicken or something for supper and you could come over and we could catch up."

He remembered the afternoons sitting on the bench seat of her grandmother's picnic table, trying to get her to understand equations. He remembered spring breezes and autumn winds, but most of all he remembered how nice it was just to be with her. For a man working to get beyond a protracted divorce, it might not be a bad idea to spend some time with a woman who reminded him of good things. Happy times.

He smiled. "That would be nice."

He made his way back to his house and headed to his grandmother's bedroom again. Because she'd lived eight months of the year in Florida and four months in Maryland, her house was still furnished as it always had been. An outdated floral bedspread matched floral drapes. Lacy lamps sat on tables by the bed. And the whole place smelled of potpourri.

With a grimace, he walked to the mirrored dresser. He'd looked in the jewelry box the night before. He could check the drawers today, but he had a feeling these lockets and necklaces were something his grandmother had squirreled away. He toed the oval braided rug beneath her bed.

Could she have had a secret compartment under there? Floorboards that he could lift, and find a metal box?

Looking for that was better than flipping through his grandmother's underwear drawer.

He pushed the bed to the side, off the rug, then knelt and began rolling the carpet, hoping to find a sign of a loose floorboard. With the rug out of the way, he felt along the hardwood, looking for a catch or a spring or something that would indicate a secret compartment. He smoothed his hand along a scarred board, watching the movement of his fingers as he sought a catch, and suddenly his hand hit something solid and stopped.

His gaze shot over and there knelt Owen.

"Hey."

He rocked back on his heels. "Hey. Does your mom know you're here?"

The little boy shook his head.

Wyatt sighed. "Okay. Look. I like you. And from what

I saw of your house this morning, I get it. You're a bored guy in a houseful of women."

Owen's big brown eyes blinked.

"But you can't come over here."

"Yes I can. I can get through the bushes."

Wyatt stifled a laugh. Leave it to a kid to be literal. "Yes, you *can* walk over here. It is possible. But it isn't right for you to leave without telling your mom."

Owen held out a cell phone. "We can call her."

Wyatt groaned. "Owen, buddy, I hate to tell you this, but if you took your mom's phone, you might be in a world of trouble."

He shoved up off the floor and held out his hand to the little boy. "Sorry, kid. But I've got to take you and the phone home."

Wyatt pulled the hedge back and walked up the steps to Missy's kitchen, holding Owen's hand. Knocking on the screen door, he called, "Missy?"

Drying her hands on a dish towel, she appeared at the door, opened it and immediately saw Owen. "Oh, no. I'm sorry! I thought he was in the playroom with the girls."

She stooped down. "O-ee, honey. You have to stay here with Mommy."

Owen slid his little arm around Wyatt's knee and hugged.

And fifty percent of Wyatt's childhood came tumbling back. He hadn't been included in the neighbor kids' games, because he was a nerd. And Owen wasn't included in his sisters' games, because he wasn't a girl. But the feeling of being excluded was the same.

Wyatt's heart squeezed. "You know what? I didn't actually bring him home to stay home." He knew a cry for help when he heard it, and he couldn't ignore it. He held out her cell phone and she gasped. "I just want you to know where he is, and I wanted to give back your phone."

She looked up at him. "Are you saying you'll keep him at your house for a while?"

"Sure. I think we could have fun."

Owen's grip on his knee loosened.

She caught her son's gaze again. "If I let you go to Mr. McKenzie's house for a few hours, will you promise to stay here this afternoon?"

Owen nodded eagerly.

Her gaze climbed up to meet Wyatt's. "What are you going to do with a kid for a couple of hours?"

"My grandmother kept everything. She should still have the video games I played as a boy. And if she doesn't, I saw a sandbox out there in your yard. Maybe we could play in that."

Owen tugged on his jeans. "I have twucks."

Missy gave Wyatt a hopeful look. "He loves to play in the sand with his trucks."

He shrugged. "So sand it is. I haven't showered yet this morning. I can crawl around in the dirt for a few hours."

Missy rose. "I really appreciate this."

"It's no problem."

Twenty minutes later, Missy stood by her huge mixer waiting for her gelatin mix to cool, watching Owen and Wyatt out her kitchen window. Her eyes filled with tears. Her little boy needed a man around, but his dad had run and wanted nothing to do with his triplets. Her dad was a drunk. Her pool of potential men for Owen's life was very small.

Owen pushed a yellow toy truck through the sand as Wyatt operated a pint-size front-end loader. He filled the back of the truck with sand and Owen "drove" it to the other side of the sandbox, where he dumped it in a growing pile.

Missy put her elbow on the windowsill and her chin on her open palm. *She* might not want to get involved with Wyatt, but it really would help Owen to have him around for the next month.

Still, he was a rich, good-looking guy, who, if he wanted to play with kids, would have had some by now. It was wrong to even consider asking him to spend time with Owen. Especially since the time he spent with Owen had to be on her schedule, not his.

She took a pitcher of tropical punch and some cookies outside. "I hate to say this," she said, handing Owen the first glass of punch, "but somebody needs a nap."

Wyatt yawned and stretched. "Hey, no need to worry about hurting my feelings. I know I need a nap."

Owen giggled.

Wyatt rose. "Wanna play for a few hours this afternoon?"

Owen nodded.

"Great. I'll be back then." He grabbed two cookies from the plate Missy held before he walked over to the hedge, pulled it back and strode through.

Watching him go, Missy frowned thoughtfully. He really wasn't a bad guy. Actually, he behaved a lot like the Wyatt she used to know. And he genuinely seemed to like Owen. Which was exactly what she wanted. Somebody to keep her little boy company.

She glanced at the plate, the empty spot where the two cookies he'd taken had been sitting. Maybe she did know a way to keep him around. Since he was in his grandma's house alone, and there was only one place in town to get food—the diner—it might be possible to keep him around just by feeding him.

That afternoon Missy watched Wyatt emerge through the hedge a little after three. Owen was outside, so he didn't even come inside. He just grabbed a ball and started a game of catch.

Missy flipped the chicken breasts she was marinating, and went back to vacuuming the living room and cleaning bathrooms. When she was done, Owen and Wyatt were sitting at the picnic table.

Marinated chicken in one hand and small bag of charcoal briquettes in the other, she raced out to the backyard. "You wouldn't want to help me light the briquettes for the grill, would you?"

Wyatt got up from the table. "Sure." Grabbing the bag from her arm, he chuckled. "I didn't know anybody still used these things."

"It's cheaper than a gas grill."

He poured some into the belly of the grill. "I suppose." He caught her gaze. "Got a match?"

She went inside and returned with igniting fluid and the long slender lighter she used for candles.

He turned the can of lighter fluid over in his hand. "I forgot about this. We'll have a fire for you in fifteen minutes."

"If it takes you any longer, you're a girl."

He laughed. "So we're back to high school taunts."

"If the shoe fits. By the way, I've marinated enough chicken for an army and I'm making grilled veggies, if you want to join us for dinner."

"I think if I get the fire going, you owe me dinner."

She smiled. She couldn't even begin to tell him how much she owed him for his help with Owen, so she only said, "Exactly."

She returned to the kitchen and watched out the window as Wyatt talked Owen through lighting the charcoal. She noticed with approval that he kept Owen a safe distance away from the grill. But also noticed that he kept talking, pointing, as if explaining the process.

And Owen soaked it all in. The little man of the house.

Tears filled her eyes again. She hoped one month with a guy would be enough to hold Owen until…

Until what she wasn't sure, but eventually she'd have to find a neighbor or teacher or maybe somebody from church who could spend a few hours a week with her son.

Because she wasn't getting romantically involved with a man again until she had her business up and running. Until she could be financially independent. Until she could live with a man and know that even if he left her she could support her kids. And with her business just starting, that might not be for a long, long time.

While the chicken cooked, Wyatt ran over to his grand-mother's house for a shower. He liked that kid. Really liked him. Owen wasn't a whiny, crying toddler. He was a cool little boy who just wanted somebody to play with.

And Wyatt had had fun. He'd even enjoyed Missy's company. Not because she was flirty or attracted to him, but because she treated him like a friend. Just as he'd thought that morning, a platonic relationship with her could go a long way to helping him get back to normal after his divorce.

He put his head under the spray. Now all he had to do was keep his attraction to her in line. He almost laughed. In high school, he'd had four years of keeping his attrac-tion to her under lock and key. While she'd been dating football stars, he'd been her long-suffering tutor.

This time he did laugh. He wasn't a long-suffering kind of guy anymore. He was a guy who got what he wanted. He liked her. He wanted her. And he was now free. It might be a little difficult telling his grown-up, spoiled self he couldn't have her....

But maybe he needed some practice with not getting his own way? His divorce had shown him, and several lawyers, that he wasn't fond of compromise. And he absolutely, positively didn't like not getting his own way.

He really did need a lesson in compromise. In stepping back. In being honorable.

Doing good things for Missy, and *not* acting on his attraction, might be the lesson in self-discipline and control he needed.

Especially since he had no intention of getting married again. The financial loss he'd suffered in his divorce was a setback. He would recover from that with his brains and talent. The hurt? That was a different story. The pain of losing the woman he'd believed loved him had followed him around like a lost puppy for two years. He had no intention of setting himself up for that kind of pain again. Which meant no permanent relationship. Particularly no marriage. And if he got involved with Missy, he would hurt her, because she was the kind of girl who needed to be married.

So problem solved. He would not flirt. He would not take. He would be kind to her and her kids. And expect nothing, want nothing, in return.

And hopefully, he'd get his inner nice guy back.

When he returned to Missy's backyard in a clean T-shirt, shorts and flip-flops, she had the veggies on the table and was pulling the chicken off the grill.

"Grab a paper plate and help yourself."

He glanced over. "The kids' plates aren't made yet."

"I can do it."

"I can help."

With a little instruction from her about how much food

to put on each, Wyatt helped prepare three plates of food for the kids. Owen sat beside him on the bench seat and Missy sat across from them with the girls.

It honest to God felt like high school all over again. Girls on one side. Boys on the other.

Little brown-eyed, blond Claire said, "We have a boys' side and a girls' side."

Wyatt caught Missy's gaze. "Is that good or bad?"

"I don't know. We've never had another boy around."

"Really?"

She shrugged and pretended great interest in cutting Helaina's chicken.

Interesting. She hadn't had another man around in years? Maybe if Wyatt worked this right, their relationship didn't have to be platonic—

He stopped that thought. Shut it down. Getting involved with someone like Missy would be nothing but complicated. While having a platonic relationship would do them both good.

So the conversation centered around kid topics while they ate. Wyatt helped clean up. Then he announced that it was time to go back to his grandmother's house.

"To hunt for hidden treasure," he told Owen.

Owen's head almost snapped off as he faced Missy. "Can I go look for hidden tweasure, too?"

"No. It's bath time then story time then bedtime."

Owen groused. But Wyatt had an answer for this, if only because he understood negotiating. Give the opposing party something they wanted and everybody would be happy.

He caught Owen by the shoulders and stooped to his height. "You need to get some rest if we're going to build the high-rise skyscraper tomorrow."

Owen's eyes lit up as he realized Wyatt intended to play

with him again the next day. He threw his arms around Wyatt's neck, hugged him and raced off.

An odd tingling exploded in Wyatt's chest. It was the first time in his life he'd been close enough to a child to get a hug. And the sensation was amazing. It made him feel strong, protective…wanted. But in a way he'd never felt before. His decision to be around this little family strengthened. He could help Owen, and being around Owen and Missy and the girls could help him remember he didn't always need to get his own way.

It was win-win.

Missy sighed with contentment. "Thanks."

"You're welcome."

With the kids so far ahead of her, she motioned to her back door. "Sorry, but I've got to get in there before they flood the bathroom."

Wyatt laughed. "Got it."

He walked to the hedge, pulled it aside and headed for his gram's house. He went into her bedroom again and started pulling shoe boxes filled with God knew what out of her overstuffed closet. But after only fifteen minutes, he glanced out the big bedroom window and saw Missy had come out to her back porch. She wearily sat on one of the two outdoor chairs.

Wyatt stopped pulling shoe boxes out of his gram's closet.

She looked exhausted. Claire had said they'd never had another man around, which probably meant Missy didn't date. But looking at her right now, he had to wonder if she ever even took a break.

He sucked in a breath. If he really wanted to help her, he couldn't just do the things he knew would help him get back his rational, calm, predivorce self. He had to do the things *she* needed.

And right now it looked as if she needed a drink.

He dropped the box, pulled two bottles of beer from the refrigerator and headed for the hedge. It rustled as he pushed it aside.

She didn't notice him walking across the short expanse of yard to the back porch, so he called up the steps. "Hey, I saw you come out here. Mind if I join you?"

"No. Sure. That'd be great."

He heard the hesitation in her voice, but decided that was just her exhaustion speaking.

He held up the two bottles of beer. "I didn't come empty-handed." He climbed the steps, offered her a beer and fell to the chair beside hers. "Your son could wear out a world-class athlete."

She laughed. "He's a good kid and he likes you. I really appreciate you spending time with him." She took a swig of beer. "Wow. I haven't had a beer in ages."

Happiness rose in him. He *had* done something nice for her.

"A person has to have all her wits to care for three kids at once. One beer is fine. Two beers would probably put me to sleep."

"Okay, good to know. This way I'll limit you to one." He eased back on the chair. "So tell me more about the cake business."

She peeked at him and his heart turned over in his chest. In the dim light of her back porch, her gray-blue eyes sort of glowed. The long hair she kept in a ponytail while she worked currently fell to her back in a long, smooth wave. He didn't dare glance down at her legs, because his intention was to keep this relationship platonic, and those legs could be his undoing.

"I love my business." She said it slowly, carefully meeting his gaze. "But it's a lot of work."

He swallowed. Her eyes were just so damned pretty. "I'll bet it is."

"And what's funny is I learned how to do most of it online."

That made him laugh. "No kidding."

He turned on his chair to face her, and suddenly their legs were precariously close. Nerves tingled through him. He desperately wanted to flirt with her. To feel the rush of attraction turn to arousal. To feel the rush of heat right before a first kiss.

Their gazes met and clung. Her tongue peeked out and moistened her lips.

The tingle dancing along his skin became a slow burn. Maybe he wasn't the only one feeling this attraction?

She rose from her chair and walked to the edge of the porch, propping her butt on the railing, trying not to look as if she was running from him.

But she was.

She was attracted to him and he wasn't having any luck hiding his attraction to her. This attraction was mutual, so why run?

"There are tons and tons of online videos of people creating beautiful one-of-a-kind cakes. If you have the basic know-how about cake baking, the decorating stuff can be learned."

He rose from his seat, too. He absolutely, positively wanted to help her with Owen, but a platonic relationship wouldn't get him over his bad divorce as well as a new romance could. And from the looks of things, she could use a little romance in her life, too. Even one that ended. Good memories could be a powerful way to get a person from one difficult day to the next.

He ambled over beside her. Edged his hip onto the railing. "So you baked a lot of trial cakes?"

She laughed nervously. "I probably should have. But I worked with a woman whose sister was getting married, and when she heard I was learning to bake wedding cakes she asked if I'd bake one for the wedding." Missy caught his gaze, her blue-gray eyes filled with heat. Her breath stuttered out.

He smiled. In high school he'd have given anything to make her breath stutter like that. And now that he had, he couldn't just ignore it. Particularly since he definitely could get back to normal a lot quicker with a new romance.

"Because it was my first cake, I did it for free." Her soft voice whispered between them. "Luckily, it came out perfectly. And I got several referrals."

He slid a little closer. "That's good."

She slid away. "That was last year. My trial and error year. This year I have enough referrals and know enough that I was comfortable quitting my job, doing this full-time."

He nodded, slid closer. He wouldn't be such an idiot that he'd seduce her tonight, but he did want a kiss.

But she scooted farther away from him. "You're not getting what I'm telling you."

He frowned. Her crisp, unyielding voice didn't match the heat bubbling in his stomach right now.

Had he fantasized his way into missing part of the conversation?

"What are you telling me?"

"I was abandoned by my husband with three kids. We've been as close to dead broke as four people can be for four long years. It was almost a happy accident that the first bride asked me to bake her cake. Over the past year I've been building to this point where I had a whole summer of cakes to bake. A real income."

She slid off the railing and walked away from him. "I like you. But I have three kids and a new business."

His chest constricted. He'd definitely fantasized his way into missing something. He hadn't heard anything even close to that in their conversation. But he heard it now. "And you don't want a man around, screwing that up?"

She winced. "No. I don't."

The happy tingle in his blood died. He wasn't mad at her. How could he be mad at her when what she said made so much sense?

But he wasn't happy, either.

He collected the empty beer bottles and left.

CHAPTER THREE

THE NEXT MORNING, Owen blew through the kitchen and out the back door like a little boy on a mission, and Missy's heart twisted. He was on his way to the sandbox, expecting to find Wyatt.

She squeezed her eyes shut in misery. The Wyatt she remembered from their high school days never would have hit on her the way he had the night before. Recalling the sweet, shy way he'd asked her to the graduation party, she shook her head. That Wyatt was gone. This Wyatt was a weird combination of the nice guy he had been, a guy who'd seen Owen's plight and rescued him, and a new guy. Somebody she didn't know at all.

Still, she knew men. She knew that when they didn't get their own way they bolted or pouted or got angry. Wyatt wasn't the kind to get angry the way her dad had gotten angry, but she'd bet her next cake referral that she'd ruined Owen's chances for a companion today. Hell, she might have wrecked his chances for a companion all month. All because she didn't want to be attracted to Wyatt McKenzie.

Well, that wasn't precisely true. Being attracted to him was like a force of nature. He was gorgeous. She was normal. Any sane woman would automatically be attracted to him. Which was why she couldn't let Wyatt kiss her. One really good kiss would have dissolved her into a puddle of need, and she didn't want that. She wanted the security of knowing she could support her kids. She wouldn't get that security if she lost focus. Or if she fell for a man before she was ready.

So she'd warned him off. And now Owen would suffer.

But when she lifted the kitchen curtain to peek outside, there in the sandbox was Wyatt McKenzie. His feet were bare. His flip-flops lay drunkenly in the grass. Worn jeans caressed his perfect butt and his T-shirt showed off wide shoulders.

She dropped the curtain with a groan. Why did he have to be so attractive?

Still, seeing him with her son revived her faith in him. Maybe he was more like the nice Wyatt she remembered?

Unfortunately, until he proved that, she believed it was better to keep her distance.

After retrieving her gum paste from the refrigerator, she broke it into manageable sections. Once she rolled each section, she put it through a pasta machine to make it even thinner. Then she placed the pieces on plastic mats and put them into the freezer for use on Friday, when she would begin making the flowers.

She peeked out the window again, and to her surprise, Owen and Wyatt were still in the sandbox.

Okay. He might not be the old shy Wyatt who'd stumbled over his words to ask her out. But he was still a good guy. She wouldn't hold it against him that he'd made a pass at her. Actually, with that pass out of the way, maybe they could go back to being friends? And maybe she should take him a glass of fruit punch and make peace?

When Missy came out to the yard with a pitcher and glasses, Wyatt wasn't sure what to do. He hadn't worked out how he felt about her rebuffing him. Except that he couldn't take it out on Owen.

She offered him a glass. "Fruit punch?"

She smiled tentatively, as if she didn't know how to behave around him, either.

He took the glass. "Sure. Thanks."

"You're welcome." She turned away just as her two little girls came running outside. "Who wants juice?"

A chorus of "I do" billowed around him. He drank his fruit punch like a man in a desert and put his glass under the pitcher again when she filled the kids' glasses.

Their gazes caught.

"Thirsty?"

"Very."

"Well, I have lots of fruit punch. Drink your fill."

But don't kiss her.

As she poured punch into his glass, he took a long breath. He was happy. He liked Owen. He even found it amusing to hear the girls chatter about their dolls when they sat under the tree and played house. And he'd spent most of his life wanting a kiss from Missy Johnson and never getting one.

So, technically, this wasn't new. This was normal.

Maybe he was just being a pain in the butt by being upset about it?

And maybe that was part of what he needed to learn before he returned home? That pushing for things he wanted sometimes made him a jerk.

Sheesh. He didn't like the sound of that. But he had to admit that up until he'd lost Betsy, he'd gotten everything he wanted. His talent got him money. His money got him the company that made him the boss. Until Betsy cheated on him, then left him, then sued him, his life had been perfect. Maybe this time with Missy was life balancing the scales as it taught him to gracefully accept failure.

He didn't stay for lunch, though she invited him to. Instead, he ate a dried-up cheese sandwich made from cheese in Gram's freezer and bread he'd gotten at the 7-Eleven the day he'd bought the beer and champagne. When he was finished, he returned to his work of taking everything out of his grandmother's closet, piling things on the bed. When that was full he shifted to stacking them on the floor beside the bed. With the closet empty, he stared at the stack in awe. How did a person get that much stuff in one closet?

One by one, he began going through the shoe boxes, which contained everything from old bath salts to old receipts. Around two o'clock, he heard the squeals of the kids' laughter and decided he'd had enough of being inside. Ten minutes later, he and Owen were a Wiffle ball team against Lainie and Claire.

Around four, Missy came outside with hot dogs to grill for supper. He started the charcoal for her, but didn't stay. If he wanted to get back his inner nice guy, to accept that she had a right to rebuff him, he would need some space to get accustomed to it.

Because that's what a reasonable guy did. He accepted his limits.

Once inside his gram's house, tired and sweaty, he headed for the bathroom to shower. Under the spray, he thought about how much fun Missy's kids were, then about how much work they were. Then he frowned, thinking about their dad.

What kind of man left a woman with three kids?

What kind of man didn't give a damn if his kids were fed?

What kind of man expected the woman he'd gotten

pregnant to sacrifice everything because she had to be the sole support of his kids?

A real louse. Missy had married a real louse.

Was it any wonder she'd warned Wyatt off the night before? She had three kids. Three energetic, hungry, busy kids to raise alone because some dingbat couldn't handle having triplets.

If she was smart, she'd never again trust a man.

A funny feeling slithered through Wyatt.

They were actually very much alike. She'd never trust a man because one had left her with triplets, and he'd never trust a woman because Betsy's betrayal had hurt a lot more than he liked to admit.

Even in his own head he hadn't considered wooing Missy to marry her. He wanted a kiss. But not love. In some ways he was no better than her ex.

He needed to stay away from her, too.

He walked over to her yard the next morning and played with Owen in the sandbox. He and Missy didn't have much contact, but that was fine. Every day that he spent with her kids and saw the amount of work required to raise them alone, he got more and more angry with her ex and more and more determined to stay away from her, to let her get on with her life. She ran herself ragged working on the wedding cake every morning and housecleaning and caring for the kids in the afternoon.

So when she invited him to supper every day, he refused. Though he was sick of the canned soup he found in Gram's pantry, and dry toasted-cheese sandwiches, he didn't want to make any more work for Missy. He also respected her boundaries. He wouldn't push to get involved with her, no matter that he could see in her eyes that she was attracted to him. He would be a gentleman.

Even if it killed him.

But on Saturday afternoon, he watched her carry the tiers of a wedding cake into her rattletrap SUV. Wearing a simple blue sleeveless dress that stopped midthigh, and high, high white sandals, with her hair curled into some sort of twist thing on the back of her head, she looked both professional and sexy.

Primal male need slid along his nerve endings and he told himself to get away from the window. But as she and the babysitter lugged the last section of the cake, the huge bottom layer, into the SUV, their conversation drifted to him through the open bedroom window.

"So what do you do once you get there?"

"Ask the caterer to lend me a waiter so I can carry all this into the reception area. Then I have to put it together and cut it and serve it."

By herself. She didn't have to say the words. They were implied. And if the caterer couldn't spare a waiter to help her carry the cake into the reception venue, she'd carry that alone, too.

Wyatt got so angry with her ex that his head nearly exploded. Though he was dressed to play with Owen, he pivoted from the window, slapped on a clean pair of jeans and a clean T-shirt and marched to her driveway.

As she opened the door to get into the driver's side of her SUV, he opened the door on the passenger's side.

"What are you doing?"

He slammed the door and reached for his seat belt. "Helping you."

She laughed lightly. "I'm fine."

"Right. You're fine. You're run ragged by three kids and a new business. Now you have to drive the cake to the wedding, set it up, and wait for the time when you can cut it and serve it." He flicked a glance at her. "All in an SUV that looks like it might not survive a trip to Frederick."

"It—"

He stopped her with a look. "I'm coming with you."

"Wyatt—"

"Start the SUV and drive, because I'm not getting out and you don't have another car to take."

Huffing out a sigh, she turned the key in the ignition. She waved out the open window. "Bye, kids! Mommy will be back soon. Be nice for Miss Nancy."

They all waved.

She backed out of the driveway and headed for the interstate.

Now that the moment of anger had passed, Wyatt shifted uncomfortably on his seat. Even though it had been for her own good, he'd been a bit high-handed. Exactly what he was trying to stop doing. "I'm not usually this bossy."

She laughed musically. "Right. You own a company. You have to be bossy."

"I suppose." Brooding, he stared out the window. She wanted nothing to do with him, and he wasn't really a good bet for getting involved with her. And they were about to spend hours together.

She probably thought he'd volunteered to help in order to have another chance to make a pass at her.

He flicked a glance at her. "I know you think I'm nuts for pushing my way into this, but I overheard what you told the babysitter. This is a lot of work."

"I knew that when I started the company. But I like it. And it's the only way I have to earn enough money to support my kids."

Which took him back to the thing that made him so mad. "Your ex should be paying child support."

Irritation caused Missy's chest to expand. She might have been able to accept his help because he was still the nice guy he used to be. But he hadn't offered because he was a nice guy. He'd offered because he felt sorry for her, and she *hated* that.

"Don't feel sorry for me!"

He snorted in disgust. "I don't feel sorry for you. I'm angry with your ex."

Was that any better? "Right."

"Look, picking a bad spouse isn't a crime. If it was, they'd toss me in jail and throw away the key."

She almost laughed. She'd forgotten he had his own tale of woe.

"I'm serious. Betsy cheated on me, lied to me, tried to set my employees against me. All while she and her lawyers were negotiating for a piece of my company in a divorce settlement. She wanted half."

Wide-eyed, Missy glanced over at him. "She cheated on you and tried to get half your company?" Jeff emptying their tiny savings account was small potatoes compared to taking half a company.

"Yes. She only ended up with a *third*." Wyatt sighed. "Feel better?"

She smiled sheepishly. "Sort of."

"So there's nobody in this car who's better than anybody else. We both picked lousy spouses."

She relaxed a little. He really didn't feel sorry for her. They were kind of kindred spirits. Being left with triplets might seem totally different than having an ex take a third of your company, but the principle was the same. Both had been dumped and robbed. For the first time in four years she was with somebody who truly "got it." He wasn't helping her because he thought she was weak. He wasn't helping her because he was still the sort of sappy kid she'd known in high school. He was helping her because he saw the injustice of her situation.

That pleased her enough that she could accept his assistance. But truth be told, she also knew she needed the help.

When they arrived at the country club, she pulled into a parking space near the service door to facilitate entry. She opened the back of her SUV and he gasped.

"Wow."

Pride shimmied through her. Though the cake was simple—white fondant with pink dots circling the top of each layer, and pink-and-lavender orchids as the cake top—it was beautiful. A work of art. Creating cakes didn't just satisfy her need for money; it gave expression to her soul.

"You like?"

"Those flowers aren't real?"

"Nope. Those are gum paste flowers."

"My God. They're so perfect. Like art."

She laughed. Hadn't she thought the same thing? "It will be melted art if we don't get it inside soon."

They took the layers into the event room and set up the cake on the table off to the right of the bride and groom's dinner seating. Around them, the caterers put white cloths on the tables. The florist brought centerpieces. The event room transformed into a glorious pink-and-lavender heaven right before their eyes.

Around four, guests began straggling in. They signed the book and found assigned seats as the bar opened.

At five-thirty the bride and groom arrived. A murmur rippled through the room. Missy sighed dreamily. This was what happened when a bride and groom were evenly matched. Happiness. All decked out in white chiffon, the beautiful bride glowed. In his black tux, the suave and sophisticated groom could have broken hearts. Wyatt looked at his watch.

"We have about two hours before we get to the cake," Missy told him.

He groaned. "Wonder what Owen's doing right now?"

"You'd rather be in the sandbox?"

"All men would rather be playing in dirt than making nice with a bunch of people wearing monkey suits."

She laughed. That was certainly not the old nerdy Wyatt she knew in high school. That kid didn't play. He read. He studied. He did not prefer dirt to anything.

She peeked over at him with her peripheral vision. She supposed having money would change anybody. But these changes were different. Not just a shift from a nerdy kid to a sexy guy. But a personality change. Before, he'd seen injustice and suffered in silence. Now he saw injustice—such as Owen being alone—and he fixed it. Even his helping her was his attempt at making up for her ex abandoning her.

Interesting.

White-coated waiters stood at the ready to serve dinner. The best man gave the longest toast in recorded history. In the background, a string quartet played a waltz.

Wyatt looked at his watch again. Silence stretched between them. Missy knew he was bored. She was bored, too. But standing around, waiting to cut the cake, was part of her job.

Suddenly he caught her hand and led her outside, but a thought stopped her short. "Is the wedding bringing up bad marriage memories?"

He laughed and spun her in a circle and into his arms. "Actually, I'm bored and I love to dance."

"To waltz?" If her voice came out a bit breathless, she totally understood why. The little spin and tug he'd used to get her into his arms for the dance had pressed her flush against him. His arm rested on her waist. Her hand sat on his strong shoulder. And for a woman who'd been so long deprived of male-female contact, it was almost too much for her nerves and hormones to handle. They jumped and popped.

She told herself to think of the old Wyatt. The nice kid. The geeky guy who'd taught her algebra. But she couldn't. This Wyatt was taller, broader, stronger.

Bolder.

He swung her around in time with the string quartet music, and sheer delight filled her. Her defenses automatically rose and the word *stop* sprang to her tongue, but she suddenly wondered why. Why stop? Her fear was of a relationship, and this was just a dance to relieve boredom. Mostly his. To keep it from becoming too intimate, too personal, she'd simply toss in a bit of conversation.

"Where'd you learn to dance like this?"

"Florida. I can dance to just about anything."

She pulled back, studied him. "Really?"

"I go to a lot of charity events. I don't want to look like a schlep."

"Oh, trust me. You're so far from a schlep it's not even funny."

He laughed. The deep, rich, sexy sound surrounded her and her heart stuttered. Now she knew how Cinderella felt dancing with the prince. Cautiously happy. No woman in her right mind really believed the prince would choose her permanently. But, oh, who could resist a five-minute dance when this sexy, bold guy was all hers?

His arms tightened around her, brought her close again, and she let herself go. She gave in to the rush of attraction. The scramble of her pulse. The heat that reminded her she was still very much a woman, not just a mom.

He whirled them around, along the stone path to a colorful garden. As they twirled, he caught her gaze and the whole world seemed to disappear. There was no one but him, with his big biceps, strong shoulders and serious brown eyes, and her with her trembling heart and melting knees. Their gazes locked and a million what-if's shivered through her.

What if he hadn't gone away after college?

What if she'd been able to keep their date?

What if she wasn't so afraid now to trust another man?

Could she fall in love with him?

The dance went on and on. They never broke eye contact. She thought of him being good first to Owen and then to all three of her kids. She thought of him angry when he'd jumped into her SUV. Righteously indignant on her behalf, since her ex was such an idiot. She thought of him wanting to kiss her the other night, and her already weak knees threatened to buckle. If it felt this good to dance with him, what would a kiss be like?

Explosive?

Passionate?

Soul searing?

"Excuse me? Are you the lady who did the cake?"

Brought back to reality, she jumped out of Wyatt's arms and faced the woman who'd interrupted them, only to find a bridesmaid.

Missy's senses instantly sharpened. "Yes. Is there something wrong? Do I need to come inside?"

"No! No! The cake is gorgeous. Perfect." The woman in the pink gown handed her a slip of paper. "That's my name and phone number. I'm getting married next year. The third week in June. I'd love for you to do my cake. Could you call me?"

Happiness raced through her. Her cheeks flushed. "I'd love to. But I have to check my book first and make sure I don't have another cake scheduled for that day."

The pretty bridesmaid said, "Well, I'm hoping you don't." Then she slipped back into the ballroom.

Slapping the little slip of paper against her hand, Missy joyfully faced Wyatt again.

He leaned against a stone retaining wall, watching her with hooded eyes.

"Look! I'm already starting to get work for next year."

He eased away from the wall. "Yeah. I see that."

She'd expected him to be happier for her. Instead he appeared annoyed. Her heart beat against her ribs. Surely he wasn't upset that they'd been interrupted?

She licked her lips and fanned the little slip of paper. "She hasn't tasted the cake yet. This might not pan out."

"Everybody who ate at the diner loved your cakes. You know they're good."

She grinned. "I do!"

"So you're a shoo-in."

"Yeah."

She took a breath. He glanced around awkwardly.

Then she remembered they'd been dancing. Her heart had been pounding. Their gazes had been locked. Something had been happening between them. But the moment had officially been broken.

And now that she was out of his arms, away from his enticing scent, away from the pull of their attraction, she was glad. Really. This wasn't a happily-ever-after kind of relationship. He'd be around only a short time, then he'd go back to Florida. And her divorce had left her unable to trust. Even if she could trust, she wouldn't get involved in something that might distract her from her wedding cake business. She'd never, ever find herself in a position of depending upon a man again.

She turned to go back into the country club ballroom. "It's about time for the bride and groom to cut the cake. Once they get pictures, our big job starts."

She didn't even look back, just expected him to follow

her. Even Wyatt with his sexy brown eyes couldn't make her forget the night she'd sat staring at the babies' cribs, knowing she didn't have formula for the next day—or money to buy it.

She would build her business, then maybe work on her trust issues. But for now, the business came first.

CHAPTER FOUR

AFTER THE BRIDE AND GROOM cut the cake, Missy sliced the bottom layer, set the pieces on plates and the plates on trays. Waiters in white shirts scrambled over, grabbed the trays and served the cake.

Wyatt glanced around. "What can I do?"

"How about if I cut the cake and put it on dessert plates, and you put the plates on the trays?"

It wasn't rocket science, but it was better than standing around watching her slender fingers work the knife. Better than wrestling with the hunger gnawing at his belly. And not hunger for food. Hunger for a kiss.

A kiss she owed him. Had she not stood him up, their date would have ended in a kiss.

Hence, she owed him.

When the last of the cake was served, she packaged the top layer, the one with the intricate orchids, into a special box. They packaged the remainder of the uncut cake into another, not quite as fancy, one. The bride's mom took both boxes, complimented Missy on the cake, then strode away to secure the leftovers for the bride.

As the music and dancing went on, Missy and Wyatt gathered up her equipment and slid it into the back of her SUV.

Just as they were closing the door, a young woman in a blue dress scrambled over. "You made the cake, right?"

Missy smiled. "Yes."

"It was wonderful! Delicious and beautiful."

Her cheeks flushed again. Her eyes sparkled with happiness. "Thanks."

"I don't suppose you have a card?"

She winced. "No. Sorry. But if you write down your name and number, I can call you." She headed for the driver's side door. "I have a pen and paper."

The young woman eagerly took the pad and pen and scribbled her name and phone number.

"Don't forget to put your wedding date on there."

After another quick scribble, the bride-to-be handed the tablet to Missy, but another young woman standing beside her grabbed the pad and pen before she could take them.

"I'll give you my name and number and wedding date, too. That was the most delicious cake I've ever eaten."

"Thanks."

When the two brides-to-be were finished heaping praise on Missy, she and Wyatt climbed into the SUV and headed home.

He'd never been so proud of anyone in his life. He didn't think he'd even been this proud of himself when he'd bought the comic book company. Of course, the stakes weren't as high. As Missy had said, she had three kids to support and no job. He'd been publishing comic books for at least six years before he bought the company, and by then, given how much influence he had over what they published, it was almost a foregone conclusion that he'd someday take over.

But this—watching Missy start her company from nothing—it was energizing. Emotional.

"You need to get business cards."

She glanced over at him, her cheeks rosy, her eyes shining. "What?"

"Business cards. So that people can call you."

She laughed her musical laugh, the one that reminded him he liked her a lot more than he should.

"It's better for them to give me their numbers. This way they don't get lost, and I control the situation."

He sucked in a breath. She liked control, huh? Well, she certainly had control of him, and it confused him, didn't fit his plans. Probably didn't fit her plans. "That's good thinking."

"I'm just so excited. I'm already starting to get work for next year." She slapped the steering wheel. "This is so great!" But suddenly she deflated.

He peered over. "What?"

"What if all the weddings are on the same day? I can't even do two cakes a week. Forget about three. I'd have to turn everybody down."

"Sounds to me like you're borrowing trouble."

"No. I'm thinking ahead. I might look like an uneducated bumpkin to you, but I've really thought through my business. I know what I can do and what I can't, and I'd have to turn down any cake for a wedding on the same day as another booking."

He nodded, curious about why her fear had sent a rush of male longing through him. He wanted to fix everything that was wrong in her life. The depth of what he felt for her didn't make sense. He could blame it on his teenage crush. Tell himself that he felt all this intensity because he already knew her. That his feelings had more or less picked up where they'd left off—

Except that didn't wash. They were two different people. Two new people. Fifteen years had passed. Technically, they didn't "know" each other. The woman she'd become from the girl she had been was one smart, sexy, beautiful female. And how he felt right now wasn't anything close to what he'd felt when he was eighteen, because he was older, more experienced.

So this couldn't be anything but sexual attraction.

A very tempting sexual attraction.

But only sexual attraction.

She had goals. She had kids. She'd already warned him off. And he didn't want another relationship...

Unless she'd agree to something fast and furious, something that would end when he left?

He snorted to himself. Really? He thought she'd go for an affair?

Was he an idiot?

He lectured himself the whole way home. But when they had unloaded the SUV and stood face-to-face, her in her pretty blue dress, with her hair slipping from its pins and looking sexily disheveled, his lips tingled with the need to kiss her.

She smiled. Her full mouth bowed up slowly, easily. "Thanks for your help."

"Thanks for..." He stopped. Damn. Idiot. She hadn't done anything for him. He'd done a favor for her. He sniffed a laugh to cover his nervousness. "Thanks for letting me go with you?"

She laughed, too. "Seriously. I appreciated your help."

He nodded, unable to take his eyes off her. The way she glowed set off crackling sparks of desire inside him. Even though he knew he wasn't supposed to kiss her, his head began to lower of its own volition.

Her blue-gray eyes shimmered up at him. Her lips parted as she realized what he was about to do. He could all but feel the heat from her body radiating to his—

She stepped back. Smiled weakly. "Thanks again for your help."

Then she spun away and raced into the house.

He stood frozen.

It took a while before he realized he probably looked like an idiot, standing there staring at her back porch. So he walked into his grandmother's house and dropped onto the guest room bed without even showering. He was tired. Crazed. Crazy to be so attracted to someone he couldn't have, and it was driving him insane that this attraction kept getting away from him.

Two minutes before he fell asleep that night, he wondered if somehow her excitement for her business had gotten tangled up in his feelings for her and morphed into something it shouldn't be.

That would really explain things for him. Normally, when he decided someone was off-limits, he could keep her off-limits. So it had to be the excitement of the day that had destroyed his resolve. That was the only thing that made sense.

The next morning he strode over to her house. Ostensibly, he'd come to get Owen to play. In reality, he had decided to test out this attraction. If it had been seeing her excitement about her business that had pushed it over the line the day before, then he'd be fine this morning.

Her door was open, so he knocked on the wood frame of the screen door. "Hey. Anybody home?"

"Come in, Wyatt."

Her voice was soft but steady. No overwhelming attraction made her breathless. In the light of day, they were normal. Or at least she was.

Now to test him.

He pulled open the screen door. "I came for Owen...."

Papers of all shapes, sizes and colors littered her kitchen

table. But she had a pretty, fresh, early morning look that caused his heart to punch against his breastbone. So much for thinking it was her excitement about her wedding cake opportunities that had gotten to him the day before. It was her. Whatever he felt for her was escalating.

He carefully made his way to the table. "What's up?"

She peeked up, her blue eyes solemn, serious. "Doing some figuring."

He sat on the chair across from hers. "Oh?"

She rose, took a cup from her cupboard, filled it with coffee and placed it in front of him.

"What I need is an assistant."

"Do you think—" Because his voice squeaked, his cleared his throat. "Do you think your business is going to pick up that fast?"

She refilled her own coffee cup and sat again. "I plan for contingencies. I don't want to be known as the wedding cake lady who can't take your wedding."

He laughed. "There's something to be said for playing hard to get...." Maybe that's why she was suddenly so attractive to him? Didn't he always want what he couldn't have? Maybe he'd only been kidding himself into thinking he was trying to get his inner nice guy back? And her playing hard to get had just fed his inner selfish demon? "Everybody wants what they can't have. You could charge more money—"

"The more cakes I bake, the more referrals I get. I don't need to be exclusive. I want to start a business, a real business. Someday have a building with a big baking area and an office."

Their knees bumped when she shifted, and her gaze jumped to his as she jerked back. Her voice was shaky when she said, "I've been going over my figures, and if I didn't save money for the winter I could hire someone."

He tried to answer, but no words formed. Mesmerized by the gaze of those soft blue eyes, everything male in him just wanted to hold her.

He frowned. *Hold her. Protect her. Save her.*

Was he falling into the same pattern he'd formed with Betsy? Once they'd started dating, he got her a great apartment, a new car. All because he didn't want to see her do without.

And he knew how that had ended.

Owen came running into the room. "I made my bed!" He jumped from one foot to the other, so eager to play that energy poured from him.

Wyatt scraped his chair away from the table. "Then let's go."

Missy swallowed and she rose, too. "Yeah. You guys go on outside. Mommy has some things to think about."

Wyatt's gut jumped again. He could solve all her problems with one call to his bank. He glanced at the papers on the table. Was it really an accident that she'd picked today, this morning, after he'd nearly kissed her the night before, to run some numbers?

He sucked in a breath. He had become a suspicious, suspicious man.

But after Betsy, was that so bad? Especially if it caused him to slow down and analyze things, so neither he nor Missy got hurt?

"Come on, O. Let's go haul some dirt."

He and Owen left the kitchen and Missy squeezed her eyes shut. Since that dance, she'd had trouble getting and keeping her breath when he was around. And she knew why. He was good-looking, but she was needy. Four years with no romance in her life, four years of not feeling like a woman, melted away when he looked at her. His dark, dark eyes seemed to see right through her, to her soul. And since that dance, every time he looked at her she knew he was as attracted to her as she was to him.

They could be talking about the price of potato chips and she would know he was thinking about their attraction.

And everything inside her would swing in that direction, too.

Luckily, she had a brain that wouldn't let her do anything stupid.

They hardly knew each other. What they felt had to be purely sexual. She had kids who needed protecting. And the only way she could truly protect her kids was to make her business so successful she'd never have to depend on a man. Keeping her eye on the ball, creating the best wedding cake company in Maryland, that's what would keep her safe, independent. Eventually, she might want a relationship. She might even marry again, if she didn't have to be dependent on a man. But it would be pretty damned hard not to become dependent on Wyatt when she was broke and he had millions.

He had to be off-limits.

No matter how good-looking he was. And no matter how much she kept noticing.

Playing with Owen cleared Wyatt's mind enough that he made a startling realization as he was eating another dry sandwich for lunch, this one peanut butter from a jar he'd found in a cabinet.

His relationship with Betsy ultimately had become all about money. But so did a lot of his relationships. He hired friends who became employees, and the friendships became working relationships. He invested in the companies of friends and those friendships became business relationships.

Because money changed things. If he really wanted his

feelings for Missy to cool, all he had to do was give her money for her business. Then his internal businessman would recategorize her.

Sadness washed through him. He didn't want to recategorize her. He wanted to like her. But he ignored those thoughts. He was recently divorced. With his limited time, all he and Missy would have would be a fling. She deserved better.

Walking to the back door of his grandmother's house, he sniffed a laugh. It looked as if he'd gotten what he wanted. His inner nice guy was back. He was putting Missy's needs ahead of his.

He strode through her empty backyard, knowing the kids were probably napping. He and Missy wouldn't just have time to talk privately; they could go over real numbers to determine exactly how much money she'd need.

His heart pinched again. He kept walking. This was the right thing to do.

On her porch, he knocked on the wood frame of the screen door.

She turned and saw him.

Time stopped. Her eyes widened with pleasure. When he opened the door and stepped inside, he watched them warm with desire. Her gaze did a quick ripple from his face to his toes, and his gut coiled.

"Hey."

"Hey."

"I didn't expect you back until the kids woke up."

He scrubbed his hand across the back of his neck. Offering her money suddenly seemed so wrong. She was pretty and she liked him and he'd always liked her. The house was quiet. He could slide his hand under that thick ponytail, nudge her to him and kiss her senseless within seconds.

The very presumptuousness of that thought got him

back on track. She'd already rebuffed him twice. She knew what she wanted and was going after it. She wouldn't sleep with him on a whim. No matter how attracted they were.

He needed to behave himself, think rationally and get them both beyond this attraction.

"I've been considering what you said this morning about hiring someone."

"Oh?"

"Yeah. Can we sit?"

"Sure."

She sat on the chair she'd been in earlier that morning. He sat across from her again.

"You need to buy a new vehicle. Maybe a van."

She laughed. "No kidding."

"So the way I figure this, you need salary for an assistant, day care for the kids in the morning and a new van."

She nodded. "Okay. I get it. You just talked me out of spending my winter money on an assistant. It won't work to hire an assistant if the SUV breaks down."

"Actually, that's why I'm here." He took one last look at her face—turned up nose, full lips, sensual blue-gray eyes. His hormones protested at the easy way he gave up on a relationship, but he trudged on. "Rather than you using your winter money, which isn't enough anyway, I'd like to give you a hundred thousand dollars."

He expected a yelp of happiness. Maybe a scream. He got a confused stare.

"You want to *give* me a hundred thousand dollars?"

"There are hidden costs in having an employee. I'm guessing a good baker doesn't come for minimum wage. Add benefits and employer taxes and you're probably close to fifty thousand. A van will run you about thirty thousand and I'm not sure about day care."

She rose. "You're kidding me."

"No. Employer taxes and benefits will about double your expense for an assistant's salary."

"I'm not talking about the taxes. I'm talking about the money." She spun away, then pivoted to face him again. "For Pete's sake! I don't want your money! I want to be independent."

"Your business can't stand on its own."

"Maybe not now, but it will."

"Not if you don't get an influx of cash."

She gasped. "I thought you had some faith in me!"

"I do!"

"You don't!" She leaned toward him and the hot liquid he saw in her eyes had nothing to do with sexual heat. She was furious with him. "If you did, you'd give me a few months to work through the bugs and get this thing going! You wouldn't offer me money."

"You're taking this all wrong. I'm trying to help you."

"So this is charity?" She looked away, then quickly looked back again. "Get out."

"No. I..." Confused, he ran his hand along the back of his neck. What had just happened?

"Get out. Now. Or I won't even send Owen out to play with you."

Wyatt headed for the door, so baffled he turned to face her, but she'd already left the room.

She sent Owen out to play after his nap, but she didn't even peek out the window. Confusion made Wyatt sigh as he trudged up the steps at suppertime. He opened another can of the soup he'd found in the pantry. Seeing the sludgelike paste, he checked the expiration date and with a groan of disgust threw it out.

What the hell was going on? Not only was he eating junk, things that had been in cupboards for God knew how long, but he was attracted to a woman who seemed equally attracted but kept rebuffing him. So he'd offered her money, to give them a logical reason to keep their relationship platonic, and instead of making her happy, he'd made her mad. *Mad*. Most people would jump for joy when they'd been offered money.

She should have jumped for joy.

Maybe what he needed was to get out of this house? He hadn't really cared to see a lot of the people from his high school days, but he was changing his mind. A conversation about anything other than Missy Johnson and her wedding cakes and her cute kids might be just what he needed to remind him he wasn't an eighteen-year-old sap anymore, pining over a pretty girl who didn't want him. When it came to women, he could have his pick. He didn't need one Missy Johnson.

He straddled his motorcycle and headed for the diner. He ambled inside and found the place almost empty. Considering that it was a sunny Sunday afternoon, Wyatt suspected everybody was outside doing something physical. A waitress in a pink uniform strolled over. He ordered a hot roast beef sandwich and mashed potatoes smothered in brown gravy. For dessert he ate pie.

After a good meal, he felt a hundred percent better. He hadn't seen anybody he recognized or who recognized him, but it didn't matter. All he'd needed to get himself back to normal was some real food.

He paid the bill, but curiosity stopped him from heading for the door. Instead, he peeked into the kitchen. "Hey, Monty. It's me. Wyatt McKenzie."

Missy's dad set his spatula on the wood-topped island in the center of the diner kitchen. "Well, I'll be damned."

Tall, balding and wearing a big apron over jeans and a white T-shirt, he walked over and slapped Wyatt on the back. "How the hell are you, kid?"

"I'm fine. Great." He looked around. "Wow. The place hasn't changed one iota in fifteen years."

"People like consistency."

"Yep." He knew that from running his own company, but there was a difference between consistent and run-down. Still, it wasn't his place to mention that. "I'm surprised you don't have any of Missy's cakes in here."

Monty stepped back. Returning to the wood-topped island, he picked up his spatula. "Oh, she doesn't bake for me anymore."

"Too busy with her own cakes, I guess."

Monty glanced up. "Is she doing good? I mean, one businessman to another?"

Wyatt laughed. Having seen a bit of her pride that morning, he guessed she probably hadn't told her father anything about her business beyond the basics. Maybe he'd also made the mistake of offering her money?

"She's doing great. Three future brides corralled her when she tried to leave yesterday's wedding reception."

"Wow. She is doing well."

"Exceptionally well. She's a bit stubborn, though, about some things."

"Are you helping her?"

He winced. "She's not much on taking help."

Monty snorted. "Never was."

Well, okay. That pushed his mood even further up the imaginary scale. If she wouldn't take help from her dad, why should Wyatt be surprised she wouldn't take help from him?

The outing got him back to normal, but not so much that he braved going into Missy's house the next morning. He went to the sandbox and five minutes later Owen, Lainie and Claire came racing out of the house.

While playing Wiffle ball with the kids, he ascertained that their mom was working on a new cake.

"This one will be yellow," Lainie said.

Not knowing what else to do, he smiled. "Yellow. That's nice. I like yellow."

"I like yellow, too."

"Me, too."

"Me, too."

He laughed. He didn't for one minute think yellow was that important to any one of the triplets, but he did see how much they enjoyed being included, involved. His heart swelled. He liked them a lot more than he ever thought he could like kids. But it didn't matter. He and their mother might be attracted, but they didn't see eye to eye about anything. Maybe it was time to step up the jewelry search and get back to Tampa?

CHAPTER FIVE

WYATT THREW HIMSELF into the work of looking for the Scottish heirlooms in the mountain of closet boxes.

He endured the scent of sachets, billowing dust and boxes of things like panty hose—who saved old panty hose and why?—and found nothing even remotely resembling jewelry.

To break up his days, he played with Owen every morning and all three kids every afternoon, but he didn't go anywhere near Missy.

Still, on Saturday afternoon, when she came out of the house dressed in a sunny yellow dress that showed off her shoulders and accented her curves, lugging the bottom of a cake with the babysitter, he knew he couldn't let her go alone. Particularly since her SUV had already had trouble starting once that week.

While she brought the rest of the cake to her vehicle, he changed out of his dirty clothes into clean jeans and a T-shirt. Looking at himself in the mirror, he frowned. His hair was growing in and looked a little like Owen's, poking out in all directions. He also needed a shave. But if he took the time to shave, she'd be gone by the time he was done.

No shave. No comb. Since he usually didn't have hair, he didn't really own a comb. So today he'd be doing grunge.

Once again, he didn't say anything. Simply walked over

to her SUV and got in on the passenger's side as she got in on the driver's side.

"Don't even bother to tell me one person can handle this big cake. I watched you and the babysitter cart it out here. I know better. If the caterer can't spare a waiter you'll be in a world of trouble."

She sighed. "You don't have to do this."

"I know."

"You haven't spoken to me since we fought on Sunday."

He made a disgusted noise. "I know that, too."

"So why are you going?"

He had no idea. Except that he didn't want to see her struggle. Remembering her fierce independent streak, he knew that reply wouldn't be greeted with a thank-you, so he said, "I like cake."

Apparently expecting to have to fend off an answer that in some way implied she needed help, she opened her mouth, but nothing came out. After a few seconds, she said, "I could make you a cake."

He peered over at her. In her sunny yellow dress, with her hair all done up, and wearing light pink lipstick, she was so cute his selfish inner demon returned. He'd forgotten how hard it was to want something he couldn't have.

"Oh, then that would be charity and we can't have that. If you can't take my money, I can't take your cake."

She sighed. "Look, I know I got a little over-the-top angry on Sunday when you offered me money. But there's a good reason I refused. I need to be independent."

"Fantastic."

She laughed. "It is fantastic. Wyatt, I need to be able to support myself and my kids. And I can. That's what makes it fantastic. *I can do this.* You need to trust me."

"Great. Fine. I trust you."

"Good, because I feel I owe you for playing with the

kids, and a cake would be a simple way for me to pay that back."

He gaped at her. "Did you hear what you just said? You want to pay me for playing."

She shoved her key into the ignition and started the SUV. "You're an idiot."

"True. But I'm an idiot who is going to get cake at this wedding."

But in the car on the way to the reception venue, he stared out the window. He couldn't remember the last time anybody had ordered him around like this. Worse, he couldn't remember a time a *woman* had ordered him around like this—and he *still* liked her.

He sighed internally. And there it was. The truth. He still liked her.

The question was what did he do about it?

Avoiding her didn't work. She wouldn't take his money so he could recategorize her. And even after not seeing her all week, the minute he was in the same car with her all his feelings came tumbling back.

He was nuts.

Wrong…

Really? Wrong? They were healthy, single, attracted people. Why was liking her wrong?

Because she didn't want to like him.

They arrived at the wedding reception more quickly than the week before because this venue was closer. As they unloaded the square layers with black lace trim, Missy gazed at each one lovingly. In high school, she'd hated having to bake fancy cakes for the diner, but now she was so glad she had. At age thirty-three she had twenty years of cake-baking experience behind her. And she was very, very good.

"The kids told me this one is yellow."

She peeked over at Wyatt, relieved he was finally talking. "It is. It's a yellow cake...with butter cream fondant and rolled fondant to make the black lace."

"How do you make lace?"

His question surprised her. Most people saw the finished product and didn't care how it got that way.

"There are patterns and forms you can buy, but I made my own."

He studied the intricate design. "That couldn't have been easy."

"I do things like this when you're playing with the kids."

He shot her a funny look and she turned away. The little spark of attraction she'd felt when she'd seen his scruffy day-old beard and butt-hugging jeans that morning flared again. With his sexy, fingers-run-through-it-in-frustration hair and his long, lean body, he was enough to drive her to distraction.

But she wouldn't be distracted.

Well, maybe a little. She was a normal woman and he was extremely sexy. Was it so wrong to be attracted? No. The trick would be not letting him see.

They arranged the black-and-white cake from the big square layer to the smallest layer, which had a top hat and sparkly wedding veil at the peak.

"Cute."

She stood back. "Different. I'll say that."

"You act as if you didn't know how it would turn out."

"I didn't. The bride is a Goth who wanted something black with hints of Victorian. She told me what she wanted and I made it."

"Can you eat the top hat?"

"Yep. And the veil, too."

"Amazing."

Their gazes caught. The flare of attraction became a

flicker of need. She tried to squelch it, but in four years she hadn't felt anything like this. Oh, who was she kidding? She'd never felt anything like this. Wyatt was bold, sexy, commanding. And he liked her. The real her. Not the pretend version most men saw when they looked at her. He'd seen her stubborn streak, and still helped her—was still attracted to her.

What if there really was something going on between them? Something real. He could walk away. Hell, after she'd yelled at him on Sunday he should have walked away. But he hadn't. Even though they'd had a fairly nasty difference of opinion—which they'd yet to get beyond—here they were. He was still attracted to her. She was still attracted to him.

The bride arrived in her black-and-white wedding gown with her tuxedo-clad groom in tow. At least fourteen tattoos were visible above the bodice of her strapless gown.

Wyatt's eyebrows rose. "Different."

"Very her," Missy replied, standing beside him, off to the left of the cake, out of the way so they didn't detract from it.

He looked at the bride, looked at the cake. "You're really very good at this."

Missy's smile came slowly. Anybody could throw batter into a pan and get a cake. But not everybody could match baking ability with artistry. It was a gift. She never took it for granted.

"I know."

"I can see why you're so confident."

"Thanks."

"Someday you are going to be the best."

She laughed. There was an unimaginable joy in having something she was good at. But an even greater joy at having people appreciate it. "Thanks."

He growled and she frowned at him. "What?"

"I can never seem to say the right thing to you."

Music from the string quartet blended with the noise of wedding guests taking seats. The best man took the microphone, hit it to make sure it was live. The tap, tap, tap rolled into the room like thunder.

Wyatt caught Missy's hand. "Let's go outside."

Confused, she let him lead her through the French doors to a wide wooden deck, which was filled with milling wedding guests. Avoiding them, he guided her to the steps, and they clambered down until they stood in a quiet garden.

She looked around. She hadn't done a lot of exploring of the country clubs and other wedding venues where she took her cakes, but seeing how beautiful, and inspiring, this garden was, maybe she should.

"This is nice."

He sighed heavily. "Let's not change the subject until I get out what I want to say."

She peeked over at him, suddenly realizing how alone they were. All her nerve endings sprang to life. She'd never been attracted to a man like this. And he wasn't just nice, he was thoughtful. Or trying. When he made a mistake he wanted to fix it. He didn't just walk away.

Her thoughts from before popped into her brain again. *What if something really was happening between them? Something real? Something important? Something permanent?*

"I understand why my offering you money doesn't fit your plan. But I still feel like we're not beyond the insult."

She pressed her lips together. She was right. He didn't walk away. He fixed what he broke. So different from her dad and her ex.

"What you said in the car today about being able to support yourself...I thought it was pride, but I finally get it. I see the bride-cake connection. You don't want money or help because you *know* this is going to work because you have that instinct. The thing that's going to push you above the rest. You are going to be one of the best in your business. You don't *need* help."

Her insides melted. She loved it when a bride gushed over a cake, or wedding guests sought her out to compliment her, but this wasn't just a compliment. This was Wyatt. A successful entrepreneur. Somebody who knew good work when he saw it. Somebody who saw that she had what it took to be successful.

Her blood warmed with pleasure that quickly turned to yearning. He was gorgeous and attracted to her. Plus, he understood her. Would it be so wrong to start something with him?

It had been so long since she'd wanted something for herself, purely for herself, that she instinctively tried to talk herself out of it. She told herself it felt wrong, because she knew she had to be self-sufficient before she started anything serious with a man.

But this was Wyatt. This was a guy who understood. A guy who didn't run. A guy who fixed things. A guy who liked her and believed in her. The little voice in her heart told her to relax and let it happen.

She smiled sheepishly, not quite sure what a woman did nowadays to let a man know she'd changed her mind and was willing to go after what they both seemed to want. "Thanks for the compliment."

He sighed again, this time as if relieved. "You're welcome."

Silence settled over them. It should have been the nice, comfortable silence of two friends. But her stomach quivered and her nerve endings lit up, as if begging to be touched. She'd never before felt this raw, wonderful need, and she wished with all her might that he'd kiss her.

As if reading her mind, he stepped close again. He laid a hand on her cheek. "Missy."

His head began to descend.

She swallowed hard. Even as the sensations rushing through her begged to be explored, new fear leaped inside her. It had been four long years since she'd kissed someone. *Four years.*

And she wasn't just considering kissing. What burned between them was so hot she knew they'd end up in bed sooner rather than later. With their faces mere inches apart, her heart hit against her ribs. Was she ready for this?

His mouth met hers and liquid heat filled her. Like lava, it erupted from her middle and poured through her veins. She put her hands on his cheeks, just wanting to touch him, but when his tongue slipped inside her mouth, she used them to bring him closer.

She'd never felt anything like this. The pleasure. The passion. The pure, unadulterated sensuality that left her breathless and achy.

His hands roamed from her shoulders to her waist and back up again. Hers fell from his cheeks to his shoulder, down his long, lean back, and slowly—enjoying every smooth demarcation of muscle and sinew beneath his T-shirt—drifted up again. He was so strong. So solid. Everything inside her wept with yearning. For four years she'd been nothing but a mom. A busy mom. Right now she felt like a woman. Flesh and blood. Heat and need.

As his mouth continued to plunder hers, she pictured them tangled in the covers of her big four-poster bed. Desire whooshed through her. Everything was happening so fast that her head spun.

She thought she knew him...but did she?

He thought he knew her…but he didn't. Nobody did.

She stopped kissing him, squeezed her eyes shut. *That* was the real reason she shied away from men. Nobody knew her. Sure, Wyatt had seen her stubborn streak. He'd seen her with the kids, in full mom mode, but nobody knew about her dad. Nobody knew about the beatings, the alcoholism, the gambling that had colored her childhood and had formed who she was. And at this stage in her life, she wasn't sure she could tell anybody. Just as she was equally sure Wyatt, this Wyatt who fixed things, who probed into things, who wanted to make everything right, would never let her get away with the usual slick answers she gave when anyone asked her if she'd seen her dad lately.

Wyatt would realize there'd been trouble in her past and he'd demand she talk about it.

She stepped away. "I'm sorry. I can't do this."

He caught her hand and tugged her back. "Seems to me you were 'doing' it just fine."

She couldn't help it; she laughed. He was such a fun guy, but her past was just too much to handle. Even for him.

She slipped away from him. "I'm serious. I don't want a relationship—"

He caught her hand and yanked her back. "That's perfect, because I don't want a relationship, either."

That confused her so much she frowned. "You don't want a relationship?"

He chuckled. "No."

She pointed at him, then herself, then back at him. "Then what's this?"

"A fling?"

She blinked. A fling? While she was worried about telling him her deepest, darkest secret, he was thinking fling?

"Look, I've only been divorced for two weeks—"

She stepped back, her mind reeling. Before thoughts of her secret had ruined the moment, she'd felt things she'd never felt before. And he wanted a fling? "But—"

"But what? We're single, adults and attracted to each other. There's no reason we can't enjoy each other while I'm here."

She blinked again. The emotions careening through her didn't match up with the word *fling*. "Let me get this straight. You want to sleep with me, no strings attached, no thought of a relationship. No possibility of falling in love?"

His face scrunched. "You're making it sound tawdry."

She'd never once considered sex just for the sake of sex. Even though it solved the problem of telling him about her dad, her stomach took a little leap. He didn't want to love her. He wasn't even considering it.

He caught her shoulders and forced her to look at him. "You said that your ex leaving you with three kids and no money made you independent?"

She nodded.

"Well, think about this. Think about working for something from the time you're sixteen, and one mistake—picking the wrong person to trust—causes you to lose one-third of it. But it's about more than the money. My ex cheated on me. Lied to me. Tried to undermine me with people in the industry, saying that when she got half the company she could take over with a little bit of help, positioning herself to take everything I'd worked for. She didn't just want money. She wanted to boot me from my own company. She wanted to ruin me."

"Oh." Hearing the hurt in his voice, understanding rose in Missy, but it didn't salve the emptiness, the letdown she felt from realizing he didn't even want to *consider* loving her. It seemed in her life there'd been nobody who'd ever really loved her. At home, her dad wasn't ever sober enough to have a real emotion. Her mom stayed too busy keeping up appearances that if she kissed her or hugged her, Missy always knew it was for show, not for real. Her sister locked herself away. Like Wyatt, she'd studied. The first chance she'd gotten, she'd left.

In going along, living the lie, Missy had been alone.

Alone.

Confused.

Not wanted.

He sighed. "I just don't believe relationships last, and I don't want either one of us to get hurt."

"Sure." She understood. She really did. No one wanted to be taken for granted, and hurt as he'd been by his ex. It could be years before he would trust again.

Which was why she stepped back. "I get it."

He sighed with relief. "Good."

But when he reached for her, she moved farther away. Put a distance between them that was as much emotional as physical.

"I can't have a fling." At his puzzled look, she added, "The things you didn't factor into your fling are my kids."

He frowned. "Your kids?"

"I can't leave them to be with you and you can't…well, sleep over."

His frown deepened. "I can't?"

"No. They're kids. Sweet. Impressionable. I don't want to confuse them."

"So you won't have a fling because of your kids?"

"I don't want them confused." Tears welled behind her eyes and she struggled to contain them. She hadn't ever quite realized how alone she was until a real relationship, a real connection, seemed to be at her fingertips, only to disappear in a puff. "I don't want them involved. And until they're old enough, I'm…well, I'm just not going to…" She reddened to the roots of her hair. "You know."

"Sleep with anybody." He shook his head. "You're not going to sleep with anybody until your kids are teenagers."

"I hadn't really thought it through, but I guess that's what I'm saying." Determined to be mature about this, she held out her hand to shake his. "No hard feelings?"

He took it. Squeezed once. "Lots of regret, but no hard feelings."

She nodded, but when he released her hand, disappointment rattled through her.

She liked him. But he didn't want to like her.

CHAPTER SIX

SUNDAY MORNING, Wyatt wanted nothing more than to stay in bed. He looked at the clock, saw it was only seven, and pulled the covers over his head. Then a car door slammed and he realized he'd woken because he'd heard a vehicle pull into the drive. He bounced out of bed, confused about who'd be coming to his Gram's house at seven o'clock on a Sunday morning. But when he walked to the kitchen window and peered out, he realized the caller had parked in Missy's driveway.

Who would visit Missy at seven o'clock on a Sunday?

With a sigh he told himself not to care about her. Ever. For Pete's sake. She'd rebuffed him twice, and the night before out-and-out told him she didn't want anything to do with him. She even made him shake on it.

Did he have no pride?

He ambled to the counter, put on a pot of coffee and opened the back door to let the stale night air out and the cool morning air in.

Leaning against the counter, he waited for his jolt of caffeine. When the coffeemaker gurgled its final release, he poured himself a cup.

Turning to walk to the table, he almost tripped over Owen.

Still wearing his cowboy pajamas, the little boy grinned. "Hey."

"Hey." He stooped down to Owen's height. "What are you doing here?"

"There's a man talking to my mom."

Even as Owen spoke, dark-haired Lainie opened Wyatt's screen door and stepped inside. Dressed in a pink nightgown, she said, "Hi," as if it were an everyday occurrence for her to walk into his house in sleepwear.

"Hi."

Before he could say anything else, Claire walked in. Also in a pink nightgown, she smiled sheepishly.

Still crouched in front of Owen, Wyatt caught the little boy's gaze. "So your mom's talking to somebody and I'm guessing she didn't see you leave."

"She told us to go to our woom."

At Wyatt's left shoulder, Lainie caught his chin and turned him to face her. "He means room."

"Your mom sent you to your room?"

Owen nodded. "While she talks to the man."

Wyatt's blood boiled. For a woman who didn't want to get involved with him, she was engrossed enough in today's male guest that she hadn't even seen her kids leave.

Maybe he'd just take her kids back and break up her little party?

Telling himself that was childish, he nonetheless set his coffee cup on the counter and herded the three munchkins to the door. Missy would go nuts with worry if she realized they were gone. Albeit for better reasons than to catch her in the act, he had to take her kids back.

"Let's go. Your mom will be worried if she finds you gone."

Owen dug in his heels. "But she's talking to the man. She doesn't want us to sturb her."

His eyebrows rose in question and he glanced at Helaina, the interpreter.

Who looked at him as if he was crazy not to understand. "Yeah. She doesn't want us to sturb her."

"Sturb?"

"Dee-sturb." Claire piped in.

"Oh, disturb."

Lainie nodded happily.

Well. Well. Little Miss I-Don't-Want-A-Fling didn't want to be disturbed. Maybe his first guess hadn't been so far off the mark, after all? She might not want a relationship with *him,* but she was with somebody.

Wyatt corralled the kids and directed them to the porch.

When they were on the sidewalk at the bottom of the steps, Helaina caught his hand. "We stay together when we walk."

Claire shyly caught his other hand.

Warmth sputtered through him. He seriously wasn't the kind of guy to hang out with kids, but not only was he playing in dirt and organizing Wiffle ball games, now he was holding hands.

Owen proudly led the way. He skipped to the hedge and pulled it aside.

Lainie stooped and dipped through. Claire stooped and dipped through. Owen grinned at him.

Wyatt took one look at the opening provided and knew that wasn't going to work. "You go first. I need to hold it up higher for myself."

Owen nodded and ducked down to slip through.

Wyatt pushed the hedge aside and stepped into Missy's backyard, where all three kids awaited him.

He pointed at the porch. "Let's go."

But only a few feet across the grass, Missy's angry

shout came from the house, as if she was talking to someone on the enclosed front porch.

"I don't care who you are! I don't care what you think you deserve! You're not getting one dime from me!"

Wyatt's blood ran cold. That didn't sound like the words of a lover. It didn't even sound like the words of a friend.

Could the man in her house be her ex? Returning for money? From her? After draining their accounts?

His nerve endings popped with anger. He dropped Claire's and Helaina's hands. "Wait here."

But when he looked down at their little faces, he saw Claire's eyes had filled with tears. Owen's and Helaina's eyes had widened in fear. The shouting had scared them. He couldn't leave them out here alone when they were obviously frightened.

"Oh, come on, darlin'. You know I should have gotten this house when your grandmother died. I'm just askin' for what you owe me."

Wyatt's mouth fell open. That was Monty.

"I heard you've got a sweet deal going with this wedding cake thing you're doing. I just want what's coming to me."

"What should be coming to you is jail time!"

"Aren't you being a little melodramatic?"

"Melodramatic? You beat Mom to within an inch of her life so often I'm not surprised her heart gave out. And you beat me and Althea." She stopped. A short cry rang out.

Then Missy said, "You get the hell away from me! Now. Mom may not have wanted to call the police, but the next time you show up here I'll not only call the police, I'll quite happily tell every damned person in this town that you beat us. Regularly. They'll see that the happy-go-lucky diner owner everybody loves doesn't really exist."

"You'd never get anybody to believe you."

"Try me."

By now the kids had huddled around the knees of Wyatt's sweatpants. No sound came from the house, but the front door slammed shut. With his hands on the kids' shoulders, Wyatt quickly shepherded them to his side of the shrubs, where Monty couldn't see them.

As her father screeched out of the driveway, Missy came barreling out the kitchen door. Standing on the porch, she screamed, "Owen! Lainie! Claire!" as if she'd gone looking for them after Monty left, found them gone and was terrified.

Wyatt quickly stepped out from behind the thin leafy branches, three kids at his knees. "We're here. They came to get me to play in the sandbox."

She ran down the porch steps and gathered her children against her. "They haven't eaten breakfast yet."

"I didn't know that or I would have given them cereal. I have plenty." Not knowing what else to do, he babbled on. "Gram had enough for an army, and most of it still hasn't hit the expiration date."

She looked up at him. Tears poured from her blue eyes, down her cheeks and off her chin.

He stooped down beside her and the kids. "Hey." His heart thudded against his breastbone. What did a man say to a woman when he'd just heard that her dad had beaten her when she was a child?

Wyatt didn't have a clue. But he did have a sore, aching heart. She'd had a crappy husband and a rotten father. While he'd had two perfect parents, talent, brains and safety, she'd lived in fear.

The knowledge rattled through him like an unwanted noise in an old car. He couldn't deny it, but he didn't know how to fix it.

And the last thing he wanted to do was say the wrong thing.

He set his hand on her shoulder. "You go inside. Take a shower. I'll feed the kids."

"I'm fine."

"You're crying." He hated like hell stating the obvious, but sometimes there was no way around that. "Give yourself a twenty-minute break. I told you I have lots of cereal. We'll be okay for twenty minutes."

Owen broke out of her hug. "We'll be okay, Mommy."

Fresh tears erupted. She gave the kids one last hug, then rose. Her voice trembled as she said, "If you're sure."

"Hey, we'll make a game out of it."

Owen tugged on the leg of his sweatpants. "Can we wook for tweasure?"

Wyatt laughed. "Yeah. We'll wook for treasure."

She'd never abandoned her kids.

Never handed them over to another person just to give herself time to pull herself together. But she also hadn't had a visit from her dad in…oh, eight years?

And he'd decided to show up today? Knowing she had money in her checking account? Demanding that she give it to him?

How the hell did he know she had money?

She put her head under the shower spray. Now that she'd had a minute to process everything, she wasn't as upset as she was surprised. Shocked that he'd shown up at her house like that. But now that she knew she was on his radar again, she wouldn't cower as her mom had. She'd stand her ground. And she *would* call the police. If he touched her or—God forbid—her kids, he'd be in jail so fast his head would spin.

She got out of the shower and dried her hair. In ten minutes she had on clean shorts and a T-shirt. Her hair was combed. Her tears were dry.

She headed outside.

She expected to find Wyatt and the kids in the yard. Instead, they were nowhere in sight. When she knocked on his kitchen door there was no answer, so she stepped inside.

"Wyatt?"

"Back here."

She followed the sound of his voice to the large corner bedroom, the 1960s version of a master suite, just like the one in her house. Old-fashioned lamps and lacy curtains reminded her of the room she'd inherited herself.

But the bed was covered in boxes, and more boxes were piled on the floor. Taking a bite of cereal from a bowl on the bedside table, Owen saw her. He grinned. "Hi, Mommy."

Lainie popped up from behind the bed. Claire peeked around a tall stack of shoe boxes. "We're looking for treasure."

Missy walked into the room. "In the boxes?"

Owen said, "Yeah. But Lainie spilled her milk."

Wyatt came running out of the bathroom, holding a roll of toilet paper. "Okay, everybody stand back…." Then he saw Missy. "Hey."

She took the toilet paper from him and rushed to the other side of the bed, where rolling milk rapidly approached the edge of the area rug. She spun off some tissue and caught the milk just in time.

Wyatt rubbed his index finger across his nose. "Things look worse than they really are."

On her way to dump the milk-sodden tissue in the bathroom, she said, "What is all this?"

"This," Wyatt said, following her to the bathroom, "is everything I found in the closet."

"Are you kidding me? How'd your gram get all that in a closet?"

"She was quite the crafty packer."

"I suppose." Missy glanced around. "So it looks like you haven't found the jewelry from Scotland yet."

"Nope. And the kids were fine. Great, actually, until Lainie spilled her milk."

"She gets overeager."

He laughed. "She wants to do everything at once."

"I can take them home now."

"Why? We're having fun. And I'm actually getting through three boxes a minute."

"Three boxes a minute?"

"They open, dump, get bored and move on to the next one. And that leaves me to collect up everything they dumped, and get it back in the box. As I'm collecting, I'm checking for jewelry. At this rate I'll have this whole room done by noon."

She laughed.

And he sighed with relief. But the relief didn't last long. With her tears dry and her mood improved, he knew she'd never tell him about her dad. And he couldn't just say, "Hey, I saw Monty running out of your house this morning." It would be awkward for her, like dropping someone in an ice-cold swimming pool.

Still, he couldn't let this go. He'd been the one to tell Monty she was doing well. He'd thought he was doing her a favor. Turns out he had everything all wrong. And somehow he had to fix it.

"So what happened this morning?"

She strolled back into the bedroom and walked over to Helaina, who'd dumped out a box of panty hose.

"What is this?"

He grabbed the ball of panty hose and stuffed it back

into the shoe box. "My grandmother never met a pair of panty hose she didn't want to save."

"My grandmother saved them, too. She used them as filler when she made stuffed animals or couch pillows."

"Thank God. I was beginning to think my grandmother was nuts." And he'd also noticed Missy had changed the subject. "So what happened this morning?"

She sucked in a breath, ruffling Lainie's dark hair as the little girl picked up another shoe box, popped the lid and dumped the contents.

Bingo. Jewelry.

He swung around to that side of the bed. Beads and bobbles rolled across the floral comforter. "Well, what do you know?"

Missy caught his gaze. "Don't get your hopes up. Most of this looks like cheap costume jewelry."

He picked up a necklace, saw a chip in the paint on a "pearl."

"Drat."

"Finding jewelry is a good sign, though. At least you know it's here somewhere."

He dropped the string of fake pearls to the bed. "Yeah, well, she has three furnished bedrooms. I found clothes in the drawers in the dressers in each room. All the closets are full of boxes like these." He sighed. "Who wants to go play in the yard?"

Missy laughed. "Is that how you look for jewelry? In the yard?"

He faced her. "In case you haven't noticed, I'm sort of, kind of, the type of guy who doesn't do anything he doesn't want to do."

Shaking her head, she laughed again. "So how do you intend to find the jewelry?"

He shrugged. "Not sure yet. But I'm an idea guy. That's

how I got rich." It was true. Even his writing was a form of coming up with ideas and analyzing them to see if they'd work. "So eventually I'll figure out a way to find the jewelry without having to look through every darned drawer and box in this house."

"Well, I'd volunteer to help you, but I have some thinking of my own to do today."

"Oh, yeah." He sat on the bed, patted the spot beside him. That was as good of an opening as any to try again to get her to talk to him. "I just told you I'm a good idea man. Maybe I could help you with that thinking."

"No. You and I have already been over this. Your idea to solve my financial problem was to give me money."

He remembered—and winced.

"So this morning I need to go over my books again, think through how I can get a van and an assistant."

"Why the sudden rush?"

She shrugged. "No reason." She clapped her hands. "Come on, kids. Let's go."

A chorus of "Ah, Mom," echoed around him.

He rose from the bed, suddenly understanding that maybe she didn't want to talk about her dad because the kids were around. Which meant they wouldn't talk until the triplets took their naps. "I promised them time in the sandbox."

She sighed. "They're not even out of their pajamas yet."

"How about if you go get them dressed while I clean up some of this mess? Then I'll take them when you're done."

"I do want that thinking time this morning." She blew her breath out in another sigh. "I don't know how to pay you back for being so good to them."

"I already told you it makes me feel weird to hear you say you want to pay me for playing. So don't say it again."

She laughed. Then she faced the kids. "All right. Let's

go. We'll get everybody into clean shorts, then you can go out to the sandbox with Wyatt."

Owen jumped. "Yay!"

Lainie raced to the door.

Claire took her mom's hand.

Wyatt watched them go, then fell to the bed again. She'd been beaten by her dad, left by her husband with three babies, and now struggled with growing a business. It didn't seem right that he couldn't give her money. But that ship had sailed. Worse, he had to confess that he was the one who'd told her dad how well she was doing.

Wyatt looked at his watch, counting down the hours till naptime, feeling as if he was counting down the hours to doomsday.

CHAPTER SEVEN

STILL TOO WORKED UP to sit at a table and run numbers, Missy pulled a box of flour from her pantry, along with semisweet chocolate chips, sugar and cornstarch. Wyatt taking the kids without pushing for answers as to why she was so upset was about the nicest thing anyone had ever done for her, so she would repay him with a cake. A fancy chocolate cake with raspberry sauce.

While the cake baked, she took snacks and juice boxes out to the kids, with an extra for Wyatt. Though he accepted the cookies and juice box, he more or less stayed back, but she understood why. Not only had he seen her sobbing that morning, but she'd rejected his advances the night before. She didn't blame him for not wanting to talk to her.

But the cake would bring them back to their normal footing.

As it cooled, she put raspberry juice, cornstarch and a quarter cup of sugar into a saucepan. After it had boiled, she strained it to remove the seeds, then set it aside. Using more chocolate chips, she made the glaze for the cake.

By the time the kids returned to the house for lunch, the cake was ready. As usual, Wyatt didn't come inside with them. He went to his own house for lunch. But that was okay. While the kids napped, she'd take the baby monitor receiver with her and deliver the cake to him.

The kids washed up, ate lunch, brushed their teeth and crawled into their little beds.

Missy took a breath and tucked the monitor under her arm. She grabbed the cup of sauce in one hand and the cake in the other and carried the best looking cake she'd ever baked across her yard, under the shrub branch and to his porch.

She lightly kicked the door with her foot. "Wyatt?"

He appeared on the other side of the screen. "Yeah?"

She presented the cake. "I made this for you."

He glanced down at the cake, then back at her. "I thought we talked about you baking me a cake?"

She laughed. "It's a thank-you for helping me out this morning. Not a thank-you for playing, because we both know that's wrong. It's thanks for helping me."

When he said nothing, she laughed again. "Open the door, idiot, so we can cut this thing and see if it tastes as good as it looks."

He opened the door and she stepped inside the modest kitchen. She set the cake on the table. "Where did your gram keep her knives?"

He walked to the cabinets, opened a drawer and retrieved a knife.

"Might as well get two forks and two plates while you're gathering things."

He silently did as he was told. She happily cut the cake. Dewy and moist, it sliced like a dream. She placed a piece on each plate, then drizzled raspberry sauce over them.

Handing one to Wyatt, she said, "There was supposed to be a whipped cream flower on each piece, but I didn't have enough hands to carry the whipped cream."

He sniffed a laugh, but didn't say anything.

That was when she felt the weirdness. Something was definitely up.

"The cake really is just a simple thank-you. No strings attached." She paused, pointing at his piece. "Try it."

He slid his fork into it and put a bite in his mouth. His eyes closed and he groaned. "Good God. That's heaven on a fork."

Pride tumbled through her. "I know! It's a simple recipe I found online. But it tastes like hours of slave labor."

She laughed again, but Wyatt set down his fork. "We have to talk."

At the stern tone of his voice, her appetite deserted her. She set her fork down, too. "You want to know what made me cry this morning."

He squeezed his eyes shut again, then popped them open. "Actually, that's the problem. I already know what made you cry this morning. When I was bringing the kids back after their surprise visit to my house, I overhead you and Monty."

"Oh." Embarrassment replaced pride. Heat slid up her cheeks. Her chest tightened.

"I heard him ask for money."

She said nothing, only stared at the pretty cake between them.

"I also heard what you said about him beating your mom, you and your sister."

She pressed her lips together.

"But that's not the worst of it."

Her head shot up and she caught his gaze. "Really? What can be worse than my dad beating me? About living a lie? About worrying every damn night that he was going to kill my mom, until she finally did die? What can be worse than that?"

"Look. I know it was a terrible thing."

"You know nothing." And she didn't want him to know anything. If she believed there was a chance for them to have a relationship, she might have told him. The timing was perfect. He already knew the overall story. She might have muddled through the humiliating details, if only because she was sick to death of living a lie. But knowing there was no chance for them, not even the possibility of love, she preferred to keep her secrets and her mortification to herself.

"I don't want to talk about it."

"Okay." His quiet acceptance tiptoed into the room. From his tone she knew he wasn't happy with her answer, but he accepted it. "But I have to tell you one more thing." He dragged in another breath. "One day last week I ate at the diner. When I was done, I went back to the kitchen to say hello to your dad, and somehow the subject of you and your business came up—"

She jumped out of her seat. "Oh, my God! *You* told him?"

"I'm sorry."

She gaped at him, horrible things going through her brain. She'd spent years staying away from her dad, not going to town picnics and gatherings or anything even remotely fun to protect her kids. And in one casual conversation, Wyatt had ruined years of her sacrifice.

She grabbed the monitor and turned to leave.

"I'm sorry!"

She spun to face him. "He's a leech. A liar. A thief. I don't want him in my life! I especially don't want him around the kids!"

"Well, you know what?" Wyatt shot out of his chair and was in front of her before she could blink. "Then you should tell people that. Because normal people don't keep secrets from their dads. Which means other normal people don't suspect you're keeping a secret from yours."

Her chin rose. "I guess that means I'm not normal, then. Thanks for that." She pivoted and smacked her hands on his screen door, opening it. "I need to get back to the kids."

When she was gone, Wyatt fell to his chair. Part of him insisted he shouldn't feel bad. He hadn't known. She hadn't told him.

But he remembered his charmed childhood. He might not have been well liked at school, but he was well loved at home. What the hell did he know about being abused? What did he know about the dark reasons for keeping secrets?

He'd been born under a lucky star and he knew it.

He scrubbed his hands down his face. Looked over at the cake. It was the best thing he had ever tasted. Missy had talent. With a little help, she would succeed. Maybe even beyond her wildest dreams.

But like an idiot, he'd blocked his chance to help her, by offering her money so he could stop being attracted to her.

Her life was about so much more than sex and marriage and who was attracted to whom. It was about more than being praised and admired. All she wanted to do was make a living. Be safe. Keep her kids safe.

And Wyatt kept hurting her.

He was an idiot.

Missy spent the rest of the kids' nap in tears. Not because Wyatt had ratted her out to her dad. He couldn't have ratted her out. As he'd said, he hadn't known she kept her success a secret from her dad. Because she didn't tell anybody about him.

And if she really dug down into the reasons she was

suddenly so sad, so weary of it all, that hit the top of the list.

She didn't talk to anybody. At least not beyond surface subjects. No one knew her. It was the coldest, emptiest, loneliest feeling in the world, to exist but not be known. In high school, she could pretend that the life she led during the day, in classes, at football games, cheering and being chosen to be homecoming queen, snowball queen and prom queen, was her real life. But as she got older, her inability to have real friends, people she could talk to, wore on her. And when she really got honest with herself, she also had to admit that her company was a nice safe way of having to connect with people in only a superficial way. Once a wedding was over, she moved on to new people. No one ever stayed in her life.

Of course, she had wanted to connect with Wyatt, but he didn't want a relationship. He wanted a fling.

She swiped away her tears. It didn't matter. She was fine. When her dad was out of the picture, her life was good. And that morning she'd scared him off. He wouldn't be back. And if he did come back, testing to see if she was serious about her threats, she'd call the police. After a night or two in jail he would stay away for good. Because he was a coward.

Then the whole town would know and she'd be forced to deal with it. But at least her life wouldn't be a lie anymore.

And maybe she could come out from under this horrible veil of secrets that ended with nothing but loneliness.

When the kids awoke, she kept them inside, working on a special project with them: refrigerator art. She got out the construction paper, glue and little round-edged plastic scissors. They made green cats and purple dogs. Cut out yellow flowers and white houses. And glued everything

on the construction paper, creating "art" she could hang
for Nancy to see on Saturday when she babysat.

And outside, Wyatt sat on the bench seat of his gram's
old wooden picnic table, peering through the openings in
the tall shrubs, waiting for them to appear.

But the kids and Missy didn't come outside. Because
she was angry? Or sad? Or in protection mode?

He didn't know.

All he knew was that it was his fault.

He rose from the picnic table and walked into his house,
back to the bedroom littered with shoe boxes. He sat on the
bed and began the task for looking for the jewelry, trying
to get his mind off Missy.

It didn't work. He was about to give up, but had nothing else to do—damn his mother for canceling the cable.
So he forced himself to open one more box, and discovered a stack of letters tied with a pink ribbon. He probably would have tossed them aside except for the unique
return address.

It was a letter from his grandfather, Sergeant Bill Mc-
Kenzie, to his grandmother, sent from Europe during
World War II.

Wyatt sat on the bed, pulled the string of the bow.

Though his grandfather had died at least twenty years
before, Wyatt remembered him as a tall, willowy guy who
liked to tell jokes, and never missed a family event like a
birthday party or graduation. He'd liked him. A lot. Some
people even said Wyatt "took after" him.

He opened the first letter.

Dear Joni...

I hope this letter finds you well. Things here are
quiet, for now. That's why I have time to write. I
wanted to thank you and everyone at home for your

efforts with the war bonds. I also know rationing is hard. I recognize what a struggle it is to do without and to work in the factories. Tell everyone this means a great deal to those of us fighting.

The letter went on to talk about personal things, how much he missed her, how much he loved her, and Wyatt had to admit he got a bit choked up. A kid never thought of his grandparents loving each other. He'd certainly never pictured them young, fighting a war and sacrificing for a cause. But he could see his grandmother working in a factory, see his grandfather fighting for freedom.

What Wyatt hadn't expected to find, in letter after letter, was how much encouragement his grandfather had given his grandmother. Especially since, of the two, she was safer.

Still, his gram would have been a young woman. Working in a factory. Going without nylons—which might explain why she saved old panty hose. Getting up at the crack of dawn, doing backbreaking labor. He'd never thought of his grandparents this way, but now that he had, their lives and their love took on a new dimension for him.

Hours later, feeling hungry, he ambled to the kitchen and saw the cake. He took a chunk of the half-eaten slice he'd left behind. Flavor exploded on his tongue like a recrimination.

He sat at the table, staring at the cake. His grandfather was such a people-smart guy that he never would have let anyone suffer in silence the way Missy was. Sure, she baked cakes and attended weddings, looking pretty and perky, as if everything was fine. But everything wasn't fine. She worked her butt off to support her kids, and probably lived her life praying her dad would forget she existed.

And Wyatt had blown that in a one-minute conversation after eating pie.

He had to do something to make that up to her. He had to do something to make her life better. He already watched her kids while she worked every morning, but from the way she'd kept them inside after their naps, she might be changing her mind about letting him do even that.

So that left her business. If he wanted to do something to help her, if he wanted to do something to make up for the things he'd done wrong, then he had to figure out how she could afford to hire an assistant and buy a van.

Without him giving her money.

The next morning, Missy got up, put on a pot of coffee, poured three bowls of cereal and three glasses of milk, and sat at the table.

"So what are you going to do today?"

Owen said, "Pway with Wyatt."

She stirred her coffee. "That sounds like a lot of fun, but he might not come over, so you should think about what you'd like to do with your sisters."

Lainie's head shot up and she gave her mom a wide-eyed look. Claire's little mouth fell open. For the past two weeks, they'd enjoyed a small heaven, playing dolls without being forced to also entertain their brother. Neither seemed happy to have that change.

A knock at the door interrupted them, turning Missy around to see who it was.

Wyatt opened the door. "I brought your cake plate and sauce cup back."

She rose, wiped her sweating palms down her denim shorts. She took the plate and cup from him. "Thanks."

He smiled slightly. "Aren't you going to offer me a cup of coffee?"

Actually, she hoped he'd just go. Like Owen, she'd gotten accustomed to having someone to talk to, to be with. She hadn't even realized it until the night before, when she'd thought about how everybody came into her life, then left again. Even Wyatt would soon leave. But as they were jointly caring for her kids, and he helped her deliver her cakes, spending entire Saturdays with her, she'd been so preoccupied with her work that she'd been growing accustomed to having him around.

But he'd told her he didn't want to be in her life, and she had accepted that. She wished he'd just leave, so she could start her healing process.

Still, after years of working at the diner as a teenager, if someone asked for coffee, she poured it. "Sure. I have plenty of coffee."

He ambled to the table. "Hey, kids."

Lainie said, "Hi, Wyatt!"

Owen said, "Hey, Wyatt."

Claire smiled.

Owen said, "Are we going to pway?"

Wyatt pulled out a chair and sat. "As soon as I talk to your mom about some things." He pointed at the boy's bowl. "Are you done eating?"

Owen picked up his little plastic bowl and drank the contents in about ten seconds. Then he slapped the bowl on the table and grinned at Wyatt from behind a milk mustache.

Wyatt laughed. "Now you need to go wash up."

"You can all wash up, brush your teeth and head outside. Wyatt won't be far behind."

Missy knew that probably sounded rude. At the very least high-handed. But she'd made up her mind the night of the wedding. Even before he'd seen her dad at her door. If she got involved with him, she wanted something more.

He didn't. Plus, in another day or week, he'd be gone. He wasn't really her friend, didn't want to be her lover, except temporarily. She had to break her attachment to him.

The kids scrambled along the short hall to their bathroom. She sat across from Wyatt.

"I'm not going to talk about my dad."

"That's not what I came to talk about."

"It isn't?"

"No. You know yesterday how I told you I was a thinker?"

"I thought you were just bragging."

He winced. "I was…sort of."

Her eyebrows rose, as if she was silently asking him what the hell that had to do with anything.

He squirmed uncomfortably. "The thing is, last night as I thought about your situation…"

"You can't help me. I have to handle my dad alone."

"I'm not talking about your dad. I'm talking about your business."

"And I thought we'd already been over this, too. I don't want your money."

"I'm not offering you money. I solve business problems all the time. And sitting there last night, I realized that if I'm such a hotshot, I should be able to solve yours, too."

She laughed. That hadn't occurred to her, but it was true. If he was such a hotshot he should be able to muddle through her measly little expansion problem. "Without offering me money."

"Right. We took that off the table the first week I was here."

"So. Now you're going to think about my problem?"

He picked up the saltshaker, turned it over in his hands as if studying it. "Actually, I solved it."

She snorted a laugh. "Right."

He finally caught her gaze. "I did. I don't know if you're going to be happy with the answer, but I took all the variables I knew into consideration, and realized that if I were in your position, I'd use the house as collateral for a line of credit."

She gasped. "Use my house?"

"I woke up my chief financial officer last night and had him run some numbers."

Wyatt pulled a paper from his back pocket. "He checked the value of your house against comps in the area, and estimates your house's value here." Wyatt pointed at the top number. "Which means you could easily get a hundred thousand dollar line of credit with the house as collateral."

She raised her gaze to his slowly. "But then I'd have a payment every month."

"You'd also have a van and an assistant, and you could take more weddings."

The truth of that hit her with a happy lift of her spirits. Though part of her struggled against it, her mind shifted into planning mode. "And maybe birthday cakes."

"And birthday cakes." He smiled sheepishly. "I ate that whole damned cake."

"Wyatt! That much sugar's not good for you."

"I know, but I'm out of food except for cereal, and I couldn't go to the diner."

Her face heated. "You can go wherever you want."

"I'll be damned if I'll give money to a guy who beat his family."

Owen came barreling into the kitchen. "Ready to pway?"

Wyatt pointed at the door. "You get everything set up outside. I'll be there in a minute." Owen raced out the door as Claire and Lainie appeared with their dolls.

"Are you going outside?"

They nodded.

Missy straightened the collar of Claire's shirt. "Okay. You know the rules. Stay in the yard."

They left and Wyatt caught her hand. "So? What do you think? Could you be okay with a line of credit?"

The warmth of his hand holding hers rendered her speechless for a few seconds, but she reminded herself he wasn't interested in her romantically, unless it was for an affair. What he was doing now was making up for talking about her to her dad.

Of course, that was sort of nice, too. If he didn't think of her as a friend, he'd blow off what he'd done. Instead, he was making it up to her. As a friend would.

She relaxed a bit. It wasn't wrong to take advice from a friend. Especially a friend who had business expertise. "It's a big step. I don't want to lose this house."

"Hey, who yelled at me for not having faith in you?"

"I did."

"Then have some faith in yourself. And diversify. I have a couple of people on staff who could look into markets for your cakes. Or you could just go to the grocery stores and restaurants in neighboring towns and offer them a cake or two. Make the first week's free. When they see the reaction to them, they'll order."

Warmth spread through her. A feeling of normalcy returned. "You think I can do this?"

"Hell, yeah." Wyatt rose. "But it's more important that you know you can do it."

CHAPTER EIGHT

AT LUNCHTIME SHE FED the kids, wondering what Wyatt was eating. Then she saw him leave on his bike. She wouldn't let herself consider that he might be going to the diner. He'd said he wouldn't, but in her life people said a lot of things, then did the opposite. She just hoped he'd respect her enough not to say anything to her dad, not to warn him away or yell at him.

Twenty minutes later, when he returned with a bag from the grocery store, she relaxed. From the size of the bag, she knew he hadn't had enough time to shop as well as visit her dad. Maybe he really was a guy true to his word?

Falling into her normal daily routine, she straightened up the house while the kids napped. She picked up toys and vacuumed the living room and playroom floors. When she walked into the kitchen, she saw Wyatt at the door.

"How long have you been standing there?"

"Long enough to know you're a thorough vacuumer."

She laughed and opened the screen door. "Did you get lunch?"

"I stopped at the store for bread and deli meat. Do you know they don't have an in-house bakery anymore? They could use some homemade cakes in their baked goods section."

"You can stop spying for me. Once I get an assistant I'll investigate every store in the area."

"So you've decided to get the line of credit?"

"Yes. Using the house as collateral."

He walked to the table. "Can we sit?"

"Why? Are you going to help me call the bank?"

He pulled some papers from his back pocket. "Actually, I'd like to be the bank."

She gasped. "I told you I don't want your money."

"And I told you that I feel responsible for the mess with your dad yesterday. This is my way of making that up to you." He caught her gaze. "Besides, I'm going to give you a point and a half below the current interest rate at the bank, and my people have worked out a very flexible repayment schedule. No matter what happens with your business, you will not lose this house."

Her heart tripped over itself in her chest. *She wouldn't lose her house?* She didn't know a bank that promised that. And Wyatt hadn't gone to the diner. He'd bought deli meat. Even though she knew he was growing tired of not eating well, he'd been true to his word.

"And it's a loan?"

He handed the papers to her. "Read the agreement. Though I promise not to take the house if you default, a new payment schedule will be created. But if you sell the house, you have to pay me the balance of the loan with the proceeds. No matter what happens, you have to pay back the hundred grand." He pointed to a paragraph at the bottom of page one. "And you have to take out a life insurance policy in the amount of a hundred thousand dollars with me as beneficiary, if you die."

Hope filled her. He hadn't merely stayed away from her dad; he'd listened to everything she'd been saying the past few weeks. "So it really is a business deal?"

"Albeit with very good terms for you. I know you don't want any special favors, but even you have to admit I owe you."

She licked her lips. Lots of people had done her wrong, but no one had ever even acknowledged that, let alone tried to make up for it.

"You can take that to an attorney, if you want."

She smiled up at him. "I could take it to my former boss at the law firm."

Wyatt rose. "Smart businesswoman that you are, I would expect no less from you."

That night, Wyatt sat on the big wicker chair on his back porch, once again wishing his mom hadn't canceled the cable. He'd dug through more boxes, read a few more of his grandfather's letters and still wasn't tired enough for bed. Leaning back in the big chair, he closed his eyes.

"Hey, are you asleep?"

He bounced up with a short laugh. Missy stood at the bottom of his porch steps, holding two bottles of beer and the papers he'd given her that afternoon.

"I guess I was."

She waved the papers. "Can I come up?"

He rose. "Sure. Your lawyer's already looked at those?"

She wore a pink top and white shorts, and had the front of her hair tied back in some sort of clip contraption, but her smile was what caught him. Bright and radiant as the closest star, it raised his hopes and eased his guilt.

She handed him a beer. "To celebrate. My old boss squeezed me in, read the papers in about ten minutes and told me I'd be a fool not to sign." She clanked her beer bottle against Wyatt's. "He's read your comics, by the way. He called you a genius."

Wyatt scuffed his tennis shoe on the old gray porch planks. "I don't know about genius."

"Oh, don't go getting all modest on me now."

He laughed. "So you're signing?"

She handed the papers to him. "It's already signed and notarized. My lawyer kept a copy and made a copy for me."

Wyatt took the papers, glanced down at her signature. "Good girl." Then he clanked his bottle to hers again. "Congratulations. Someday you're going to be the superstar this town talks about."

She fell into one of the big wicker chairs. "This town doesn't care about superstars. We're all about making ends meet."

He sat, too. It was the first time since he'd been home that she'd been totally relaxed with him. He took a swig of his beer, then said, "There's no shame in that."

"I think about ninety percent of America lives that way."

The conversation died and he really wished it hadn't. There was a peace about her, a calmness that he'd never seen before.

"So you're happy?"

"I'm ecstatic. Within the next month I'll have a van, an assistant and day care for the kids." She turned to him. "Do you know how good it is for kids to socialize?"

He didn't. Not really. He knew very little about kids. What he knew was business and comics. So he shrugged. "I guess pretty important."

"Owen will have other boys to play with."

Though Wyatt got a stab of jealousy over that, he also knew he was leaving soon. With or without the jewelry, he couldn't stay away from his work more than a month, five weeks tops.

"That can't be anything but good."

Another silence fell between them. After a few minutes

she turned to face him. "I don't know how to deal with someone who knows about my dad."

"Really?"

"Yeah. I've been keeping the secret so long it feels odd that another person knows. It's almost like who I am around you is different."

He laughed. "That's funny, because I've been thinking the same thing since I came here."

"That I'm different?"

"No. More that I can't get my footing. In Florida I'm king of my company. Here, I know nothing about kids or cakes or weddings. Plus, I'm the guy you remember as a nerd."

"You're so not a nerd."

"Geek then."

She shook her head. "Have you looked at yourself in the mirror lately?"

He glanced down at his jeans, then back at her. "I wore jeans in high school."

"Yeah. But not so well."

He laughed.

She smiled. "It's like you're the first person in my life to know the whole me. Past and present."

"And you're the first person to know the whole me. Geek and sex god."

She laughed and rose from her seat. "Right." Reaching for his empty beer bottle, she said, "Before that little display of conceit, I was going to ask if you wanted to help me van shop."

"I'd *love* to help you van shop."

"See? Old Wyatt wouldn't have been able to do that."

"Old Wyatt?"

"The geeky high school kid."

"Right."

"But older, wiser Wyatt can."

He chuckled. No one ever called him old, let alone wise. But he sort of liked it. Just as she had her fortes with kids and cakes, he had his expertise, too. "So you're going to let me go with you?"

"Yes." She turned and started down the stairs. "And don't go getting any big ideas about buying some tricked out supervan. I saw the clause in the agreement where you can raise the amount of the loan to accommodate expansion. I don't want any more money. I have to grow the business in stages. We get a normal van. I hire a normal assistant. The kids go to local day care."

By the time she finished she was at the bottom of the steps. She turned to face him.

He saluted her. "Aye, aye, Captain."

She laughed. "I also like your new sense of humor. Young Wyatt didn't laugh much."

He leaned on the porch railing. Since they were being honest, it was time to admit the truth. "He was always too busy being nervous. Especially around you. You're so beautiful you probably make most men nervous."

She shook her head as if she thought he was teasing, then pointed at the hedge. "I've gotta go. See you tomorrow."

"See you tomorrow."

He pushed away from the railing, smiling to himself. She was correct. He felt odd around her because she was the first, maybe the only person in his life to know both sides of him.

But now he also knew her secret. Instead of that scaring him the way he knew it probably should, because her secret was dark and frightening and needed to be handled with care, he felt a swell of pride. She hadn't told him her secret, but she clearly trusted him with it. He felt honored.

* * *

"Hi, Mommy."

Missy opened her eyes and smiled down at the foot of the bed. Claire grinned at her. She never awoke after the kids. She couldn't imagine why she'd slept so late. Except that being honest with Wyatt about her dad, and accepting the loan, had relaxed her. She didn't have to pretend that everything was fine around him. She could be herself.

"Hey, sweetie. Want some cereal?"

Her daughter's grin grew and she nodded.

Missy rolled out of bed. Normally she was already in shorts and a T-shirt before she went to the kitchen. Today she was so far behind she didn't have time to change. Still, she slept in pajama pants and a tank top. There was no reason to change or even to find a robe. She sleepily padded from her bedroom in the back corner of the downstairs into the kitchen. As she got cereal from the cupboard and Claire climbed onto a chair, Lainie and Owen ambled into the kitchen. They also climbed onto chairs.

She'd barely gotten cocoa chunks cereal into three bowls and a pot of coffee on before there was a knock at her door. Without waiting for her to invite him in, Wyatt entered.

"Are you here to mooch coffee?"

He laughed. "No, but I wouldn't say no if you'd offer me a cup."

She motioned for him to take a seat at the table, grabbed a cup from the cupboard and poured some coffee into it for him.

When she set it in front of him, his gaze touched on her tank top, then rippled down to her pajama pants. "I guess I'm early for the van shopping."

She stifled the warmth and pleasure that saturated her at his obvious interest. Saturday they'd decided against any kind of relationship because they wanted two different things. Yesterday, when she'd signed the line of credit papers, they'd cemented that. Even if he wanted to get involved with her—which he didn't—she wouldn't get involved with a man who owned the "mortgage" on her house.

"You want to go today?"

"No time like the present. My bank wire transferred the hundred grand into a new account set up for you. We can stop at the bank for you to sign the paperwork, and the money will be at your disposal immediately."

Her attraction to him was quickly forgotten as her heart filled with joy. This was really happening. She was getting a van, a helper... She would expand her business!

"Let me call Nancy to babysit." Missy popped out of her chair and raced back to the bedroom to get her phone. After Nancy agreed to come over, she hopped into the shower. Halfway done shampooing her hair, she realized she'd left the kids with Wyatt. Without thinking.

She trusted him.

She ducked her hair under the spray. She did trust him.

She waited for her tummy to twist or her breathing to become painful at the thought of trusting someone so easily, so completely, that she didn't even think to ask him to mind the kids, but nothing happened.

She finished her shower, fixed her hair and slid into jeans and a blue T-shirt. In a way she was glad they'd decided on Saturday night against a relationship, because her feelings for him had nothing to do with her attraction—or his. The trust she felt for him was simple, honest. Just as she'd realized his lending her money was like something a friend would do to make up for a wrong, her leaving her kids without thought was also the act of a friend.

They were becoming *friends*.

Tucking her hair behind her ears, she walked into the kitchen to find Wyatt filling the sink with soapy water as her children brought their cereal bowls to him.

"How'd you get them to do that?"

"Bribery."

Her mouth fell open. "Wyatt—"

"Relax. I promised them another trip to my grandmother's house to look through boxes. Nothing sinister like ice cream."

She casually walked to the table. "Ice cream isn't a bad idea."

He turned from the sink. "It isn't?"

"No. There's a nice place a mile or so out of town." She peeked at him, testing this friendship they were forming. Though her stomach jumped a bit at how handsome he was, she reminded herself that was normal. "Maybe we could take the kids there when I get the van. You know? Use getting ice cream as a maiden voyage."

He appeared surprised. "Sounds great."

Nancy knocked on the door and walked into the kitchen. "I heard there's a bunch of kids here who want to play house with me."

The girls jumped for joy. "Yay!"

But Owen deflated.

Wyatt stooped down to talk to him. "Don't worry. Van shopping won't take all day. And when we get back you can do whatever you want."

"Wook for tweasure?"

"Sure."

Missy's heart swelled. If they hadn't had the talk about their relationship she'd be in serious danger of falling in love with this guy. But they had had the talk. Then he'd overheard her argument with her father. And now they were friends.

Outside, she rummaged through her purse for her SUV keys. But when she reached the driver's side door, she noticed he hadn't followed.

"Aren't you sick of that beast yet?"

She laughed. "What?"

He jangled his keys. "It's such a beautiful day. Let's take the bike."

Happiness bubbled in her veins. "I haven't been on a bike since high school."

He grabbed the thin shrub branch and pushed it aside for her. "Then it's time."

With a laugh, she dipped under and walked over to the garage door. He opened it and there sat his shiny black bike.

"I don't have a helmet."

"You can use mine."

He handed her the helmet and straddled the bike.

She licked her suddenly dry lips. For all her fancy, happy self-talk that morning about being glad they were becoming friends, the thought of straddling the bike behind him sent shivers up her spine.

She'd danced with him. She'd kissed him. She knew the potency of his nearness.

And in spite of all that happy self-talk, she was susceptible. He was good to her. He was good to her kids. And around him she felt like a woman. Not just a mom.

She liked that feeling as much as she liked the idea of being his friend.

"Come on! Don't be a chicken."

Glad that he mistook her hesitancy for fear, she sucked in a breath. She could stop this just by saying she'd changed her mind and wanted to take the SUV. But then she'd miss the chance to hold him without worry he'd get the wrong impression. The chance to slide her cheek against his back. The chance to inhale his scent.

And the chance to enjoy him for a few minutes without consequences. Because, God help her, she did like him as more than a friend. He was the one who didn't want her. And if she refused this chance to be close to him, she'd regret it.

She slid onto the bike.

He revved the engine as she plopped the helmet on her head. Within seconds they shot out of the garage and onto the quiet street. She wrapped her arms around his middle, not out of a desire to hold him, but out of sheer terror.

Then the wind caught her loose hair beneath the helmet and whooshed along her limbs. Gloriously free, she raised her arms, let them catch the breeze and yelled, "Woo hoo!"

She felt rather than heard him laugh. In under five minutes, they were at the bank. She pulled off the helmet and he wrapped the straps around the handlebars before they walked into the lobby.

The customer service representative quickly found her file. Missy signed papers. Wyatt signed papers. And within what seemed like seconds they were on the bike again.

He pulled out onto Main Street and stopped at the intersection. He turned his head and yelled, "What car dealer do you want to go to?"

"I thought you'd know."

"I haven't been around here for a while." He revved the bike and smiled at her. His dark eyes shone with devilishness that called to her. "We could just get on the highway and drive until we find something."

Part of her wanted to. The kids were cared for. She was in a wonderful, daring mood. And he was so close. So sweet. So full of mischief...

Mischief with someone she really liked was dangerous to a mother of three who was knee-deep in a fledgling business. She pulled out her phone. "Or I could look up dealers online."

"Spoilsport." He revved the bike. "I like my idea better." He shot out into the street again. They flew down Main Street and again she had to stifle the urge to put her hands in the air and yell, "Woo hoo!"

But she stifled it. Because as much fun as this was, she had to get a van and get home to her kids.

A little voice inside her head disagreed. She didn't need to get home. Nancy was at the house. The kids were fine. And Missy was out. Out of the house. On her way to buy a van. On her way to having a wonderful future because her business would succeed. She knew it would.

Then she remembered the look of mischief in Wyatt's eyes. That was why she needed to get home. She liked him. Really liked him. And he wanted an affair. That was a bad combo. She hit a few buttons on her phone and began looking for a used car dealer.

Wyatt got them on the highway. The bike's speed picked up. Wind rushed at her. The sun warmed her arms. She put her face up and inhaled.

"Find a place yet?"

When Wyatt's voice whispered in her ear, she almost flew off the bike. He chuckled. "I turned on the mic." He showed her the mouthpiece hanging from the phone piece in his ear.

She said, "Oh." She shouldn't have been surprised by the communications equipment. In his real world, Wyatt probably had every gadget known to mankind. After a few flips through the results of her internet search on her phone screen, she said, "There's a place right off the highway about a mile down the road."

"Then that's where we'll go."

They drove the mile, took the exit ramp and stopped in the parking lot of a car dealer. Shiny new cars, SUVs, trucks and vans greeted them.

She slid off the bike. "Wow. There are so many cars here."

Wyatt smoothed his hand along the fender of a brand-new red truck. "Too bad you need a van." He whistled as he walked along the back panels. "Look at this thing."

She laughed. "You should buy it for yourself."

He lovingly caressed some chrome. "I should." He turned toward the big building behind the rows and rows of vehicles. "I think I'll just go find a salesman."

He came back ten minutes later with a salesman who first told him all the finer points of the brand-new red truck, then turned to her as Wyatt climbed into the truck cab.

"I hear you need a van."

She smiled slightly. "Yes."

"Do you know what you want?"

"Yes. A white one."

He laughed. "No. I was talking about engine size, cargo bay versus seating."

Wyatt jumped out of the truck. "She wants a V-8, with seats that retract so that she has enough space to deliver goods."

"What kind of goods? How much space?"

"She bakes wedding cakes. The space doesn't need to be huge. We just need to know that the van can be easily air-conditioned."

"Are you sure she doesn't want to order a refrigerated van?"

Missy opened her mouth to speak, but Wyatt said, "She's on a limited budget. She doesn't need to go overboard."

They looked at several vans. Test drove three. In the end, she bought a white van that was used rather than new. She didn't know anything about refrigerated vans, but it sounded like something she might need in the future. Given that the used van was twelve thousand dollars less than a new one, she wouldn't be wasting as much if she decided a year or two from now to get the refrigerated van. Exclusively for business. She might even be able to keep the used van for her kids.

She suddenly felt like a princess—buying what she needed, planning to buy something even better in the future.

They walked into the office to write up the papers for her van. She called the bank and made arrangements to do a wire transfer of the purchase price, then signed on the dotted line.

The salesman stapled her papers together and gave her a set. "Okay. Van will be delivered tomorrow morning."

He then passed a bunch of papers to Wyatt. "And for the truck."

He said, "Thanks," and signed a few things.

The salesman handed him the keys. "Pleasure doing business with you, Mr. McKenzie. You know, if you get tired of the red one, I also have it in blue and yellow."

Wyatt laughed.

It was then that it hit her how rich he was. Sure, she'd always known in an abstract way that he had money. But watching him see something he wanted and buy it without a moment's hesitation or a single second thought made it real. This guy she liked, someone who was a friend, had more money than she could even imagine.

They walked out into the bright sunshine. He slid onto the bike. She put the helmet on her head and got on behind him. As he started off, she slid her arms around his waist and squeezed her eyes shut. He was so far out of her league. So different than anybody she knew.

Sadness made her sigh. Still, she leaned in close to him. Because he couldn't see her, she let her eyes drift shut, and enjoyed the sensation of just holding him. Because he was tempting. Because she was grateful. Because for once in her life, she really, really wanted somebody, but she was smart enough to know she couldn't have him.

And if she didn't take this chance to hold him, to feel the solidity of him beneath her chest, she might not ever get another.

When they returned to his gram's, she removed the helmet. He looped the strap over the handlebars.

"So? Fun?"

She refused to let her sadness show and spoil their day. "Oh, man. So much fun. I loved the bike ride, but I loved buying the van even more. I've never been able to get what I wanted. I've always had to take what I could afford."

He grinned. "It's a high, isn't it?"

"Yeah, but I'm not going to let myself get too used to it. For me, it's all part of getting my business up and running."

He nodded. "So, go feed the kids lunch and I'll be over around two to play with Owen."

She said, "Okay," and turned to go, but then faced Wyatt again. He was great. Honest. Open. Generous. And she'd always had her guard up around him. But now he knew her secret. He knew the real her. And he still treated her wonderfully.

She walked over and stood on her tiptoes. Intending to give him a peck on his check, in the last second she changed her mind. When her toes had her tall enough to reach his face, she kissed his lips. One soft, quick brush of her mouth across his that was enough to send electricity to her toes.

"Thanks."

He laughed. "I'd say you're welcome, but you owed me that kiss."

"I did?"

"If you'd kept our date graduation night, you'd have kissed me."

"Oh, really?"

"I might have been a geek, but that night I knew what I wanted and I was getting it."

She laughed, but stopped suddenly.

"What?"

She shook her head, turned away. "It's nothing."

He caught her hand and hauled her back. "It's something."

She stared at the front of his T-shirt. "The first day you arrived, I wanted to say I was sorry I broke that date." She swallowed. "I was all dressed to go, on my way to the door…" She looked up. "But my dad hit my mom. Bloodied her lip."

Wyatt cursed. "You don't have to tell me this."

"Actually, I want to. I think it's time to let some of this out." She held his gaze. "I trust you."

"Then why don't we go into the house and you can tell me the whole story?"

She almost told him she should get back to the kids, but her need to rid herself of the full burden of this secret told her to take a few minutes, be honest, let some of this go.

She nodded and they walked to the back door of his grandmother's house and into her kitchen. He made a pot of coffee, then leaned against the counter.

"Okay…so what happened that night?"

"We'd had a halfway decent graduation. It was one of those times when Dad had to be on his best behavior because we were in public, so everything went well. I actually felt normal. But driving home, he stopped at a bar. When he got home, he freaked out. He'd been on good behavior so long he couldn't keep up the pretense anymore and he exploded. He slammed the kitchen door, pivoted and hit my mom. Her lip was bleeding, so I took her to the sink to wash it off and get ice, and he just turned and punched Althea, slamming her into the wall." Missy squeezed her eyes shut, remembering. "It was a nightmare, but then again lots of times were like that."

"Scary?"

She caught his gaze. "More than scary. Out of control. Like playing a game where the rules constantly change. What made him happy one day could make him angry the next. But even worse was the confusion."

"Confusion worse than changing rules?"

She swallowed. "Emotional, personal confusion."

Wyatt said nothing. She sucked in a breath. "Imagine what it feels like to be a little girl who wants nothing but to protect her mom, so you step in front of a punch."

He cursed.

"From that point on, I became fair game to him."

"He began to beat you, too?"

She nodded. "It was like I'd given him permission when I stepped into the first punch." She licked her lips. "So from that point on, my choice became watch him beat my mom, or take some of the beating for her."

Wyatt's eyes squeezed shut, as if he shared her misery through imagining it. "And you frequently chose to be beaten."

"Sometimes I had to."

She walked to the stove, ran her finger along the shiny rim. "But that night he couldn't reach me. I'd taken my mother to the sink, stupidly believing that without anyone to hit, he'd get frustrated and head for the sofa. But he went after Althea."

"How old was she?"

"Twelve. Too young to take full-fist beating from a grown man."

"I'm sorry."

Missy sucked in another breath. Hearing the truth coming from her own mouth, her anger at herself, disappointment in herself, and the grief she felt over losing Althea began to crumble. She'd been young, too. Too young to take the blame for things her father had done.

She loosened her shoulders, faced Wyatt again. "I could see her arm was broken, so I didn't think. I didn't speak. I didn't ask permission or wait for instructions. I just grabbed the car keys to take her to the hospital, and my dad yanked the bottle of bleach off the washer by the back door." Missy looked into Wyatt's dark, solemn eyes. "He took off the cap and, two seconds before I would have been out of range, tossed it at me. It ran down my skirt, washing out the color, eating holes right through the thin material."

Wyatt shook his head. "He was insane."

"I'd earned that dress myself." Her voice wobbled, so she paused long enough to strengthen it. She was done being a victim, done being haunted by her dad. It appeared even her ghosts of guilt over Althea leaving were being exorcized. "I worked for every penny I'd needed to buy it. But when he was drunk, he forgot things like that. As I was scrambling out of the dress, before the bleach burned through to my skin, he called me a bunch of names. I just tossed the dress in the trash and walked to my room. I put on jeans and a T-shirt and took Althea to the hospital. His screams and cursing followed us out the door and to the car."

Wyatt said nothing.

She stayed quiet for a few seconds, too, letting it soak in that she'd finally told someone, and that in telling someone she'd seen that she wasn't to blame. That she had no sin. No part in any of it except victim. And she was strong enough now not to accept that title anymore.

"At the hospital, a social worker came into the cubicle. Althea wanted to tell, to report our dad. I wouldn't let her." Missy glanced up at him again. "I feared for Mom. I knew the social worker would take us away, but Mom would be stuck there. And because we'd embarrassed him, he'd be even worse to her than he already was."

"Why didn't your mom leave?"

"She was afraid. She had no money. No skills. And he really only beat her about twice a month."

Wyatt sniffed in derision. "He's a bastard."

"I left the next day. Got a clerical job in D.C. and an apartment with some friends. Althea spent every weekend with us. I guess that was enough for my dad to realize we didn't need him—didn't depend on him—and we could report him, because he stopped hitting Mom. When Althea graduated, she left town. Went to college in California. We haven't really heard from her since." Saying that aloud hurt. Missy loved and missed her sister. But she wasn't the reason Althea had gone. She could let go of that now. "When one of my roommates moved out, I tried to get my mom to move in with me, but she refused. A few weeks later she had a heart attack and died."

Wyatt gaped at her. "How old was she?"

"Not quite fifty. But she was worn down, anorexic. She never ate. She was always too worried to eat. It finally killed her."

With her story out, exhaustion set in. Missy's shoulders slumped.

He turned to the coffeepot, poured two cups. "Here."

She smiled shakily. "That wasn't so bad."

"Secrets are always better if you tell them."

She laughed. "How do you know?"

He shrugged. "School, I guess. In grade school I hid the fact that I was bullied from my parents. But in high school I knew I couldn't let it go on. The kids were bigger, meaner, and I was no match. So I told them. They talked to the school principal. At first the bullies kept at me, but after enough detention hours, and seeing that I wasn't going to be their personal punching bag anymore, they stopped."

Missy laughed, set her cup on the counter beside him and flattened her hands on his chest. "Poor baby."

"I'd have paid good money to have you tell me that in high school."

"I really did like you, you know. I thought of you as smart and honest."

"I was."

She peeked up at him. "You are now, too."

The room got quiet. They stood as close as lovers, but something more hummed between them. Emotionally, she'd never been as connected to anyone as she was to him right now. She knew he didn't want anything permanent, but in this minute, she didn't, either. All she wanted was the quiet confirmation that, secrets shared, she would feel in the circle of his arms. She wanted to feel. To be real. To be whole.

Then she heard the kids out in the yard. Her kids. Her life. She didn't need sex to tell her she was real, whole. She had a life. A good life. A life she'd made herself. She _____ cake to bake this Saturday. Soon she'd have an as- _____ She'd make cakes for grocery stores and restau- _____ Her life had turned out better than she'd expected.

She had good things, kids to live for, a business that made her happy.

She stepped away. A one-night stand would be fun. But building a good life was better. "I've gotta go."

He studied her. "You're okay?"

"I'm really okay." She smiled. "I'm better than okay. Thanks for letting me talk to you."

"That's what friends do."

Her smile grew. The tension in her chest eased. "Exactly. So if you have any deep, dark secrets, I'm here for you, friend."

"You know my story. Stood up to bullies in high school, made lots of money, bad marriage, worse divorce—which I'm beginning to feel better about, thank you for asking."

She laughed and headed for the door. "Well, if you ever need to talk, you know where I am."

"Like I said, I have no secrets."

She stopped, faced him again. He might not have secrets, but he did have hurts. Hurts he didn't share.

Were it not for those hurts, she probably wouldn't push open the door and walk away. She'd probably be in his arms right now. But she did push on the screen door, did leave his kitchen. They were both too smart to get involved when he couldn't let go of his past.

nad a
sistant
rants.

CHAPTER NINE

SATURDAY MORNING Wyatt didn't wait until Missy was ready to leave to get dressed to help deliver her cake. She hadn't yet hired an assistant. She'd put an ad in the papers for the nearby cities, and a few responses had trickled in. But she wasn't about to jump into anything. She wanted time for interviews and to check references.

He couldn't argue with that. Which meant he'd need to help her with that week's wedding.

So Friday he'd bought new clothes, telling himself he was tired of looking like a grunge rocker. Saturday morning, after his shower, he had black trousers, a white shirt and black-and-white print tie to put on before he ambled to her house. As had become his practice, he knocked twice and walked in.

Then stopped.

Wearing an orange-and-white-flowered strapless sundress, and with her hair done up in a fancy do that let curls fall along the back of her neck, she absolutely stopped his heart. In a bigger city, she would have been the "it" girl. In a little town like Newland, with nowhere to go but the grocery store or diner, and no reason to dress up, she sort of disappeared.

"You look amazing." He couldn't help it; the words tumbled out of their own volition.

She smiled sheepishly. "Would you believe this is an old work dress? Without the little white jacket, it's perfect for a garden wedding."

He looked her up and down once again, his heart pitter-pattering. "I should get a job at that law firm if everyone looks that good."

Because he'd flustered her, and was having a bit of trouble keeping his eyes off her, he searched for a change of subject. Glancing around her kitchen, he noticed the five layers of cake sitting in a row on her counter. Oddly shaped and with what looked to be steel beams trimming the edges, it wasn't her most attractive creation.

"Is the bride a construction worker?"

"That's the Eiffel Tower." Missy laughed. "The groom proposed there."

"Oh." Wyatt took a closer look. "Interesting."

"It is to them."

Owen skipped into the room. "Hey, Wyatt."

"Hey, kid." He faced Missy, asking, "When's Nancy get here?" But his heart sped up again just from looking at her. She had the kind of legs that were made to be shown off, and the dress handled that nicely. Nipped in at the waist, it also accented her taut middle. The dip of the bodice showed just enough cleavage to make his mouth water.

And he thought *he* looked nice. She put him and his white shirt and black trousers to shame—even with a tie.

"She should be here in about ten minutes. If you help me load up, we can get on the road as soon as she arrives."

Making several trips, Missy and Wyatt put the layers of cake into the back of her new van. Together they carried the bottom layer, which had little people and trees painted on the side, mimicking street level around Paris's most famous landmark.

"Cute."

"It is cute. To the bride and groom." She grinned. "And it's banana walnut with almond filling."

He groaned. "I'll bet that's delicious."

Sixteen-year-old Nancy walked up the drive. Her dark hair had been pulled into a ponytail. In a pair of shorts and oversize T-shirt, she was obviously ready to play.

"Hi, Missy. Wyatt."

The kids came barreling out. She scooped them into her arms. "What first? Cartoons or sandbox?"

Owen said, "Sandbox."

The girls whined. But Nancy held her ground. "Owen has to get the chance to pick every once in a while."

After a flurry of goodbyes and a minute for Missy to find her purse, she and Wyatt boarded the van. He glanced around with approval. "So much better than the SUV."

"I know."

She started the engine and pulled out of the driveway onto the street. In a few minutes they were on the highway.

She peeked over at him. "So...you look different. Very handsome."

Her compliment caused his chest to swell with pride. He'd had hundreds of women come on to him since he'd become rich, but none of their compliments affected him as Missy's did. But that was wrong. They'd decided to be friends.

Pretending to be unaffected, he flipped his tie up and let it fall. "You know, I don't even dress like this for my own job."

"That's because you're the boss. Here I'm the boss."

"You never told me you wanted me to dress better."

"I think it was implied by the way everybody around you dressed. It's called positive peer pressure."

He chuckled, then sneaked a peek at her. Man. He'd never seen anybody prettier. Or happier. And what made it even better was knowing he'd played a part in her happiness. She wanted this business to succeed and it would. Because she'd let him help.

Pride shimmied through him, but so did his darned attraction again, stronger and more potent than it had been before she complimented him. But they'd already figured out they wanted two different things. The night before, she'd even offered to listen to his troubles. Smart enough not to want to get involved with him, she'd offered them the safe haven of friendship. He shouldn't be thinking of her any way, except as a friend.

It took two hours to get to the country club where the reception was being held. The party room of the clubhouse had been decorated in green and ivory, colors that flowed out onto the huge deck. The banister swirled with green and ivory tulle, down stairs that led guests to a covered patio where tables and chairs had been arranged around two large buffet tables.

As they carried the cake into the clubhouse, Missy said, "Wedding was at noon. Lunch will be served around one-thirty. Cake right after that, then we're home."

He snorted. "After a two-hour drive."

"Now, don't be huffy. Because we get home early, I'm making dinner and insisting you eat with us."

"You are?"

"Yep. And I'm not even cooking something on the grill. I'm making real dinner."

"Oh, sweetheart. You just said the magic words. *Real dinner.* You have no idea how hungry I am."

She laughed. They put the cake together on a table set up in a cool, shaded section of the room. When the wedding guests arrived, however, no one came into the building or even climbed up to the deck. Instead, they gathered on the patio, choosing their lunch seats, getting drinks from the makeshift bar.

The bride and groom followed suit. On the sunny, beautiful May day, no one went any farther than the patio.

"One of two things has to happen here," Missy said as she looked out the window onto the guests who were a floor below them. "Either we need to get people in here or we need to get the cake out there."

He headed for the door. "I'll go talk to somebody."

She put her hand on his forearm to stop him. "*I'll* go talk to somebody."

She walked through the echoing room and onto the equally empty deck, down the stairs to the covered patio. Wyatt watched her look through the crowd and finally catch the attention of a tuxedo-clad guy.

She smiled at him and began talking. Even from a distance Wyatt saw the sparkle in her eyes, and his gaze narrowed in on the guy she was talking to. Tall, broad-shouldered, with dark curly hair, he wasn't bad looking... Oh, all right, he was good-looking, and was wearing a tux. Wyatt knew how women were about men in tuxes. He'd taken advantage of that a time or two himself. And Missy was a normal woman. A woman he'd rejected. She had every right to be attracted to this guy.

Even if it did make Wyatt want to punch something.

As she and the man in the tux walked up the stairs to the deck, he scrambled away from the window. She opened the door and motioned around the empty room.

"See? No one's even come in here."

The man in the tux glanced around, his gaze finally alighting on her creation. "Is that the cake?"

She smiled. "Yes."

Tux man strolled over. He examined the icing-covered

Eiffel Tower, then looked over his shoulder at Missy, who had followed him. "You're remarkable."

Her cheeks pinkened prettily. Wyatt's eyes narrowed again.

"I wouldn't say remarkable." She grinned at him. "But I am good at what I do."

"And beautiful, too."

Unable to stop himself, Wyatt headed for the cake table.

Missy's already pink cheeks reddened. "Thanks. But as you can see, the cake—"

"I don't suppose you'd give a beleaguered best man your phone number?"

Her eyes widened. Wyatt's did, too. Beleaguered best man? Did he think he was in a Rodgers and Hammerstein play?

"I—"

He slid his hand into his pocket. "I have a pen."

Wyatt finally reached them. "She's got a pen, too, bud. If she wanted to give you her phone number, she could. But it seems she doesn't want to."

Missy shot Wyatt a stay-out-of-this look, then smiled politely at the best man. "What my assistant is trying to say is that I'm a very busy person. I keep a pen and paper for brides-to-be, who see my cakes and want to talk about me baking for them."

The best man stiffened. "So you wanting to get the cake downstairs, into the crowd, is all about PR for you?"

"Heavens, no." She laughed airily. "I want the bride to see the cake she designed."

But the best man snorted as if he didn't believe her. He shoved his hands into his pockets, casually, as if he held all the cards and knew it. "I guess you'll just have to figure out a way to get the bride up here yourself, then."

But Missy didn't bite. She smiled professionally and

said, "Okay." Not missing a beat, she walked over to the French doors leading to the deck and went in search of the bride.

His threat ignored, the best man deflated and headed for the door, too.

Wyatt chuckled to himself. She certainly was focused. The best man might have temporarily knocked her off her game, but she'd quickly rebounded.

A few minutes later, Missy returned to the room in the clubhouse, the bride and groom on her heels.

"As you can see, nobody's here."

The bride stopped dead in her tracks. "That's my cake?"

Missy pressed her hand to her throat. "You said you wanted the Eiffel tower."

The bride slowly walked over. She ambled around the table, examining the cake. Wyatt stifled the urge to pull his collar away from his neck. In the quiet, empty room, the click of the bride's heels as she rounded the table was the only sound. Her face red, Missy watched helplessly.

Finally the bride said, "It's beautiful. So real. Isn't it, Tony?"

Tony said, "Yeah. It's cool. I like it."

"I think I'll have the band announce that we're cutting the cake up here, and ask everyone to join us."

Missy sighed with relief. "Sounds good."

Tony caught the bride's hand and they went back to the patio.

As soon as they were gone, Missy turned on Wyatt. "And *you*."

"Me?" This time he did run his fingers under his shirt collar to release the strangled feeling. "What did I do?"

She stalked over to him. In her pretty orange-and-white-flowered dress and her tall white sandals, with her hair all done up, she looked like a Southern belle on the warpath.

"I fight my own battles. He was a jerk, but I handled him. Professionally. Politely."

"He was a letch."

She tossed her hands in the air. "I've handled letches before. Sheesh! Do you think he's the first best man to come on to me?"

Wyatt's blood froze, then heated to boiling and roared through his veins. "Best men come on to you?"

"And ushers and fathers of the bride—or groom." She stepped into his personal space. "But I'm a big girl. I can handle myself with bad boys."

He snorted. "Oh, really?"

"You think I can't?"

His hands slipped around the back of her neck, pulling her face to his as he lowered his head. His lips met hers in a flurry of passion and desire. He expected her to back off, to be stunned—at the very least surprised. Instead, she met him need for need. When his tongue slipped into her mouth, she responded like someone as starved for this as he was.

Heat exploded in his middle, along with a feeling so foreign he couldn't have described it to save his life. Part need, part entitlement, part something dark and wonderful, it fueled the fire in his soul and nudged him to go further, take what he wanted, salve this crazy ache that dogged him every time he was around her.

The door opened and sounds from the wedding below billowed inside. Missy jerked away, her eyes filled with fire. From passion or from anger, Wyatt couldn't tell.

She pulled a tissue from her pocket, quickly dabbed her lips, turned and faced the bride, groom and photographer with a smile.

"Come in. We're all set up."

* * *

What the hell was that?

Missy smiled at the bride and groom, leading them and the wedding party to the Eiffel Tower cake. As the crowd gushed, complimenting the detail, retelling the story of how the groom had proposed, her thoughts spun away again.

Had Wyatt kissed her out of jealousy?

Her stomach knotted. He'd absolutely been jealous. But she'd bet her bottom dollar the kiss hadn't been out of jealousy, but was meant to teach her a lesson. She'd responded to prove she was able to take care of herself. And instead...

Well, she'd knocked them both for a loop.

The question was—

How did they deal with it?

The bride and groom posed for pictures with the cake, along with their parents and the bridal party. They served each other a bite of the cake as the photographer snapped more pictures. Almost as quickly as they'd come, they left, taking the bridal party with them.

And the room went silent.

Missy sighed, calmly walking to the cake table, though inside she was scrambling for something to say. Anything to get both their minds off that kiss.

"My best cake ever and I won't be getting any referrals from it."

He didn't even glance at her. "How do you know?"

Either he wasn't happy about being jealous or he wasn't happy that this kiss had been better than their first. "Only the wedding party and the bride and groom saw it."

He sniffed a laugh. "Give people time to taste it. You'll get your referrals."

"That's just it. They didn't leave instructions to serve it." She sighed. "I'm going to find the bride's mom."

With that, she left, and Wyatt collapsed against the silent, empty bar behind him. He didn't need to wonder what had happened when they kissed. He didn't need to probe why he'd been jealous. He was falling for her. A few weeks past his divorce and like a sucker he was falling for somebody new.

He couldn't let it happen. Not just to protect himself, but to protect her. She didn't want to fall in love with a guy who wasn't ready for a commitment, any more than he wanted to fall in love so soon after he'd ended his marriage. Only beginning to get her feet wet with her business, she wanted the fun, the thrill, of stepping into her destiny. Of making money. Running the show.

Her response to his kiss had started out as a way to tell him to back off, that she could handle herself. No matter that it ended up with both of them aroused and needy. The original intent had been clear. Now he had to return them to sanity.

Though he was starving, he begged off her homemade dinner and drove ten miles to the next town over to eat meat loaf that was a disgrace. Sunday, he played with the kids but avoided seeing Missy. On Monday morning, however, he arrived at her back door as soon as he saw the kitchen light go on. He knocked twice, then let himself inside.

Without turning around, she said, "Come in, Wyatt."

The laugh in her voice told him she wasn't as afraid to be around him as he was to be around her. That served to strengthen his resolve. Wrapped up in her new business venture, she was too busy to dwell on runaway emotions the way he was. Not just the rumble of attraction, the longing to kiss her senseless and make her his, but the urge to protect her, bring her into his home…really make her his.

He knew these urges were wrong. With the ink barely

dried on his divorce papers, they could simply be rebound needs. So he had to get hold of himself. To protect himself, but also to protect her. Whether she knew it or not, she was vulnerable. He could be a real vulture when he went after something he wanted. She wouldn't stand a chance.

And after he got what he wanted, he'd get bored, and he'd leave her hurt and broken.

He would not do that to her.

Since their biggest temptation time seemed to be weddings, there was an easy answer.

"This week we're going to have to find that assistant for you."

She walked away from the coffeepot, holding two steaming mugs. She handed one to him and they sat at the table, where all three kids sleepily played with cereal that swam in milk made chocolate by the little bites bobbing in it.

"Did you get any responses to your ad?"

"Lots. I'm just not sure where to interview people."

"Since you're going to be baking here at your house, I think the interviews should take place here."

"Okay." She sipped her coffee, then smiled. "Want some cocoa bites?"

"I thought you'd never ask."

They called the four candidates Missy deemed best suited for her company, and set up interviews for Tuesday, Wednesday and Thursday.

Wyatt sat with her through the interview for the first candidate, Mona Greenlee, a short, squat woman who clearly loved food. But after a comment or two at the beginning of the meeting, he stopped talking and let Missy ask her questions, give Mona a tour of the house and introduce her to the kids.

Mona laughed about how unusual it was to bake from a

house, but Missy assured her that her kitchen had passed inspection. After she left, Wyatt headed for the door.

"Where are you going?"

He turned slowly. When he finally caught her gaze, she saw a light in his eyes that caused her heart to stutter. His focus fell from her eyes to her mouth, then rose again. "You can handle these interviews on your own."

Though complimented by his faith in her, she got a funny feeling in her stomach. Was he leaving because he was thinking about kissing her?

Remembering the kiss from Saturday made her stomach flip again. That was one great kiss. A kiss she wouldn't mind repeating. But they'd been attracted to each other right from the beginning and they'd managed to work together in spite of it. Wanting to kiss shouldn't cause him to leave.

"You don't want to help?"

"You're fine without me."

But I like spending time with you. I like your goofy comments. I like you.

The words swirled around in Missy's head so much, she almost said them. But she didn't. First, the intensity of her feelings surprised her, and she needed to think them through. Second, if she'd grown so accustomed to having him around that she didn't mind having him neb his nose into her business, then maybe things had gone further than she wanted them to.

He didn't want a relationship. She didn't want a fling. It was better not to encourage these feelings. And maybe he was right. They shouldn't spend so much time together.

She did the next interview alone and didn't have a problem until Jane Nelson left. Then she scurried outside to find Wyatt. Not to ask for help, but to talk. To tell hi about Jane. To show him that she could handle all this alone, and how excited she was.

But when she walked into the backyard where he was playing Wiffle ball with the kids, he barely spoke to her. He complimented the job she had done interviewing Jane, but he didn't ask questions or go into detailed answers. He was distancing himself from her.

Disappointment followed her back into the house. She didn't *need* him, but suddenly everything she did felt empty without him.

At the end of the next two interviews, she didn't bother looking for Wyatt, but that didn't stop the emptiness. After so many weeks of having him underfoot, it seemed wrong that he was pulling away from her.

Except he'd be leaving in a few days. Maybe he was preparing them both?

That would be okay, except she didn't want to be prepared. She wanted to enjoy the last few days she had with him. What was the point of starting the empty feeling early? It would find a home in her soon enough, when he really did leave.

Thursday evening she offered Elaine Anderson the job. She'd blended in best with the chaos and the kids, and was able to start immediately.

To celebrate, Missy made fried chicken, and sent Owen over to get Wyatt. She knew that was a tad underhanded, but after several days of not seeing him, she was tired of wasting the precious little time they had left together. Plus, spending a few days without him had forced her to see that she liked him a lot more than she thought she did. So tonight she intended to figure out what was really going on with him.

If he was upset about their kiss and didn't want to repeat it, she would back off.

But if he was struggling with jealousy and the lines they'd drawn about their relationship, maybe it was time to change things. He didn't want a relationship. She didn't want a fling, but surely they could find a compromise position? Maybe agree to date long distance for a few months to see if this thing between them was something they should pursue.

He strolled over to the picnic table behind bouncing Owen, who was thrilled to be getting his favorite fried chicken, and in general thrilled with life these days. She no longer worried about his transition after Wyatt left. With money to put the kids in day care for four hours every morning, she knew Owen would find friends. Her life was perfect.

Except for the empty feeling she got every time she thought about Wyatt leaving.

But tonight she intended to set this relationship onto one course or another. Either ask him to work something out with her or let him go. And then stick by that decision.

"I hope you like fried chicken."

He reached for two paper plates, obviously about to help her dish up food for the kids. "I don't think there's a person in the world who doesn't like fried chicken."

Watching him help Owen get his dinner, she pressed her lips together. There was so much about Wyatt that was likable, perfect. And she wasn't just talking about his good looks, charm and sex appeal. He liked her kids. Genuinely liked them. Plus, with the exception of the last wedding, they always had fun together. They understood each other.

Hell, he was the first person—the only person—to know her whole story. It didn't seem right that this had to end.

She put three stars on the plus column for a relationship.

He liked her kids. He was fun to be around. He knew her past and didn't think any less of her for it.

They settled on the worn bench seats, said grace and dug into dinner.

He groaned with ecstasy.

She smiled. Whoever said the way to a man's heart was his through stomach must have known tall, perpetually hungry Wyatt.

"This is fantastic."

"Just a little something I can whip up at a moment's notice." Not that she was bragging, but it never hurt to remind him that she wasn't just a businesswoman and mother. There were as many facets to her as there were to any of the women he dated in Florida. She smoothed her palms down the front of her shorts. After cooking the chicken, she'd changed into her best pink shirt, the one her former coworkers told her bought out the best in her skin tones. And thinking of the bikini-clad beach bunnies he probably met in Florida, she was glad she looked her best. But sitting across from him, acknowledging the realities of his life, she fought the doubts that beat at her brain.

How did a thirty-three-year-old mother of triplets compete with beach bunnies?

Should she even try?

Wasn't she setting herself up for failure?

They ate dinner with Owen and the girls giggling happily. Owen grinned with his mouth full and made Lainie say, "Oh, gross! Tell him to stop that."

But Missy only smiled, glad to have her mind off Wyatt for a few seconds. It was good to see Owen behave like a little boy. Gross or not.

When they were done eating, Wyatt helped her clear the picnic table and bring everything into the kitchen. She persuaded him to help her tidy up, delaying his visit, but she could see he was eager to go.

Fears and doubts pummeled her. He'd talked so little she was beginning to believe he'd already made up his mind. And if he'd set his course on forgetting her, wouldn't it be embarrassing to talk about thinking of a compromise for them? That kiss on Saturday, the one that had gotten away from them and knocked both of them to their knees, proved there was something powerful between them. Something she wanted. Something he seemed to be afraid of.

And even now he was straining toward the door.

Owen popped into the kitchen, already bathed. His sisters were now in the tub. With his pajama top on backward, he raced to Wyatt with a huge storybook. Big and shiny, with a colorful cover, it hid half his body.

"You wead this to me?"

"I don't know, buddy. I should get going."

Missy waited in silence. She could nudge Wyatt into reading the book, but this was a big part of what she'd want in any man she let into her life. A real love for her kids. Wyatt had shown he loved to play. He'd also shown a certain kinship with Owen. But when the chips were down, when he wanted to leave, would he stay?

He stooped down. "I'm kinda tired."

Owen rolled his eyes. "It takes five minutes."

Then the most wonderful thing happened. Wyatt laughed. He laughed long and hard. When he was done, he scooped Owen up, book and all, and carried him down the hall. "Which one's your room?"

Missy scrambled behind them. "They all still sleep in the same room. I'm waiting until Owen's a little older before I make him sleep by himself."

When they reached the bedroom, Wyatt tossed Owen on his bed. He giggled with delight.

The girls ran into the bedroom. Dressed in their pink nighties, they raced to their beds and slid under the covers.

Wyatt sat on the edge of Owen's bed. He opened the book.

"'The adventures of Billy Bunny,'" he read, and Missy leaned against the door frame, "'began behind the barn.'"

He glanced back at Missy. "A lot of alliteration in this thing."

"Kids like that…and things that rhyme."

He nodded. "Point taken."

He turned his attention back to the book. "'A curious bunny, he spent his days exploring.'"

Missy watched silently, noting how the girls laid on their backs and closed their eyes, letting the words lead them to dreamland. But Owen sat up, looked at the pages, looked at Wyatt with real love in his eyes.

And that's when Missy fell in love. Or maybe admitted the love she'd had for Wyatt ever since they'd been on his bike and she'd laid her head on his back. This guy wasn't just sexy and smart. He had a real heart. For her kids. For her—if that kiss was anything to go by.

And she suddenly knew that was why he'd been so closed off. He was falling for her and he didn't want to be. What he felt for her was about more than sex. And it scared him.

When the story ended, he shut the book. Owen had snuggled into his side, but his eyes drooped.

"Wead it again."

Wyatt rose, shifting Owen to his pillow as he did so. "You're sleepy."

"But I wike it."

He pulled the covers to Owen's chin. "And you can hear it again tomorrow."

Owen's eyes drifted shut. Missy pushed away from the

door frame, smiling at Wyatt as he flicked off the bedside lamp and walked out of the room.

"Thanks."

He stepped into the hall.

She closed the door behind him. If what he felt for her was about more than sex, more than a fling, then she definitely wanted it. "Want a beer?"

He cleared his throat. "I need to get home."

"Please? Just five minutes."

He rubbed his hand along the back of his neck. "Let's talk on the porch."

On the way to her kitchen door, she grabbed two bottles of beer. She understood why he was afraid. If falling for him had scared and confused her, she could only imagine what it felt like to be a newly divorced guy falling for a woman with three needy kids. But she wasn't asking him to marry her. At least not now. All she wanted was a little time. A visit or two after he returned to his real life, and maybe the option for her and the triplets to visit him this winter.

As the screen door slapped closed behind her, she handed him a beer.

He looked at the bottle, looked at her. "We shouldn't do this."

"What? Drink? We're both over twenty-one. Besides, we limited ourselves to a bottle. We're strong, mature and responsible that way."

He let out a sigh. "That's just it. You are strong and mature and responsible. I am not."

"You think you're not, but I see it every day."

"Trust me. You're seeing a side of me that few people ever do."

She smiled. "I suspected that."

As if wanting to prove himself to be irresponsible and

immature, he guzzled his beer and handed the empty to her.

"In Florida I'm moody, bossy and pushy."

"You've been pretty moody, bossy and pushy here, too, but you're also good to the kids, good to me, fun to be around, considerate."

He groaned and turned away. When he faced her again frustration poured from him. "Don't make me into something I'm not!"

At his shout, she backed up a step. "I'm not."

"You are! What you see as good things, I see as easy steps. Who wouldn't enjoy a few weeks of playing with kids, no stress, no pressure? Even helping you with cakes and money and finding a van—those things were fun. But in a few days I go home, and when I do, I'll be back to working ten- and twelve-hours days, pushing my employees, making my parents crazy when I bow out of invitations I'd agreed to because they suddenly don't suit me." His voice softened on the last words. He reached out and gently stroked Missy's cheek. "I wish I was the guy you think I am. But I'm not." He snorted. "Just ask my ex-wife."

He took one final long look at her, then bounded off the porch, down the steps and across her yard. She stood watching him, her heart sighing in her chest.

His anger had surprised her, but the way his voice had softened and his eyes filled with longing meant more than his words. He talked about a person she didn't know. Someone impossible to get along with. He'd been a little pushy and bossy around her, but not so much that he was offensive or even hard to handle. Yet it was clear he saw himself as impossible to get along with.

So how could the guy who was so good to her kids, so good to her, think himself impossible to get along with?

Running his company couldn't make him feel that way.

He'd never been anything but calm, cool and collected when discussing her business. He knew he was smart. He knew what he was doing.

Unless dealing with a scheming wife, a woman who'd insinuated herself into his company, had made him suspicious, bossy, difficult—out of necessity?

And being away from his ex and the business had brought back the nice guy he was?

That had to be it. It was the only theory that made sense.

Around his ex-wife, he'd always had to be on guard and careful, so he didn't see how good he was. But Missy did. And somehow between now and the day he left, she was going to have to get him to see it, too.

CHAPTER TEN

WHEN WYATT GLANCED OUT the window Saturday afternoon, Missy wasn't carrying a cake with Nancy, the babysitter. She and her assistant, Elaine, lugged the huge violet creation to the back of her new van.

Pride enveloped him. This week's cake was huge and fancy. Flowers made ropes of color that looped from layer to layer. It reminded him of the Garden of Eden.

But as he admired her in her pretty pink dress, a dress that complemented the cake, he realized he wouldn't be scrambling to put on clean clothes, or driving with her to a wedding reception, helping to set up, telling her how much he liked her latest cake, dancing, almost kissing—actually kissing. His breath stalled. That last kiss had been amazing.

Still, forcing her to hire her assistant quickly had been the right thing to do. He didn't want any more time with her. He didn't want to lead her on and he didn't want her getting any more wild ideas that he was a nice guy. This—her leaving without him—was for the best.

She got behind the steering wheel and her assistant jumped into the passenger's side. As Missy put the van into reverse and started out of the driveway, she called, "See you later, kids!"

He watched her leave, his heart just heavy enough to

make him sad, but not so heavy that he believed he'd done the wrong thing in standing her on her own two feet and then stepping back.

He turned to face another bed full of boxes, this one in the first of two extra bedrooms. His grandmother might have been a neat, organized hoarder, but she'd been a hoarder all the same. He worked for hours, until his back began to ache. Then he glanced out the window longingly. On this sunny May afternoon, he had no intention of spending any more time inside, looking for jewelry that he was beginning to believe did not exist.

He slid into flip-flops and jogged down his back porch steps. Ducking under the shrub, he noticed the kids were in the sandbox. Nancy sat on the bench seat of the old wooden picnic table.

He ambled over. "Hey."

Owen's head shot up. "Hey, Wyatt."

"Hey, Owen." He faced the babysitter. "Can I play?"

Nancy rose from the picnic table. "Actually, I was hoping you'd come over."

He peeked at her. Sixteen, pretty and probably very popular, she reminded Wyatt of the sitters his mom used to hire when he was a kid. Young. Impressionable.

He wasn't sure he should be glad she was hoping he'd come over. "You were?"

She winced. "Tomorrow's Mother's Day and I forgot to get my mom a gift."

"Oh, shoot!" He winced with her, happy her gladness at seeing him was innocent, but also every bit as guilty as she was about the Mother's Day gift. "I forgot, too."

"I'll tell you what. You give me fifteen minutes to run to the florist and I'll order both of our moms flowers."

He waved his hand in dismissal. "That's okay. I can do

mine online. You go, though. There's nothing worse than forgetting Mother's Day."

"My mother would freak."

He laughed. "My mother would double freak."

"So you're okay with the kids? The florist is on Main Street and I can be there and back in fifteen minutes."

"If they're not crowded."

She grimaced. "Yeah. If they're not crowed."

He slid out of his flip-flops. "Take your time. We'll be fine."

When she was gone, the triplets shifted and moved until there was enough space for Wyatt in the sandbox. They decided to build a shopping center, which made Owen happy and also pleased the girls, who—though he hadn't thought them old enough to understand shopping—seemed to have the concept down pat.

After five minutes of moving sand, Owen suddenly said, "What's Mother's Day?"

"That's the day you buy your mom…" Wyatt stopped, suddenly understanding the three big-eyed kids who hung on his every word. He didn't have to do the math to know that they'd never bought their mother a gift for Mother's Day. Their dad had been gone on their first Mother's Day. Missy's mom was dead, so they'd never seen Missy buy a Mother's Day gift. Missy's dad was worthless, so there had been no one to tell them about Mother's Day, let alone help them choose gifts.

"It's the day kids buy their mom a present—usually flowers—so she knows that they love her."

Owen studied him solemnly. "We love our mom."

Wyatt's heart squeezed. The temptation to help them order flowers was strong, but this was exactly the kind of thing he shouldn't be doing. It was easy, goofy things like this that made Missy think he was nice.

He wasn't. He was a cutthroat businessman.

He cleared his throat. "Yeah. I know you love your mom."

Lainie tapped on his knee. "So we should get her flowers."

The desire to do that rumbled through him. He didn't just want to help these kids; he also knew Missy deserved a Mother's Day gift.

Ah, hell. Who was he kidding? Wild horses couldn't stop him from helping them. Somehow he'd downplay his role in things.

He pulled out his phone. "And that's why we're going to order some."

All three kids stared at him, hope shining from their big eyes. He looked down at the small screen before him. It seemed too impersonal to buy their first ever Mother's Day gift from a tiny screen on a phone. Particularly since the babysitter had said the florist was a five-minute walk away.

He rose, dusted off his butt. "You know what? I think we should do a field trip."

Lainie gaped at him as if he'd grown a second head. "We're going to a field?"

He laughed. "We're going to the florist." He looked down. All three kids had on tennis shoes. They were reasonably clean. He had credit cards in his wallet in his back pocket. They were set.

He caught Lainie's hand, then Claire's. "Owen, can you be a big boy and walk ahead of us?"

His chest puffed out with pride. "Yeth."

Lainie dropped his hand. "I can walk ahead, too."

Wyatt laughed. The little brunette had definitely inherited her mother's spunk—and maybe a little of her competitiveness. "Go for it."

They strode out of the drive, Claire holding his hand,

Owen sort of marching and Lainie pirouetting ahead of him. Wyatt directed them to turn right, then herded them across the quiet street and turned right again.

The walk took more like ten minutes, not the five Nancy had said, and Wyatt ended up carrying Claire, but they made it.

Owen opened the door to the florist shop and a bell sounded as they entered.

Because it was late afternoon, probably close to closing time, the place was almost empty. Nancy was at the counter, paying for her flowers.

She grinned when she saw the kids. "Hi, guys." Then she glanced at Wyatt. "What's up?"

"We've decided to get flowers, too. For Missy."

Her eyes widened with understanding. "What a great idea! Do you want me to stay and help?"

"No. We'll meet you back at the house."

She kissed each kid's cheek, then headed for the door, a huge purple flowery thing in her hands.

Wyatt faced the clerk. "What was that?"

The fifty-something woman smiled. "Hydrangeas." She peered into Claire's face. "I recognize the little Brooks kids, but I'm not familiar with you."

"I'm Wyatt…" His eyes narrowed as he read her name tag. "Mrs. Zedik?"

"Yes?"

"You taught me in fourth grade."

She looked closer. "I can't place you."

"That's because I wear contacts instead of big thick glasses. I'm Wyatt McKenzie."

She gasped. "Well, good gravy! Wyatt McKenzie. What brings you home?"

"Looking through things in Gram's house. Making sure she doesn't have a Rembrandt that gets sold for three dollars and fifty cents at the garage sale the real estate agent is going to have once we put the house on the market."

The woman laughed. "And what are you doing with the Brooks triplets?"

Lainie and Owen blinked up at her.

From her position on Wyatt's arm, Claire said, "We're shopping for Mother's Day flowers."

Mrs. Zedik came out from behind the counter. "And what kind of flowers do you want?"

Lainie said, "Pink."

Claire said, "Yellow."

Owen pointed at a huge bushlike thing. "Those."

Mrs. Zedik laughed. "Well, I might be able to find the azaleas the boy wants in pink. That way two kids would get what they want."

Claire caught Wyatt's face and turned it to her. "I want yellow."

He said to Mrs. Zedik, "She wants yellow."

"So we'll pick two flowers."

"How about if we let each kid get the flower they want?" He set Claire on the floor and reached for his credit card. "Sky's the limit on this thing."

With a chuckle she took the card. "I heard you made some money."

"Yeah. And it's no fun having money if you can't use it to make people happy." He stooped to the kids' level. "Pick what you want. Everybody gets a flower to give to your mom." Then he rose. "Any chance I can get these delivered?"

She winced. "Depends on how soon you want them. Van's out making deliveries now. Won't be back for at least two hours."

"It would be nice if she'd get them tomorrow morning."

Mrs. Zedik made a face. "We don't actually deliver on Mother's Day. It's Sunday."

"How about this? You deliver these flowers to my house this evening and I'll take care of the kids getting them to their mom in the morning."

"That sounds good."

Even as he spoke, Lainie called out, "I want this one."

Claire said, "I want this one."

Lainie looked at Claire's flower, then her own. "I want that one, too."

Mrs. Z walked up behind him. "I do have two of those."

"Okay, we'll get two of those and Owen's bush."

Owen said, "I want one of these, too." He pointed at an arrangement.

Lainie said, "I want one of those, too."

Mrs. Z's eyebrows rose.

Wyatt sucked in a quick breath. "Might be easier to let them each pick two."

"Can I have one of those?" This time Owen pointed at a vase in a cooler with a long-stemmed red rose.

"Owen, that would be three flowers."

He nodded.

Wyatt laughed.

Mrs. Z smiled. "You said money was no fun unless you spent it."

"I'm just hoping you have a van big enough to get them everything they want."

"I think it's sweet."

He didn't like thinking about how sweet it was. He'd told Missy the last time they'd talked that he was grouchy and bossy, and usually he was. But how could he resist helping her kids show her that they love her? "Actually, it's more of a necessity, since I haven't yet figured out how to tell these kids no."

Mrs. Z rounded the counter. "Just let me get a tablet and start writing some of this down."

In the end, they bought nine flower arrangements, three long-stemmed roses in white vases, three Mother's Day floral arrangements and three plants.

He walked the kids back to the house, Owen in the lead with Lainie pirouetting behind him. But when Wyatt slid Claire to the ground again, another thought hit him. He directed them to sit on the bench seat of the picnic table, and crouched in front of them.

"Mother's Day is a special day when moms don't just get flowers, they also aren't supposed to work."

The kids gave him a blank stare.

"At the very least somebody should take them out to breakfast or lunch. So I was thinking we could—"

Owen interrupted him. "We can make breakfast."

"Yeah, we can make breakfast."

Claire tugged on his hand. "I can make toast."

"Well, that would be really cute, but it might be even cuter if—"

The sound of a vehicle pulling into the driveway stopped him. He turned and saw Missy's new van.

He rose as she got out. "What are you doing home so early?"

"Garden wedding. Fifteen-minute service. Then an hour for pictures. Then cake and punch and we were done."

"Where's Elaine?"

"I dropped her off at home."

Missy stooped down and opened her arms. The kids raced into them. "So did you have fun today?"

"We went to—"

"We played in the sandbox," Wyatt interrupted, giving Owen a significant look. "Why don't you go wash up? At least get out of that dress?"

She glanced down at herself. "I guess I should."

"Great. The kids and I will be out here when you're done."

When she was gone, he whirled to face the kids. "The flowers are a secret."

Lainie frowned. "A secret?"

"So that tomorrow morning, we can have a big surprise. We'll hide the flowers at my house tonight, then tomorrow morning I'll sneak them over and we can have them on the kitchen table and your mom will be so surprised."

Owen frowned at him.

"Trust me. Secrets are fun." He paused to let that sink in. "Okay?"

They just looked at him.

Nancy came out of the back door and ambled over. "If you're trying to get them to keep a secret, it's not going to work. Your best bet is to entertain them so well they forget what you did today. And above all else don't say the one word that will trigger the memory."

This time he frowned. "What word is that?"

"F-l-o-w-e-r-s."

He got it. "Okay. Keep them busy, don't remind them of what we did."

Nancy ambled away, tucking her babysitting money in the back pocket of her jeans.

Heeding her advice, Wyatt said, "So, aren't we building a shopping mall?"

All three kids raced to the sandbox. When Missy came out, he kept them superinvolved in digging sand. She told Wyatt a bit about the wedding and the cake and the bride and groom, but then got bored and went into the house to make supper.

Wyatt all but breathed a sigh of relief, but fifteen minutes later she brought out hamburger patties and asked him to light the grill.

He didn't want to stay for dinner, and give him and Missy so much time together that his feelings overwhelmed him again, but he had no choice.

The girls picked up their dolls and began to follow Missy into the house. Panicking, he said, "Hey, wanna learn how to grill?"

The girls stopped, grinned and raced back to him.

Missy stopped, too, and faced him. "I was okay with you showing Owen how to light the grill, because he doesn't get to do a lot of boy things, but honestly, they're a little young to learn how to light charcoal briquettes."

"Maybe. But I don't want them to help with the grill so much as I...want to finish our shopping center."

She laughed. "Really? It's that important to you to be done?"

"We're about to lose the light."

"It's early. You have plenty of light."

"We also have lots of work to do."

She shook her head. "Suit yourself. But everybody has to wash up before they eat."

When she was gone, he directed the kids to the sandbox. "That was close."

Lainie said, "What was close?"

"Nothing." He pointed at some blocks in the sand. "Aren't you building a Macy's?"

She grinned and picked up the blocks.

All three kids got back to work as easily as if building block shopping malls was their real job. Wyatt waited fifteen minutes before he checked on the grill, found the briquettes a nice hot white and set the hamburgers on to cook.

Just as the hamburgers were getting done, Missy came out with buns and potato salad. His mouth watered.

"Are those buns homemade?"

She said, "Mmm-hmm."

His mouth really watered and he made a mental note to find himself a half-decent restaurant, because everything inside him was really liking this. And he knew he could have it, all of it, the kids, Missy, good food, if he could just pretend that he was the nice guy she thought he was.

But he wasn't.

They sat down to eat and Wyatt forced himself not to gush with praise over how delicious the food was. Then Owen unexpectedly said, "Hey, you know where we went today?"

It was everything Wyatt could do not to slap his hand over Owen's mouth to keep him quiet. Instead he said, "We went for a walk," as he gave Owen a look he hoped would remind him they weren't supposed to talk about the florist.

Owen's eyes widened, then he sheepishly looked away. But Lainie said, "I danced in the street."

Missy's head jerked up. "What?"

"When we went for our walk, I let her walk ahead of me and she sort of did those circle things ballet dancers do," Wyatt said.

"In the street?"

"There were no cars coming."

"No. But you're teaching them bad habits if you let them get too casual about crossing the street."

"Good point," he said, hoping that his easy acquiescence would smooth things over. "So your bride really liked your cake?"

Missy took a breath. Wyatt couldn't tell if it was an annoyed breath or a relieved breath.

Then she said, "Yes. The bride loved the cake." She set her fork down and smiled. "I told you I got four referrals."

"So how's your calendar looking these days?"

"Really good. I'll have to work with Elaine a lot to see if she can handle setting up a cake alone, but that's all part of being a start-up business. Everything's an experiment."

"Do you like yellow flowers?"

Wyatt's gaze jumped to Claire, who was sliding her fork around her plate as if she was bored, then over to Missy.

Missy's gaze had gone to the rows of yellow flowers around her house. She laughed. "Yes. I obviously love yellow flowers."

Claire grinned and glanced at Owen. "Told you."

Lainie said, "I like pink."

Wyatt jumped from his seat. "You know what? I think we should help your mom with these dishes."

Missy laughed. "Sit. We have plenty of time. Besides, they're paper plates. We'll toss them."

"I know, but shouldn't we get this potato salad into the refrigerator?"

She frowned. "Because of the mayonnaise?"

He didn't have a clue in hell, but he said, "Yes."

"Hmm." She rose. "Maybe."

He waved her down. "Sit! The kids and I will do it."

"Why are you spoiling me?"

"We're not spoiling you. We're—" Shoot. He almost said something about starting Mother's Day early. He wasn't any better at this than the kids.

"We know you worked hard."

Owen tugged on his jeans. "I worked hard."

"We all worked hard," Wyatt agreed. "But your mom's the only one who got paid for her work, so the rest of us are freeloaders."

Owen's face scrunched in confusion.

"Which is why we need to earn our supper by cleaning up."

Not entirely on board with the idea, Owen nonetheless

got up from the table and helped Wyatt and his sisters clear away the paper plates and gather the silverware. In the kitchen, he gave each triplet a dish towel and stood over them as they dried silverware.

Missy came in carrying the potato salad. "I thought the whole purpose of getting up from the table was to bring this in."

He winced. "Sorry."

She laughed. "Your memory's about as good as mine."

They finished the silverware and cleared the kitchen table, and then there was nothing to do.

No reason to keep himself in their company.

No way he could make sure none of the kids talked about their surprise.

Owen tugged on his jeans. "You weed me a stowwy?"

Right! Story! "Only if you take your bath first."

Owen's head swiveled to Missy. "Can we?"

She frowned. "It's carly."

"I never heard of a mother thinking her kids were settling in for the night too early."

Her frown deepened. "I suppose not. It's just not like them."

"Well, we did have a busy day."

She sighed. "Okay."

"Yippee!" Owen raced to the bathroom. Missy tried to fill the tub, but Wyatt shooed her away. "I'll bathe Owen. You do the girls."

When Owen was bathed and in his pj's, Wyatt stood at the closed bathroom door, listening to the girls' chatter, hoping they didn't mention the flowers.

Apparently the promise of a story was enough to take their minds in another direction. Both Claire and Lainie raced through their baths. He smiled, listening to them talk to their mom, who told them about the bride's dress and how handsome the groom looked in his tux, making her work that day seem like part of a big fairy tale. A sweet, wonderful fairy tale where moms loved their kids and grooms didn't get divorced.

Wouldn't that be nice?

"What are you doing?"

Wyatt glanced down at Owen, who had the big Billy Bunny book again. "Waiting for the girls."

"Oh." He grinned. "I'll wait, too."

Wyatt almost argued, but with the little boy quiet beside him, he decided to take his victories where he could. When the doorknob rattled, he turned Owen toward the bedroom and they scooted down the hall. When the girls arrived in their pink nighties, he and Owen were on Owen's bed, looking as if they'd been there the whole time.

Owen handed him the book.

He frowned. "Billy Bunny again?"

"We wike it."

"Yeah," Claire said as she climbed into her bed. "We like it."

He opened the book. "Okay."

He read it twice, dragging out the story as much as he could, hoping to tire the kids. By the end of the second read through, the girls were asleep and Owen was nodding off.

When Wyatt finished, he slid out of bed, put Owen's head on the pillow and leaned down to brush a kiss across his forehead. For three kids who loved to talk, keeping their secret had probably been something akin to torture, but they'd come through like three little troupers.

He straightened away and saw Missy in the doorway, watching him with a smile. He remembered her portrayal for the girls of that day's wedding, with the handsome groom and the love-struck bride. He could almost see him and Missy standing in a flower-covered gazebo, him in a tux, her in a gown. Lainie pirouetting everywhere.

He shook his head to clear the picture. That was so wrong.

As he reached the door, he shooed her into the hall and closed the door behind him. Faking a yawn, he said, "I guess I better get going, too."

"Seriously? If I didn't know better I'd think the four of you really had been working on a shopping mall."

"Actually, I think keeping track of three kids for eight hours is harder than building a shopping mall."

She laughed, her pretty blue eyes filled with delight. "It's how I keep my girlish figure."

He glanced down, took in every curve of her nearly perfect form and swallowed hard. "You should write a book. It could be the newest diet craze. You could call it 'how to look eighteen even though you're thirty-three.'"

"You think I look eighteen?"

I think you look fantastic. The words tickled his tongue, pirouetted like Lainie across his teeth. He held them back only because he knew it was for her own good that she didn't know how beautiful he thought she was.

"Listen, I really have to go."

"Oh."

The disappointment in her voice nearly did him in. He hesitated, but gritted his teeth. He wasn't right for her. She deserved somebody better.

He headed for the door. "I'll see you tomorrow."

"Oh?"

Damn it! He really wasn't any better at this than the kids. Worse, he knew the flowers the next day would make her like him again.

He really wasn't very good at this.

That night he set his alarm for five o'clock, wanting

to get up before Missy did. Still tired, he groaned when it rang, but he forced himself out of bed. Missy deserved a Mother's Day.

One by one, he carried the flower arrangements to her porch. When he realized he didn't have a key, he felt along the top of the door, looked under the mat and finally found one under an odd-looking rock in the small flower garden beside the bottom step to her porch.

He let himself in and began carrying flowers into the kitchen. With all nine pots and vases on the table, he found eggs in her refrigerator and bread for the toaster and started their simple breakfast.

Before even the first two slices of bread popped, Owen sleepily ambled into the kitchen. Claire followed a few seconds behind him and Lainie a few seconds after that.

"Everybody has to be quiet," he whispered as the kids raced to the table filled with their flowers.

Missy awakened to the oddest noise. She could have sworn it was a pop. Or was it a bang?

Oh, Lord. A woman with three kids did not like to hear a bang. She whipped off her covers and ran to the kitchen, only to find a table full of flowers, Wyatt with his arms up to the elbows in sudsy water and Claire standing on the step stool making toast.

Missy walked into the kitchen. "What's this?"

Everybody froze at the sound of her voice.

Wyatt said, "What did we practice?"

All three kids shouted, "Happy Mother's Day."

Owen raced over and caught her around the knees, hugging for all he was worth. Claire bounced off the step stool and ran over, too. Lainie danced to the flowers. "These are yours."

Her heart stuttered. Tears pricked her eyelids. She

pressed her fingers to her lips. Three azalea bushes tow-
ered over the lower "fancy" arrangements, which had plastic decorations stuck among the flowers that proclaimed
Happy Mother's Day! Three long-stemmed red roses sat
in tall milk-glass vases.

She swallowed. Four Mother's Days had come and gone
with no recognition, and truth be told, she'd been too busy
to notice. If anything, she mourned her mom on Mother's
Day.

She walked to the table, ran her fingers along the velvety
petal of one of the roses. How could a man who thought
to help her kids get her flowers for Mother's Day—a man
who was making her breakfast, which she could smell was
now burning—think he wasn't nice?

Her eyes filled with tears, half from the surprise and
half from sorrow for him. His ex had really done a number on him.

She peeked over at Wyatt. "Thanks."

Flipping scrambled eggs, which smoked when he
shifted them, he said, "It was nothing."

It was everything. But she couldn't tell him that.

This guy, who was probably the kindest, most considerate person she'd ever known, didn't have any idea how
good he was.

She looked at him—organizing the kids, tossing Claire's
burned toast into the trash, starting over with the scrambled eggs—and something happened inside her chest.

She'd already realized that she loved him. She'd tried a
few halfhearted attempts to let him know, and even an attempt to ask him if she could visit him or if he could visit
her again. But somehow she'd never been able to get out
the right words. And she'd never actually led him into the
will-you-visit-us or can-we-visit-you conversation.

Still, the sense she had this time, the strong sense that

burst inside her and caused her spine to straighten and her brain to shift into gear, told her the days of halfhearted attempts were gone. She wanted this man in her life forever. And by God, she would figure out a way to keep him.

CHAPTER ELEVEN

AFTER BREAKFAST, Owen and his sisters directed Missy to the living room recliner. Wyatt handed her the Sunday paper. Lainie found the side controller and flipped up the footrest.

Missy laughed. "You're spoiling me."

"Oh, I have a feeling one day of spoiling won't hurt you." Wyatt turned to the door. "We'll clean the kitchen, then get the kids out of pj's into shorts so that we can play outside."

Laughing again, she opened the paper and read until Wyatt had all three kids dressed and on their way out the door.

As soon as they were gone, she leaped out of the chair and found her cell phone.

"Nancy? It's me, Missy Brooks. Are you busy tonight?"

If she was going to seduce Wyatt McKenzie, she couldn't do it with a baby monitor in her right hand. She needed a sitter.

A little after nine that night, a knock on the door surprised Wyatt. He was in bedroom number three now. After caring for the kids that afternoon, giving Missy a break, his heart had hurt so much he'd come home and begun digging. He needed to find his grandmother's jewelry and get home before he said or did something he'd regret. Something that would ultimately hurt Missy.

The knock sounded again. "I'm coming! I'm coming!"

He raced to the door and whipped it open. There stood Missy, her hair wet from the unexpected spring rain, her eyes shining with laughter.

She displayed a bottle of wine. "It's a thank-you."

He looked at the bottle. What he'd done for her, the flowers, the breakfast, those were simple things someone should have thought to do four years ago. Yet she didn't let a kindness go unnoticed. She took the time to do something nice in return.

That was part of why he liked her so much. Part of why she was so tempting. Part of why she was too good for him.

He opened the door and took it. "Thanks. But I'm—"

But as he tried to close the door again, she wedged her way inside. "I brought the wine for *us* to drink."

"Oh." That couldn't happen. Wine made him romantic. And after an afternoon with three kids he was coming to adore, and an emotional morning of being proud of himself for helping her kids give her a real Mother's Day, the two of them alone with a bottle of wine was not such a good idea.

Thinking fast, he said, "Well, then we'll have to drink it while we look for jewelry. That's the agenda for tonight."

She rolled up her sleeves. "I don't mind."

Of course she didn't. She might like him, but she didn't seem to be experiencing the heart-stopping, fiery attraction he had for her. Drinking wine like two friends, digging through boxes for Scottish jewelry that may or may not exist, was a fun evening for her.

Watching her, hearing her laugh, wanting her so much he ached all over, would be an evening of torture for him.

Still, he got two glasses, pulled the cork from the wine and led her to the bedroom.

He poured two glasses of wine and handed one to her.

She peeked up and smiled. "Thanks."

His heart zigzagged through his chest. Her eyes sparkled. Her face glowed with happiness. He knew he was responsible for her happiness and part of him just wanted to take the credit for what he'd done, to accept her gratitude by kissing her senseless and—

Oh, boy. That "and" was exactly where they shouldn't go.

He turned away. "You're welcome." He put his glass to his lips, but instead of taking a sip, he gulped, then had to refill his glass.

She laughed. "I know you hate looking for this jewelry, but be careful with the wine."

"I'm not going anywhere." He couldn't keep his voice from sounding just a tad childish and bitter. And why shouldn't he be? The woman he'd always loved was at his fingertips, but he was too much of a gentleman to take her.

Damn his stupid manners! He was going to have a long talk with his mother when he got home.

"Let's just get to work."

She looked around with a smile, sipped her wine, then turned her smile on him. "Where do we start?"

"Those boxes there." He pointed at a tall stack. "Are all things I've gone through." He pointed at another stack. "So start there."

She walked over to the pile, sat on the floor and went to work on the shoe boxes, popping lids, pouring out junk, sifting through it for jewelry, and then moving on to the next box, as he'd explained to her the day her kids had helped him.

They worked in silence for at least twenty minutes. Done with her stack, she moved to the one beside it.

"I had to go through a lot of junk when my gram died, too."

Her voice eased into the silent room. Okay with the neutral comment, he said, "Really?"

"Yep. She wasn't quite the packrat your gram seemed to be, but she kept a lot of mason jars in the basement."

He laughed. "So she was a jelly maker."

"And she loved to can her own spaghetti sauce." Missy sighed. "She was such a bright spot in my life."

"My gram was, too. That's why I moved her down to Florida with us."

"So what do you have down there to fit all these people? A mansion?"

He laughed again. "No one lives with me. I got my gram a town house and my parents have a house near mine on the Gulf."

"Sounds nice."

He glanced over. Usually when he told someone he had a house on the Gulf, they oohed and ahhed. She seemed happy for him, but not really impressed. "It's a six-thousand-square-foot mansion with walls of windows to take advantage of the view."

She winced. "You're lucky you can afford to hire someone to clean that."

His gaze winged over to her. Was she always so practical? "I don't get it very dirty."

"Was that the house you shared with your wife?"

"She got the big house."

Missy gaped at him. "She didn't think six thousand square feet was good enough?"

"She didn't think anything was good enough." He

stopped himself. Since when did he talk about Betsy? About his marriage?

Missy shrugged. "Makes sense."

Cautious, but curious, because to him nothing about Betsy made sense, he said, "What makes sense?"

"That you divorced. It sounds like you had two different ideas of what you wanted."

He'd never thought of it that way. "I guess we did."

"So what was she like?"

"Tall, pretty." The words were out before he even thought to stop them. "She'd been a pageant girl."

"Oh, very pretty then."

He laughed. "Why are you asking questions about my ex?"

Missy caught his gaze. "Scoping out the competition."

He choked on his wine. "The competition?"

"Yeah. I like you." She said it naturally, easily, as if it didn't make any difference in the world. "I really like you. And I don't want to find out what to do or not do to get you to like me. I'm just trying to figure out what makes you you."

He set his wineglass down on the table. "Don't."

"Why not?"

"Because we've already been over this. My ex did a number on me. Even if I wasn't only a month out of a divorce, I wouldn't want to get involved again."

"It might be a month since you divorced, but if you fought over the settlement for four years, you haven't been married for four years."

"What?"

"You heard me. You keep saying you've only been divorced a month, but you've been out of your relationship a lot longer." She took a sip of wine. "Have you dated?"

His eyebrows rose. "I was separated. I was allowed to date."

"I'm not criticizing. I'm just helping you to understand something." She paused with a gasp. "Hey, look at this!"

The enthusiasm in her voice drew his gaze. She held up a small round thing with a woman's face on it.

She beamed. "It's a cameo."

He cautiously said, "That's good?"

"Not only does it look really old, but it's clear it was expensive." She examined it. "Wow."

He scrambled over. "What else is in that box?"

She rose, taking the box with her, and sat on the bed. He sat beside her.

She pulled out matching combs. "These are hair combs." She studied them. "They're so pretty."

He reached in and retrieved a delicate necklace. Reddish stones and silver dominated the piece. "No wonder my mom wanted them."

"Yeah."

Missy's voice trembled on the one simple word, and even though she hadn't said it, he knew what troubled her. He set the necklace back in the box, as sadness overwhelmed him, too. "So. I found what I came for."

"Yeah. You did."

And now he could go home.

Silence settled over them. Then he peeked at her and she peeked at him. He'd never see her again. Oh, tomorrow morning after he packed, he'd walk over and say goodbye to her and the kids. But this was the very last time they'd be alone together. Once he returned to Florida, he wasn't coming back. He had a life that didn't include her, and in that life he wasn't this normal, selfless guy she was falling in love with. He was a bossy, moody, selfish businessman who now had to deal with an ex-wife who owned one-third of his company. She might not have controlling interest, but she had enough of a say to make his life miserable.

And he wouldn't waste the ten or so minutes he had with the genuinely kind, selfless woman sitting beside him, by thinking about his bad marriage.

Though Missy had paid him back for the kiss they should have had graduation night, he bent and brushed his lips across hers. He went to pull back, but she caught him around the neck and kept him where he was, answering his kiss with one that was so soft and sweet, his chest tightened.

When her tongue peeked out and swiped across his lips, his control slipped. This was the one person he'd felt connected to since he was a geek and she was a prom queen. For once, just once, he wanted to feel what it would be like to be hers. He took over the kiss, and suddenly they were both as greedy as he'd always wanted to be.

As his mouth plundered hers, his hands ran down her arms, then scrambled back up again. Her velvety skin teased him with the promise of other softer skin hidden beneath her clothes. She wrapped her arms around his back and the feelings he'd had when she'd clung to him that day on the motorcycle returned. All that trust, all that love, in one simple gesture.

She loved him.

The thought stopped him cold. No matter what he did now, she would be hurt when he left. So would it be so bad to make love, to give them both a memory?

Yes. It would be bad. It would give her false hope. It would tear him up inside to leave her.

When he pulled away, he didn't merely feel the physical loss, he felt the emotional loss. But he knew he'd done the right thing.

Missy rose from the bed. She paced around the little

room as if deliberating, then swung to face him. "You know, I never felt alone. Not once in the four years after my husband left, until I began missing you."

The sadness in her voice pricked his heart. He'd deliberately held himself back the past few days. He knew that's why she'd missed him. Still, he said, "I'm not even gone yet."

"No, but you always pull away."

"I have to. One of us has to be smart about this."

"How do you know I want to be smart? Couldn't I once, just once, get something I want without worrying about tomorrow?"

Yearning shuddered through him. He wanted this night, too. And if she didn't stop pushing, he would take it. "Right from the beginning you've told me your kids come first, and the best way to protect them is to keep yourself from doing stupid things."

She faced him with sad blue eyes. "Would making love with the first guy I've been attracted to in four years really be stupid?"

His blasted need roared inside him. For fifteen years he'd wished she was attracted to him. Now that she was, he had to turn her away. Everything inside him rebelled at the idea. Everything except the gentleman his mother had raised. He knew this was the right thing. "That's not a reason to do this."

"Okay, then." She smiled. "How about this? I love you."

The very thought stole his breath. Missy Johnson, prettiest girl he'd ever met, girl he'd been in love with forever, woman who'd made the past four weeks fun, loved him.

He'd guessed that already, but hearing her say it was like music. Still, practicality ruled him. He snorted a laugh. "Right. In four weeks, you've fallen in love?"

"What's so hard to believe about that?"

"It's not hard to believe. It's just not love. Since I've been here, you haven't merely had company, you've also had an ally for your business. Somebody who saw your potential and wouldn't let you back down or settle for less than what you deserve."

"You know, in some circles that might be taken to mean you love me, too."

Oh, he did. Part of him genuinely believed he did. And the words shivered on his tongue, begging to be released. But his practical side, the rational, logical, hard-nosed businessman, argued that this wasn't love. That everything he believed he felt was either residual feelings from his teen years or rebound feelings. Feelings that would disappear when he went home. Feelings that would get her hopes up and then hurt her.

"I care about you. But I didn't have a good marriage. And for the past four years I've been trapped in hearings and negotiations to keep my wife—ex-wife—from taking everything I'd worked for. In the end we compromised, but I'd be lying if I said I wasn't bitter. And what you think I feel—" He snorted a laugh. "Hell, what I think I feel isn't love. It's rebound. You're everything she wasn't. And I need to go home. Get back to my real life."

Hurt to her very core, Missy walked around the bedroom. There was no way she could let the conversation end like this. She picked up one of the broaches that meant so much to his family. He had roots. He'd always had stability. He didn't know what it was like to be alone and wanting. So he didn't know how desperate she was to hang on to the first person in her life she really loved. And the first person, she believed, to really love her.

"You've never once seemed bitter around me."

"That's because I've been happy around you." When

her gaze darted to his, he held up his hand to stop what she wanted to say. "Or maybe it was more that around you I was occupied." He ran his fingers through his hair. "Look, I'm not going to lie to you by telling you leaving will be easy. It won't. You and the kids mean more to me than anybody ever has. But the timing is wrong. And if I stay or ask you to come with me, one of us is going to get hurt." He sucked in a breath. "And it won't be me. I'm selfish. I'm stubborn. I usually take what I want, so be glad I'm giving you a way out."

Her lips trembled. She'd presented all her best arguments and he wasn't budging. She had a choice. Stay and embarrass herself by crying in front of him, maybe even begging him to stay, or go—lose any chance of keeping him here, but salvage her pride.

She glanced up at him, saw the look of sadness on his face and knew the next step was pity. Pity for the woman who was left by her ex. Pity for the woman who was only now getting her life together after her father's abuse.

Pride rescued her. She would never settle for anybody's pity.

She softly sucked in a breath to hold off the tears, and smiled. Though it killed her, she forced her lips to bow upward, her tears to stay right where they were, shimmying on her eyelids.

"You know what? You're right. You probably are a totally different guy in Florida. I *am* just starting out. It is better not to pursue this."

"Two years from now you'll be so busy and so successful you'll forget who I am."

Oh, he was wrong about that. She'd never forget him. But he was also right. She would be busy. Her kids would be well dressed, well loved, happy. She would have all the shiny wonderful toys every baker wanted. Hell, she'd probably have her own building by then.

Still, she wouldn't let him off the hook. In some ways she believed he needed to be loved even more than she did. She loved him and he needed to know that. "I will be busy, but I won't forget you."

Her heart caught in her throat and she couldn't say any more. She turned to the door and walked out.

He didn't try to follow her.

CHAPTER TWELVE

MISSY AWAKENED before the kids, rolled out of bed and began baking. Wyatt rejecting her again the night before had stung, but the more she examined their conversation, the tortured expression on his face, the need she felt rolling from him, the more she knew he loved her.

That was the thing that bothered her about his rejecting her. Not her own loss. His. He kept saying he was protecting her from hurt, but in her own sadness she hadn't seen his loss. It took her until three o'clock in the morning to realize that to keep her from hurt he was hurting himself.

If she really believed he didn't want her, she'd let him go without a second thought. But she wasn't going to let him walk away just to protect her. Risk was part of love. Unfortunately, both of them had been in relationships that hadn't panned out, so they were afraid to risk.

Well, she wasn't. Not with Wyatt. He was good, kind, loving. He would never leave her. And she would never leave him. She loved him.

In her pantry, she found the ingredients for lemon cake and meringue frosting. When the kids woke at eight, she fed them, then shooed them out the door to play.

As they sifted through the sand, she took a few peeks outside to see when Wyatt came out to be with them. He didn't. But that didn't bother her. He'd found his jewels the night before. He could be on the phone with his mom or even his staff, making plans to go home.

Which was why she had to get her lemon cake to him as soon as possible so she would have one more chance to talk him out of leaving, or one more chance to talk him into staying in touch, visiting her every few weeks or letting her and the kids visit him.

Elaine arrived at nine. Missy brushed her hands on her apron, then removed it. "Would you mind watching the kids while I quickly deliver this cake next door to Wyatt?"

With a laugh, Elaine said, "No. Go."

Pretty yellow-and-white cake in hand, she walked through the backyard and dipped through the hole in the shrub. Sucking in a breath for courage, she pounded up the back porch steps and knocked on the kitchen door.

"He's not here."

She spun around to find Owen on her heels. "What?"

"He just weft."

"He just weft?"

Owen nodded. "He said to tell you goodbye."

"Oh."

Wow. Her chest collapsed, as if someone had punched it. Wyatt wasn't even going to tell her goodbye? Shock rendered her speechless, but also prevented her from overtly reacting.

"Well, then let's go home. We'll eat this cake for dessert at suppertime."

Owen eagerly nodded.

But as they clomped down the stairs, the shock began to wear off. Her throat closed. Tears filled her eyes.

It really was over. He didn't want her. All the stuff she'd convinced herself of, that he loved her, that he was protecting her, it was crap.

How many times had he told her he was a spoiled man,

accustomed to getting what he wanted? How many times had he warned her off?

God, she was stupid! What he'd been saying was that if he wanted her, he would have her. And all that pain over leaving her that she'd been so sure she'd seen the night before? She hadn't.

She set the cake on the counter, gave Elaine a list of chores for the day and went to her bedroom. About to throw herself across the bed and weep, she faltered. A shower would cover the noise of her crying. Then she wouldn't have to worry about yet another person, Elaine, feeling sorry for her. She stripped, got into the shower and let the tears fall.

He might not have loved her, but like a fool, she'd fallen for him.

Wyatt had decided to take the bike home. He loved the truck, but he needed the bike. He needed the feeling of the wind on his face to remind him of who he was and what he did and why he hadn't taken what Missy had offered.

Damn it! She'd have slept with him, even after all his warnings.

He stifled the urge to squeeze his eyes shut. She was such a good person. Such a wonderful person. And such a good mom.

A vision of his last five minutes with Owen popped into his head. He'd thought he could slide out the front door, zoom down the steps and get on the bike without being noticed. But the little boy had been at the opening in the shrubs. Just as he had been the day Wyatt arrived.

"Where you goin'?"

He'd stopped, turned to face him. "Home."

"You didn't give me a wide."

No longer having trouble understanding Owen's lisp,

he'd laughed, dropped his duffel bag in the little pouch that made the back of the bike's seat, and headed to the opening. When he reached Owen he'd crouched down.

"Actually, I think you're too small to ride a bike."

Owen looked at his tennis shoes. "Oh."

"But don't worry, someday you'll be tall. Not just big enough to ride a bike, but tall."

The little boy grinned at him.

Wyatt ruffled his hair. He started to rise to go, but his heart tightened and he stopped. He opened his arms and Owen stepped into them. He wrapped them around the boy, his eyes filling with tears. This time next week, when the kids went to day care, Owen would forget all about him. But Wyatt had a feeling he'd never forget Owen.

He let him go and rose. "See ya, kid."

"See ya."

Then he'd gotten on his bike and rode off.

Damn it. Now his head was all cloudy again and his chest hurt from wanting. Wanting to stay with Missy. Wanting to be around her kids. Wanting to stay where he was instead of return to the home that was supposed to be paradise, but he knew would be empty and lifeless.

Seeing a sign for a rest stop, he swung off the highway and drove up to the small brick building.

He took off his helmet and headed for the restroom. Parked beside the sidewalk was a gray-blue van. As he approached, the side door slid open and six kids rolled out. Three girls. Three boys. They barreled past him and giggled their way to the building.

"Might as well mosey instead of running." The man exiting the van smiled at him. "They'll be taking up most of the bathroom stalls and all the space in front of the vending machines for the next twenty minutes."

Last month that would have made Wyatt grouchy. This

month it made him smile. He could see Missy's kids doing the same thing a few years from now. "Yours?"

"Three grandkids. Three kids with my new wife." He pointed at the tall, willowy redhead who followed the kids, issuing orders and in general looking out for them.

"Oh." Wyatt was all for polite chitchat, but he wasn't exactly sure what to say to that. The closer the stranger got to Wyatt the more obvious it was that he wasn't in his twenties, as the redhead was. Early fifties probably. Plus, he'd admitted three of those kids were his *grandkids*.

The man batted a hand in dismissal. "Everybody says raising kids is a younger man's game, and that might be true, but I love them all."

"Bet your older kids aren't thrilled."

He laughed. "Are you kidding? Our house is the in place to be. We have movie night every Friday, so every Friday both of my daughters get a date night with their husbands."

"Well, that's handy."

"And I feel twenty-eight again."

Wyatt laughed. He guessed that was probably the redhead's age.

"Didn't think I'd pull through after my first wife left me." He tossed Wyatt a look. "Dumped me for my business partner, tried to take the whole company from him." He chuckled. "My lawyers were better than theirs."

Wyatt couldn't stop the guffaw that escaped. It was nice to see somebody win in divorce wars.

"But now I have a wife I know really loves me. Three new kids to cement the deal. And very good relationships with my older kids, since I am a convenient babysitter for weekends."

"That's nice."

The older man sucked in a breath. "It is nice." He slapped Wyatt on the back. "I'm telling you, second chances are the best. Just when you think you're going to be alone forever, love finds you in the most unexpected ways." He stopped, his mouth fell open and he began racing up the sidewalk. "Come on, Tommy! You know better than that."

By the time Wyatt got out of the restroom, the van, the older man and the kids were gone. He shook his head with a laugh, thinking the guy really was lucky. Then he walked up to a vending machine and inserted the coins to get a two-pack of chocolate cupcakes. He pushed the selection button. They flopped down to the takeaway tray.

He opened them and shoved an entire cupcake into his mouth, then nearly spit it out.

Compared to the cake he'd been eating the past few weeks, it was dry, tasteless. And made him long for Missy with every fiber of his being. Not because he wanted cake, but because she made him laugh, made him think, made him yearn for things he didn't even realize he wanted.

He wanted kids.

Someday he wanted to be the dad in the van taking everyone on an adventure. He wanted his house to be the one that hosted Friday night movie night—with the triplets' friends.

He wanted to have a bigger family than his parents and Missy's parents had given them. So his grandkids could have cousins and aunts and uncles. Things he didn't have.

But most of all he wanted her. He wanted to laugh with her, to tease with her, to wake up beside her every morning and fall asleep with her at night. He didn't want the noise in Tampa. He didn't want to fight any more battles in courtrooms or in his boardroom. He wanted a real life.

He glanced around the crowded rest stop. What the hell

was he doing here? He never ran away from something he wanted. He went after it.

And the first step was easy. He climbed on his bike, but before he started the engine, he pulled out his cell phone. He hit Betsy's speed dial number.

When she answered, he said, "Here's the deal. You come up with ten percent over the market value for my shares, or you sell me yours for their real value."

She sputtered. "What?"

"You heard me. If you want to play hardball, I'm countering your offer. I'll buy your shares for market value. If that doesn't suit you, then you buy me out. But I'm not working with you. And I'm not running the company for you. One of us takes all. The other gets lost. I don't care which way it goes."

"We're not supposed to negotiate without our lawyers."

"Yeah, well, I found something I want more than my company. I'd be happy to keep it and run it, as long as I don't have to deal with you. We never were a good match. We're opposites who argue all the time. If we try to run the company together, all we'll do is fight. And I'm done fighting. If you don't want to buy my shares, I'll find somebody who will."

She sighed. "Wyatt—"

"You have ten seconds to answer. Either let me buy your shares for what they're really worth or you buy mine and I disappear. Or I sell them to a third party."

"I don't want your company."

"Clock's ticking."

"Fine. I'll take market value."

"I'll call my accountant and lawyer."

He clicked off the call with a grin. He was free. Finally free to walk into the destiny he'd known was his since ninth grade. He was gonna marry Missy Johnson.

He started the bike and zipped onto the highway, this time going in the opposite direction, back home.

He was going to get his woman.

Missy cried herself out in the shower, put on clean clothes and set about making gum paste. While it cooled, she could have made a batch of cupcakes. Her plan was to deliver the cupcakes to every restaurant in a three-county area this week, but her heart wasn't in it. After Wyatt's rejection, she needed to feel loved, wanted. So as Elaine gathered the ingredients for a batch of chocolate cupcakes, she went outside to plant the azalea bushes the kids had bought her for Mother's Day.

The problem was she could see splashes of red through the shabby hedge. Her heart stuttered a bit. Wyatt's truck. He'd have to come home for that.

She stopped the happy thoughts that wanted to form. Even if he did come home, he wouldn't come over to see her. He'd made his choices. Now she had to live with them. With her pride intact. She didn't beg. She'd never begged. She sucked it up and went on.

She would go on now, too.

But one of these days she'd dig up those shrubs and replace them with bushes thick enough that she couldn't see the house on the other side. True, it would take years for them to grow tall enough to be a fence, but when they grew in they would be healthy and strong…and full. So she wouldn't be able to see into the McKenzie yard, and any McKenzie who happened to wander home wouldn't be able to see into hers.

She snorted a laugh. No McKenzie would be coming home. He'd probably send somebody to pick up the truck, and hire a Realtor to sell the house. She had no reason to protect herself from an accidental meeting. There would be no accidental meeting.

The roar of a motorcycle in her driveway brought her back to the present. Her first thought was that someone had chosen to turn around in her drive. Still, curious, she spun around to see who was.

Wyatt.

Her heart cartwheeled. *Wyatt.*

She removed her gardening gloves and tossed them on the picnic table, her heart in her throat.

As he removed his helmet and headed into her yard, all three kids bounced up with glee. He got only midway to the picnic table before he was surrounded. He reached down and scooped up Claire. Helaina and Owen danced around him as he continued toward the picnic table.

"Are we going to play?" Owen's excited little voice pierced her heart. This was just like Wyatt. Come back for two seconds, probably to give her keys to the truck for whoever he sent up to retrieve it, and undo all the progress she'd made in getting the kids to understand that he'd left and wasn't coming back.

"In a minute." He slid Claire to the ground again. "I need to talk to your mom."

All three kids just looked at him.

He laughed. "If you go play now, I'll take you for ice cream later."

Owen's eyes widened. "In the twuck?"

Missy sighed. Now he was just plain making trouble for her. "The truck doesn't have car seats."

Wyatt sat on the bench across from hers and casually said, "We'll buy some."

That was good enough for the triplets. With a whoop of delight from Owen and a "Yay!" from Claire and Lainie, the three danced over to the sandbox.

"Why are you here?" There was no point delaying the inevitable. "Did you forget something?"

He laughed. "Yes. I forgot you guys."

"Right." She glared at him across the table. "What the hell is that supposed to mean?"

"It means I don't want to go back without you."

Her heart tripped. She caught herself. She hadn't precisely misinterpreted everything he'd said and done to this point, but she had done a lot of wishful thinking. She liked him. But they were at two different places in their lives. And even if they weren't, they lived in two different parts of the country.

"I shouldn't have gone."

She sniffed a laugh. "You seemed pretty certain about it last night."

"Last night I was an idiot. This morning I left without talking to you because I didn't want to hurt you. Turns out I hurt myself the most by leaving."

She shook her head. "So this is all about you?"

"This is all about us. About how we fit. About how we would be a family."

For the first time since he'd walked over from her driveway, hope built in her heart. But hope wasn't safe. She'd spent her childhood hoping her dad would change. Her marriage hoping her husband would stay with her. Every time she hoped, someone hurt her or left her.

"Hey." His soft voice drifted over to her as his strong hand reached across the table and caught hers. "I'm sorry. I shouldn't have gone. I didn't even want to leave. But something inside me kept saying I couldn't do this. That I'd hurt you and hurt the kids."

She didn't look at him. She couldn't. If she glanced over and saw those big brown eyes sad, she'd melt. And she didn't want to melt. She needed to be strong to resist whatever nonsense he was about to say.

"Then I saw this guy and his family at a rest stop on I-95. His first wife had dumped him for his business partner and he married this really hot chick who had to be at least thirty years younger than he was."

Missy couldn't help it. She looked over at him with a laugh. "Are you kidding me?"

"No. Listen." He rose from his side of the picnic table and walked over to hers. Sitting almost on top of her, he forced her to scoot over to accommodate him. "He had six kids in a van that sort of looked like yours."

"Six kids?"

"Half of them were his with his new wife."

"Half?"

"The other half were grandkids."

That made her laugh out loud. "Grandkids?"

"Grandkids and kids all mingled together, and they were having a blast."

She suddenly realized they were talking like normal people again. Just two old friends, sitting on her picnic table, talking about the daily nonsense that happens sometimes.

It hurt her heart because this was what she wanted out of life. A companion. A lover, sure. But more than that, every woman wanted a guy who talked, shared his day, shared his hopes, his dreams. And the easy, casual way Wyatt sat with her, talked with her, got her hopes up more than any apology.

If she didn't leave now, she'd let those hopes take flight and she'd end up even more hurt than she already was.

She rose. "Well, that's great."

He grabbed her hand and tugged her back down again. "You're not listening to what I'm telling you."

Annoyed, she turned on him. "So what are you telling me?"

"Well, I was going to say I love you, but you seem a little too grouchy to hear it."

She huffed a laugh. "You don't love me. You said so last night. You said you *cared* about me but didn't love me."

"Geez, did you memorize everything I said verbatim?"

"A woman doesn't forget the words that hurt her."

He caught her chin and made her look at him. "I do love you. I love you more than anybody or anything I've ever thought I loved. I got confused because I thought I wasn't ready or supposed to love. That guy in the van, the guy with all the kids and enough family to be an organizational chart for a Fortune 500 company? He showed me that you don't have to be ready. Sometimes you can't be ready. When life and love find you, you have to grab them. Inconvenience, messiness, problems and all."

The hope in her heart swelled so much it nearly exploded. "Are you saying we're inconvenient?"

"Good God, woman, you have triplets. Of course this is inconvenient. You're starting a business here, which means you can't leave. My business is a thousand miles away. You haven't met my parents. Not that they won't love you, but it's going to be a surprise to suddenly bring three kids into their world. Especially since if we're going to make this work, I'm going to be spending a big chunk of my time up here." He shook his head. "They moved to Florida to be with me and now I'm going to be living at least half the year up here."

She laughed a bit. That was sort of ironic.

His serious brown eyes met her gaze. "But I love you. I want what you bring to my world."

"Messiness, inconvenience and problems?"

"Happiness, joy and a sense of belonging."

With every word he said his face got closer. Until when he said, "Belonging," their lips met.

This time there was no hesitation. There was no sense that as soon as he got the chance he would pull away. This time there was only real love. The love she'd been searching for her whole life was finally here.

Finally hers.

EPILOGUE

Two years later they got married on a private island about an hour down the coast from Tampa. The triplets, now six, were more than happy to be the wedding party. Owen looked regal in his little black tux that matched Wyatt's, and the girls really were the princesses they wanted to be, dressed in pale pink gowns with tulle skirts.

Nancy, their longtime babysitter, now a college sophomore, had been invited to the wedding as a guest, but ended up herding the triplets into submission as they stood at the end of the long white runner that would take Missy to the gazebo on the beach, where she would marry the love of her life.

She and Wyatt had decided to date for a year, then had been engaged for a year. Not just to give her a chance to get her company running smoothly, with a baking supervisor and actual delivery staff, but also to give the two of them time to enjoy being in love. Though Wyatt spent most of his time in her house when he visited, he'd kept his gram's house. He was very sentimental when it came to Missy, to their past, and especially to the picnic tables where he'd taught her how to solve equations.

"Okay, Owen, you're first."

Nancy gave him a small push to start him on his journey down the white runner to the gazebo, where Wyatt and the minister waited. Owen hesitated at first, but when he saw all the people urging him on, especially Wyatt's parents, his first grandparents, it was as if someone had flashed a light indicating it was showtime. He grinned and waved, taking his time as he went from the back of the beach to the gazebo.

Wyatt caught him by the shoulders and got him to stand still, but he couldn't stop Owen's grin. This was the day they officially became a family. A mom and dad, three kids and actual grandparents more than happy to spoil them rotten. Yeah. Owen was psyched for this.

Then the girls ambled up the aisle, more serious than their brother. They had rose petals to drop. Nancy had skirted the rows of folding chairs to get to the end of the runner and help the girls up the two steps into the gazebo.

Owen gave the thumbs-up signal. The crowd laughed.

Missy smiled. Then she pressed her hand to her tummy as she circled behind the last row of chairs to the runner. When she stood at the threshold of her journey up the aisle, she saw Wyatt, and all her fears, all her doubts disappeared.

His black tux accented his dark good looks, but with Owen standing just a bit above knee height beside him, and the girls a few feet away, waiting for their mom, he also looked like the wonderful father that he was.

She watched his eyes travel from her shoulders to the bodice of her strapless gown and down the tangle of tulle and chiffon that created the short skirt. His gaze paused at her knees, where the dress stopped, and he smiled before he raised his eyes and their gazes locked.

She walked down the aisle alone, because that's what she was without Wyatt. Then she carefully navigated the two steps to the gazebo and handed the two bouquets she carried to the girls.

Wyatt took her hands.

They said their vows and exchanged rings with the sound of the surf behind them. Then they posed for pictures in the gazebo, on the shore, with the kids, without the kids, with his parents and even with Nancy.

In the country club ballroom, they greeted a long line of guests, mostly Wyatt's friends and employees, as well as a swell of friends she'd made once she felt comfortable in Tampa.

As they walked to the main table for dinner, she guided Wyatt along a path that took them past their cake.

"Banana walnut?" he whispered hopefully.

"With a layer of chocolate fudge, a layer of almond, a layer of spice and an extra banana walnut layer at the top for us to take home for our first anniversary." She paused, her critical gaze passing over every flower of the five-layer cake.

He nudged her to get moving. "Everybody knows what you're doing."

She stopped, faced him with a smile. "Really?"

"You're judging that cake! Elaine was paralyzed with fear that she'd somehow ruin it."

"That's not what I'm doing."

He frowned, then his eyes narrowed. "So what are you doing?"

"I'm deciding if she's good enough to take responsibility for the wedding-cake division."

He gaped at her. "You'd give that up?"

"Not give up per se. I'd like to go back to baking. Let her supervise."

"Wow."

"It means I'd be home all winter."

His stupefied expression became a grin. "Here? In Florida?"

Her hands traveled up his lapels and to his neck. "It is our home."

"Our home. I like the sound of that."

"I want cake!"

Missy didn't even have to glance down to know the triplets had gathered at their knees.

She ruffled Owen's hair. "You always want cake. Just like your dad."

Wyatt smiled. "I like the sound of that."

"What? That you have a son?"

"Nope. I like that he already takes after me."

He stooped to Owen's height. "Don't worry. I'm guessing the guests won't eat even half that thing. You and I will be eating cake for a week."

Owen high-fived him. "All right."

They walked to the main table, raised enough for all the guests to see them. They settled Lainie and Claire in chairs to the right of Missy, and Owen between Wyatt and his parents.

When Owen grinned, Missy knew, of all the people at the wedding, herself and Wyatt included, her son was the happiest. He hadn't just gotten a dad and a grandpa; finally he wasn't the only man in the family.

* * * * *

FIRST COMES
BABY…

BY
MICHELLE DOUGLAS

At the age of eight **Michelle Douglas** was asked what she wanted to be when she grew up. She answered, 'A writer.' Years later she read an article about romance writing and thought, *Ooh, that'll be fun*. She was right. When she's not writing she can usually be found with her nose buried in a book. She is currently enrolled in an English Master's programme for the sole purpose of indulging her reading and writing habits further. She lives in a leafy suburb of Newcastle, on Australia's east coast, with her own romantic hero—husband Greg, who is the inspiration behind all her happy endings.

Michelle would love you to visit her at her website: www.michelle-douglas.com.

To my editor, Sally Williamson,
for her keen editorial eye and all her support.
Many, many thanks.

CHAPTER ONE

'BEN, WOULD YOU consider being my sperm donor?'

Ben Sullivan's head rocked back at his best friend's question. He thrust his glass of wine to the coffee table before he spilled its contents all over the floor, and spun to face her. Meg held up her hand as if she expected him to interrupt her.

Interrupt her?

He coughed. Choked. He couldn't breathe, let alone interrupt her! When he'd demanded to know what was on her mind this wasn't what he'd been expecting. Not by a long shot. He'd thought it would be something to do Elsie or her father, but...

He collapsed onto the sofa and wedged himself in tight against the arm. Briefly, cravenly, he wished himself back in Mexico instead of here in Fingal Bay.

A sperm donor? Him?

A giant hand reached out to seize him around the chest, squeezing every last atom of air out of his lungs. A loud buzzing roared in his ears.

'Let me tell you first why I'd like you as my donor, and then what I see as your role in the baby's life.'

Her no-nonsense tone helped alleviate the pressure in his chest. The buzzing started to recede. He shot forward and stabbed a finger at her. 'Why in God's name do you need a sperm donor? Why are you pursuing IVF at all? You're not even thirty!' She was twenty-eight, like him. 'There's loads of time.'

'No, there's not.'

Everything inside him stilled.

She took a seat at the other end of the sofa and swallowed. He watched the bob of her throat and his hands clenched. She tried to smile but the effort it cost her hurt him.

'My doctor has told me I'm in danger of becoming infertile.'

Bile burned his throat. Meg had always wanted kids. She owned a childcare centre, for heaven's sake. She'd be a great mum. It took an enormous force of will to bite back the angry torrent that burned his throat. Railing at fate wouldn't help her.

'I'm booking in to have IVF so I can fall pregnant asap.'

Hence the reason she was asking him if he'd be her sperm donor. *Him*? He still couldn't get his head around it. But... 'You'll make a brilliant mum, Meg.'

'Thank you.' Her smile was a touch shy. It was the kind of smile that could turn the screws on a guy. 'Not everyone will be as understanding, I fear, but...' She leaned towards him, her blonde hair brushing her shoulders. 'I'm not scared of being a single mum, and financially I'm doing very well. I have no doubt of my ability to look after not only myself but whoever else should come along.'

Neither did he. He'd meant it when he'd said she'd be a great mother. She wouldn't be cold and aloof. She'd love her child. She'd fill his or her days with love and laughter, and it would never have a moment's doubt about how much it was cherished.

His chest burned. An ache started up behind his eyes. She'd give her child the kind of childhood they had both craved.

Meg straightened. 'Now, listen. For the record, if you hate the idea, if it makes you the slightest bit uncomfortable, then we just drop the subject, okay?'

His heart started to thud.

'Ben?'

She had her bossy-boots voice on and it almost made him smile. He gave a hard nod. 'Right.'

'Right.' Her hands twisted together and she dragged in a

deep breath. Her knuckles turned white. Ben's heart thumped harder.

'Ben, you're my dearest friend. I trust you with my life. So it somehow only seems right to trust you with another life—a life that will be so important to me.'

He closed his eyes and hauled in more air.

'You're healthy, fit and intelligent—everything I want for my child.'

He opened his eyes again.

She grinned. 'And, while you will never, ever get me to admit this in front of another living soul, there isn't another man whose genes I admire more.'

Behind the grin he sensed her sincerity. And, just like every other time he visited, Meg managed to melt the hardness that had grown in him while he'd been away jetting around the world.

'I want a baby so badly I ache with it.' Her smile faded. 'But having a baby like this—through IVF—there really isn't anyone else to share the journey with me. And an anonymous donor...' She glanced down at her hands. 'I don't know—it just seems a bit cold-blooded, that's all. But if that donor were you, knowing you were a part of it...'

She met his gaze. He read in her face how much this meant to her.

'Well, that wouldn't be so bad, you know? I mean, when my child eventually asks about its father I'll at least be able to answer his or her questions.'

Yeah, but *he'd* be that father. He ran a finger around the collar of his tee shirt 'What kind of questions?'

'Hair colour, eye colour. If you were fun, if you were kind.' She pulled in a breath. 'Look, let me make it clear that I know you have absolutely no desire to settle down, and I know you've never wanted kids. That's not what I'm asking of you. I'm not asking you for any kind of commitment. I see your role as favourite uncle and nothing more.'

She stared at him for a moment. 'I know you, Ben. I promise your name won't appear on the birth certificate unless you want to. I promise the child will never know your identity. Also,' she added, 'I would absolutely die if you were to offer me any kind of financial assistance.'

That made him smile. Meg was darn independent—he'd give her that. Independent *and* bossy. He suspected she probably thought she made more money than him too.

The fact was neither one of them was crying poor.

'I know that whether you agree to my proposition or not you'll love and support any child of mine the way you love and support me.'

That was true.

She stared at him in a way that suddenly made him want to fidget.

She curled her legs beneath her. 'I can see there's something you want to say. Please, I know this is a big ask so don't hold back.'

Her words didn't surprise him. There'd never been any games between him and Meg. Ben didn't rate family—not his mother, not his father and not his grandmother. Oh, he understood he owed his grandmother. Meg lectured him about it every time he was home, and she was right. Elsie had fed, clothed and housed him, had made sure he'd gone to school and visited the doctor when he was sick, but she'd done it all without any visible signs of pleasure. His visits now didn't seem to give her any pleasure either. They were merely a duty on both sides.

He'd make sure she never wanted for anything in her old age, but as far as he was concerned that was where his responsibility to her ended. He only visited her to make Meg happy.

He mightn't rate family, but he rated friendship—and Meg was the best friend he had. Megan Parrish had saved him. She'd taken one look at his ten-year-old self, newly abandoned on Elsie's doorstep, and had announced that from that day forth they were to be best friends for ever. She'd given his starved heart all the companionship, loyalty and love it had needed. She'd nurtured them both with fairytales about families who loved one another; and with the things they'd do, the adventures they'd have, when they grew up.

She'd jogged beside him when nothing else would ease the burn in his soul. He'd swum beside her when nothing else would do for her but to immerse herself in an underwater world—where she would swim for as long as she could before coming up for air.

And he'd watched more than once as she'd suffered the crippling agony of endometriosis. Nothing in all his life had ever made him feel so helpless as to witness her pain and be unable to ease it. His hands clenched. He hadn't realised she still suffered from it.

'Ben?'

'I'm concerned about your health.' Wouldn't her getting pregnant be an unnecessary risk at this point? 'That's what I want to talk about.'

He shifted on the sofa to survey her more fully. She held her glass out and he topped it up from the bottle of Chardonnay they'd opened during dinner. Her hand shook and something inside him clenched. He slammed the bottle to the coffee table. 'Are you okay?' he barked without preamble.

She eyed him over the glass as she took a sip. 'Yes.'

His tension eased. She wouldn't lie to him. 'But?'

'But it's a monthly problem.' She shrugged. 'You know that.'

But he'd thought she'd grown out of it!

Because that's what you wanted to think.

His hands fisted. 'Is there anything I can do?'

Her face softened in the dim light and he wanted to reach across and pull her into his arms and just hold her…breathe her in, press all of his good health and vitality into her body so she would never be sick again. 'No doubt Elsie's told you that I've had a couple of severe bouts of endometriosis over the last few months?'

His stomach rolled and roiled. He nodded. When he'd roared into town on his bike earlier in the day Meg had immediately sent him next door to duty-visit his grandmother, even though they all knew he only returned to Fingal Bay to visit Meg. Elsie's two topics of conversation had been Meg's health and Meg's father's health. The news had been chafing at him ever since.

'Is the endometriosis the reason you're in danger of becoming infertile?'

'Yes.' She sat back, but her knuckles had turned white again. 'Which is why I'm lusting after your genes and...'

'And?' His voice came out hoarse. How could fate do this to his best friend?

'I don't know what to call it. Maybe there isn't actually a term for it, but it seems somehow wrong to create a child with an anonymous person. So, I want your in-their-prime genes and your lack of anonymity.'

Holding her gaze, he rested his elbows on his knees. 'No fathering responsibilities at all?'

'God, no! If I thought for one moment you felt pressured in that direction I'd end this discussion now.'

And have a baby with an anonymous donor? He could see she would, but he could also see there'd always be a worry at the back of her mind. A fear of the unknown and what it could bring.

There was one very simple reason why Meg had turned to him—she trusted him. And he trusted her. She knew him, and knew how deftly he avoided commitment of any kind. She knew precisely what she was asking. And what she'd be getting if he went along with this scheme of hers.

If he agreed to be her sperm donor it would be him helping her become a mother. End of story. It wouldn't be his child. It would be Meg's.

Still, he knew Meg. He knew she'd risk her own health in an attempt to fall pregnant and then carry the child full term and give birth to it. Everything inside him wanted to weep at the thought of her never becoming a mother, but he couldn't be party to her risking her health further. He dragged a hand back through his hair and tried to find the words he needed.

'I will tell you something, though, that is far less admirable.' She sank back against the arm of the sofa and stretched her legs out until one of them touched his knee. 'I'm seriously looking forward to not having endometriosis.'

It took a moment for her words to reach him. He'd been too intent on studying the shape of her leg. And just like that he found himself transported to that moment ten years ago when he'd realised just how beautiful Meg had become. A moment that had started out as an attempt at comfort and turned passionate. In the blink of an eye.

The memory made him go cold all over. He'd thought he'd banished that memory from his mind for ever. That night he'd almost made the biggest mistake of his whole sorry life and risked destroying the only thing that meant anything to him— Meg's friendship. He shook his head, his heart suddenly pounding. It was stupid to remember it now. *Forget it!*

And then her words reached him. He leaned forward, careful not to touch her. 'What did you just say about the endometriosis?'

'You can't get endometriosis while you're pregnant. Pregnancy may even cure me of it.'

If he did what she asked, if he helped her get pregnant, she might never get endometriosis again.

He almost hollered out his assent before self-preservation kicked in. Not that he needed protecting from Meg, but he wanted them on the same page before he agreed to her plan.

'Let me just get this straight. I want to make sure we're working on the same assumptions here. If I agree to be your sperm donor I'd want to be completely anonymous. I wouldn't want anyone to know. I wouldn't want the child to ever know. Just like it wouldn't if you'd gone through a sperm bank.'

'Not all sperm banks are anonymous.' She shrugged. 'But I figured you'd want anonymity.'

She had that right. If the child knew who its father was it would have expectations. He didn't *do* expectations.

'And this is *your* baby, Meg. The only thing I'd be doing is donating sperm, right?'

'Absolutely.'

'I'd be Uncle Ben, nothing more?'

'Nothing more.'

He opened and closed his hands. Meg would be a brilliant mother and she deserved every opportunity of making that dream come true. She wasn't asking for more than he could give.

He stood. 'Yes,' he said. 'I'll help out any way I can.'

Meg leapt to her feet. Her heart pounded so hard and grew so big in her chest she thought she might take off into the air.

When she didn't, she leapt forward and threw her arms around all six-feet-three-inches of honed male muscle that was her dearest friend in the world. 'Thank you, Ben! Thank you!' Dear, *dear* Ben.

She pulled back when his heat slammed into her, immediately reminded of the vitality and utter life contained by all that honed muscle and hot flesh. A reminder that hit her afresh during each and every one of Ben's brief visits.

Her pulse gave a funny little skip and she hugged herself. A baby!

Nevertheless, she made herself step back and swallow the excess of her excitement. 'Are you sure you don't want to take some time to think it over?' She had no intention of railroading him into a decision as important as this. She wanted—needed—him to be comfortable and at peace with this decision.

'He shook his head. 'I know everything I need to. Plus I

know you'll be a great mum. And you know everything you need to about me. If you're happy to be a single parent, then I'm happy to help you out.'

She hugged herself again. She knew her grin must be stupidly broad, but she couldn't help it. 'You don't know what this means to me.'

'Yes, I do.'

Yes, he probably did. His answering grin made her stomach soften, and the memory of their one illicit kiss stole through her—as it usually did when emotions ran high between the two of them. She bit back a sigh. She'd done her best to forget that kiss, but ten years had passed and still she remembered it.

She stiffened. Not that she wanted to repeat it!

Good Lord! If things had got out of control that night, as they'd almost threatened to, they'd—

She suppressed a shudder. Well, for one thing they wouldn't be having this conversation now. In fact she'd probably never have clapped eyes on Ben again.

She swallowed her sudden nausea. 'How's the jet lag?' She made her voice deliberately brisk.

He folded his arms and hitched up his chin. It emphasised the shadow on his jaw. Emphasised the disreputable bad-boy languor—the cocky swing to his shoulders and the loose-limbed ease of his hips. 'I keep telling you, I don't get jet lag. One day you'll believe me.'

He grinned the slow grin that had knocked more women than she could count off their feet.

But not her.

She shook her head. She had no idea how he managed to slip in and out of different time zones so easily. 'I made a cheese and fruit platter, if you're interested, and I know it's only spring, and still cool, but as it's nearly a full moon I thought we could sit out on the veranda and admire the view.'

He shrugged with lazy ease. 'Sounds good to me.'

They moved to the padded chairs on the veranda. In the

moonlight the arc of the bay glowed silver and the lights on the water winked and shimmered. Meg drew a breath of salt-laced air into her lungs. The night air cooled the overheated skin of her cheeks and neck, and eventually helped to slow the crazy racing of her pulse.

But her heart remained large and swollen in her chest. A baby!

'Elsie said your father's been ill?'

That brought her back to earth with a thump. She sliced off a piece of Camembert and nodded.

He frowned. The moonlight was brighter than the lamp-only light of the living room they'd just retired from, and she could see each and every one of his emotions clearly—primarily frustration and concern for her.

'Elsie said he'd had a kidney infection.'

Both she and Ben called his grandmother by her given name. Not Grandma, or Nanna, or even an honorary Aunt Elsie. It was what she preferred.

Meg bit back a sigh. 'It was awful.' It was pointless being anything other than honest with Ben, even as she tried to shield him from the worst of her father and Elsie. 'He became frail overnight. I moved back home to look after him for a bit.' She'd given up her apartment in Nelson Bay, but not her job as director of the childcare centre she owned, even if her second-in-command *had* had to step in and take charge for a week. Moving back home had only ever been meant as a temporary measure.

And it hadn't proved a very successful one. It hadn't drawn father and daughter closer. If anything her father had only retreated further. However, it had ensured he'd received three square meals a day and taken his medication.

'How is he now?'

'It took him a couple of months, but he's fit as a fiddle again. He's moved into a small apartment in Nelson Bay. He said he wanted to be closer to the amenities—the doctor, the shops, the bowling club.'

Nelson Bay was ten minutes away and the main metropolitan centre of Port Stephens. Fingal Bay crouched at Port Stephens' south-eastern edge—a small seaside community that was pretty and unspoilt. It was where she and Ben had grown up.

She loved it.

Ben didn't.

'Though I have a feeling that was just an excuse and he simply couldn't stand being in the same house as his only daughter any longer.'

Ben's glass halted halfway to his mouth and he swore at whatever he saw in her face. 'Hell, Meg, why do you have to take this stuff so much to heart?'

After all this time. She heard his unspoken rider. She rubbed her chest and stared out at the bay and waited for the ache to recede.

'Anyway—' his frown grew ferocious '—I bet he just didn't want you sacrificing your life to look after him.'

She laughed. Dear Ben. 'You're sure about that, are you?' Ever since Meg's mother had died when she was eight years old her father had…What? Gone missing in action? Given up? Forgotten he had a daughter? Oh, he'd been there physically. He'd continued to work hard and rake in the money. But he'd shut himself off emotionally—even from her, his only child.

When she glanced back at Ben she found him staring out at the bay, lips tight and eyes narrowed to slits. She had a feeling he wasn't taking in the view at all. The ache in her chest didn't go away. 'I don't get them, you know.'

'Me neither.' He didn't turn. 'The difference between you and me, Meg, is that I've given up trying to work them out. I've given up caring.'

She believed the first statement, but not the second. Not for a moment.

He swung to glare at her. 'I think it's time you stopped trying to understand them and caring so much about it all too.'

If only it were that easy. She shrugged and changed the topic. 'How was it today, with Elsie?'

His lip curled. 'The usual garrulous barrel of laughs.'

She winced. When she and Ben had been ten, his mother had dumped him with his grandmother. She'd never returned. She'd never phoned. Not once. Elsie, who had never exactly been lively, had become even less so. Meg couldn't never remember a single instance when Elsie had hugged Ben or showed him the smallest sign of affection. 'Something's going on with the both of them. They've become as thick as thieves.'

'Yeah, I got that feeling too.'

Her father had come to fatherhood late, Elsie had come to motherhood early, and her daughter—Ben's mother—had fallen pregnant young too. All of which made her father and Elsie contemporaries. She shook her head. They still seemed unlikely allies to her.

'But...' Ben shifted on his chair. 'Do we really care?'

Yes, unfortunately she did. Unlike her father, she couldn't turn her feelings off so easily. Unlike Ben, she couldn't bury them so deep they'd never see the light of day again.

Ben clenched a fist. 'You know what gets me? That you're now stuck looking after this monstrosity of a white elephant of a house.'

She stilled. Ben didn't know? 'I'm not precisely stuck with it, Ben. The house is now mine—he gifted it to me. He had the deeds transferred into my name before he left.'

His jaw slackened. 'He what? Why?'

She cut another slice of Camembert, popped it in her mouth and then shrugged. 'Search me.'

He leaned forward. 'And you accepted it?'

She had. And she refused to flinch at the incredulity in his voice. Some sixth sense had told her to, had warned her that something important hinged on her accepting this 'monstrosity of a white elephant of a house', as Ben called it.

'Why?'

She wasn't sure she'd be able to explain it to Ben, though. 'It seemed important to him.'

Dark blue eyes glared into hers. She knew their precise colour, even if she couldn't make it out in the moonlight.

'You're setting yourself up for more disappointment,' he growled.

'Maybe, but now nobody can argue that I don't have enough room to bring up a baby, because I most certainly do.'

He laughed. Just as she'd meant him to. 'Not when you're living in a five-bedroom mansion with a formal living room, a family room, a rumpus and a three car garage,' he agreed.

'But?'

'Hell, it must be a nightmare to clean.'

'It's not so bad.' She grinned. 'Confession time—I have a cleaning lady.'

'Give me a tent any day.'

A tent was definitely more Ben's style.

She straightened. 'You're home for a week, right?' Ben never stayed longer than a week. 'Do you mind if I make us an appointment with my doctor for Wednesday or Thursday?'

'While I'm in Fingal Bay, Meg, I'm yours to command.'

The thing was, he meant it. Her heart swelled even more. 'Thank you.' She stared at him and something inside her stirred. She shook it away and helped herself to more cheese, forced herself to stare out at the bay. 'Now, you've told me how you ended up in Mexico when I thought you were leading a tour group to Machu Picchu, but where are you heading to next?'

Ben led adventure tours all around the world. He worked on a contract basis for multiple tour companies. He was in demand too, which meant he got to pick and choose where he went and what he did.

'The ski fields of Canada.'

He outlined his upcoming travel plans and his face lit up. Meg wondered what he'd do once he'd seen everything. Start at the beginning again? 'Have you crewed on a yacht sailing around the world yet?'

'Not yet.'

It was the goal on his bucket list he most wanted to achieve. And she didn't doubt that he eventually would. 'It must take a while to sail around the world. You sure you could go that long without female company?'

'Haven't you heard of a girl in every port?'

She laughed. She couldn't help it. The problem was with Ben it probably wasn't a joke.

Ben never dated a woman for longer than two weeks. He was careful not to date any woman long enough for her to become bossy or possessive. She doubted he ever would. Ben injected brand-new life into the word footloose. She'd never met anyone so jealous of his freedom, who fought ties and commitment so fiercely—and not just in his love-life either.

Her stomach clenched, and then she smiled. It was the reason he was the perfect candidate.

She gripped her hands together. A baby!

CHAPTER TWO

I'm pregnant!!!

The words appeared in large type on Ben's computer screen and a grin wider than the Great St Bernard Pass spread across his face.

Brilliant news, he typed back. *Congratulations!!!*

He signed off as *Uncle Ben*. He frowned at that for a moment, and then hit 'send' with a shake of his head and another grin. It had been a month since his visit home, and now... Meg—a mum-to-be! He slumped in his chair and ran a hand back through his hair. He'd toast her in the bar tonight with the rest of the crew.

He went to switch off his computer but a new e-mail had hit his inbox: *FAVOURITE Uncle Ben! Love, M xxx*

He tried the words out loud. 'Favourite Uncle Ben.' He shook his head again, and with a grin set off into the ice and snow of a Canadian ski slope.

Over the next two months Ben started seeing pregnant women everywhere—in Whistler ski lodges, lazing on the beaches of the Pacific islands, where he'd led a diving expedition, on a layover in Singapore, and in New Zealand before *and* after he led a small team on a six day hike from the Bay of Islands down to Trounson Kauri Park.

Pregnant women were suddenly everywhere, and they filled his line of vision. A maternal baby bulge had taken on the same fascination for him as the deep-sea pearls he collected for himself, the rare species of coral he hunted for research purposes, and his rare sightings of Tasmanian devils in the ancient Tasmanian rainforest. He started striking up conversations with pregnant women—congratulating them on the upcoming addition to their family.

To a woman, each and every one of them beamed back at him, their excitement and the love they already felt for their unborn child a mirror of how he knew Meg would be feeling. Damn it! He needed to find a window in his schedule to get home and see her, to share in her excitement.

In the third month he started hearing horror stories.

He shot off to Africa to lead a three-week safari tour, clapping his hands over his ears and doing all he could to put those stories out of his mind. Meg was healthy. And she was strong too—both emotionally and physically. Not to mention smart. His hand clenched. She'd be fine. Nothing bad would happen to her or the baby.

It wouldn't!

'You want to tell me what's eating you?' Stefan, the director of the tour company Ben was contracted to, demanded of Ben on his second night in Lusaka, Zambia. 'You're as snarly as a lion with a thorn in its paw.'

Ben had worked for Stefan for over five years. They'd formed a friendship based on their shared love of adventure and the great outdoors, but it suddenly struck Ben that he knew nothing about the other man's personal life. 'Do you have any kids, Stefan?'

He hadn't known he'd meant to ask the question until it had shot out of his mouth. Stefan gave him plenty of opportunity to retract it, but Ben merely shoved his shoulders back and waited. That was when Stefan shifted on his bar stool.

'You got some girl knocked up, Ben?'

He hadn't. He rolled his shoulders. At least not in the way Stefan meant. 'My best friend at home is pregnant. She's ecstatic about it, and I've been thrilled for her, but I've started hearing ugly stories.'

'What kind of stories?'

Ben took a gulp of his beer. 'Stories involving morning sickness and how debilitating it can be. Fatigue.' Bile filled his mouth and he slammed his glass down. 'Miscarriages. High blood pressure. Diabetes. Sixty-hour labours!' He spat each word out with all the venom that gnawed at his soul.

His hand clenched. So help him God, if any of those things happened to Meg...

'Being a father is the best thing I've ever done with my life.'

Ben's head rocked up to meet Stefan's gaze. What he saw there made his blood start to pump faster. A crack opened up in his chest. 'How many?' he croaked.

Stefan held up three fingers and Ben's jaw dropped.

Stefan clapped him on the shoulder. 'Sure, mate, there are risks, but I bet you a hundred bucks your friend will be fine. If she's a friend of yours she won't be an airhead, so I bet you'll find she's gone into all this with her eyes wide open.'

Meg had, he suddenly realised. But had he? For a moment the roaring in his ears drowned out the noise of the rowdy bar. It downed out everything. Stefan's lips moved. It took an effort of will to focus on the words emerging from them.

'...and she'll have the hubby and the rest of her family to help her out and give her the support she'll need.'

Ben pinched the bridge of his nose and focused on his breathing. 'She's going to be a single mum.' She had no partner to help her, and as far as family went...Well, that had all gone to hell in a hand basket years ago. Meg's father and Elsie? Fat lot of good they'd be. Meg had no one to help her out, to offer her support. No one. Not even him—the man who'd helped get her pregnant.

A breath whistled out of Stefan. 'Man, that's tough.'

All the same, he found himself bristling on Meg's behalf. 'She'll cope just fine. She's smart and independent and—'

'I'm not talking about the mum-to-be, mate. I'm talking about the baby. I mean it's tough on the baby. A kid deserves to have a mother *and* a father.'

Ben found it suddenly hard to swallow. And breathe. Or speak. 'Why?' he croaked.

'Jeez, Ben, parenting is hard work. When one person hits the wall the other one can take over. When one gets sick, the other one's there. Besides, it means the kid gets exposed to two different views of the world—two different ways of doing things and two different ways of solving a problem. Having two parents opens up the world more for a child. From where I'm sitting, every kid deserves that.'

Ben's throat went desert-dry. He wanted to moisten it, to down the rest of his beer in one glorious gulp, but his hands had started to shake. He dragged them off the table and into his lap, clenched them. All he could see in his mind's eye was Meg, heavily pregnant with a child that had half his DNA.

When he'd agreed to help her out he hadn't known he'd feel this...*responsible*.

'But all that aside,' Stefan continued, 'a baby deserves to be loved unconditionally by the two people who created it. I know I'm talking about an ideal world, here, Ben, but...I just think every kid deserves that love.'

The kind of love he and Meg hadn't received.

The kind of love he was denying his child.

He swiped a hand in front of his face. No! *Her* child!

'You'll understand one day, when you have your own kids, mate.'

'I'm never—'

He couldn't finish the sentence. Because he *was*, wasn't he? He was about to become a father. And he knew in his bones with a clarity that stole his breath that Uncle Ben would never make up for the lack of a father in his child's life.

His child.

He turned back to Stefan. 'You're going to have to find

someone to replace me. I can't lead Thursday's safari.' Three weeks in the heart of Africa? He shook his head. He didn't have that kind of time to spare. He had to get home and make sure Meg was all right.

He had to get home and make sure the baby was all right.

CHAPTER THREE

A MOTORBIKE TURNED in at the end of the street. Meg glanced up from weeding the garden and listened. That motorbike sounded just like Ben's, though it couldn't be. He wasn't due back in the country for another seven weeks.

She pressed her hands into the small of her back and stretched as well as she could while still on her knees. This house that her father had given her took a lot of maintenance—more than her little apartment ever had. She'd blocked out Saturday mornings for gardening, but something was going to have to give before the baby came. She just wouldn't have time for the upkeep on this kind of garden then.

She glanced down at her very small baby bump and a thrill shot through her. She rested a hand against it—*her baby*—and all felt right with the world.

And then the motorbike stopped. Right outside her house.

She leapt up and charged around to the front of the house, a different kind of grin building inside her. Ben? One glance at the rangy broad-shouldered frame confirmed it.

Still straddling his bike, he pulled off his helmet and shook out his too-long blond-streaked hair. He stretched his neck first to the left and then to the right before catching sight of her. He stilled, and then the slow grin that hooked up one side of his face lit him up from the inside out and hit her with its impact.

Good Lord. She stumbled. No wonder so many women had fallen for him over the years—he was gorgeous! She knew him so well that his physical appearance barely registered with her these days.

Except...

Except when his smile slipped and she read the uncertainty in his face. Her heart flooded with warmth. This was the first time he'd seen her since she'd become pregnant. Was he worried she wouldn't keep her word? That she'd expect more from him than he was willing or able to give?

She stifled a snort. *As if!*

While she normally delighted in teasing him—and this was an opportunity almost too good to pass up—he had made this dream of hers possible. It was only fair to lay his fears to rest as soon as she could.

With mock-seductive slowness she pulled off her gardening gloves one finger at a time and tossed them over her shoulder, and then she sashayed down the garden path and out the gate to where he still straddled his bike. She pulled her T-shirt tight across her belly and turned side-on so he could view it in all its glory.

'Hello, *Uncle Ben.* I'd like you to meet *my baby* bump—affectionately known as the Munchkin.'

She emphasised the words 'Uncle Ben' and 'my', so he'd know everything remained the same—that she hadn't changed her mind and was now expecting more from him than he could give. He should have more faith in her. She knew him. *Really* knew him. But she forgave him his fears. Ben and family? That'd be the day.

He stared at her, frozen. He didn't say anything. She straightened and folded her arms. 'What you're supposed to say, *Uncle Ben*, is that you're very pleased to meet said baby bump. And then you should enquire after my health.'

His head jerked up at her words. 'How are—?' He blinked. His brows drew together until he was practically glaring at her. 'Hell, Meg, you look great! As in *really* great.'

'I feel great too.' Pregnancy agreed with her. Ben wasn't the only one to notice. She'd received a lot of compliments over the last couple of months. She stuck out a hip. 'What? Are you saying I was a right hag before?'

'Of course not, I—'

'Ha! Got you.'

But he didn't laugh. She leaned forward to peer into his face, took in the two days' worth of stubble and the dark circles under his eyes. Where on earth had he flown in from? 'How long since you had any sleep?' She shuddered at the thought of him riding on the freeway from Sydney on that bike of his. Ben took risks. He always had. But some of those risks were unnecessary.

His eyes had lowered to her abdomen again.

She tugged on his arm. 'C'mon, Ben. Shower and then sleep.'

'No.'

He didn't move. Beneath his leathers his arm flexed in rock-hardness. She let it go and stepped back. 'But you look a wreck.'

'I need to talk to you.'

His eyes hadn't lifted from her abdomen and she suddenly wanted to cover herself from his gaze. She brushed a hand across her eyes. *Get a grip. This is Ben.* The pregnancy hormones might have given her skin a lovely glow, but she was discovering they could make her emotionally weird at times too.

'Then surely talking over a cup of coffee makes more sense than standing out here and giving the neighbours something to talk about.'

Frankly, Meg didn't care what any of the neighbours thought, and she doubted any of them, except perhaps for Elsie, gave two hoots about her and Ben. She just wanted him off that bike.

'You look as if you could do with a hot breakfast,' she added as a tempter. A glance at the sun told her it would be a late breakfast.

Finally Ben lifted one leg over the bike and came to stand beside her. She slipped her arm through his and led him towards the front door. She quickly assessed her schedule for the following week—there was nothing she couldn't cancel. 'How long are you home for this time, Uncle Ben?' She kept her voice light because she could feel the tension in him.

'No!' The word growled out of him as he pulled out of her grasp.

She blinked. What had she said wrong?

'I can't do this, Meg.'

Couldn't do what?

He leaned down until his face was level with hers. The light in his eyes blazed out at her. 'Not Uncle Ben, Meg, but Dad. I'm that baby's father.' He reached out and laid a hand across her stomach. '*Its father*. That's what I've got to talk to you about, because father is the role I want to take in its life.'

The heat from his hand burned like a brand. She shoved it away. Stepped back.

He straightened. 'I'm sorry. I know it's not what I agreed to. But—'

'Its father?' she hissed at him, her back rigid and her heart surging and crashing in her chest. The ground beneath her feet was buckling like dangerous surf. 'Damn it, Ben, you collected some sperm in a cup. That doesn't make you a father!'

She reefed open the door and stormed inside. Ben followed hot on her heels. Hot. Heat. His heat beat at her like a living, breathing thing. She pressed a hand to her forehead and kept walking until she reached the kitchen. Sun poured in at all the windows and an ache started up behind her eyes.

She whirled around to him. 'A father? *You?*' She didn't laugh. She didn't want to hurt him. But Ben—a father? She'd never heard anything more ridiculous. She pressed one hand to her stomach and the other to her forehead again. 'Since when have you ever wanted to be a father?'

He stared back at her, his skin pallid and his gaze stony.

Damn it! How long since he'd slept?

She pushed the thought away. 'Ben, you don't have a sin-

gle committed bone in your body.' What did he mean to do—
hang around long enough to make the baby love him before
dashing off to some far-flung corner of the globe? He would
build her baby's hopes up just to dash them. He would do that
again and again for all of its life—breezing in when it suited
him and breezing back out when the idea of family started to
suffocate him.

She pressed both hands to her stomach. It was her duty to
protect this child. Even against her dearest friend. 'No.' Her
voice rang clear in the sunny silence.

He shook his head, his mouth a determined line. 'This is
one of the things you can't boss me about. I'm not giving way.
I'm the father of the baby you're carrying. There's nothing you
can do about that.'

Just for a moment wild hope lifted through her. Maybe they
could make this work. In the next moment she shook it off.
She'd thought that exact same thing once before—ten years
ago, when they'd kissed. *Maybe they could make this work.
Maybe she'd be the girl who'd make him stay. Maybe she'd
be the girl to defeat his restlessness.* All silly schoolgirl nonsense, of course.

And so was this.

But the longer she stared at him the less she recognised the
man in front of her. Her Ben was gone. Replaced by a lean,
dark stranger with a hunger in his eyes. An answering hunger
started to build through her. She snapped it away, breathing
hard, her chest clenching and unclenching like a fist. A storm
raged in her throat, blocking it.

'I am going to be a part of this baby's life.'

She whirled back. She would fight him with everything
she had.

He leant towards her, his face twisted and dark. 'Don't make
me fight you on this. Don't make me fight you for custody,
Meg, because I will.'

She froze. For a moment it felt as if even her heart had stopped.

The last of the colour leached from Ben's face. 'Hell.' He backed up a step, and then he turned and bolted.

Meg sprang after him and grabbed his arm just before he reached the back door. She held on for dear life. 'Ben, don't.' She rested her forehead against his shoulder and tried to block a sob. 'Don't look like that. You are not your father.' The father who had—

She couldn't bear to finish that thought. She might not think Ben decent father material, but he wasn't his father either.

'And stop trying to shake me off like that.' She did her best to make her voice crisp and cross. 'If I fall I could hurt the baby.'

He glared. 'That's emotional blackmail.'

'Of the worst kind,' she agreed.

He rolled his eyes, but beneath her hands she felt some of the tension seep out of him. She patted his arm and then backed up a step, uncomfortably aware of his proximity.

'I panicked. You just landed me with a scenario I wouldn't have foreseen in a million years. And you...You don't look like you've slept in days. Neither one of us is precisely firing on all cylinders at the moment.'

He hesitated, but then he nodded, his eyes hooded. 'Okay.'

This wasn't the first time she and Ben had fought. Not by a long shot. One of their biggest had been seven years ago, when Ben had seduced her friend Suzie. Meg had begged him not to. She'd begged Suzie not to fall for Ben's charm. They'd both ignored her.

And, predictably, as soon as Ben had slept with Suzie he'd lost all interest and had been off chasing his next adventure. Suzie had been heartbroken. Suzie had blamed Meg. Man, had Meg bawled him out over *that* one. He'd stayed away from her girlfriends after that.

This fight felt bigger than that one.

Worse still, just like that moment ten years ago—when they'd kissed—it had the potential to destroy their friendship.

Instinct told her that. And Ben's friendship meant the world to her.

'So?'

She glanced up to find him studying her intently. 'So...' She straightened. 'You go catch up on some Zs and I'll—'

'Go for a walk along the spit.'

It was where she always went to clear her head. At low tide it was safe to walk all the way along Fingal Beach and across the sand spit to Fingal Island. It would take about sixty minutes there and back, and she had a feeling she would need every single one of those minutes plus more to get her head around Ben's bombshell.

Her hands opened and closed. She had to find out what had spooked him, and then she needed to un-spook him as quickly as she could. Then life could get back to normal and she could focus on her impending single motherhood.

Single. Solo. She'd sorted it all straight in her mind. She knew what she was doing and how she was going to do it. She would *not* let Ben mess with that.

'Take a water bottle and some fruit. You need to keep hydrated.'

'And you need to eat something halfway healthy before you hit the sack.'

'And we'll meet back here...?'

She glanced at her watch. 'Three o'clock.' That was five hours from now. Enough time for Ben to grab something to eat and catch up on some sleep.

He nodded and then shifted his feet. 'Are you going to make me go to Elsie's?'

She didn't have the energy for another fight. Not even a minor one. 'There are four guest bedrooms upstairs. Help yourself.'

They'd both started for their figurative separate corners when the doorbell rang. Meg could feel her shoulders literally sag.

Ben shot her a glance. 'I'll deal with it. I'll say you're not available and get rid of whoever it is asap.'

'Thanks.'

She half considered slipping out through the back door while he was gone and making her way down to the bay, but that seemed rude so she made herself remain in the kitchen, her fingers drumming against their opposite numbers.

Her mind whirled. *What on earth was Ben thinking?* She closed her eyes and swallowed. *How on earth was she going to make him see sense?*

'Uh, Meg?'

Her eyes sprang open as Ben returned, his eyes trying to send her some message.

And then Elsie and her father appeared behind him. It took an effort of will to check her surprise. Her father hadn't been in this house since he'd handed her the deeds. And Elsie? Had Elsie *ever* been inside?

Her father thrust out his jaw. 'We want to talk to you.'

She had to bite her lip to stop herself adding please. Her father would resent being corrected. She thrust her jaw out. Well, bad luck, because she resented being spoken to that way and—

'We brought morning tea,' Elsie offered, proffering a bakery bag.

It was so out of character—the whole idea of morning tea, let alone an offering of cake—that all coherent thought momentarily fled.

She hauled her jaw back into place. 'Thank you. Umm… lovely.' And she kicked herself forward to take the proffered bag.

She peeked inside to discover the most amazing sponge and cream concoction topped with rich pink icing. *Yum!* It was the last kind of cake she'd have expected Elsie to choose. It was so frivolous. She'd have pegged Elsie as more of a date roll kind of person, or a plain buttered scone. Not that Meg was complaining. No sirree. This cake was the bee's knees. Her mouth watered. Double *yum*.

She shook herself. 'I'll…um…go and put the percolator on.'

Ben moved towards the doorway. 'I'll make myself scarce.'

'No, Benjamin, it's fortunate you're here,' her father said. 'Elsie rang me when she heard you arrive. That's why we're here. What we have to say will affect you too.'

Ben glanced at Meg. She shrugged. All four of them in the kitchen made everything suddenly awkward. She thought fast. Her father would expect her to serve coffee in the formal lounge room. It was where he'd feel most comfortable.

It was the one room where Ben would feel least comfortable.

'Dad, why don't you and Elsie make yourselves comfortable in the family room? It's so lovely and sunny in there. I'll bring coffee and cake through in a moment.' Before her father could protest she turned to Ben. Getting stuck making small talk with her father and Elsie would be his worst nightmare. 'I'd appreciate it if you could set a tray for me.'

He immediately leapt into action. She turned away to set the percolator going. When she turned back her father and Elsie had moved into the family room.

'What's with them?' Ben murmured.

'I don't know, but I told you last time you were here that something was going down with them.'

They took the coffee and cake into the family room. Meg poured coffee, sliced cake and handed it around.

She took a sip of her decaf and lifted a morsel of cake to her mouth. 'This is *very* good.'

Her father and Elsie sat side by side on the sofa, stiff and formal. They didn't touch their coffee or their cake. They didn't appear to have a slouchy, comfortable bone between them. With a sigh, Meg set her fork on the side of her plate. If she'd been hoping the family room would loosen them up she was sorely disappointed.

She suddenly wanted to shake them! Neither one of them

had asked Ben how he was doing, where he'd been, or how long he'd been back. Her hand clenched around her mug. They gave off nothing but a great big blank.

She glanced at Ben. He lounged in the armchair opposite, staring at his cake and gulping coffee. She wanted to shake him too.

She thumped her mug and cake plate down on the coffee table and pasted her brightest smile to her face. She utterly refused to do *blank*. 'While it's lovely to see you both, I get the impression this isn't a social visit. You said there's something you wanted to tell us?'

'That's correct, Megan.'

Her father's name was Lawrence Samuel Parrish. If they didn't call him Mr Parrish—people, that was, colleagues and acquaintances—they called him Laurie. She stared at him and couldn't find even a glimpse of the happy-go-lucky ease that 'Laurie' suggested. Did he resent the familiarity of that casual moniker?

It wasn't the kind of question she could ever ask. They didn't have that kind of a relationship. In fact, when you got right down to brass tacks, she and her father didn't have any kind of relationship worth speaking of.

Her father didn't continue. Elsie didn't take up where he left off. In fact the older woman seemed to be studying the ceiling light fixture. Meg glanced up too, but as far as she could tell there didn't seem to be anything amiss—no ancient cobwebs or dust, and it didn't appear to be in imminent danger of dropping on their heads.

'Well!' She clapped her hands and then rubbed them together. 'We're positively agog with excitement—aren't we, Ben?'

He started. 'We are?'

If she'd been closer she'd have kicked him. 'Yes, of course we are.'

Not.

Hmm... Actually, maybe a bit. This visit really was unprecedented. It was just that this ritual of her doing her best to brisk them up and them steadfastly resisting had become old hat. And suddenly she felt too tired for it.

She stared at *Laurie* and Elsie. They stared back, but said nothing. With a shrug she picked up her mug again, settled back in her *easy* chair and took a sip. She turned to Ben to start a conversation. *Any* conversation.

'Which part of the world have you been jaunting around this time?'

He turned so his body was angled towards her, effectively excluding the older couple. 'On safari in Africa.'

'Lions and elephants?'

'More than you could count.'

'Elsie and I are getting married.'

Meg sprayed the space between her and Ben with coffee. Ben returned the favour. Elsie promptly rose and took their mugs from them as they coughed and coughed. Her father handed them paper napkins. It was the most animated she'd ever seen them. But then they sat side-by-side on the sofa again, as stiff and formal as before.

Meg's coughing eased. She knew she should excuse herself for such disgusting manners, but she didn't. For once she asked what was uppermost in her mind. 'Are you serious?'

Her father remained wooden. 'Yes.'

That was it. A single yes. No explanation. No declaration of love. Nothing.

She glanced at Ben. He was staring at them as if he'd never seen them before. He was staring at them with a kind of fascinated horror, as if they were a car wreck he couldn't drag his gaze from.

She inched forward on her seat, doing all she could to catch first her father's and then Elsie's eyes. 'I don't mean to be impertinent, but...*why*?'

'That *is* impertinent.' Her father's chin lifted. 'And none of your business.'

'If it's not my business then I don't know who else's it is,' she shot back, surprising herself. Normally she was the keeper of the peace, the smoother-over of awkward moments, doing all she could to make things easy for this pair who, it suddenly occurred to her, had never exactly made things easy for either her or Ben.

'I told you they wouldn't approve!' Elsie said.

'Oh, it's not that I don't approve,' Meg managed.

'I don't,' Ben growled.

She stared at him. 'Yeah, but you don't approve of marriage on principle.' She rolled her eyes. Did he seriously think he wanted to be a father?

Think about that later.

She turned back to the older couple. 'The thing is, I didn't even know you were dating. Why the secrecy? And…and… I mean…'

Her father glanced at Elsie and then at Meg. 'What?' he rapped out.

'Do you love each other?'

Elsie glanced away. Her father's mouth opened and closed but no sound came out.

'I mean, surely that's the only good reason to marry, isn't it?'

Nobody said anything. Her lips twisted. *Have a banana, Meg.* Was she the only person in this room who believed in love—good, old-fashioned, rumpy-pumpy love?

'Elsie and I have decided that we'll rub along quite nicely together.'

She started to roll her eyes at her father's pomposity, but then he did something extraordinary—he reached out and clasped Elsie's hand. Elsie held his hand on her lap and it didn't look odd or alien or wrong.

Meg stared at those linked hands and had to fight down a

sudden lump in her throat. 'In that case, congratulations.' She rose and kissed them both on the cheek.

Ben didn't join her.

She took her seat and sent him an uneasy glance. 'Ben?'

He shrugged. 'It's no business of mine.' He lolled in his chair with almost deliberate insolence. 'They're old enough to know what they want.'

'Precisely,' her father snapped.

She rubbed her forehead. No amount of smoothing would ease this awkward moment. She decided to move the moment forward instead. 'So, where will you live?'

'We'll live in my apartment at Nelson Bay.'

She turned to Elsie. 'What will you do with your house?'

Before he'd retired Meg's father had been a property developer. He still had a lot of contacts in the industry. Maybe they'd sell it. Maybe she'd end up with cheerful neighbours who'd wave whenever they saw her and have young children who'd develop lifelong friendships with her child.

'I'm going to give it to Ben.'

Ben shot upright to tower over all of them. 'I don't want it!'

Her father rose. 'That's an ungracious way to respond to such a generous gift.'

Ben glared at his grandmother. 'Is he railroading you into this?'

'Most certainly not!' She stood too. 'Meg's right. She's seen what you haven't—or what you can't. Not that I can blame you for that. But...but Laurie and I love each other. I understand how hard you might find that to believe after the way the two of us have been over the years, but I spent a lot of time with him when he was recuperating.' She shot Meg an almost apologetic glance that made Meg fidget. 'When you were at work, that is. We talked a lot. And we're hoping it's not too late for all of us to become a family,' she finished falteringly, her cheeks pink with self-consciousness.

It was one of the longest speeches Meg had ever heard her utter, but one glance at Ben and she winced.

'A family?' he bellowed.

'Sit!' Meg hollered.

Everyone sat, and then stared at her in varying degrees of astonishment. She marvelled at her own daring, and decided to bluff it out. 'Have you set a date for the wedding?'

Elsie darted a glance at Meg's father. 'We thought the thirtieth of next month.'

Next month? The end of March?

That was only six weeks away!

'We'll be married by a celebrant at the registry office. We'd like you both to be there.' Her father didn't look at her as he spoke.

'Of course.' Though heaven only knew how she'd get Ben there. He avoided weddings like the plague—as if he thought they might somehow be catching.

'And where have you settled on for your honeymoon?'

'I…' He frowned. 'We're too old for a honeymoon.'

She caught his eye. 'Dad, do you love Elsie?'

He swallowed and nodded. She'd never seen him look more vulnerable in his life.

She blinked and swallowed. 'Then you're not too old for a honeymoon.' She hauled in a breath. 'And, like Elsie, are you hoping to rebuild family ties?'

'I sincerely hope so, Megan. I mean, you have a baby on the way now.'

Correction—she'd never seen him look more vulnerable until *now*. He was proffering the olive branch she'd been praying for ever since she was eight years old, and she found all she wanted to do was run from the room. A great ball of hardness lodged in her stomach. Her father was willing to change for a grandchild, but not for *her*.

'Meg.'

She understood the implicit warning Ben sent her. He didn't

want her hurt or disappointed. *Again.* She understood then
that the chasm between them all might be too wide ever to
be breached.

She folded her arms, her brain whirling. Very slowly, out of
the mists of confusion and befuddlement—and resentment—a
plan started to form. She glanced at the happy couple. A plan
perfect in its simplicity. She glanced at Ben. A plan devious
in design. *A family, huh?* They'd see about that. All of them.
Laurie and Elsie, and Ben too.

She stood and moved across to Ben's chair. 'You must allow
Ben and I to throw you a wedding—a proper celebration to
honour your public commitment to each other.'

'What the—?'

Ben broke off with a barely smothered curse when she sur-
reptitiously pulled his hair.

'Oh, that's not necessary—' Elsie started.

'Of course it is!' Meg beamed at her. 'It will be our gift to
you.'

Her father lumbered to his feet, panic racing across his face.
Meg winked at Elsie before he could speak. 'Every woman
deserves a wedding day, and my father knows the value of
accepting generosity in the spirit it's given. Don't you, Dad?'
Family, huh? Well, he'd have to prove it.

He stared at her, dumbfounded and just a little...afraid?
That was when it hit her that all his pomposity and stiffness
stemmed from nervousness. He was afraid that she'd reject him.
The thought made her flinch. She pushed it away.

'We'll hold the wedding here,' she told them, lifting her
chin. 'It'll be a quiet affair, but classy and elegant.'

'I...' Her father blinked.

Ben slouched down further in his chair.

Elsie studied the floor at her feet.

Meg met her father's gaze. 'I believe thank you is the phrase
you're looking for.' She sat and lifted the knife. 'More cake,

anyone?' She cut Ben another generous slice. 'Eat up, Ben. You're looking a bit peaky. I need you to keep your strength up.'

He glowered at her. But he demolished the cake. After the smallest hesitation, Elsie forked a sliver of cake into her mouth. Her eyes widened. Her head came up. She ate another tiny morsel. Watching her, Laurie did the same.

'What the hell do you think you're doing?' Ben rounded on her the instant the older couple left.

She folded her arms and nodded towards the staircase. 'You want to go take that nap?'

He thrust a finger under her nose. 'What kind of patsy do you take me for? I am *not* helping you organise some godforsaken wedding. You got that?'

Loud and clear.

'The day after tomorrow I'm out of here, and I won't be back for a good three months.'

Exactly what she'd expected.

'Do you hear me, Meg? Can I make myself any clearer?'

'The day after tomorrow, huh?'

'Yes.'

'And you won't be back until around May?'

'Precisely.' He set off towards the stairs.

She folded her arms even tighter. She waited until he'd placed his foot on the first riser. 'So you've given up on the idea of fatherhood, then?'

He froze. And then he swung around and let forth with a word so rude she clapped her hands across her stomach in an attempt to block her unborn baby's ears. *'Ben!'*

'You…' The finger he pointed at her shook.

'I *nothing,*' she shot back at him, her anger rising to match his. 'You can't just storm in here and demand all the rights and privileges of fatherhood unless you're prepared to put in the hard yards. Domesticity and commitment includes dealing with my father and your grandmother. It includes helping out at the odd wedding, attending baptisms and neighbourhood pool parties and all those other things you loathe.'

She strode across to stand directly in front of him. 'Nobody is asking you to put in those hard yards—least of all me.'

His eyes narrowed. 'I know exactly what you're up to.'

He probably did. That was what happened when someone knew you so well.

'You think the idea of helping out at this wedding is going to scare me off.'

She raised an eyebrow. Hadn't it?

'It won't work, Meg.'

They'd see about that. 'Believe me, Ben, a baby is a much scarier proposition than a wedding. Even this wedding.'

'You don't think I'll stick it out?'

Not for a moment. 'If you can't stick the wedding out then I can't see how you'll stick fatherhood out.' And she'd do everything she could to protect her child from that particular heartache. 'End of story.'

The pulse at the base of his jaw thumped and his eyes flashed blue fire. It was sexy as hell.

She blinked and then took a step back. Stupid pregnancy hormones!

He thrust out his hand. 'You have yourself a deal, Meg, and may the best man win.'

She refused to shake it. Her eyes stung. She swallowed a lump the size of a Victorian sponge. 'This isn't some stupid bet, Ben. This is my baby's life!'

His face softened but the fire in his eyes didn't dim. 'Wrong, Meg. Our baby. It's *our* baby's life.'

He reached out and touched the backs of his fingers to her cheek. And then he was gone.

'Oh, Ben,' she whispered after him, reaching up to touch the spot on her cheek that burned from his touch. He had no idea what he'd just let himself in for.

CHAPTER FOUR

BEN SLEPT IN one of Meg's spare bedrooms instead of next door at Elsie's.

He slept the sleep of the dead.

He slept for twenty straight hours.

When he finally woke and traipsed into the kitchen, the first thing he saw was Meg hunched over her laptop at the kitchen table. The sun poured in at the windows, haloing her in gold. She glanced up. She smiled. But it wasn't her regular wide, unguarded smile.

'I wondered when you'd surface.'

He rubbed the back of his neck. 'I can't remember the last time I slept that long.' Or that well.

'Where were you?'

He frowned and pointed. 'Your back bedroom.'

Her grin lit her entire face. 'I meant where exactly in Africa were you before you flew home to Australia?'

Oh, right. 'Zambia, to be exact.' He was supposed to be leading a safari.

She stared at him, but he couldn't tell what she was thinking. He remembered that conversation with Stefan, and the look of fulfilment that had spread across his friend's face when he'd spoken about his children. It had filled Ben with awe, and the sudden recognition of his responsibilities had changed everything.

He had to be a better father than his own had been. He had to or—

His stomach churned and he cut the thought off. It was too early in the day for such grim thoughts.

'Exciting,' she murmured.

He shifted his weight to the balls of his feet. 'Meg, are we okay—you and me?'

'Of course we are.' But she'd gone back to her laptop and she didn't look up as she spoke. When he didn't move she waved a hand towards the pantry. 'Look, we need to talk, but have something to eat first while I finish up these accounts. Then we'll do precisely that.'

He'd stormed in here yesterday and upended all of her plans. Meg liked her ducks in neat straight rows. She liked to know exactly where she was going and what she was working towards. He'd put paid to all of that, and he knew how much it rattled her when her plans went awry.

Awry? His lips twisted. He'd blown them to smithereens. The least he could do was submit to her request with grace, but...

'You're working on a Sunday?'

'I run my own business, Ben. I work when I have to work.'

He shut up after that. It struck him how much Meg stuck to things, and how much *he* never had. As soon as he grew bored with a job or a place he moved on to the next one, abuzz with the novelty and promise of a new experience. His restlessness had become legendary amongst his friends and colleagues. No wonder she didn't have any faith in his potential as a father.

All you did was collect sperm in a cup.

He flinched, spilling cereal all over the bench. With a muffled curse he cleaned it up and then stood, staring out of the kitchen window at the garden beyond while he ate.

You never planned to have a child.

He hadn't. He'd done everything in his power to avoid that

kind of commitment. Bile rose in his throat. So what the hell was he doing here?

He stared at the bowl he held and Stefan's face, words, rose in his mind. *A baby deserves both a mother and a father.* He pushed his shoulders back and rinsed his bowl. He might not have planned this, but he had no intention of walking away from his child. He couldn't.

He swung to Meg, but she didn't look up from her computer. He wasn't hungry but he made toast. He ate because he wanted his body clock to adjust to the time zone. He ate to stop himself from demanding that Meg stop what she was doing and talk to him right now.

After he'd washed and dried the dishes Meg turned off her computer and pushed it to one side. He poured two glasses of orange juice and sat down. 'You said we have to talk.' He pushed one of the glasses towards her.

She blinked. 'And you don't think that's necessary?'

'I said what I needed to say yesterday.' He eyed her for a moment. 'And I don't want to fight.'

She stared at him, as if waiting for more. When he remained silent she blew out a breath and shook her head.

He rolled his shoulders and fought a scowl. 'What?'

'You said yesterday that you want to be acknowledged as the baby's father.'

'I do.'

'And that you want to be a part of its life.'

He thrust out his jaw. 'That's right.'

'Then would you kindly outline the practicalities of that for me, please? What precisely are your intentions?'

He stared at her blankly. What was she talking about?

She shook her head again, her lips twisting. 'Does that mean you want to drop in and visit the baby once a week? Or does it mean you want the baby to live with you for two nights a week and every second weekend? Or are you after week-about parenting?' Her eyes suddenly blazed with scorn. 'Or do you mean to flit in and out of its life as you do now, only instead of calling you Uncle Ben the child gets the privilege of calling you Daddy?'

Her scorn almost burned the skin from his face.

She leaned towards him. 'Do you actually mean to settle down and help care for this baby?'

Settle down? His mouth went dry. He hadn't thought...

She drew back and folded her arms. 'Or do you mean to keep going on as you've always done?'

She stared at him, her blazing eyes and the tension in her folded arms demanding an answer. He had to say something. 'I...I haven't thought the nuts and bolts of the arrangements through.' It wasn't much to give her, but at least it was the truth.

'You can't have it both ways, Ben. You're either globe-trotting Uncle Ben or one hundred per cent involved Daddy. I won't settle for anything but the best for my child.'

He leapt out of his chair. 'You can't demand I change my entire life!'

She stared at him, her eyes shadowed. 'I'm not. I've never had any expectations of you. You're the one who stormed in here yesterday and said you wanted to be a father. And a true father is—'

'More than sperm in a cup.' He fell back into his seat.

She pressed her fingers to her eyes. 'I'm sorry. I put that very crudely yesterday.'

Her guilt raked at him. She hadn't done anything wrong. He was the one who'd waltzed in and overturned her carefully laid plans.

She lifted her head. 'A father is so much more than an uncle, Ben. Being a true father demands more commitment than your current lifestyle allows for. A father isn't just for fun and games. Being a father means staying up all night when your child is sick, running around to soccer and netball games, attending parent and teacher nights.'

His hands clenched. His stomach clenched tighter. He'd

stormed in here without really knowing what he was demanding. He still didn't know what he was demanding. He just knew he couldn't walk away.

'Ben, what do you even know about babies?'

Zilch. Other than the fact that they were miracles. And that they deserved all the best life had to give.

'Have you ever held one?'

Nope. Not even once.

'Do you even know how to nurture someone?'

He stiffened. *What the hell...?*

'I don't mean do you know how to lead a group safely and successfully down the Amazon, or to base camp at Everest, or make sure someone attaches the safety harness on their climbing equipment correctly. Do you know how to care for someone who is sick or who's just feeling a bit depressed?'

What kind of selfish sod did she think him?

His mouth dried. What kind of selfish sod *was* he?

'I'm not criticising you. Those things have probably never passed across your radar before.' Her brow furrowed. 'You have this amazing and exciting life. Do you really want to give it up for nappies, teething, car pools and trips to the dentist?'

He couldn't answer that.

'Do you *really* want to be a father, Ben?'

He stared at his hands. He curled his fingers against his palms, forming them into fists. 'I don't know what to do.' He searched Meg's eyes—eyes that had given him answers in the past. 'What should I do?' Did she think he had it in him to become a good father?

'No way!' She shot back in her chair. 'I am not going to tell you what to do. I am not going to make this decision for you. It's too important. This is something you have to work out for yourself, Ben.'

His mouth went drier than the Kalahari Desert. Meg meant to desert him?

Her face softened. 'If you don't want that level of involvement I will understand. You won't be letting me down. We'll carry on as we've always done and there'll be no hard feelings. At least not on my side.'

Or his!

'But if you do want to be a proper father it only seems fair to warn you that my expectations will be high.'

He swallowed. He didn't *do* expectations.

She reached out and touched his hand. He stared at it and suddenly realised how small it was.

'I'm so grateful to you, Ben. I can't tell you how much I'm looking forward to becoming a mother—how happy I am that I'm pregnant. You helped make that possible for me. If you do want to be a fully involved father I would never deny that to you.'

It was a tiny hand, and as he stared at it he suddenly remembered the fairytales she'd once spun about families—perfect mothers and fathers, beautiful children, loving homes—when the two of them had been nothing but children themselves. She'd had big dreams.

He couldn't walk away. She was carrying *his* child. But could he live up to her expectations of what a father should be? Could he live up to his own expectations? Could he do a better job than his father had done?

His heart thumped against his ribcage. It might be better for all concerned if he got up from this table right now and just walked away.

'I realise this isn't the kind of decision you can make overnight.'

Her voice hauled him back from the brink of an abyss.

'But, Ben, for the baby's sake...and for mine...could you please make your decision by the time the wedding rolls around?'

His head lifted. Six weeks? She was giving him six weeks? If he could cope with six weeks living in Fingal Bay, that was.

He swallowed. If he couldn't he supposed they'd have their answer.

'And speaking of weddings…' She rose and hitched her head towards the back door.

Weddings? He scowled.

'C'mon. I need your help measuring the back yard.'

'What the hell for—?'

He broke off on an expletive to catch the industrial tape measure she tossed him—an old one of her father's, no doubt—before it brained him. She disappeared outside.

Glowering, he slouched after her. 'What for?' he repeated.

'For the marquee. Elsie and my father can be married in the side garden by the rose bushes, weather permitting, and we'll set up a marquee out the back here for the meal and speeches and dancing.'

'Why the hell can't they get married in the registry office?'

She spun around, hands on hips. The sun hit her hair, her eyes, the shine on her lips. With her baby bump, she looked like a golden goddess of fertility. A *desirable* goddess. He blinked and took a step back.

'This is a wedding. It should be celebrated.'

'I have never met two people less likely to want to celebrate.'

'Precisely.'

He narrowed his eyes. 'What are you up to?'

'Shut up, Ben, and measure.'

They measured.

The sun shone, the sky was clear and salt scented the air, mingling with the myriad scents from Meg's garden. Given the sobering discussion they'd just had, he'd have thought it impossible to relax, but as he jotted down the measurements that was exactly what he found himself doing.

To his relief, Meg did too. He knew he'd freaked her out with his announcement yesterday—that he'd shocked and stressed her. He paused. And then stiffened. He'd *stressed* her. She was pregnant and he'd stressed her. He was an idiot! Couldn't he have found a less threatening and shocking way of blurting his intentions out?

His hands clenched. He was a tenfold idiot for not actually working out the nuts and bolts of those intentions prior to bursting in on her the way he had—for not setting before her a carefully thought-out plan that she could work with. She'd spend the next six weeks in a state of uncertainty—which for Meg translated into stress and worry and an endless circling litany of 'what-ifs'—until he made a decision. He bit back a curse. She'd dealt with him with more grace than he deserved.

He shot a quick glance in her direction. She didn't look stressed or fragile or the worse for wear at the moment. Her skin glowed with a health and vigour he'd never noticed before. Her hair shone in the sun and...

He rolled his shoulders and tried to keep his attention above neck level.

It was just... Her baby bump was small, but it was unmistakable. And it fascinated him.

'Shouldn't you be taking it easy?' he blurted out in the middle of some soliloquy she was giving him about round tables versus rectangular.

She broke off to blink at him, and then she laughed. 'I'm pregnant, not ill. I can keep doing all the things I was doing before I became pregnant.'

Yeah, but she was doing a lot—perhaps more than was good for her. She ran her own childcare centre—worked there five days a week and heaven only knew how many other hours she put into it. She had to maintain this enormous house and garden. And now she was organising a wedding.

He folded his arms. It was just as well he had come home. He could at least shoulder some of the burden and make sure she looked after herself. Regardless of any other decision he came to, he could at least do that.

She started talking again and his gaze drifted back towards her baby bump. But on the way down the intriguing shadow of cleavage in the vee of her shirt snagged his attention. His breath jammed in his throat and a pulse pounded at his groin. The soft cotton of her blouse seemed to enhance the sweet fullness of her breasts.

That pulse pounded harder as he imagined the weight of those breasts in his hands and the way the nipples would harden if he were to run his thumbs over them—back and forth, over and over, until her head dropped back and her lips parted and her eyes glazed with desire.

His mouth dried as he imagined slipping the buttons free and easing that blouse from her shoulders, gazing at those magnificent breasts in the sun and dipping his head to—

He snapped away. *Oh, hell!* That was *Meg* he was staring at, lusting after.

He raked both hands back through his hair and paced, keeping his eyes firmly fixed on the ground in front of him. Jet lag—that had to be it. Plus his brain was addled and emotions were running high after the conversation they'd had.

And she was pregnant with *his* child. Surely it was only natural he'd see her differently? He swallowed and kept pacing. Once he'd sorted it all out in his head, worked out what he was going to do, things would return to normal again. His hands unclenched, his breathing eased. Of course it would.

He came back to himself to find her shaking his arm. 'You haven't heard a word I've said, have you? What's wrong?'

Her lips looked plump and full and oh-so-kissable. He swallowed. 'I…uh…' They were measuring the back yard. That was right. 'Where are we going to find enough people to fill this tent of yours?'

'Marquee,' she corrected. 'And I'm going to need your help on that one.'

His help. *Focus on that—not on the way her bottom lip curves or the neckline of her shirt or—*

Keep your eyes above her neck!

'Help?' he croaked, suddenly parched.

'I want you to get the names of ten people Elsie would like to invite to the wedding.'

That snapped him to. 'Me?'

'I'll do the same for my father. I mean to invite some of my friends, along with the entire street. Let me know if there's anyone you'd like to invite too.'

'Dave Clements,' he said automatically. Dave had thrown Ben a lifeline when he'd most needed one. It would be great to catch up with him.

But then he focused on Meg's order again. Ten names from Elsie? She had to be joking right? 'Does she even *know* ten people?'

'She must do. She goes to Housie one afternoon a week.'
She did?

'Who knows? She might like to invite her chiropodist.'
Elsie had a chiropodist?

'But how am I going to get her to give me two names let alone ten?' He and his grandmother could barely manage a conversation about the weather, let alone anything more personal.

'That's your problem. You're supposed to be resourceful, aren't you? What do you do if wild hyenas invade your camp in Africa? Or if your rope starts to unravel when you're rock-climbing? Or your canoe overturns when you're white-water rafting? This should be a piece of cake in comparison.'

Piece of cake, his—

'Besides, I'm kicking you out of my spare room, so I expect you'll have plenty of time to work on her.'

He gaped at her. 'You're not going to let me stay?'

'Your place is over there.' She pointed across the fence. 'For heaven's sake, Ben, she's *giving* that house to you.'

'I don't want it.'

'Then you'd better find a more gracious way of refusing it than that.'

She stood there with hands on hips, eyes flashing, magnificent in the sunlight, and it suddenly occurred to him that moving out of her spare bedroom might be a very good plan. At least until his body clock adjusted.

She must have read the capitulation in his face because her shoulders lost their combativeness. She clasped her hands together and her gaze slid away. He wondered what she was up to now.

'I…um…' She glanced up at him again and swallowed. 'I want to ask you something, but I'm afraid it might offend you—which isn't my intention at all.'

He shrugged. 'Ask away, Meg.'

She bent down and pretended to study a nearby rosebush. He knew it was a pretence because he knew Meg. She glanced at him and then back at the rosebush. 'We're friends, right? Best friends. So that means it's okay to ask each other personal questions, don't you think?'

His curiosity grew. 'Sure.' For heaven's sake, they were having a baby together. How much more personal could it get?

'You really mean to stay in Fingal Bay for the next six weeks?'

'Yes.'

She straightened. 'Then I want to ask if you have enough money to see you through till then. Money isn't a problem for me, and if you need a loan…' She trailed off, swallowing. 'I've offended you, haven't I?'

He had to move away to sit on a nearby bench. Meg thought him some kind of freeloading loser? His stomach churned. He pinched the bridge of his nose. No wonder she questioned his ability to be any kind of decent father to their child.

'I'm not casting a slur on your life or your masculinity,' she mumbled, sitting beside him, 'but you live in the moment and go wherever the wind blows you. Financial security has never been important to you. Owning things has never been important to you.'

He lifted his head to survey the house behind her. 'And they are to you?' It wasn't the image he had of her in his mind. But her image of *him* was skewed. It was just possible they had each other completely wrong.

After all, how much time had they really spent in each other's company these last five to seven years?

She gave a tiny smile and an equally tiny shrug. 'With a baby on the way, financial security has become very important to me.'

'Is that why you let your father gift you this house?'

'No.'

'Then why?' He turned to face her more fully. 'I'd have thought you'd hate this place.' The same way he hated it.

She studied him for a long moment. 'Not all the associations are bad. This is where my mother came as a new bride. This is where I met my best friend.'

Him.

'Those memories are good. And look.' She grabbed his hand and tugged him around the side of the house to the front patio. 'Look at that view.'

She dropped his hand and a part of him wished she hadn't. The crazy mixed-up, jet lagged part.

'This has to be one of the most beautiful places in the world. Why wouldn't I want to wake up to that every day?'

He stared at the view.

'Besides, Fingal Bay is a nice little community. I think it's a great place to raise a child.'

He stared out at the view—at the roofs of the houses on the street below and the curving bay just beyond. The stretch of sand bordering the bay and leading out to the island gleamed gold in the sun. The water sparkled a magical green-blue. He stared at the boats on the water, listened to the cries of the seagulls, the laughter of children, and tried to see it all objectively.

He couldn't. Every rock and curve and bend was imbued with his childhood.

But...

He'd travelled all around the world and Meg was right. The picturesque bay in front of him rivalled any other sight he'd seen.

He turned to her. 'It's as simple as that? This is where you want to live so you accepted this house as a gift?'

A sigh whispered out of her, mingling with the sounds of the waves whooshing up onto the sand. 'It's a whole lot more complicated than that. It was as if…as if my father *needed* to give me this house.'

He leant towards her. 'Needed to?'

She shrugged, her teeth gnawing on her bottom teeth. 'I haven't got to the bottom of that yet, but…'

She gazed up at him, her hazel eyes steady and resolute, her chin at an angle, as if daring him to challenge her.

'I didn't have the heart to refuse him.'

'The same way you're hoping I won't refuse Elsie.'

'That's between you and her.'

'Don't you hold even the slightest grudge, Meg?'

'Don't you think it's time you let yours go?'

He swung away. Brilliant. Not only did she think him financially unsound, but she thought him irresponsible and immature on top of it.

At least he could answer one of those charges. 'Early in my working life I set up a financial security blanket, so to speak.' He'd invested in real estate. Quite a bit of it, actually.

Her eyes widened. 'You did?'

He had to grit his teeth at her incredulity. 'Yes.'

She pursed her lips and stared at him as if she'd never seen him before. 'That was very sensible of you.'

He ground his teeth harder. He'd watched Laurie Parrish for many years and, while he might not like the man, had learned a thing or two that he'd put into practice. Those wise investments had paid off.

'I have enough money to tide me over for the next six weeks.' And beyond. But he resisted the impulse to brag and tell her exactly how much money that financial security blanket of his held—that really would be immature.

'Okay.' She eyed him uncertainly. 'Good. I'm glad that's settled.'

'While we're on the subject of personal questions—' he rounded on her '—you want to tell me what you're trying to achieve with this godforsaken wedding?'

She hitched up her chin and stuck out a hip. 'I'm joying this "godforsaken wedding" up,' she told him. 'I'm going to *force* them to celebrate.'

He gaped at her. 'Why?'

'Because there was no joy when we were growing up.'

'They were never there for us, Meg. They don't deserve this—the effort you put in, the—'

'Everyone deserves the right to a little happiness. And if they truly want to mend bridges, then...'

'Then?'

'Then I only think it fair and right that we give them that opportunity.'

Ben's face closed up. Every single time he came home Meg cursed what his mother had done to him—abandoning him like she had with a woman who'd grown old before her time. Usually she would let a topic like this drop. Today she didn't. If Ben truly wanted to be a father, he needed to deal with his past.

She folded her arms, her heart pounding against the walls of her chest. 'When my mother died, my father just shut down, became a shell. Her death—it broke him. There was no room in his life for joy or celebration.'

Ben pushed his face in close to hers, his eyes flashing. 'He should've made an effort for you.'

Meg's hand slid across her stomach. She'd make every effort for *her* child, she couldn't imagine ever emotionally abandoning it, but maybe men were different—especially men of her father's generation.

She glanced at Ben. If a woman ever broke his heart, how would he react? She bit back a snigger. To break his heart a woman would have to get close to Ben, and he was never going to let that happen.

Ben's gaze lowered to where her hand rested against her stomach. His gaze had kept returning to her baby bump all morning. As if he couldn't get his fill. She swallowed. It was disconcerting, being the subject of his focus.

Not her, she corrected, the baby.

That didn't prevent the heat from rising in her cheeks or her breathing from becoming shallow and strained.

She tried to shake herself free from whatever weird and wacky pregnancy hormone currently gripped her. *Concentrate.*

'So,' she started, 'while my father went missing in action, your mother left you with Elsie and disappeared. She never rang or sent a letter or anything. Elsie must've been worried sick. She must've been afraid to love you.'

He snapped back. 'Afraid to—?'

'I mean, what if your mother came back and took you away and she never heard from either of you again? What if, when you grew up, you did exactly what your mother did and abandoned *her*?'

'My mother abandoned me, not Elsie.'

'She abandoned the both of you, Ben.'

His jaw dropped open.

Meg nodded. 'Yes, you're right. They both should've made a bigger effort for us. But at least we found each other. At least we both had one friend in the world we could totally depend upon. And whatever else you want to dispute, you can't deny that we didn't have fun together.'

He rolled his shoulders. 'I don't want to deny that.'

'Well, can't you see that my father and Elsie didn't even have that much? Life has left them crippled. But...' She swallowed. 'I demand joy in my life now, and I won't compromise on that. If they refuse to get into the swing of this wedding then I'll know those bridges—the distance between us—can never be mended. And I'll have my answer.'

She hauled in a breath. 'One last chance, Ben, that was what I'm giving them.' And that's what she wanted him to give them too.

Ben didn't say anything. She cast a sidelong glance at him and bit back a sigh. She wondered when Ben—*her* Ben, the Ben she knew, the Ben with an easy smile and a careless saunter, without a care in the world—would return. Ever since he'd pulled his bike to a halt out at the front of her house yesterday there'd been trouble in his eyes.

He turned to her, hands on hips. He had lean hips and a tall, rangy frame. With his blond-tipped hair he looked like a god. No wonder women fell for him left, right and centre.

Though if he'd had a little less in the charm and looks department maybe he'd have learned to treat those women with more sensitivity.

Then she considered his mother and thought maybe not.

'When was the last time *you* felt joyful?' she asked on impulse.

He scratched his chin. He still hadn't shaved. He should look scruffy, but the texture of his shadowed jaw spoke to some yearning deep inside her. The tips of her fingers tingled. She opened and closed her hands. If she reached out and—

She shook herself. Ben *did* look scruffy. Completely and utterly. He most certainly didn't look temptingly disreputable with all that bad-boy promise of his.

Her hands continued to open and close. She heaved back a sigh. Okay, we'll maybe he did. But that certainly wasn't the look she was into.

Normally.

She scowled. Darn pregnancy hormones. And then the memory of that long ago kiss hit her and all the hairs on her arms stood to attention.

Stop it! She and Ben would never travel down that road again. There was simply too much at stake to risk it. *Ever.*

She folded her arms and swallowed. 'It can't be that hard, can it?' she demanded when he remained silent. Ben was the last person who'd need lessons in joy, surely?

'There are just so many to choose from,' he drawled, with that lazy hit-you-in-the-knees grin.

The grin was too slow coming to make her heart beat faster. Her heart had already started to sink. Ben was lying and it knocked her sideways. She'd always thought his exciting, devil-may-care life of freedom gave him endless pleasure and joy.

'The most recent instance that comes to mind is when I bungee-jumped over the Zambezi River from the Victoria Falls Bridge. Amazing rush of adrenaline. I felt like a superhero.'

She scratched a hand back through her hair. What was she thinking? Of *course* Ben's life gave him pleasure. He did so many exciting things. Did he really think he could give that all up for bottles and nappies?

'What about you? When was the last time you felt joyful?'

She didn't even need to think. She placed a hand across her stomach. And even amid all her current confusion and, yes, fear a shaft of joy lifted her up. She smiled. 'The moment I found out I was pregnant.'

She was going to have a baby!

'And every single day after, just knowing I'm pregnant.' Ben had made that possible. She would never be able to thank him enough. Ever.

She set her shoulders. When he came to the conclusion she knew he would—that he wasn't cut out for domesticity—she would do everything in her power to make sure he felt neither guilty nor miserable about it.

Ben shaded his eyes and stared out at the perfect crescent of the bay. 'So you want to spread the joy, huh?'

'Absolutely.' Being pregnant had changed her perspective. In comparison to so many other people she was lucky. Very lucky. 'We know how to do joy, Ben, but my father and Elsie—well, they've either forgotten how or they never knew the secret in the first place.'

'It's not a secret, Meg.'

Tell her father and Elsie that.

'And if this scheme of yours doesn't work and they remain as sour and distant as ever?'

'I'm not going to break my heart over it, if that's what you're worried about. But at least I'll know I tried.'

He shifted his weight and shoved his hands into the pockets of his jeans, making them ride even lower on his hips. The scent of leather slugged her in the stomach—which was odd, because Ben wasn't wearing his leather jacket.

'And what if it does work? Have you considered that?'

She dragged her gaze from his hips and tried to focus. 'That scenario could be the most challenging of all,' she agreed. 'The four of us...five,' she amended, glancing down at her stomach, 'all trying to become a family after all this time. It'll be tricky.'

She wanted to add, *but not impossible*, but her throat had closed over at the way he surveyed her stomach. Her chest tightened at the intensity of his focus. The light in his eyes made her thighs shake.

She cleared her throat and dragged in a breath. 'If it works I'll get a warm and fuzzy feeling,' she declared. Warm and fuzzy was preferable to hot and prickly. She rolled her shoulders. 'And perhaps you will too.'

Finally—*finally*—his gaze lifted to hers. 'More fairytales, Meg?'

Did he still hold that much resentment about their less than ideal childhood? 'You still want to punish them?'

'No.' Very slowly he shook his head. 'But I don't think they deserve all your good efforts either. Especially when I'm far from convinced anything either one of us does will make a difference where they're concerned.'

'But what is it going to hurt to try?'

'I'm afraid it'll hurt *you*.'

He'd always looked out for her. She couldn't help but smile at him. 'I have a baby on the way. I'm on top of the world.'

He smiled suddenly too. A real smile—not one to trick or beguile. 'All right, Meg, I'm in. I'll do whatever I can to help.'

She let out a breath she hadn't even known she'd held.

'On one condition.'

She should've known. She folded her arms. 'Which is…?' She was *not* letting him sleep in her spare bedroom. He belonged next door. Besides… She swallowed. She needed her own space.

'You'll let me touch the baby.'

CHAPTER FIVE

MEG COULDN'T HELP her sudden grin. Lots of people had touched her baby bump—happy for her and awed by the miracle growing inside her. Why should Ben be any different?

Of course he'd be curious.

Of course he'd be invested.

He might never be Daddy but he'd always be Uncle Ben. *Favourite* Uncle Ben. Wanting to touch her baby bump was the most natural thing in the world.

She didn't try to temper her grin. 'Of course you can, Ben.'

She turned so she faced him front-on, offering her stomach to him, so to speak. His hands reached out, both of them strong and sure. They didn't waver. His hands curved around her abdomen—and just like that it stopped being the most natural thing in the world.

The pulse jammed in Meg's throat and she had to fight the urge to jolt away from him. Ben's hands suddenly didn't look like the hands of her best friend. They looked sensual and sure and knowing. They didn't feel like the hands of her best friend either.

Her breath hitched and her pulse skipped and spun like a kite-surfer in gale force winds. With excruciating thoroughness he explored every inch of her stomach through the thin cotton of her shirt. His fingers were hot and strong and surprisingly gentle.

And every part of her he touched he flooded with warmth and vigour.

She clenched her eyes shut. Her *best friend* had never looked at her with that possessive light in his eyes before. Not that it was aimed at her per se. Still, the baby was inside *her* abdomen.

He moved in closer and his heat swamped her. She opened her eyes and tried to focus on the quality of the light hitting the water of the bay below. But then his scent swirled around her—a mix of soap and leather and something darker and more illicit, like a fine Scotch whisky. She dragged in a shaky breath. Scotch wasn't Ben's drink. It was a crazy association. That thought, though, didn't make the scent go away.

Her heart all but stopped when he knelt down in front of her and pressed the left side of his face to her stomach, his arm going about her waist. She found her hand hovering above his head. She wanted to rest it there, but that would make them seem too much of a trio. Her throat thickened and tears stung her eyes. They weren't a trio. Even if by some miracle Ben stayed, they still wouldn't be a trio.

But he wouldn't stay.

And so her hand continued to hover awkwardly above his head.

'Hey, little baby,' he crooned. 'I'm your—'

'No!' She tried to move away but his grip about her tightened.

'I'm…I'm pleased to meet you,' he whispered against her stomach instead.

She closed her eyes and breathed hard.

When he climbed back to his feet their gazes clashed and locked. She'd never felt more confused in her entire life.

'Thank you.'

'You're welcome.'

Their gazes continued to battle until Ben finally took a step away and seemed to mentally shake himself. 'What's the plan for the rest of the day?'

The plan was to put as much distance between her and Ben as she could. Somewhere in the last day he'd become a stranger to her. A stranger who smelled good, who looked good, and who unnerved her.

This new Ben threatened more than her equilibrium. He threatened her unborn child's future and its happiness.

The Ben she knew would never do anything to hurt her. But this new Ben? She didn't trust him. She wanted to be away from him, to get her head back into some semblance of working order. She knew exactly how to accomplish that.

'I'm going into Nelson Bay to start on the wedding preparations.'

'Excellent plan. I'll come with you.'

She nearly choked. 'You'll what?'

'You said you wanted my help.' He lifted his arms. 'I'm yours to command.'

Why did that have to sound so suggestive?

'But—' She tried to think of something sensible to say. She couldn't, so she strode back around the side of the house.

'Time is a-wasting.' He kept perfect time beside her.

'It's really not necessary.' She tucked her hair back behind her ears, avoiding eye contact while she collected the tape measure along with the measurements he'd jotted down for her. 'You only got back from Africa yesterday. You are allowed a couple of days to catch your breath.'

'Are you trying to blow me off, Meg?'

Heat scorched her cheeks. 'Of course not.'

He grinned as if enjoying her discomfiture. 'Well, then…'

She blew out a breath. 'Have it your own way. But we're taking my car, not the bike, and I'm driving.'

'Whatever you say.'

He raised his hands in mock surrender, and suddenly he was her Ben again and it made her laugh. 'Be warned—I *will* make you buy me an ice cream cone. I cannot get enough of passionfruit ripple ice cream at the moment.'

He glanced at his watch. 'It's nearly lunchtime. I'll buy you a kilo of prawns from the co-op and we can stretch out on the beach and eat them.'

'You'll have to eat them on your own, then. And knowing how I feel about prawns, that'd be too cruel.'

He followed her into the house. 'They give you morning sickness?'

She patted her stomach. 'It has something to do with mercury levels in seafood. It could harm the baby. I'm afraid Camembert and salami are off the menu too.'

He stared at her, his jaw slack, and she could practically read his thoughts—shock that certain foods might harm the baby growing inside her—and his sudden confrontation with his own ignorance. Her natural impulse was to reassure him, but she stifled it. Ben was ignorant about babies and pregnancy, and it wasn't up to her to educate him. If he wanted to be a good father he would have to educate himself, exercising his own initiative, not because she prompted or nagged him to.

But she didn't want the stranger back, so she kept her voice light and added, 'Not to mention wine and coffee. All of my favourite things. Still, I seem to be finding ample consolation in passionfruit ripple ice cream.'

She washed her hands, dried them, stowed the measurements in her handbag and then lifted an eyebrow in Ben's direction. 'Ready?'

He still hadn't moved from his spot in the doorway, but at her words he strode across to the sink to pump the strawberry-scented hand-wash she kept on the window ledge into his hands. The scent only seemed to emphasise his masculinity. She watched him wash his hands and remembered the feel of them on her abdomen, their heat and their gentleness.

She jerked her gaze away.

'Ready.'

When she turned back he was drying his hands. And there was a new light in his eyes and a determined shape to his mouth. Normally she would take the time to dust a little powder on her nose and slick on a coat of lipstick, but she wanted to be out of the house and into the day. Right now!

She led the way to her car.

'Okay, the plan today is to hire a marquee for the big event—along with the associated paraphernalia. Tables chairs and whatnot,' she said as they drove the short distance to the neighbouring town. 'And then we'll reward ourselves with lunch.'

'Do you mind if we do a bit of shopping afterwards? I need to grab a few things.'

She glanced at him. Ben and shopping? She shook her head. 'Not at all.'

To Meg's utter surprise, Ben was a major help on the Great Marquee Hunt. He zeroed in immediately on the marquee that would best suit their purposes. The side panels could be rolled up to allow a breeze to filter through the interior if the evening proved warm. If the day was cool, however—and that wasn't unheard of in late March—the view of the bay could still be enjoyed through the clear panels that acted like windows in the marquee walls.

Ben insisted on putting down the deposit himself.

Given the expression on his face earlier, when she'd asked him about his financial circumstances, she decided it would be the better part of valour not to argue with him.

Furniture was next on the list, and Meg chose round tables and padded chairs. 'Round tables means the entire table can talk together with ease.' Hopefully it would promote conversation.

Ben's lips twisted. 'And they'll make the marquee look fuller, right?'

Exactly.

'What else?' he demanded.

'We need a long table for the wedding party.'

'There's only four of us. It won't need to be *that* long.'

'And tables for presents and the cake.'

Ben pointed out tables, the salesman made a note, and then they were done—all in under an hour.

Ben's hands went to his hips. 'What now?'

To see him so fully focused on the task made her smile. 'Now we congratulate ourselves on having made such excellent progress and reward ourselves with lunch.'

'That's it?'

She could tell he didn't believe her. 'It's one of the big things ticked off. It's all I had scheduled for today.'

'What are the other big things?'

'The catering, the cake, the invitations. And...' A grin tugged at her lips.

He leaned down to survey her face. His own lips twitched. 'And?'

'And shopping for Elsie's outfit.'

He shot away from her. 'Oh, no—no, no. You're *not* dragging me along on that.'

She choked back a laugh. 'Fat lot of use you'd be anyway. I'll let you off the hook if you buy me lunch.'

'Deal.'

They bought hot chips smothered in salt and vinegar, and dashed across the road to the beach. School had gone back several weeks ago, but it was the weekend and the weather was divine. The long crescent of sand that bordered the bay was lined with families enjoying the sunshine, sand and water. Children's laughter, the sounds of waves whooshing up onto the beach and the cries of seagulls greeted them. *Divine!* She lifted her face to the sun and breathed it all in.

They found a spare patch of sand and Meg stretched out her legs, relishing the warmth of the sun on the bare skin of her arms and legs. She glanced at Ben as he hunkered down beside her. He must be hot.

'You should've changed into shorts.'

He unwrapped the chips. 'I'm good.'

Yeah, but he'd look great in shorts, and—

She blinked. What on earth...? And then the scent of salt and vinegar hit her and her stomach grumbled and her mouth watered. With a grin he held the packet towards her.

They ate, not saying much, just listening to the familiar sounds of children at play and the splashing of the tiny waves that broke onshore. Nearby a moored yacht's rigging clanged in the breeze, making a pelican lift out of the water and wheel up into the air. It was summer in the bay—her favourite time of year and her favourite patch of paradise.

She wasn't sure when they both started to observe the family—just that at some stage the nearby mother, father and two small girls snagged their attention. One of the little girls dashed down the beach towards them, screaming with delight when her father chased after her. Seizing her securely around the waist, he lifted her off her feet to swing her above his head.

'Higher, Daddy, higher!' she squealed, laughing down at him, her face alive with delight.

The other little girl, smaller than the first, lurched across the sand on chubby, unsteady legs to fling her arms around her father's thigh. She grinned and chortled up at him.

Meg swallowed and her chest started to cramp. Both of those little girls literally glowed with their love for their father.

She tore her gaze away to stare directly out in front of her, letting the sunlight that glinted off the water to dazzle and half-blind her.

'More?' Ben's voice came out hoarse and strained as he held the chips out to her.

She shook her head. Her appetite had fled.

He scrunched the remaining chips and she was aware of every crackle the paper made. And how white his knuckles had turned. She went back to staring directly out in front of her, tracking a speedboat as it zoomed past.

But it didn't drown out the laughter of the two little girls.

'Did you ever consider what you were depriving your child of when you decided to go it alone, Meg?'

His voice exploded at her—tight and barely controlled. She stiffened. And then she rounded on him. 'Don't take that high moral tone with me, Ben Sullivan! Since when in your entire adult life, have you *ever* put another person's needs or wants above your own?'

He blinked. 'I—'

'I didn't twist your arm. You had some say in the matter, you know.'

Her venom took him off guard. It took her off guard too, but his question had sliced right into the core of her. She'd thought she'd considered that question. She'd thought it wouldn't matter. But after seeing that family—the girls with their father, their love and sense of belonging—she felt the doubt demons rise to plague her.

'Families come in all shapes and sizes,' she hissed, more for her own benefit than his. Her baby would want for nothing! 'As for depriving my child of a father? Well, I don't rate my father very highly, and I sure as heck don't rate yours. There are worse things than not having a father.'

Ben's head rocked back in shock. Meg's sentiment didn't surprise him, but the way she expressed it did.

He clenched his jaw so hard he thought he might break teeth. A weight pressed against his chest, making it difficult to breathe.

'Just like you don't rate me as a father, right?' he rasped out, acid burning his throat.

Eventually he turned to look at her. She immediately glanced away, but not before he recognised the scepticism stretching through her eyes. The weight in his chest grew heavier. If Meg didn't have any faith in him...

No, dammit! He clenched his hands. Meg didn't have all the answers.

He swore.

She flinched.

He kept his voice low. 'So I'm suitable as a sperm bank but not as anything more substantial?' Was *that* how she saw him?

She stared straight back out in front of her. 'That surprises you?'

'It does when that's your attitude, Meg.'

That made her turn to look at him.

Dammit it all to hell, she was supposed to *know* him!

A storm raged in the hazel depths of her eyes. He watched her swallow. She glanced down at her hands and then back up. 'How long have you wanted to be a father, Ben? A week?'

It was his turn to glance away.

'I've wanted to be a mother for as long as I can remember.'

'And you think that gives you more rights?'

'It means I know what to expect. It means I know I'm not going to change my mind next week. It means I know I'm committed to this child.' She slapped a hand to the sand. 'It means I know precisely what I'm getting into—that I've put plans into place in anticipation of the baby's arrival, and that I've adjusted my life so I can ensure my baby gets the very best care and has the very best life I can possibly give it. And now you turn up and think you have the right to tell me I'm selfish!'

She let out a harsh laugh that had his stomach churning.

'When have you ever committed to anybody or anything? You've never even taken a job on full-time. You've certainly never committed to a woman or what's left of your family. It's barely possible to get you to commit to dinner at the end of next week!'

'I'm committed to *you*.' The words burst out of him. 'If you'd ever needed me, Meg, I'd have come home.'

She smiled then, but there was an ache of sadness behind her eyes that he didn't understand. 'Yes, I believe you would've. But once I was back on my feet you'd have been off like a flash again, wouldn't you?'

He had no answer to that.

'The thing is, Ben, your trooping all over the world having adventures is fine in a best friend, but it's far from fine in a father.'

She had a point. He knew she did. And until he knew how involved he wanted to be he had no right to push her or judge her. 'I didn't mean to imply you were selfish. I think you'll be a great mum.'

But it didn't mean there wasn't room for him in the baby's life too.

She gestured to her right, to where that family now sat eating sandwiches, but she didn't look at them again. 'Is that what you really want?'

He stared at the picture of domestic bliss and had to repress a shudder. He wasn't doing marriage. Ever. He didn't believe in it. But... The way those little girls looked at their father—their faces so open and trusting. And loving. The thought of having someone look up to him like that both terrified and electrified him.

If he wanted to be a father—a proper father—his life would have to change. Drastically.

'Ben, I want a better father for my child than either one of us had.'

'Me too.' That at least was a no-brainer.

She eyed him for a moment. Whenever she was in the sun for any length of time the green flecks within the brown of her iris grew in intensity. They flashed and sparkled now, complementing the aqua water only a few feet away.

Aqua eyes.

A smattering of freckles across her nose.

Blonde hair that brushed her shoulders.

And she smelled like pineapple and coconuts.

She was a golden goddess, encapsulating all he most loved about summer.

'Ben!'

He snapped to. 'What?'

Her nostrils flared, drawing his attention back to her freckles. She glanced away and then back again. 'I said, you *do* know that I'm not anti-commitment the way you are, right?'

'Yeah, sure.'

His attention remained on those cute freckles, their duskiness highlighting the golden glow of her skin. He'd never noticed how cute they were before—cute and kind of cheeky. They were new to him. This conversation wasn't. Commitment versus freedom. They'd thrashed it out endless time. To her credit, though, Meg had never tried to change his mind. They'd simply agreed to disagree. Even that one stupid time they had kissed.

Damn it! He'd promised never to think about that again.

'Then you should also be aware that I don't expect to "*deprive*"—' she made quotation marks in the air with her fingers '—my child of a father for ever.'

He frowned, still distracted by those freckles, and then by the shine on her lips when she moistened them. 'Right.'

She hauled in a breath and let it out again. The movement wafted a slug of coconut infused pineapple his way. He drew it into his lungs slowly, the way he would breathe in a finely aged Chardonnay before bringing the glass to his lips and sipping it.

'Just because I've decided to have a baby it doesn't mean I've given up on the idea of falling in love and getting married, maybe having more kids if I'm lucky.'

It took a moment for the significance of her words to connect, but when they did they smashed into him with the force of that imaginary bottle of Chardonnay wielded at his head. The beach tilted. The world turned black and white. He shoved his hands into the sand and clenched them.

'I might be doing things slightly out of order, but...' She let her words trail off.

He stabbed a finger at her, showering her with sand. 'You are *not* letting another man raise my child!'

He shot to his feet and paced down to the water's edge, tried to get his breathing back under control before he hyperventilated.

Another man would get the laughter…and the fun…and the love.

He dragged a hand back through his hair. Of course this schmuck would also be getting hog-tied into marriage and would have to deal with school runs, parent and teacher interviews and eat-your-greens arguments. But…

'No!'

He swung around to find Meg standing directly behind him. 'Keep your voice down,' she ordered, glancing around. 'There are small children about.'

Why the hell didn't she just bar him from all child-friendly zones? She obviously didn't rate his parenting abilities at all. His hands clenched. But giving his child—*his child*—to another man to raise? No way!

He must have said it out loud, because she arched an eyebrow at him. 'You think you can prevent me from marrying whoever I want?'

'Whomever,' he said, knowing that correcting her grammar would set her teeth on edge.

Which it did. 'You and whose army, Ben?'

'You can marry *whomever* you damn well please,' he growled, 'but this baby only has one father.' He pounded a fist to his chest. 'And that's me.'

She folded her arms. 'You're telling me that you're giving up your free and easy lifestyle to settle in Port Stephens, get a regular job and trade your motorbike for a station wagon?'

'That's exactly what I'm saying.'

'Why?'

It was a genuine question, not a challenge. He didn't know how to articulate the determination or sense of purpose that had overtaken him. He only knew that this decision was the most important of his life.

And he had no intention of getting it wrong.

He knew that walking away from their baby would be wrong.

But…

It left the rest of his life in tatters.

Meg sighed when he remained silent. She didn't believe he meant it. It was evident in her face, in her body language, in the way she turned away. Her lack of faith in him stung, but he had no one else to blame for that but himself.

He would prove himself to her. He would set all her fears to rest. And he would be the best father on the planet.

When she turned back he could see her nose had started to turn pink. Her nose always went pink before she cried. He stared at the pinkness. He glanced away. Meg hardly ever cried.

He glanced back. Swallowed. It could be sunburn. They'd been out in the sun for a while now.

He closed his eyes. He ached to wrap her in his arms and tell her he would not let either her or the baby down. Words, though, were cheap. Meg would need more than verbal assurances. She'd need action.

'We should make tracks.' She shaded her eyes against the sun. 'You said you needed to do some shopping?'

He did. But he needed a timeout from Meg more. He needed to get his head around the realisation that he was back in Port Stephens for good.

He feigned interest in a sultry brunette, wearing nothing but a bikini, who was ambling along the beach towards them.

'Ben?'

He lifted one shoulder in a lazy shrug. 'The shopping can wait.' He deliberately followed the brunette's progress instead of looking at Meg. 'Look, why don't you head off? I might hang around for a while. I'll find my own way home.'

He knew exactly what interpretation Meg would put on that.

The twist of her lips told her she had. Without another word, she turned and left.

Clenching his hands, he set off down the beach, not even noticing the brunette when he passed her.

A baby deserves to have the unconditional love of the two people who created it. If he left, who would his child have in its day-to-day life? Meg, who'd be wonderful, and Uncle Ben who'd never be there. His hands clenched. Meg's father and Elsie could hardly be relied on to provide the baby with emotional support.

He shook his head. He could at least make sure this child knew it was loved and wanted by its father. Things like that — they did matter.

And this baby deserved only good things.

When he reached the end of the beach he turned and walked back and then headed for the shops. Meg should be home by now, and he meant to buy every damn book about pregnancy and babies he could get his hands on. He wanted to be prepared for the baby's arrival. He wanted to help Meg out in any way he could.

What he didn't need was her damn superiority, or her looking over his shoulder and raising a sceptical eyebrow at the books he selected. He had enough doubt of his own to deal with.

He turned back to stare at the beach, the bay, and the water. Back in Port Stephens for good?

Him?

Hell.

CHAPTER SIX

MEG SANG ALONG to her Madonna CD in full voice. She'd turned the volume up loud to disguise the fact she couldn't reach the high notes and in an attempt to drown out the chorus of voices that plagued her—a litany of 'what ifs' and 'what the hells' and 'no ways'. All circular and pointless. But persistent. Singing helped to quiet them.

She broke off to complete a complicated manoeuvre with her crochet needle. At least as far as she was concerned it was complicated. Her friend Ally assured her that by the time she finished this baby shawl she'd have this particular stitch combination down pat.

She caressed the delicate white wool and surveyed her work so far. It didn't seem like much, considering how long it had taken her, but she didn't begrudge a moment of that time. She'd have this finished in time for the baby's arrival. Maybe only just, but it would be finished. And then she could wrap her baby in this lovely soft shawl, its wool so delicate it wouldn't irritate newborn skin. She'd wrap her baby in this shawl and it would know how much it was loved.

She lifted it to her cheek and savoured its softness.

The song came to an end. She lowered the crocheting back to her lap and was about to resume when some sixth sense had her glancing towards the doorway.

Ben.

Her throat tightened. She swallowed once, twice. 'Hey,' she finally managed.

'I knocked.' He pointed back behind him.

She grabbed the remote, turned the music down and motioned for him to take a seat. 'With the music blaring like that there's not a chance I'd have heard you.'

He stood awkwardly in the doorway. She gripped the crochet needle until the metal bit into her fingers.

'Madonna, huh?' He grinned but it didn't hide his discomfort.

'Yup.' She grinned back but she doubted it hid her tension, her uneasiness either.

He glanced around. 'We never sat in here when we were growing up.'

'No.' When they'd been growing up this had definitely been adult territory. When indoors, they'd stuck to the kitchen and the family room. 'But this is my house now and I can sit where I please.'

He didn't look convinced. Tension kept his spine straight and his shoulders tight. Last week she'd have risen and led him through to the family room, where he'd feel more comfortable. This week...?

She lifted her chin. This week making Ben comfortable was the last thing on her agenda. That knowledge made her stomach churn and bile rise in her throat. It didn't mean she wanted to make him *un*comfortable, though.

She cleared her throat. 'Have a look out of the front window.'

After a momentary hesitation he did as she ordered.

'It has the most divine view of the bay. I find that peaceful. When the wind is up you can hear the waves breaking on shore.'

'And that's a sound you've always loved.' He settled on the pristine white leather sofa. 'And you can hear it best in here.'

And in the front bedroom. She didn't mention that, though.

Mentioning bedrooms to Ben didn't seem wise. Which was crazy. But...

She glanced at him and her pulse sped up and her skin prickled. *That* was what was crazy. He sprawled against the sofa with that easy, long-limbed grace of his, one arm resting along the back of the sofa as if in invitation. Her crochet needle trembled.

She dragged her gaze away and set her crochet work to one side. Her life was in turmoil. That was all this was—a reaction to all the changes happening in her life. The fact she had a baby on the way. The fact her father was marrying Elsie. The fact Ben claimed he wanted to be a father.

Ben nodded towards the wool. 'What are you doing?'

She had to moisten her lips before she could speak. 'I'm making a shawl for the baby.'

She laid the work out for him to see and he stared at it as if fascinated. When he glanced up at her, the warmth in those blue eyes caressed her.

'You can knit?'

She pretended to preen. 'Why, yes, I can, now that you mention it. Knitting clubs were more popular than book clubs around here for a while. But this isn't knitting—it's crochet, and I'm in the process of mastering the art.'

He frowned. And then he straightened. 'Why? Are you trying to save money?'

She folded her arms. That didn't deserve an answer.

His eyes narrowed. 'Or is this what your social life had descended to?'

If she could have kept a straight face she'd have let him go on believing that. It would be one seriously scary picture of life here in Fingal Bay for him to chew over. One he'd probably run from kicking and screaming. But she couldn't keep a straight face.

He leant back, his shoulders loosening, his grin hooking

up one side of his face in that slow, melt-a-woman-to-her-core way he had. 'Okay, just call me an idiot.'

If she's had any breath left in her lungs she might have done exactly that. Only that grin of his had knocked all the spare oxygen out of her body.

'Your social life is obviously full. I've barely clapped eyes on you these last few days.'

Had he wanted to? The thought made her heart skip and stutter a little faster.

Stop being stupid! 'It's full enough for me.' She didn't tell him that Monday night had been an antenatal class, or that last night she'd cooked dinner for Ally, who was recovering from knee surgery. Ben's social life consisted of partying hard and having a good time, not preparing for babies or looking after friends.

Ben's life revolved around adrenaline junkie thrills, drinking hard and chasing women. She wondered why he wasn't out with that sexy brunette this evening—the one he'd obviously had every intention of playing kiss chase with the other day—and then kicked herself. Sunday to Wednesday? Ben would count that a long-term relationship. And they both knew what he thought about those.

'So why?' He gestured to the wool.

He really didn't get it, did he? An ache pressed behind her eyes. What the hell was he doing here? She closed her eyes, dragged in a breath and then opened them again. She settled more comfortably in her chair.

'Once upon a time...' she started.

Ben eased back in his seat too, slouching slightly, his eyes alive with interest.

'Once upon a time,' she repeated, 'the Queen announced she was going to have a baby. There was much rejoicing in the kingdom.'

He grinned that grin of his. 'Of course there was.'

'To celebrate and honour the impending arrival of the royal

heir, the Queen fashioned a special shawl for the child to be wrapped in. It took an entire nine months to make, and every stitch was a marvel of delicate skill, awe-inspiring craftsmanship and love. All who saw it bowed down in awe.'

He snorted. 'Laying it on a bit thick, Meg. A shawl is never going to be a holy grail.'

She tossed her head. 'All who saw it bowed down in awe, recognising it as the symbol of maternal love that it was.'

The teasing in Ben's face vanished. He stared at her with an intensity that made her swallow.

'When the last stitch was finished, the Queen promptly gave birth. And it was said that whenever the royal child was wrapped in that shawl its crying stopped and it was immediately comforted.' She lifted her chin. 'The shawl became a valued family heirloom, passed down throughout the generations.'

He eyed the work spread in her lap. Was it her imagination or did he fully check her chest out on the way down? Her pulse pounded. Wind rushed in her ears.

'You want to give your baby something special.'

His words pulled her back from her ridiculous imaginings. 'Yes.' She wanted to fill her baby's life with love and all manner of special things. The one thing she didn't want to give it was a father who would let it down. She didn't say that out loud, though. Ben knew her feelings on the subject. Harping on it would only get his back up. He had to come to the conclusion that he wasn't father material in his own time.

She didn't want to talk about the baby with Ben any longer. She didn't have the heart for it.

'So, how's your week been so far?'

His lips twisted. 'How the hell do you deal with Elsie?'

Ah.

'The woman is a goddamn clam—a locked box. I'm never going to get those names for you Meg.'

She'd known it would be a tough test. But if Ben couldn't pass it he had no business hanging around in Fingal Bay.

His eyes flashed. 'Is it against the rules to help me out?'

She guessed not. He'd still have to do the hard work, but…

She didn't want to help him. She stared down at her hands. She wanted him to leave Fingal Bay and not come back for seven, eight…ten months.

He's your best friend!

And he was turning her whole life upside down. Not to mention her baby's.

She remembered the way she'd ached for her father to show some interest in her life, to be there for her. And she remembered the soul-deep disappointment, the crushing emptiness, the disillusionment and the shame when he'd continued to turn away from her. Nausea swirled in her stomach. She didn't want that for her child.

Did her baby need protecting from Ben? She closed her eyes. If she knew the answer to that…

'Why didn't you come over for dinner tonight? Elsie says you come to dinner every Wednesday night.'

She opened her eyes to find him leaning towards her. She shrugged. 'Except when you're home.'

His lips, which were normally relaxed and full of wicked promise, pressed into a thin line. 'And why's that?'

'I like to give you guys some space when you're home.'

'Is that all?'

Her automatic response was to open her mouth to tell him of course that was all. She stamped on it. Ben had changed everything when he'd burst in on Saturday. She wasn't sure she wanted to shield him any more. 'Precisely how much honesty do you want, Ben?'

His jaw slackened. 'I thought we were always honest.'

She pursed her lips. 'I'm about as honest as I can be when I see you for a total of three weeks in a year. Four if I'm lucky.'

His jaw clenched. His nostrils flared. 'Why didn't you come over to Elsie's tonight?'

Fine. She folded her arms. 'There are a couple of reasons.

The first: Elsie is hard work. You're home so you can deal with her. It's nice to have a night off.'

He sagged back as if she'd slugged him on the jaw.

'I make her cook dinner for me every Wednesday night. It's a bargain we struck up. I do her groceries and she cooks me dinner on Wednesday nights. But really it's so I can make sure she's still functioning—keep an eye on her fine motor skills and whatnot. See if I can pick up any early signs of illness or dementia.'

Which proved difficult as Elsie had absolutely no conversation in her. Until one night about a month ago, when Elsie had suddenly started chatting and Meg had fled. It shamed her now—her panic and sense of resentment and her cowardice. She could see now that Elsie had tried to open a door, and Meg had slammed it shut in her face.

Ben stared at her. He didn't say a word. It was probably why Elsie had reverted to being a clam around Ben now.

Still, it wasn't beyond Ben to make an overture too, was it? Meg bit her lip. If he truly wanted to be a father.

'Look, when you breeze in for an odd week here and a few days there, I do my best to make it fun and not to bore you with tedious domestic details. But if you mean to move back to Port Stephens for good then you can jolly well share some of the load.'

He'd gone pale, as if he might throw up on her pristine white carpet. 'What's the other reason you didn't come to dinner?' he finally asked.

She swallowed. Carpets could be cleaned. It was much harder to mend a child's broken heart. But...

'Meg?'

She lifted her chin and met his gaze head-on. 'I don't like seeing you and Elsie together. It's when I like you both least.'

He stared at her, his eyes dark. In one swift movement he rose. 'I should go.'

'Sit down, Ben.' She bit back a sigh. 'Do you mean to run

away every time we have a difficult conversation? What about if that difficult conversation is about the baby? Are you going to run away then too?'

The pulse at the base of his jaw pounded. 'Couldn't you at least offer a guy a beer before tearing his character to shreds?'

She stood. 'You're right. But not a beer. You drink too much.'

'Hell, Meg, don't hold back!'

She managed a smile. Somehow. 'I'm having a hot chocolate. I'm trying to make sure I get enough calcium. Would you like one too, or would you prefer tea or coffee?'

He didn't answer, and she led the way to the kitchen and set about making hot chocolate. She was aware of how closely Ben watched her—she'd have had to be blind not to. It should have made her clumsy, but it didn't. It made her feel powerful and…and beautiful.

Which didn't make sense.

She shook the thought off and handed Ben one of the steaming mugs. 'Besides,' she started, as if there hadn't been a long, silent pause in their conversation, 'I'm not shredding your character. You're my best friend and I love you.'

She pulled a stool out at the breakfast bar and sat. 'But c'mon, Ben, what's to like about hanging out with you and Elsie? She barely speaks and you turn back into a sullen ten-year-old. All the conversation is left to me. You don't help me out, and Elsie answers any questions directed to her in words of two syllables. Preferably one if she can get away with it. Great night out for a girl.' She said it all with a grin, wanting to chase the shadows from his eyes.

'I…' Ben slammed his mug down, pulled out the stool beside her and wrapped an arm about her shoulders in a rough hug. 'Hell, Meg, I'm sorry. I never looked at it that way before.'

'That's okay.' He smelled of leather and Scotch and her senses greedily drank him in. 'I didn't mind when your visits were so fleeting—they were like moments stolen from reality. They never seemed part of the real world.'

'Which will change if I become a permanent fixture in the area?'

Exactly. She reached for her mug again. Ben removed his arm. Even though it was a warm night she missed its weight and its strength.

'I deal with Elsie by telling her stories.'

He swung around so quickly he almost spilled his drink. 'Like our fairytales?'

She shook her head. No, not like those. They were just for her and Ben. 'I talk at her—telling her what I've been up to for the week, what child did what to another child at work, what I saw someone wearing on the boardwalk in Nelson Bay, what wonderful new dish I've recently tried cooking, what book I'm reading. Just...monologues.'

It should be a tedious, monotonous rendition—a chore—but in between enquiring if Elsie had won anything at Housie or the raffles and if she'd made her shopping list yet, to amuse herself Meg dramatised everything to the nth degree. It made the time pass more quickly.

'So I should tell her what I've been up to?'

She shrugged.

'But I haven't been doing anything since I got back.'

She made her voice tart. 'Then I suggest you start doing something before you turn into a vegetable.'

A laugh shot out of him. 'Like I said earlier, don't hold back.'

She had no intention of doing so, but... She glanced at the handsome profile beside her and an icy hand clamped around her heart and squeezed. Her chest constricted painfully. She didn't want to make Ben miserable. She didn't want him feeling bad about himself. She wanted him to be happy.

And living in Fingal Bay would never make him happy.

She dragged her gaze back to the mug she cradled in her hands. 'I already have the names of ten guests from my father.'

'How'd you manage that?'

'Deceit and emotional blackmail.'

He grinned. And then he threw his head back and laughed. Captured in the moment like that he looked so alive it momentarily robbed her of breath, of speech, and of coherent thought. She never felt so alive as when Ben was home. Yearning rose inside her. Yearning for...

He glanced at her, stilled, and his eyes darkened. It seemed as if the very air between them shimmered. They swayed towards each other.

And then they both snapped away. Meg grabbed their now empty mugs and bolted for the sink, desperately working on getting her breathing back under control. They'd promised one another that they would never go *there* again. They'd agreed their friendship was too important to risk. And that still held true.

In the reflection of the window she could see Ben pacing on the other side of the breakfast bar, his hands clenched. Eventually she wouldn't be able to pretend to be washing the cups any more.

Ben coughed and then stared up at the ceiling. 'Deceit and emotional blackmail?'

She closed her eyes, counted to three and turned off the tap. She turned back to him, praying—very hard—that she looked casual and unconcerned. 'I told him that Elsie would love a small party for a reception and that if he cared about Elsie's needs then he'd give me the names of ten people I could invite to the wedding.'

'It obviously worked.'

Like a charm. Her father and Elsie might not be particularly demonstrative, but Meg didn't doubt they cared deeply for each other. She remembered their linked hands, the fire in Elsie's eyes when she'd defended Laurie to Ben, and her father's vulnerability.

She glanced at Ben. He seemed completely unfazed by that

'moment'. The hot chocolate in her stomach curdled. Maybe she'd been the only one caught up in it.

She cleared her throat. 'It worked so well he actually gave me a dozen names.'

Ben rubbed his chin. 'If I did it in reverse...'

'Worth a try,' she agreed.

'Brilliant!' He slapped a hand down on the breakfast bar. 'Thanks, Meg.'

'Any time.'

But the words sounded wooden, even to her own ears. He opened the back door, hesitated, and then turned back. 'I didn't come back to make your life chaotic on purpose, Meg.'

She managed a smile. 'I know.'

'What night do you check up on your father?'

She should have known he'd make that connection. 'Tomorrow night. He refuses to cook, or to let me cook, so we have dinner at the RSL club.'

'Would it be all right if Elsie and I came along with you tomorrow night?'

What? Like a family? She frowned and scratched the back of her neck. Eventually she managed to clear her throat again. 'The more the merrier.'

'What time should we be ready?'

'He likes to eat early these days, so I'll be leaving here at six.'

With a nod, he was gone.

Ben stood in the dark garden, adrift between Meg's house and Elsie's.

He'd wandered over to Meg's tonight because he couldn't have stood another ten minutes in Elsie's company, but...

He scratched a hand back through his hair. He hadn't expected to be confronted with his own inadequacies. With his selfishness.

He threw his head back to glare at the stars. He dragged

cleansing breaths into his lungs. No wonder Meg didn't believe he'd see this fatherhood gig through.

He rested his hands against his knees and swore. He had to start pulling his weight. Meg was pregnant. She should be focussing on things like getting ready for the baby. Resting.

While he'd been off seeing the world Meg had been taking care of everyone. He straightened. Well, her days of being a drudge were over. He'd see to that.

He glanced at his grandmother's house. Shoving his shoulders back, he set off towards it.

He found Elsie at the kitchen table, playing Solitaire—just as she'd been doing when he'd left. The radio crooned songs from the 1950s.

'Drink?' he offered, going to the fridge.

'No, thank you.'

She didn't so much as glance at him. He grabbed a beer… stopped…set it back down again and seized a can of soda instead. The silence pressed down like a blanket of cold snow. He shot a glance towards the living room and the promised distraction of the television.

You turn back into a sullen ten-year-old.

He pulled out a chair and sat at the table with Elsie—something he hadn't done since he'd returned home—and watched as she finished her game. She glanced at him and then in the wink of an eye, almost as if she were afraid he'd change his mind, she dealt them both out seven cards each.

'Can you play rummy?'

'Sure I can.'

'Laurie taught me.'

His skin tightened. He rolled his shoulders. So far this was the longest conversation they'd had all week. 'I…uh…when he was recuperating and you visited?'

'That's right.'

He wanted to get up from the table and flee. It all felt so wrong. But he remembered Meg's crack about him reverting to a sullen ten-year-old and swallowed. 'When I was in Alaska I played a form of rummy with the guys off the fishing trawlers. Those guys were ruthless.'

But Elsie, it seemed, had clammed up again, and Ben wondered if it was something he'd said.

They played cards for a bit. Finally he broke the silence. 'Meg's looking great. Pregnancy obviously agrees with her.'

Nothing.

'She's crocheting this thing—a baby shawl, I think she said. Looks hard, and progress is looking slow.' He picked up the three of spades Elsie had discarded. She still didn't say anything. He ground back a sigh. 'Can you crochet?'

'Yep.'

She could? He stared at her for a moment, trying not to rock back on his chair. 'You should ask her to bring this shawl over to show you. In fact, you should make something for the baby too.'

She didn't look up from her cards. 'Me?'

He frowned. 'And so should I.'

'You?' A snort accompanied the single syllable.

He cracked his knuckles. 'I might not be able to knit or sew, but travelling in the remote parts of the world forces a guy to become pretty handy.'

Handy? *Ha!* He could fashion a makeshift compass, build a temporary shelter and sterilise water, but what on earth could he make for the baby that would be useful? And beautiful. Because he'd want it to be beautiful too. An heirloom.

'A crib.' As the idea occurred to him he said it out loud. He knew a bit about carpentry. 'I'll build a crib for the baby.' He laid out his trio of threes, a trio of jacks and placed his final card on Elsie's sevens. 'Gin.'

Elsie threw her cards down with a sniff.

'Best of three,' Ben announced. 'You're rusty. You need the practice. Though it's got to be said those Alaskan fisherman took no prisoners.'

Elsie picked up her second hand without a word. Ben mentally rolled his eyes. Meg was right. This was hard work. But he found a certain grim enjoyment in needling Elsie too.

As they played he found himself taking note of Elsie's movements. Her hands were steady and she held herself stiffly erect. No signs of a debilitating disease there as far as he could see. When she won the game in three moves he had to conclude that, while she didn't say much, her mind was razor-sharp.

'Gin!' There was no mistaking her triumph, but she still didn't crack a smile.

He snorted. 'I went easy on you.'

Her chin came up a notch. Her eyes narrowed.

'Oh, and by the way, we're having dinner with Meg and her father tomorrow evening at the club. I said we'd be ready at six.'

'Right.'

They played in silence for several moments, and then all in a rush it suddenly occurred to Ben that he might be cramping the older couple's style. He cleared his throat. It wasn't easy imagining Elsie and Mr Parrish wanting—needing—privacy. But that didn't change the fact that they were engaged.

'Do you mind me staying here while I'm in town?'

'No.'

'Look, if it's not convenient I can arrange alternative accommodation. I might be staying a bit longer than usual.'

'How long?'

'I'm not sure yet.'

Oh, he was sure, all right. He was staying for good. Meg should be the first to know that, though. 'I'd certainly understand it if you'd like me to find somewhere else to stay.'

'No.'

He stared at her. She didn't say any more. 'Did my mother really never contact you, not even once, after she left me here?'

The question shocked him as much as it probably shocked Elsie. He hadn't known it had been hovering on his lips, waiting to pounce. He hadn't known he still even cared what the answer to the damn question might be.

Elsie folded her cards up as tight as her face and dropped them to the table. 'No.'

Without another word she rose and left the room.

'Goodnight, Ben,' he muttered under his breath. 'Goodnight, Elsie,' he forced himself to call out. 'Thanks for the card game.'

Ben and Elsie strolled across to Meg's the next evening at six on the dot. At least Ben strolled. Elsie never did anything quite so relaxed as stroll. Her gait was midway between a trudge and a march.

They waited while Meg reversed her car—a perky blue station wagon—out of the garage, and then Ben leant forward and opened the front passenger door for Elsie.

'I insist,' he said with a sweep of his arm when she started to back away. He blocked her path. Her choices were to plough through him or to subside into the front seat. She chose the latter.

'Hey, Meg.' He settled into the back seat.

'Hey, Ben.' She glanced at Elsie. 'Hello, Elsie.'

'Hello.'

He didn't need to see Elsie to know the precise way she'd just folded her hands in her lap.

'How was work?' he asked Meg as she turned the car in the direction of Nelson Bay. He was determined to hold up his end of the conversation this evening.

'Hectic...Fun.' She told them a silly story about one of the children there and then flicked a glance at Elsie. 'How was your day?'

'Fine.'

'What did you get up to?'

'Nothing new.'

In the rear vision mirror she caught Ben's glance and rolled her eyes.

'Though I did come across a recipe that I thought I might try. It's Indian. I've not tried Indian before.'

Silence—a stunned and at a loss silence—filled the car. Meg cleared her throat. 'Sounds…uh…great.' She glanced in the mirror again and Ben could almost see her mental shrug. She swallowed. 'What did *you* do today, Ben?'

'I bought some wood.'

She blinked as she stared at the road in front of her. 'Wood?'

'That's right. But don't ask me what it's for. It's a surprise.'

She glanced at Elsie. 'What's he up to? Is he building you a veggie patch?'

'Unlikely. But if he does it'll be *his* veggie patch.'

In the mirror Meg raised an eyebrow at him and he could read her mind. They were having a conversation like normal people—him, her and Elsie. He couldn't blame her for wondering if the sky was falling in.

'I'll tell you something that's surprised the pants off of me,' he said, as smoothly as he could.

In the mirror he watched her swallow. 'Don't keep me in suspense.'

'Elsie plays a mean hand of rummy.'

Meg glanced at her. 'You play rummy?'

'Yes, your father taught me.'

Just for a moment Meg's shoulders tightened, but then she rolled them and shrugged. 'Rummy is fun, but I prefer poker. Dad plays a mean hand of poker too.'

Did he? Ben wondered if he'd ever played a hand or two with his daughter.

'So Elsie kicked your butt, huh?'

'We're a game apiece. The tie-break's tonight.'

'Well, now.' Meg pulled the car to a halt in the RSL Club's parking lot. 'I expect to hear all about it tomorrow.'

'If she beats me, I'm making it the best of five.'

Elsie snorted. 'If you come to dinner next Wednesday, Meg, you can join in the fun.'

He wasn't sure who was more stunned by that offer—him, Meg or Elsie.

'Uh, right,' Meg managed. 'I'll look forward to it.'

Elsie's efforts at hospitality and conversation had thrown him as much as they'd obviously thrown Meg, but as Ben climbed out of the car he couldn't help wondering when he'd fallen into being so monosyllabic around his grandmother. Especially as he prided himself on being good company everywhere else.

He frowned and shook his head. He'd *never* been anything but monosyllabic around Elsie. It was a habit. One he hadn't even considered breaking until Meg had sent out the challenge.

He glanced at the older woman. When had she got into the habit? Maybe nobody had ever challenged her, and—

Holy crap!

Ben's jaw dropped and his skin tightened when Meg rounded the car to join them. His chest expanded. It was as if he didn't fit his body properly any more.

Holy mackerel!

She wore a short blue skirt that stopped a good three inches above her knees and swished and danced about flirty thighs.

Man, Meg had great legs!

He managed to lift a hand to swipe it across his chin. No drool. He didn't do drool. Though, that said, until this week he'd have said he didn't do ogling Meg either.

Now it seemed he couldn't do anything else.

She had legs that went on for ever. The illusion was aided and abetted by the four-inch wedge heels she wore, the same caramel colour as her blouse. He toenails were painted a sparkly dark brown.

She nudged him in the ribs. 'What's with you?'

'I...um...' He coughed. Elsie raised an eyebrow and for the first time in his life he saw her actually smile. Oh, brilliant! She'd seen the lot and knew the effect Meg was having on him.

'I...um...' He cleared his throat and pointed to Meg's feet.

'Those shoes should come with a warning sign. Are you sure pregnant women are allowed to wear those things?'

She snorted. 'Just watch me, buster.'

He didn't have any other choice.

'I've given up caffeine, alcohol, salami and Camembert, but I'm not giving up my sexy sandals.'

She and Elsie set off for the club's entrance. He trailed after, mesmerised by the way Meg's hips swayed with hypnotic temptation.

How had he never noticed *that* before?

He swallowed. He had a feeling he was in for a long night.

CHAPTER SEVEN

MEG GLANCED AT Ben sitting at the table next to her in the club, and then away again before anyone could accuse her of having an unhealthy fixation with her best friend.

But tonight he'd amazed her. He not only made an effort to take part in the conversation, he actively promoted it. He quizzed her father on the key differences between five-card draw poker, stud poker and Texas hold 'em. She hadn't seen her father so animated in a long time. And Elsie listened in with a greedy avidity that made Meg blink.

The more she watched, the more she realised how good the older couple were for each other.

She bit her lip and glanced around the crowded dining room. She wanted to be happy for her father and Elsie. She gritted her teeth. She *was* happy for them. But their newfound vim made her chafe and burn. It made her hands clench.

Ben trailed a finger across one of her fists, leaving a burning path of awareness in his wake. She promptly unclenched it. He sent her a smile filled with so much understanding she wanted to lay her head on his shoulder and bawl her eyes out.

Pregnancy hormones.

Do you mean to use that as an excuse for every uncomfortable emotion that pummels you at the moment?

It might not explain her unexpected resentment towards the older couple, but it was absolutely positively the reason her pulse quickened and her skin prickled at the mere sight of

Ben. It had to be. And it was absolutely positively the reason her stomach clenched when his scent slugged into her—that peculiar but evocative mixture of leather and Scotch whisky.

For pity's sake, he wasn't even wearing leather or drinking whisky.

Her lips twisted. He couldn't help it. He smelled like a bad boy—all illicit temptation and promises he wouldn't keep. That grin and his free and easy swagger promised heaven. For one night. She didn't doubt for a moment that he'd deliver on *that* particular promise either.

And darn it all if she didn't want a piece of that!

She swallowed. She didn't just want it. She craved it. Her skin, her lungs, even her fingers ached with it.

Pregnancy hormones. *It had to be.*

Just her luck. Why couldn't she be like other women who became nauseous at the smell of frying bacon? That would be far preferable to feeling like *this* when Ben's scent hit her.

Her fingers curled into her palms. She had to find a way to resist all that seductive bad-boyness. For the sake of their friendship. And for the sake of her baby.

She dragged in a breath. She'd seen smart, sensible women make absolute fools of themselves over Ben and she had no intention of joining their ranks. She could *not* let lust deflect her from the important issue—ensuring her baby had the best possible life that she could give it. She could do that and save her friendship with Ben.

But not if she slept with him.

She ground her teeth together. Why had nobody warned her that being pregnant would make her…horny?

She shifted on her chair. Horny was the perfect description. There was nothing dignified and elegant or slow and easy in what she felt for Ben.

She risked a glance at him. Her blood Mexican-waved in her veins. Heat pounded through her and she squeezed her thighs tightly together. What she felt for Ben—*her best friend*—was hot and carnal, primal and urgent.

And it had to be denied.

She dragged her gaze away and fiddled with her cutlery.

Ben nudged her and she could have groaned out loud as a fresh wave of leather and whisky slammed into her. But it occurred to her then that she'd left the entire running of the conversation up to him so far. He probably thought she was doing it to punish him, or to prove some stupid point, when the real reason was she simply couldn't string two thoughts let alone two sentences together in a coherent fashion.

'Sorry, I was a million miles away.' She made herself smile around the table. 'My girlfriends have warned me about baby brain.'

Ben cocked an eyebrow. He grinned that slow and easy grin that could reduce a woman to the consistency of warm honey, inch by delicious inch.

She swallowed and forced her spine to straighten. 'Basically it means my brain will turn to mush and I won't be able to verbalise anything but nonsense for days at a time.'

She glanced at Elsie. 'Do you remember that when you were pregnant?'

Elsie drew back, paled, and Meg tried not to wince. She'd never asked Elsie about pregnancy or motherhood before and it was obviously a touchy subject. She hadn't meant to be insensitive.

In an effort to remove attention from Elsie, she swung to her father. 'Or can *you* remember Mum having baby brain when she was pregnant with me?'

An ugly red flushed his cheeks. As if she'd reached across and slapped him across the face. Twice.

Oh, great. Another no-go zone, huh?

She wanted nothing more than to lay her head on the table, close her eyes and rest for a while.

'And what a sterling example of baby brain in action,' Ben

murmured in her ear, and she found herself coughing back a laugh instead.

'I guess that's a no on both counts,' she managed, deciding to brazen it out, hoping it would make it less awkward all round. She glanced around the crowded dining room. 'There's a good crowd in but, man, I'm hungry. I wonder when our food will be ready?'

On cue, their table buzzer rang. Ben and her father shot to their feet. 'I'll get yours,' Ben told her, placing a hand on her shoulder to keep her in her seat.

Elsie watched as the two men walked towards the bistro counter where their plates waited. Meg made herself smile. 'Well, this is nice, isn't it?'

'You shouldn't have mentioned your mother.'

Meg blinked. 'Why ever not?'

Elsie pressed her lips primly together. 'He doesn't like to talk about her.'

Wasn't that the truth? 'And yet she was *my* mother and I do. Why should my needs be subordinate to his?'

'That's a selfish way to look at it.'

Interesting…Elsie was prepared to go into battle for her father. Something in Meg's heart lifted.

But something else didn't. 'Maybe I'm tired of stepping on eggshells and being self-sacrificing.'

Elsie paled. 'Meg, I—'

The men chose that moment to return with the food and Elsie broke off. Meg couldn't help but be relieved.

Ben glanced at Elsie and then whispered to Meg, 'More baby brain?'

'"Curiouser and curiouser," said Alice,' she returned.

He grinned. She grinned back. And for a moment everything was right again—she and Ben against the world…or at least against Elsie and Laurie, who'd been the world when she and Ben had been ten-year-olds.

They ate, and her father and Elsie reverted to their customary silence. Between them Meg and Ben managed to keep up a steady flow of chatter, but Meg couldn't help wondering if the older couple heard a word they said.

When they were finished, their plates removed and drinks replenished, Meg clapped her hands. 'Okay, I want to talk about the wedding for a moment.'

Her father scowled. 'I don't want a damn circus, Megan.'

'It's not going to be a circus. It's going to be a simple celebration. A celebration of the love you and Elsie share.' She folded her arms. 'And if you can't muster the courtesy to give each other that much respect then you shouldn't be getting married in the first place.'

Elsie and Laurie stared at her in shock. Ben let forth with a low whistle.

'Elsie—not this Saturday but the one after you and I are going shopping for your outfit.'

'Oh, but I don't need anything new.'

'Yes, you do. And so do I.' Her father had multiple suits, but... She turned to Ben. 'You'll need a suit.'

He saluted. 'I'm onto it.'

She turned back to the older couple. 'And you will both need an attendant. Who would you like as your bridesmaid and best man?'

Nobody said anything for a moment. She heaved back a sigh. 'Who were you going to have as your witnesses?'

'You and Ben,' her father muttered.

'Fine. I'll be your best man, but I'll be wearing a dress.'

'And I'll be bridesmaid in a suit,' Ben said to Elsie.

He said it without rancour and without wincing. He even said it with a grin on his face. Meg could have hugged him.

'Now, Elsie, do you want someone to give you away?'

'Of course not! Who on earth would I ask to do that?'

Meg leant back. She stared at the ceiling and counted to three. 'I'd have thought Ben would be the logical choice.'

The other woman's chin shot up. 'Ben? Do you really expect him to still be here in six weeks' time?'

'If he says he will, then, yes.'

'Give me away?' Her face darkened as she glared at Ben. 'Oh, you'd like that, wouldn't you? You'd love to give me away and be done with me for ever.'

Meg took one look at her best friend's ashen face and a scorching red-hot savagery shook through her. She leant forward, acid burning her throat and a rank taste filling her mouth. 'And who could blame him? I don't know why he even bothers with you at all. What the hell have you ever given him that he couldn't have got from strangers? You never show the slightest interest in his life, never show him the slightest affection—not even a tiny bit of warmth. You have no right to criticise him. *None!*'

'Meg.'

Ben's voice burned low but she couldn't stop. Even if she'd wanted to, she couldn't have. And she didn't want to. 'It was your job to show him love and security when he was just a little boy, but did you ever once hug him or tell him you were glad he'd come to stay with you? No, not once. Why not? He was a great kid and you…you're nothing but a—'

'Megan, that's enough! You will *not* speak to my intended like that.'

'Or what?' she shot straight back at her father. 'You'll never speak to me again? Well, seeing as you barely speak to me now, I can hardly see that'd be any great loss.'

Even as the words ripped out of her she couldn't believe she was uttering them. But she meant them. Every single one of them. And the red mist held her too much in its sway for her to regret them.

She might never regret them, but if she remained here she would say things she *would* regret—mean, bitter things just for the sake of it. She pushed out of her seat and walked away, walked right out of the club. She tramped the two blocks down to the water's edge to sit on a bench overlooking the bay as the sun sank in the west.

The walking had helped work off some of her anger. The warm air caressed the bare skin of her neck and legs, and the late evening light was as soothing as the ebb and flow of the water.

'Are you okay?'

Ben. And his voice was as soothing as the water too. But it made her eyes prickle and sting. She nodded.

'Do you mind if I join you?'

She shook her head and gestured for him to take the seat beside her.

'What happened back there?' he finally asked. 'Baby brain?'

She didn't know if he was trying to make her laugh or if he was as honest-to-God puzzled as he sounded. She dragged in a breath that made her whole body shudder. 'That was honest, true-blue emotion, not baby brain. I've never told either one of them how I feel about our childhoods.'

'Well, you left them in no doubt about your feelings on the subject tonight.'

She glanced at him. 'I don't particularly feel bad about it.' Did that make her an awful person? 'I don't want revenge, and I don't want to ruin their happiness, but neither one of them has the right to criticise you or me for being unsupportive. Especially when we're bending over backwards for them.'

He rested his elbows on his knees and then glanced up at her. 'You've bottled that up for a long time. Why spill it now?'

She stared out at the water. The sky was quickly darkening now that the sun had gone down. The burning started behind her eyes again. 'Now that I'm pregnant and expecting a child of my own, their emotional abandonment of us seems so much more unforgivable to me.'

He straightened and she turned to him.

'Ben, I can't imagine not making every effort for my child,

regardless of what else is happening in my life. I love it so much already and it makes me see…'

'What?'

She had to swallow. 'It makes me see that neither one of them loved us enough.'

'Oh, sweetheart.' He slipped an arm about her shoulders and she leant against him, soaking up his strength and his familiarity, his *Ben*-ness.

'You've never blown your top like that,' she murmured into his chest. And he had so much more to breathe fire about than her—not just Elsie, but his mother and father too. 'Why not?' It obviously hadn't been healthy for *her* to bottle her anger and hurt up for so long. If he was bottling it up—

'Meg, honey.' He gave a low laugh. 'I did it with actions rather than words. Don't you remember?'

She thought about it for a while and then nodded. 'You rebelled big-time.' He'd started teenage binge-drinking at sixteen, and staying out until the wee small hours, getting into the occasional fight—and, she suspected, making himself at home in older women's beds.

The police had brought him home on more than one occasion. He'd had a couple of fathers and one husband warn him off—violently. Yes. She nodded again. Ben had gone off the rails in a big way, and she could see it now for the thumbing of his nose at his family that it had been.

Still, he'd had the strength and the sense to pull out of that downward spiral. Dave Clements—a local tour operator—had offered him a part-time job and had taken him under his wing, had encouraged Ben to finish school. And Ben had, and now he led the kind of life most people could only dream of.

But was he happy?

She'd thought so, but…She glanced up into his face and recognised the shadows there. She straightened and slipped her hand into his, held it tight. 'I'm sorry if my outburst brought up bad stuff for you. I didn't mean—'

'For me?' He swung to her. 'Hell, Meg, you were magnificent! I just...'

She swallowed. 'What?'

He released her to rest his elbows on his knees again and drag both hands back through his hair. She wanted his arm resting back across her shoulders. She wanted not to have hurt him.

'Is it my coming home and turning your nicely ordered plans on their head? Did that have a bearing on your outburst tonight? I don't mean to be causing you stress.'

'No! That had nothing to do with it. That—' she waved back behind her '—was about me and them. Not about me and you.' She moistened her lips. 'It was about me and my father.' And about her anger at Elsie for not having shown Ben any love or affection. 'You had nothing to do with that except in...'

'What?'

'When I was busy doing what you were mostly doing tonight,' she started slowly, 'making sure the conversation flowed and that there weren't any awkward moments, I didn't have the time to feel those old hurts and resentments.'

'While I, at least whenever I've been home,' he said with a delicious twist of his lips, 'have been far too busy stewing on them.'

'But when you took on my role tonight I started to wonder why I was always so careful around them, and I realised what a lie it all seemed.'

'So you exploded.'

She slouched back against the bench. 'Why can't I just make it all go away and not matter any more? It all seems so pointless and self-defeating.' She couldn't change the past any more than she could change her father or Elsie. Her hands clenched. 'I should be able to just get over it.' She wasn't ten years old any more.

'It doesn't work like that.'

She knew he was right. She lifted her chin. 'It doesn't mean I have to let it blight the future, though. I don't have to continue mollycoddling my father or Elsie. At least not at the expense of myself.'

'No, you don't.'

He'd been telling her that for years. She'd never really seen what he meant till now.

'And I have a baby on the way.' She hugged herself. 'And that's incredibly exciting and it makes me happier than I have words for.'

He stared at her. He didn't smile. *They* had a baby on the way. *They.* She could read that in his face, but he didn't correct her.

She stared back out at the bay. The last scrap of light in the sky had faded and house lights and boat lights and street lights danced on the undulating water, turning it into a kind of fairyland.

Only this wasn't a fairytale. Ben said he wanted to be involved in their baby's life, but so far he hadn't shown any joy or excitement—only agitation and unease.

'So…?'

His word hung in the air. She didn't know what it referred to. She hauled in a breath and raised one shoulder. 'I don't much feel like going back to the club and dealing with my father and Elsie.'

'You don't have to. I asked your father if he'd see Elsie home.'

She swung back to him. 'I could kiss you!'

He grinned. A grin full of a slow burn that melted her insides and sent need hurtling through her. She started to reach for him, realised what she was doing, and turned the questing touch into a slap to his thigh before leaping to her feet.

'Feel like going for a walk?' She couldn't keep sitting here next to him and not give in to temptation.

Which was crazy.

Truly crazy.

Nonetheless, walking was a much safer option.

With a shrug he rose and they set off along the boardwalk in the direction of the Nelson Bay marina, where there was a lot of distraction—lights and people and noise. Meg swallowed. Down at this end of the beach it was dark and almost deserted. It would take ten minutes to reach the marina. And then they'd have to walk back this way. In the dark and the quiet.

Her feet slowed.

But by then—after all that distraction and the exercise of walking—she'd have found a way to get her stupid hormones back under control, right?

She went to speed up again, but Ben took her arm and led her across a strip of grass and down to the sand. He kicked off his shoes, and after a moment's hesitation she eased her feet out of her wedges.

They paddled without talking very much. The water was warm. She needed icy cold rather than this beguiling warmth that brought all her senses dancing to life. Paddling with Ben in all the warmth of a late summer evening, with the scent of a nearby frangipani drenching the air, was far too intimate. Even though they'd done this a thousand times and it had never felt intimate before.

Except that one time after her high school graduation, when he'd been her white knight and taken her to the prom.

Don't think about that!

She cleared her throat. 'Tell me again how magnificent I was.' Maybe teasing and banter would help her find her way back to a more comfortable place.

Ben turned and moved back towards her. He inadvertently flicked up a few drops of water that hit her mid-calf...and higher. They beaded and rolled down her legs with delicious promise.

He halted in front of her, reaching out and cupping her cheek. 'Meg, nobody has ever stood up for me the way you did tonight. Not ever.'

In the moonlight his eyes shimmered. 'Oh, Ben,' she whispered, reaching up to cover his hand with hers. He deserved to have so many more people in his life willing to go out on a limb for him.

'You made me feel as if I could fly.'

She smiled. 'You mean you can't?'

He laughed softly and pulled her in close for a hug. She clenched her eyes shut and gritted her teeth as she forced her arms around him to squeeze him back for a moment. She started to release him, but he didn't release her. She rested her cheek on his shoulder and bit her lip until she tasted blood. It took all her concentration to keep her hands where they ought to be.

And then his hand slid down her back and it wasn't a between-friends gesture. It was…

She drew back to glance into his face. The hunger and the need reflected in his eyes made her sway towards him. She planted her hands against his chest to keep her balance, to keep from falling against him. As soon as she regained her footing she meant to push him away.

Only, her hands, it seemed, had a different idea altogether. They slid across his shirt, completely ignoring the pleasant sensation of soft cotton to revel in the honed male flesh beneath it. Ben's chest had so much *definition*. And he was hot! His heat branded her through his shirt and his heart beat against her palm like a dark throbbing promise. The pulse in her throat quivered.

She swallowed and tried to catch her breath. She should move away.

But the longer she remained in the circle of Ben's arms, the more the strength and the will drained from her body and the harder it became to think clearly and logically.

And beneath her hands his body continued to beat at her like a wild thing—a tempting and tempestuous primal force, urging her to connect with something wild and elemental within herself.

She lifted her gaze to his. A light blazed from his eyes, re vealing his need, an unchecked recklessness and his exaltation

'I've been fighting this all night,' he rasped, 'but I'm no going to fight it any more.'

He tangled his hand in her hair and pulled it back until he lips lifted, angled just so to give him maximum access, an then his mouth came down on hers—hot, hungry, unchecked

His lips laid waste to all her preconceptions. She'd though he'd taste wickedly illicit and forbidden, but he didn't tast like whisky or leather or midnight. He tasted like summer an ripe strawberries and the tang of the ocean breeze. He taste like freedom.

It was more intoxicating than anything she'd ever experi enced.

Kissing Ben was like flying.

A swooping, swirling, tumbling-in-the-surf kind of flying

He pulled her closer, positioned his body in such a wa that it pressed against all the parts of her she most wante touched—but it didn't appease her, only inflamed. His nam ripped from her throat and he took advantage of it to deepen th kiss further. She followed his lead, drinking him in greedil Her head swam. She fisted her hands in his shirt and dragge him closer. His strength was the only thing keeping them bot upright.

She needed him *now*. Her body screamed for him. Sh pressed herself against him in the most shameless way sh could—pelvis to pelvis, making it clear what she wanted. De manding fulfilment.

His mouth lifted from hers. He dragged in air and then hi teeth grazed her throat. She arched against him. 'Please, Be Please.' she sobbed.

With a growl, he scrunched her skirt in his hand. He trace the line of her panty elastic with one finger and she thougl she might explode then and there.

His finger shifted, slid beneath the elastic.

Oh, please. Please.

A car horn blared, renting the air with discord, and Ben leapt away from her so fast she'd have fallen if he hadn't shot out an arm to steady her. When she regained her balance he released her with an oath that burned her ears.

'What the *hell* were you thinking?' His finger shook as he pointed it at her.

Same as you. Only she couldn't get her tongue to work properly and utter that remark out loud.

He wheeled away, dragging both hands back through his hair.

No, no, no, she wanted to wail. *Don't turn knight on me now—you're a bad boy!*

But when he swung back his face was tense and drawn, and she was grateful she hadn't said it out loud.

Because it would have been stupid.

And wrong.

Her flesh chilled. Trembling set in. She walked away from him and up the beach a little way to sit. She needed to think. And she couldn't think and walk at the same time because her limbs were boneless and it took all her concentration to remain upright. She pulled her skirt down as far as it would go and kept her legs flat out in front of her to reveal as little thigh as possible.

He strode up to her and punched a finger at her again. 'This is not on, Meg. You and me. It's never going to happen.'

'Don't use that tone with me.' She glared at him. 'You started it.'

'You could've said no!'

'You could've not kissed me in the first place!'

She expected him to stride away into the night, but he didn't. He paced for a bit and then eventually came back and sat beside her. But not too close.

'Are we still okay?' he growled.

'Sure we are.' But her throat was tight.

'I don't know what came over me.'

'It's been an emotional evening.' She swallowed. 'And when emotions run high you always seek a physical outlet.'

He nodded. There was a pause. 'It's not usually your style, though.'

She shifted, rolled her shoulders. 'Yeah, well, it seems that being pregnant has made me...itchy.'

He stared. And then he leaned slightly away from her. 'You're joking?'

'I wish I were.'

She had to stop looking at him. She forced her gaze back to the front—to the gently lapping water of the bay. Which wasn't precisely the mood she was after. She forced her gaze upwards. Stars. She heaved out a sigh and gave up.

'So you're feeling...? Umm...? All of the time?'

She pressed her hands to her cheeks and stared doggedly out at the water, desperately wishing for some of its calm to enter her soul. 'I expected to feel all maternal and Mother Earthy. Not sexy.'

'You know, it kind of makes sense,' he said after a bit. 'All those pregnancy hormones are making you look great.'

At the moment she'd take the haggard morning sickness look if it would get things between her and Ben on an even keel again.

'You sure we're okay?' he said again.

She bit back a sigh. 'I'm not going to fall for you, Ben, if that's what you're worried about.'

'No, I—'

'For a start, I don't like the way you treat women, and I'm sure as hell not going to let any man treat me like that.'

'I do not treat women badly,' he growled.

'Wham, bam, thank you, ma'am. That's your style.'

And as far as she was concerned it was appalling. She grimaced. Even if a short time ago she'd been begging for exactly that. She massaged her temples. She found her own behaviour this evening appalling too. She'd never acted like that before—so heedless and mindless. Not with any man.

'I haven't had any complaints.'

She snorted. 'Because you don't stick around long enough to hear them.'

'Hell, Meg.' He scowled. 'I show a woman a good time. I don't make promises.'

But he didn't care if a woman did read more into their encounter. He'd used that to his advantage on more than one occasion.

'Yeah, well, I want more than that from a relationship, and that's something I know you're not in the market for.' He grabbed her arm when she went to rise. She fell back to the sand, her shoulder jostling his. 'What?'

He let her go again. 'I'm glad we're on the same page, because…'

An ache started up behind her eyes. 'Because?'

'I've made a decision and we need to talk about it.'

She smoothed her skirt down towards her knees again. Ben was going to leave right after the wedding. That was what he wanted to tell her, wasn't it?

She pulled in a breath and readied herself for his news. It was good news, she told herself, straightening her spine and setting her shoulders. Things could get back to normal again.

'I've made the decision to stay in Port Stephens. I'll find work here and I'll find a place to live. I want to be a father to our baby, Meg. A *proper* father.'

CHAPTER EIGHT

THE WORLD TILTED to one side. Meg planted a hand against shifting sand. 'Staying?' Her voice wobbled.

Living here in Port Stephens, so close to Elsie and his childhood, would make Ben miserable. She closed her eyes. In less than six months he'd go stir crazy and flee in a trail of dust.

And where would that leave her baby and their friendship?

Depending on how much under the six-month mark Ben managed to hold on for, her baby might not even have been born. She opened her eyes. In which case it wouldn't have come to rely on Ben or to love him.

It wouldn't be hurt by his desertion.

But Ben would be. His failure to do this would destroy something essential in him.

And she didn't want to bear witness to that.

She turned to find him studying her. His shoulders were hitched in a way that told her he was waiting for her to say something hard and cruel.

And the memory of their kiss—that bone-crushing kiss—throbbed in all the spaces between them.

She moistened her lips. 'You haven't been back here a full week yet. This is a big decision—huge. It's life-changing. You don't have to rush it, or make a hasty choice, or—'

'When it comes down to brass tacks, Meg, the decision itself is remarkably simple.'

It was?

'Being a parent—a father—is the most important job in the world.'

Her heart pounded. He would hate himself—*hate*—when he found out he wasn't up to the task. Her heart burned, her eyes ached and her temples throbbed.

And at the back of her mind all she could think about was kissing him again. Kissing him had been a mistake. But that didn't stop her from wanting to repeat it.

And repeat it.

Over and over again.

But if they did it would destroy their friendship. She clenched her hands in her lap and battled the need to reach out and touch him again, kiss him again, as she hungered to do.

'Coming back home this time...' He glanced down at his hands. 'I've started to realise how shallow my life really is.'

Her jaw dropped.

'I know it looks exciting, and I guess it is. But it's shallow too. I've spent my whole life running away from responsibility. I'm starting to see I haven't achieved anything of real value at all.'

She straightened. 'That's not true. You help people achieve their dreams. You give them once-in-a-lifetime experiences—stories they can tell their children.'

'And who am I going to tell *my* stories to?'

Her heart started to thud.

'I've steered clear of any thoughts of children in my future, afraid I'd turn out like my parents.' His face grew grim but his chin lifted. 'That will only happen if I let it.'

He turned to her. *Stop thinking about kissing him!*

'What I really want to know is what you're scared of, Meg. Why does the thought of my coming home for good and being a father to our child freak you out?'

Because what if I never do manage to get my hormones back under control?

She snapped away at that thought. It was ludicrous. And unworthy. This should have nothing to do with her feelings and everything to do with her baby's. She couldn't let how she felt colour that reality.

'Meg?'

The notion of Ben coming home for good *did* freak her out. It scared her to the soles of her feet. He knew her too well for her to deny it. 'I don't want to hurt you,' she whispered.

He set his shoulders in a rigid line. 'Give it to me straight.'

She glanced at her hands. She hauled in a breath. 'I'm afraid you'll hang around just long enough for the baby to love you. I'm afraid the baby will come to love and rely on you but you won't be able to hack the monotony of domesticity. I'm afraid your restlessness will get the better of you and you'll leave. And if you do that, Ben, you will break my baby's heart.'

He flinched. The throbbing behind her eyes intensified.

'And if you do that, Ben…' she forced herself to continue '…I don't know if I could ever forgive you.'

And they would both lose the most important friendship of their lives.

He shot to his feet and strode down to the water's edge.

'And what's more,' she called after him, doing what she could to keep her voice strong, 'if that's the way this all plays out, I think you will hate yourself.'

There was so much to lose if he stayed.

He strode back to where she sat, planted his feet in front of her. 'I can't do anything about your fears, Meg. I'm sorry you feel the way you do. I know I have no one to blame but myself, and that only time will put your fears to rest.' He dragged a hand back through his hair. 'But when *our* baby is born I'm going to be there for it every step of the way. I want it to love me. I want it to rely on me. I'll be doing everything to make that happen.'

She shrank from him. 'But—'

'I mean to be the best father I can be. I mean to be the kind of father to my son or daughter that my father wasn't to me. I want our baby to have everything good in life, and I mean to stick around to make sure that happens.'

Meg covered her face with her hands. 'Oh, Ben, I'm sorry. I'm so, so sorry.'

Ben stared at Meg, with her head bowed and her shoulders slumped, and knelt down on the sand beside her, his heart burning. He pulled her hands from her face. 'What on earth are you sorry for?' She didn't have anything to be sorry about.

'I'm sorry I asked you to donate sperm. I'm sorry I've created such an upheaval in your life. I didn't mean for that to happen. I didn't mean to turn your life upside down.'

The darkness in her eyes, the guilt and sorrow swirling in their depths, speared into him. 'I know that.' He sat beside her again. 'When I agreed to be your sperm donor I had no idea I'd feel this way, and I'm sorry that's turned all your plans on their head.'

She pulled in a breath that made her whole body shudder. He wanted to wrap her in his arms. She moved away as if she'd read that thought in his face. It was only an inch, but it was enough. *All because of that stupid kiss.*

Why the hell had he kissed her? He clenched a hand. Ten years ago he'd promised he would never do that again. Ten years ago, when that jerk she'd been dating had dumped her. She'd been vulnerable then. She'd been vulnerable tonight too. And he'd taken advantage of that fact.

Meg wasn't the kind of girl a guy kissed and then walked away from. He might be staying in Port Stephens for good, but he wasn't changing his life *that* much. He had to stop sending her such mixed signals. They were friends. *Just* friends. *Best friends.*

He closed his eyes and gritted his teeth. Control—he needed to find control.

And he needed to forget how divine she'd felt in his arms

and how that kiss had made him feel like a superhero, shooting off into the sky.

She cleared her throat, snagging his attention again. 'Obviously neither one of us foresaw what would happen.'

Her sigh cut him to the quick. 'I know this is hard for you, Meg, but I do mean to be a true father to our child.'

She still didn't believe him. It was in her face. In the way she opened her hands and let the sand trickle out of them. In the way she turned to stare out at the water.

'And because I do want to be a better father than my own, I need to clear the air about that kiss.'

His body heated up in an instant as the impact of their kiss surged through him again. That kiss had been—

He fisted his hands and tried to cut the memory from his mind. He was not going to dwell on that kiss again. *Ever*. He couldn't. Not if he wanted to maintain his sanity. Not if he wanted to save their friendship.

Meg slapped her hands to the sides of her knees. 'You are nothing like your father.'

How could she be so sure of that?

'You would never, *ever* put a gun to anyone's head—let alone your own child's.'

Bile rose in his throat. That had happened nearly twenty years ago, but the day and all its horror was etched on his memory as if with indelible ink. His mother and father had undergone one of the most acrimonious divorces in the history of man. In the custody battle that had ensued they had used their only son to score as many points off one another as they could. At every available opportunity.

Their bitterness and their hate had turned them into people Ben hadn't been able to recognise. They'd pushed and pushed and pushed each other, until one day his father had shown up on the front doorstep with a shotgun.

Ben's heart pounded. He could still taste the fear in his mouth when he'd first caught sight of the gun—could still feel the grip of a hard hand on the back of his neck when he'd turned to run. He'd been convinced his father would kill them.

Ben pressed a hand to his forehead and drew oxygen into his lungs. Meg wrapped her arm through his. It helped anchor him back in the present moment, drawing him out of that awful one twenty years ago.

'My parents must've cared for each other once—maybe even loved each other—but marriage for them resulted in my father being in prison and my mother dumping me with Elsie and never being heard from again.'

'Not all marriages end like that, Ben.'

'True.'

But he had the same raging passions inside him that his parents had. He had no intention of setting them free. That was why he kept his interludes with women light and brief. It was safer all round.

Gently, he detached his arm from Meg's. 'Whatever else I do, though, marriage is something I'm never going to risk.'

She shook her head and went back to lifting sand and letting it trickle through her hand. 'This is one of those circular arguments that just go round and round without ending. We agreed to disagree about this years ago.'

He heard her unspoken question. *So why bring it up now?*

'Regardless of what you think, Meg, I do mean to be a good father. But that doesn't mean I've changed my mind about marriage.'

She stopped playing with the sand. 'And you think because I'm feeling a little sexy that I'm going to weave you into my fantasies and cast you in the role of handsome prince?' She snorted. 'Court jester, more like. It'd take more than a kiss for me to fall in love with you, Ben Sullivan. I may have baby brain, but that doesn't mean I've turned into a moron. Especially—' she shot to her feet '—when I don't believe you'll hang around long enough for anyone to fall in love with you anyway.'

He didn't argue the point any further. Only time would prove to her that he really did mean to stick around.

He scrambled to his feet. He just had to make sure he didn't kiss her again. Meg didn't do one-night stands—it wasn't how she was built inside. She got emotionally involved. He knew that. He'd always known that. He pushed his shoulders back and shoved his hands into the pockets of his shorts. He'd made a lot of mistakes in his sorry life, but he wasn't making that one.

He set off after Meg. 'What would you like me to do in relation to the wedding this week?'

She'd walked back to where they'd kicked off their shoes. He held her arm as she slid hers back on. He gritted his teeth in an effort to counter the warm temptation of her skin.

She blinked up at him as she slid a finger around the back of one of her sandals. She righted herself and moved out of his grasp. 'There's still a lot to do.' She glanced at him again. 'How busy are you this coming week?'

He'd be hard at work, casting around for employment opportunities, putting out feelers and sifting through a few preliminary ideas he'd had, but he'd find time to help her out with this blasted wedding. The days of leaving everything up to her were through. 'I have loads of time.'

'Well, for a start, I need those names from Elsie.'

'Right.'

They set off back towards the club and Meg's car. 'I don't suppose you'd organise the invitations, would you? I wasn't going to worry with anything too fancy. I was just going to grab a few packets of nice invitations from the newsagents and write them out myself. Calligraphy is unnecessary—they just need to be legible.'

'Leave it to me.'

'Thank you. That'll be a big help.'

'Anything else?'

'I would be very, very grateful if you could find me a gardener. I just don't have the spare time to keep on top of it a the moment. This wedding will be that garden's last hurrah, because I'm having all those high-maintenance annuals ripped out and replaced with easy-care natives.'

He nodded. 'Not a problem.'

They drove home in silence. When Meg turned in at her driveway and turned off the ignition she didn't invite him in for a drink and he didn't suggest it either. Instead, with a quick goodnight, he headed next door.

The first thing he saw when he entered the kitchen was Elsie, sitting at the table shuffling a deck of cards. Without a word, she dealt out a hand for rummy. Ben hesitated and then sat.

'How's Meg?'

'She's fine.'

'Good.'

He shifted. 'She'd feel a whole lot happier, though, if you'd give her a list of ten people she can invite to the wedding.'

Elsie snorted. He blinked again. Had that been a *laugh*?

'She said that although her father won't admit it, he'd like more than a registry office wedding.'

Elsie snorted again, and this time there was no mistaking it—it was definitely a laugh. 'I'll make a deal with you, Ben.'

Good Lord. The woman was practically garrulous. 'A deal?'

'For every hand you win, I'll give you a name.'

He straightened on his chair. 'You're on.'

Meg glanced around at a tap on the back door. And then froze. Ben stood there, looking devastatingly delicious, and a traitorous tremor weakened her knees.

With a gulp, she waved him in. Other than a couple of rushed conversations about the wedding, she hadn't seen much of him during the last two weeks. Work had been crazy, with two of her staff down with the flu, and whenever she had seen Ben and asked what he'd been up to he'd simply answered with a cryptic, 'I've been busy.' Long, leisurely conversations obviously hadn't been on either of their agendas.

Her gaze lowered to his lips. Lips that had caressed hers. Lips that had transported her to a place beyond herself and made her yearn for more. So much more. Lips that were moving now.

'Whatever it is you're cooking, Meg, no known man would be able to resist it.'

She snapped away and forced a smile.

'Cookies?'

Her smile became almost genuine at the hope in his voice. 'Chocolate chip,' she confirmed.

'Even better.' He glanced at her baking companions. 'Sounds like you guys have been having fun in here.'

Loss suddenly opened up inside her. He was her best friend. They had to find a way to overcome this horrid awkwardness.

She swallowed and hauled in a breath, gestured to the two children. 'This is Laura, who is ten, and Lochie, who is eight.'

'We're brother and sister,' Laura announced importantly.

'And Auntie Meg used to go to school with Mummy.'

'Felicity Strickland,' Meg said at his raised eyebrow. 'Laura and Lochie—this is my friend Ben from next door. He went to school with your mummy too. What do you think? Will we let him share our cookies?'

Lochie nodded immediately. 'That means there'll be another boy.'

In Lochie's mind another boy meant an ally, and Meg had a feeling he was heartily sick of being bossed by his sister.

Laura folded her arms. 'He'll have to work for them. It's only fair, because we've all worked.'

Meg choked back a laugh. She half expected Ben to make some excuse and back out through the door.

'What would I have to do?' he asked Laura instead. 'I'll do just about anything for choc-chip cookies. Especially ones that smell this good.'

Laura glanced up at Meg.

'How about Ben sets the table?'

'And pours the milk?'

She nodded. 'Sounds fair.'

Ben tackled setting the table and pouring out four glasses of milk while Meg pulled a second tray of cookies from the oven and set them to cool on the counter. She'd hoped that baking cookies would make her feel super-maternal, but one glance at Ben threw that theory out of the water.

She still felt—

Don't think about it!

Her hands shook as she placed the first batch of cookies on a plate and handed them to Laura, who took them over to the table.

They ate cookies and drank milk.

But even over the home-baked goodness of choc-chip cookies Meg caught a hint of leather and whisky. She tried to block it from her mind, tried to ignore the longing that burned through her veins.

The children regaled Ben with stories of their Christmas trip to Bali. Meg glanced at Ben and then glanced away again, biting her lip. It was no use telling herself this was just Ben. There was no *just* Ben about it—only a hard, persistent throb in her blood and an ache in her body.

When the phone rang she leapt to her feet, eager for distraction.

Ben's eyes zeroed in on her face the moment she returned to the kitchen. 'Problem?'

She clenched and unclenched her hands. 'The caterers I had lined up for the wedding have cancelled on me, the rotten—' she glanced at the children '—so-and-sos.'

She pressed her fingers to her temples and paced up and down on the other side of the breakfast bar. The wedding was three weeks away. Less than that. Two weeks and six days. Not that she was counting or anything.

Ben stood. 'What can I do?'

She glanced at him. She glanced at the children. A plan—devious, and perhaps a little unfair—slid beneath her guard. No, she couldn't.

Two weeks and six days.

She folded her arms. 'Are you up for a challenge, Ben Sullivan?'

He rocked back on his heels. 'What kind of challenge?'

She glanced at the children and then back at him, with enough meaning in her face that he couldn't possibly mistake her message.

He folded his arms too. 'Bring it on.'

'If you keep Laura and Lochie amused for an hour or two, it'll give me a chance to ring around and find a replacement caterer.'

He glanced at the television. 'Not a problem.'

She shook her head and glanced out of the kitchen window towards the back yard. There was no mistaking the panic that momentarily filled his eyes. 'I'll need peace and quiet.'

Did he even know the first thing about children and how much work they could sometimes be? Laura truly was the kind of child designed to test Ben's patience to the limit too. And when he found out the truth that being a father wasn't all beer and skittles—all fun and laughter at the beach and I-love-you-Daddy cuddles—how long before he left?

She did what she could to harden her heart, to stop it from sinking, to cut off its protests.

Lochie's face lit up. 'Can we go to the beach? Can we go swimming?'

Relief lit Ben's face too, but Meg shook her head. 'Your mum said no swimming.' Besides, she wanted them all here, right under her nose, where she could keep an eye on them.

Ben glared at her. 'Why not?'

She reached out and brushed a hand through Lochie's hair,

pulled him against her in a hug. 'Lochie's recovering from an ear infection.'

Ben shuffled his feet. 'I'm sorry to hear that, mate.'

Lochie straightened. 'We could play Uno. Laura remembered to bring it.'

'Because you *didn't*.' She rolled her eyes. 'You never do. Do you know how to play?' she demanded of Ben.

'No idea.'

'Then I'll teach you.' She took Ben's hand. 'Get the game, Lochie.'

'Please,' Ben corrected.

Laura blinked. So did Meg. 'Get the game, *please*, Lochie,' Laura amended, leading both males outside as she waxed lyrical about the importance of good manners.

Meg grimaced. Poor Ben. Laura was ten going on eighty. It hardly seemed fair to expect him to cope with her. She glanced down at her baby bump, rested her hand on it before glancing back out of the window. It was an hour. Two hours tops. She'd be nearby, and if he couldn't deal with Laura for that length of time then he had no right remaining here in Port Stephens at all.

Still, even with that decided Meg couldn't move from the window. She watched as the trio settled on the outdoor furniture, and as Ben listened while Laura explained the rules of the game in exhaustive detail. His patience touched her. Once the game started he kept both children giggling so hard she found herself wishing she could go outside and join them.

She shook her head. Two weeks and six days. She had a caterer to find.

It took Meg forty minutes' worth of phone calls before she found a replacement caterer. She glanced at her watch and winced. How on earth was Ben surviving? She raced into the family room to peer out through the glass sliding door that afforded an excellent view of the back yard and started to laugh.

Ben had set up an old slip 'n' slide of hers—one they'd played on when they were children—and the three of them

were having the time of their lives. Laura giggled, Lochie
chortled, and Ben's whole face had come alive. It shone.

She took a step towards the door, transfixed, her hand reach
ing out to rest against the glass as if reaching for...

Ben's face shone.

Her other hand moved to cover her stomach. What if Ben
did stay? What if he kept his word and found fatherhood sat
isfying? What if he didn't run away?

Her heart thudded as she allowed the idea truly to sink in
The blood vessels in her hand pulsed against the glass. If Ben
kept his word then her baby would have a father.

A real father.

She snatched her hand away. She backed up to the sofa. But
she couldn't drag her gaze away from the happy trio in her back
yard, watching in amazement as Ben effortlessly stepped in
to prevent a spat between the children. He had them laughing
again in no time. The man was a natural.

And he had a butt that—

She waved a hand in front of her face to shoo the thought
away. She didn't have time for butts—not even butts as sub
lime as Ben's.

Or chests. She blinked and leaned forward. He really did
have the most amazing body. He'd kept his shirt on, but it was
now so wet it stuck to him like a second skin, outlining every
delicious muscle and—

She promptly changed seats and placed her back to the door
She dragged in a breath and tried to control the crazy beat
ing of her heart.

If Ben *did* overcome his wanderlust...

She swallowed. He'd never lied to her before. Why would
he lie to her now? Especially about something as important as
their child's happiness.

No! She shot to her feet. *Her* child!

She raced to the refrigerator to pour herself an ice-cold glass
of water, but when she tipped her head back to drink it her eyes

caught on the vivid blue of the water slide and the children's laughter filled her ears.

Slowly she righted her glass. This was their child. *Theirs.* She'd let fear cloud her judgement. Not fear for the baby, but fear for herself. Fear that this child might somehow damage her friendship with Ben. Fear that she might come to rely on him too heavily. Fear at having to share her child.

She abandoned her water to grip her hands together. She hadn't expected to share this baby. In her possessiveness, was she sabotaging Ben's efforts?

She moistened suddenly dry lips. It would be hard, relinquishing complete control and having to consider someone else's opinions and ideas about the baby, but behind that there would be a sense of relief too, and comfort. To know she wasn't in this on her own, that someone else would have her and the baby's backs.

She'd fully expected to be a single mum—had been prepared for it. But if she didn't have to go it alone...

If her baby could have a father...

Barely aware of what she was doing, Meg walked back to the double glass doors. Ben had a child under each arm and he was swinging them round and round until they shrieked with laughter. Laura broke away to grab the hose and aimed it directly at his chest. He clutched at the spot as if shot and fell down, feigning injury. Both children immediately pounced on him.

The longer Meg watched them the clearer the picture in her mind became. Her baby could have a mother *and* a father. Her baby could have it all!

Pictures formed in her mind—pictures of family picnics and trips to the beach, of happy rollicking Christmases, of shared meals and quiet times when the baby was put down and—

She snapped away. Heat rushed through her. *Get a grip!* Her baby might have a father, but that didn't mean she and Ben would form a cosy romantic bond and become the ideal picture-perfect family. That would never happen.

Her heart pounded so hard it almost hurt, and she had to close her eyes briefly until she could draw much needed breath into straining lungs.

Ben would never do family in the way she wanted or needed. That stupid kiss ten years ago and the way Ben had bolted from town afterwards had only reinforced what she'd always known—that he would never surrender to the unpredictability and raw emotion of romantic love, with all its attendant highs and lows. She might have baby brain and crazy hormones at the moment, but she'd better not forget that fact—not for a single, solitary moment.

Best friends.

She opened her eyes and nodded. They were best friends who happened to have a child together and they'd remain friends. They *could* make this work.

She rested her forehead against the glass, her breath fogging it so she saw the trio dimly, through a haze. If only she knew for certain that Ben wouldn't leave, that he wouldn't let them down. That he'd stay. She wanted a guarantee, but there weren't—

She froze.

She turned to press her back against the door. What did Ben want more than anything else in the world?

To be on the crew of a yacht that was sailing around the world.

Did he want that more than he wanted to be a father?

Her heart pounded. Her stomach churned. She pushed away from the door and made for the phone, dialling the number for Dave Clements' travel agency. 'Dave? Hi, it's Meg.'

'Hey, Meg. Winnie and I are really looking forward to the wedding. How are the preparations coming along?'

'Oh, God, don't ask.'

He laughed. 'If there's anything I can do?'

'Actually, I do need to come in and talk to you about organising a honeymoon trip for the happy couple.'

'Drop in any time and we'll put together something fabulous for them.'

'Thank you.' She swallowed. 'But that's not the reason I called.' Her mouth went dry. She had to swallow again. 'I've been racking my brain, trying to come up with a way to thank Ben. He's been such a help with the preparations and everything.'

'And?'

'Look,' she started in a rush, 'you know he's always wanted to crew on a round-the-world yacht expedition? I wondered if there was a way you could help me make that happen?'

A whistle travelled down the line. She picked up a pen and doodled furiously on the pad by the phone, concentrating on everything but her desire to retract her request.

'Are you sure that's what you want, Meg? When I spoke to him through the week it sounded like he was pretty set on staying in Port Stephens.'

She glanced out of the window at Ben and the children. Still laughing. Still having the time of their lives. 'It's something he's always wanted. I want him to at least have the opportunity to turn it down.'

But would he?

'Okay, leave it with me. I'll see what I can do.'

'Thanks, Dave.'

She replaced the receiver. If Ben turned the opportunity down she'd have her guarantee.

If he didn't?

She swallowed. Well, at least that would be an answer too.

CHAPTER NINE

BEN CRUISED THE road between Nelson Bay and Fingal Bay with the driver's window down, letting the breeze dance through the car and ruffle his hair. He put his foot down a centimetre and then grinned in satisfaction. This baby, unlike his motor-bike, barely responded.

Perfect.

The coastal forest and salt-hardy scrubland retreated as the road curved into the small township. On impulse he parked the car and considered the view.

As a kid, he'd loved the beach. He and Meg had spent more time down there than they had in their own homes. Maybe he'd taken it for granted. Or maybe he'd needed to leave it for a time to see some of the world's other beautiful places before he could come back and truly appreciate it.

Because Meg was right—for sheer beauty, Fingal Bay was hard to beat. The line of the beach, the rocky outcrop of Fingal Island directly opposite and the sand spit leading out to it formed a cradle that enclosed the bay on three of its sides. The unbelievably clear water revealed the sandy bottom of the bay, and the bottle-nosed dolphins that were almost daily visitors.

He'd fled this place as soon as he was of a legal age. Staring at it now, he felt as if it welcomed him back. He dragged in a breath of late-afternoon air—salt-scented and warm—then glanced at his watch and grinned. Meg should be home by now.

He drove to her house, pulled the car into her driveway

and blared the horn. He counted to five before her front door swung open.

Meg stood silhouetted in the light with the darkness of the house behind her and every skin cell he possessed tightened. Her baby bump had grown in the month he'd been home. He gazed at it hungrily. He gazed at *her* hungrily.

He gave himself a mental slap upside the head. He'd promised to stop thinking about Meg that way. He'd promised not to send her any more mixed messages. He would never be able to give her all the things a woman like her wanted and needed, and he valued their friendship too much to pretend otherwise.

If only it were as easy as it sounded.

With a twist of his lips, he vaulted out of the car.

When she saw him, her jaw dropped. She stumbled down the driveway to where he stood, her mouth opening and closing, her eyes widening. 'What on earth is that?'

He grinned and puffed out his chest. 'This—' he slapped the bonnet '—is my new car.' This would prove to her that he was a changed man, that he was capable of responsibility and stability. That he was capable of fatherhood.

He pushed his hands into the pockets of his jeans, his shoulders free and easy, while he waited for her to finish her survey of the car and then pat him on the back and meet his gaze with new respect in her eyes.

'You...' She swallowed. 'You've bought a station wagon?'

'I have.' His grin widened. He'd need room for kid stuff now. And this baby had plenty of room.

'You've gone and bought an ugly, boxy *white* station wagon?'

She stared at him as if he'd just broken out in green and purple spots. His shoulders froze in place. So did his grin. She planted her hands on her hips and glared. The sun picked out the golden highlights in her hair. Her eyes blazed, but her lips were the sweetest pink he'd ever seen.

Meg was hot. He shifted, adjusting his jeans. Not just pretty, but smokin' hot. Knock-a-man-off-his-feet hot. He needed something ice-cold to slake the heat rising through him or he'd—

'Where's your bike?' she demanded.

He moistened his lips. 'I traded it.' The icy sting of the cold current that visited the bay at this time of year might do the trick.

'You. Did. *What?*' Her voice rose on the last word. Her nostrils flared. She poked him in the shoulder. 'Have you gone mad? What on earth were you thinking?'

He leant towards her, all his easy self-satisfaction slaughtered. 'I was trying to prove to you that I've changed,' he ground out. 'This car is a symbol that I can be a good father.'

'It shows you've lost your mind!'

She dragged both hands back through her hair. She stared at him for a moment, before transferring her gaze back to the station wagon.

'Inside—now,' she ordered. 'I don't want to have this conversation on the street.'

He planted his feet. 'I'm not some child you can order about. If you want to talk to me, then you can ask me like a civilised person. I'm tired of you treating me like a second-class citizen.' Like someone who couldn't get one damn thing right.

He knew she was stressed about the wedding, about the baby, about him—about that damn kiss!—but he was through with taking this kind of abuse from her. Meg had always been a control freak, but she was getting worse and it was time she eased up.

He welcomed the shock in her eyes, but not the pain that followed swiftly on its heels. Meg was a part of him. Hurting her was like hurting himself.

She swallowed and nodded. 'Sorry, that really was very rude of me. It's just…I think we need to talk about that.' She gestured to his car. 'Would you come inside for coffee so we can discuss it?' When he didn't say anything she added, 'Please?'

He nodded and followed her into the house.

She glanced at the kitchen clock. 'Coffee or a beer?'

'Coffee, thanks.' Meg had been right about the drinking. Somewhere along the line, when he hadn't been paying attention, it had become a habit. He'd made an effort to cut back.

She made coffee for him and decaf for herself. He took in the tired lines around her eyes and mouth and the pallor of her skin where previously there'd been a golden glow and something snagged in his chest. 'What's wrong with the car?' he said, accepting the mug she handed him. 'I thought it would show you I'm serious about sticking around and being involved with the baby.'

'I think I've been unfair to you on that, Ben.'

She gestured to the family room sofas and he followed her in a daze.

She sat. She didn't tuck her legs beneath her like she normally did. She didn't lean back against the sofa's cushioned softness. She perched on the edge of the seat, looking weary and pale. Her mug sat on the coffee table, untouched. He wanted to ease her back into that seat and massage her shoulders…or her feet. Whichever would most help her to relax.

Except he had a no-touching-Meg rule. And he wasn't confident enough in his own strength to break it.

She glanced up, the green in her eyes subdued. 'You said you wanted to be an involved father and I automatically assumed…'

'That I was lying.'

'Not on purpose, no.' She frowned. 'But I didn't think you really knew what you were talking about. I didn't think you understood the reality of what you were planning to do.'

And why should she? The truth was he hadn't understood the reality at all. Not at first.

She glanced back at him and her gaze settled on his mouth for a beat too long. Blood rushed in his ears. When she realised her preoccupation she jerked away.

'I didn't think you knew your own mind.' She swallowed.

'That wasn't fair of me. I'm sorry for doubting you. And I'm sorry I haven't been more supportive of your decision.'

'Hell, don't apologise.' Coffee sloshed over the side of his mug and he mopped it up with the sleeve of his shirt. 'I needed your challenges to make me analyse what I was doing and what it is I want. I should be thanking you for forcing me to face facts.' For forcing him to grow up.

When he glanced back up he found her making a detailed inventory of his chest and shoulders. Her lips parted and fire licked along his veins.

Don't betray yourself, he tutored himself. *Don't!*

Her eyes searched his, and then the light in them dulled and she glanced away, biting her lip.

He had to close his eyes. 'You don't need to apologise about anything.'

He opened his eyes and almost groaned at the strain in her face. He made himself grin, wanting to wipe the tension away, wanting desperately for things to return to normal between them again.

'Though I have to say if I'd known that calling you on the way you've been treating me would change your thinking I'd have done it days ago.'

'Oh, it wasn't that.' She offered him a weak smile that didn't reach her eyes. 'It was watching you with Laura and Lochie last Saturday.'

He'd sensed that had been a test. He just hadn't known if he'd passed it or not.

'I had a ball.'

'I know. And so did they.'

'They're great kids.'

Just for a moment her eyes danced. 'Laura can be a challenge at times.'

'She just needs to loosen up a bit, that's all.' In the same way Meg needed to loosen up.

Who made sure Meg had fun these days? Who made sure

she didn't take herself too seriously? She'd said that the baby gave her joy, but it wasn't here yet. What else gave her joy? It seemed to him that at the moment Meg was too busy for joy, and that was no way to live a life.

He'd need to ponder that a bit more, but in the meantime…

'What's your beef with the car?'

That brought the life back to her cheeks. He sat back, intrigued.

'Could you have picked a more boring car if you'd tried?'

'*You* have a station wagon,' he pointed out.

'But at least mine is a sporty version and it's useful for work. And it's blue!'

'The colour doesn't matter.'

'Of course it does.' She leant to towards him. 'I understand you want to prove you're good father material, but that doesn't mean you have to become *beige*!'

'Beige' had been their teenage term for all things boring.

'I agree that with a baby you'll need a car. But you're allowed to buy a car you'll enjoy. A two-seat convertible may not be practical, but you're an action man, Ben, and you like speed. You could've bought some powerful V6 thing that you could open up on the freeway, or a four-wheel drive you could take off-road and drive on the beach—or anything other than that boring beige box sitting in my driveway.'

He considered her words.

'Do you think fatherhood is going to be beige?' she demanded.

'No!'

She closed her eyes and let out a breath. 'That's something, at least.'

He saw it then—the reason for her outburst. She'd started to believe in him, in his sense of purpose and determination, and then he'd turned up in that most conservative of conservative cars and he'd freaked her out.

Again.

He was determined to get things back on an even footing between them again. And he'd succeed. As long as he ignored the sweet temptation of her lips and the long clean line of her limbs. And the desire that flared in her green-flecked eyes.

'You don't have to change who you are, Ben. You might not be travelling around the globe any more, throwing yourself off mountains, negotiating the rapids of some huge river or trekking to base camp at Everest—but, for heaven's sake, it doesn't mean you have to give up your motorbike, does it?'

That—trading in his bike—had been darn hard. It was why it had taken him a full month of being back in Fingal Bay before he'd found the courage to do it. But he'd figured it was a symbol of his old life and therefore had to go. But if Meg was right...

'I want you to go back to that stupid car yard and buy it back.'

A weight lifted from his shoulders. He opened and closed his hands. 'You think I should?'

'Yes! Where else am I going to get my occasional pillion passenger thrill? All that speed and power? And, while I know you can't literally feel the wind in your hair because of the helmet, that's exactly what it feels like. It's like flying.'

He had a vision of Meg on the back of his bike, her front pressed against his back and her arms wrapped around his waist. He shot to his feet. 'If I race back now I might catch the manager before he leaves for the day.' He had to get his bike back. 'He had a nice-looking four wheel drive in stock. That could be a bit of fun.' He rubbed at his jaw. 'I could take it for a test drive.'

Meg trailed after him to the front door. 'Good luck.'

Halfway down the path, he swung back. 'What are you doing Saturday?'

'Elsie and I are shopping for wedding outfits in the morning.' She grimaced. 'It's not like we've left it to the last minute or anything, but that grandmother of yours can be darn slippery when she wants to be.'

The wedding was a fortnight this Saturday. 'And in the afternoon?'

She shook her head and shrugged.

'Keep it free,' he ordered. Then he strode back, slipped a hand around the back of her head and pressed a kiss to her brow. 'Thanks, Meg.'

And then he left before he did something stupid, like kiss her for real. That wouldn't be getting their friendship back on track.

Meg glanced up at the tap on the back door. 'How did the shopping go?' Ben asked, stepping into the family room with the kind of grin designed to bring a grown woman to her knees.

Her heart swelled at the sight of him. *Don't drool. Smile. Don't forget to smile.*

The smiling was easy. Holding back a groan of pure need wasn't. 'The shopping? Oh, it went surprisingly well,' she managed. Elsie had been remarkably amiable and co-operative. 'We both now have outfits.'

They'd found a lovely lavender suit in shot silk for Elsie. Though she'd protested that it was too young for her, her protests had subsided once Meg had pronounced it perfect. Meg had settled on a deep purple satin halter dress with a chiffon overlay that hid her growing baby bulge. It made her feel like a princess.

'How are the wedding preparation coming along? What do you need me to do this week?'

Ben had, without murmur, executed to perfection whatever job she'd assigned to him. He'd been amazing.

She thought of the request she'd made of Dave and bit her lip. Perhaps she should call that off. Ben had settled into a routine here as if…almost as if he'd never been away. The thought of him leaving…

She shook herself. The wedding. They were talking about the wedding. 'You have a suit?'

'Yep.'

'Then there's not much else to be done. The marquee is being erected on the Friday afternoon prior, and the tables and chairs will all be set up then too.'

'I'll make sure I'm here in case there are any hitches.'

'Thank you.' He eyed her for a moment. It made her skin prickle. 'What?'

He shook himself. 'Have you managed to keep this afternoon free?'

'Uh-huh.' Something in her stomach shifted—a dark, dangerous thrill at the thought of spending a whole afternoon in Ben's company. 'What do you have planned?' If both of them were sensible it would be something practical and beige boring.

Ben's eyes—the way they danced and the way that grin hooked up the right side of his face—told her this afternoon's adventure, whatever it might be, was not going to be beige.

'It's a surprise.'

Her blood quickened. She should make an excuse and cry off, but...

Damn it all, this was Ben—*her best friend*—and that grin of his was irresistible. She glanced down at her sundress. 'Is what I'm wearing okay?'

'Absolutely not.' His grin widened. 'You're going to need a pair of swimmers, and something to put on over them to protect you from sunburn.'

Her bones heated up. She really, truly should make an excuse. 'And a hat, I suppose?' she said, moving in the direction of her bedroom to change.

'You get the picture,' he said.

Meg lifted her face into the breeze and let out a yell for the sheer fun of it. Ben had driven them into Nelson Bay in his brand new *red* four-wheel drive to hire a rubber dinghy with an outboard motor for the afternoon. They were zipping across the vast expanse of the bay as if they were flying.

Ben had given her the wind in her hair for real, and she couldn't remember the last time she'd had this much fun. She released the rope that ran around the dinghy's perimeter and flung her arms back, giving herself up to sheer exhilaration.

'Meg!'

She opened her eyes at Ben's shout, saw they were about to hit the wake from a speedboat, and grabbed the rope again for balance. They bounced over the waves, her knees cushioned by the buoyant softness of the rubber base.

Eventually Ben cut the motor and they drifted. She trailed her hand in the water, relishing its refreshing coolness as she dragged the scent of salt and summer into her lungs. Silver scales glittered in the sun when a fish jumped out of the water nearby. Three pelicans watched from a few metres away, and above them a flock of seagulls cried as they headed for the marina.

The pelicans set off after them, and Meg turned around and stretched her legs out. The dinghy was only small, but there was plenty of room for Meg and Ben to sit facing one another, with their legs stretched to the side. She savoured the way the dinghy rocked and swayed, making their legs press against each other's, the warm surge that shot through her at each contact.

Ever since that kiss she'd found herself craving to touch Ben—to test the firmness of his skin, to explore his muscled leanness and discover if it would unleash the heat that could rise in her without any warning.

It was dangerous, touching like this, but she couldn't stop herself. Besides, it was summer—the sun shone, the gulls wheeled and screeched, and water splashed against the sides of the dingy. For a moment it all made her feel young and reckless.

'This was a brilliant idea, Ben.'

He grinned. 'It's certainly had the desired effect.'

She reached up to adjust the brim of her sunhat. 'Which was?'

'To put the colour back in your cheeks.'

She stilled. It was strange to have someone looking out for her, looking after her. 'Thank you.' If Ben did stay—

She cut that thought off. Whether Ben stayed or not, it wasn't his job to look after her. He might fill her with heat, but that didn't mean they had any kind of future together.

Except as friends.

He shrugged. 'Besides, it's nice to have some buddy-time.'

She gritted her teeth. Buddy-time was excellent. It *was*!

She glanced at him and tried to decipher the emotions that tangled inside her, coiling her up tight.

She started to name them silently. One: desire. Her lips twisted. *Please God, let that pass.* Two: anger that he'd turned her nicely ordered world on its head. She shook her head. *Deal with it.* Three: love for her oldest, dearest friend, for all they'd been through together, for all they'd shared, and for all the support and friendship he'd given her over the years.

And there was another emotion there too—something that burned and chafed. A throbbing sore. It was...

Hurt.

That made her blink. Hurt? She swallowed and forced herself to examine the feeling. An ache started at her temples. Hurt that he'd stay in Port Stephens for their baby in a way he'd never have stayed for her.

Oh, that was petty. And nonsensical.

She rubbed her hands up and down her arms. She hadn't harboured hidden hopes that Ben would come back for her. *She hadn't!* But seeing him now on such a regular basis...not to mention that kiss on the beach...that devastating kiss...

'Cold?'

She shook her head and abruptly dropped her hands back to her lap. She dragged in a breath. She had to be careful. She couldn't go weaving Ben into her romantic fantasies. It would end in tears. It would wreck their friendship. And that would be the worst thing in the world. It was why she hadn't let herself get hooked on that kiss ten years ago. It was why she had to forget that kiss the other night.

A romantic relationship—even if Ben was willing—wasn't worth risking their friendship over.

Deep inside, a part of her started to weep. She swallowed. Hormones, that was all.

'I can still hardly believe that Elsie and your father are marrying.'

She nodded, prayed her voice would work properly, prayed she could hide her strain. 'It shows a remarkable optimism on both their parts.'

He surveyed her for a moment. 'How are you getting on with your father?'

'Same as usual.' She lifted her face to the sun to counter a sudden chill. 'Neither he nor Elsie have mentioned my outburst. It seems we're all back to pretending it never happened.' Not that she knew what else she'd been expecting. Or hoping for. 'It's the elephant in the room nobody mentions.'

'It's had a good effect on Elsie, though.'

She straightened from her slouch. 'No?'

'Yep.' He flicked water at her. 'She's less buttoned-up and more relaxed. She makes more of an effort at conversation too.'

'*No?*'

He flicked water at her again. 'Yep.'

'I'd say that's down to the effect of her romance with my father.'

'She's even knitting the baby some booties.'

Meg leant towards him, even though she was in danger of getting more water flicked at her. 'You're kidding me?'

He didn't flick more water at her, but she realised it had been a mistake to lean towards him when the scent of leather and whisky slugged into her, heating her up...tightening her up. Making her want forbidden things.

She sat back. Darn it all! How on earth could she be so

aware of his scent out here in the vast expanse of the bay? Surely the salt water and the sun should erase it, dilute it?

She scooped up a whole handful of water and threw it at him.

And then they had the kind of water fight that drenched them both and had her squealing and him laughing and them both breathing heavily from the exertion.

'How long since you've been out on the bay like this?' he demanded, subsiding back into his corner.

'Like this?' She readjusted her sunhat. 'Probably not since the last time we did it.'

'That has to be two years ago!'

'I've been out on a couple of dinner cruises, and I've swum more times than I can count.'

'What about kayaking?'

That was one of her favourite things—to take a kayak out in the early evening, when the shadows were long, the light dusky and the water calm. Paddling around the bay left her feeling at one with nature and the world. But when had she'd actually last done that?

She cocked her head to one side. She'd gone out a few times in December, but...

She hadn't been out once this year! 'I...I guess I've been busy.'

'You need to stop and smell the roses.'

He was right. This afternoon—full of sun, bay and a beat-up rubber dinghy—had proved that to her. She wanted to set her child a good example. She had no intention of turning into a distracted workaholic mother. She thought about her father and Elsie, how easily they'd fallen into unhealthy routines and habits.

She swallowed and glanced at Ben. He always took the time to smell the roses. Her lips twisted. Sometimes he breathed them in a little too deeply, and for a little too long, but nobody could accuse him of not living life to the full.

Would he still feel life was full after he'd been living in Port Stephens for a couple of years?

She glanced around. It was beautiful here. He was having fun, wasn't he?

For today.

But what would happen tomorrow, the day after that, and next week, next month, or even next year? *Please, God, don't let Ben be miserable.*

There was still so much that had to be settled. She leant back and swallowed. 'I agree it's important to slow down and to enjoy all the best that life has to offer, but you've still got some big decisions ahead of you, Ben.' And she doubted she'd be able to relax fully until he'd made them.

'Like?'

'Like what are you going to do with Elsie's house? Will you live there on your own after the wedding?'

'I haven't thought about it.'

'And what about a job? I'm not meaning to be nosy or pushy or anything, but…'

His lips twitched. 'But?'

'I figure you don't want to live off your savings for ever.'

'I have a couple of irons in the fire.'

He did? She opened her mouth but he held up a hand to forestall her.

'Once I have something concrete to report you'll be the first to know. I promise.'

She wanted to demand a timeframe on his promise, but she knew he'd scoff at that. And probably rightly so.

'Do you think I should move into Elsie's house?'

Her mouth dried. 'I…'

'If I do, I'll be paying her rent.' He scowled. 'I don't want her to give the darn thing to me. It's hers.'

She eyed him for a moment. 'What if she gifts it to the baby?'

His mouth opened and closed but no sound came out. It obviously wasn't a scenario he'd envisaged. 'I...' He didn't go on.

She glanced away, her stomach shrinking. The two of them had to have a serious conversation. But not today. They could save it for some other time.

'You better spit it out, Meg.'

She glared at the water. Ben knowing her so well could be darn inconvenient at times. She blew out a breath and turned to him. 'There are a few things I think we need to discuss in relation to the baby, but they can wait until after the wedding. It's such a glorious afternoon.'

And she didn't want to spoil it. Or ruin this easy-going camaraderie that should have been familiar to them but had been elusive these last few weeks.

'It could be the perfect afternoon for such a discussion,' he countered, gesturing to the sun, the bay and the holiday atmosphere of these last dog days of summer. 'When we're both relaxed.'

If she uttered the C-word he wouldn't remain relaxed. Still, she knew him well enough to know he wouldn't let it drop. She glanced around. Maybe he was right. Maybe she *should* lay a few things out there for him to mull over before Dave presented him with that dream offer. It only seemed fair.

She shivered, suddenly chilled, as if a cloud had passed over the sun. 'You won't like it,' she warned.

'I'm a big boy, Meg. I have broad shoulders.'

'You want to know if I think you should live in Elsie's house? That depends on...' She swallowed.

'On?'

'On what kind of access you want to have to the baby.'

He frowned. 'What do you mean?'

She wasn't going to be able to get away with not using the C-word. Dancing around it would only make matters worse.

'What I'm talking about, Ben, are our custody arrangements.'

* * *

Custody?

Ben flinched as the word ripped beneath his guard. His head was filled with the sound of shouting and screaming and abuse.

Custody?

'No!' He stabbed a finger at her. He swore. Once. Hard. Tried to quieten the racket in his head. He swore again, the storm raging inside him growing in strength. 'What the bloody hell are you talking about? *Custody?*' He spat the word out. 'No way! We don't need *custody* arrangements. We aren't like that. You and I can work it out like civilised people.'

Meg had gone white.

He realised he was shouting. Just like his mother had shouted. Just like his father had shouted. He couldn't stop. 'We're supposed to be friends.'

She swallowed and bile filled his mouth. Was she afraid of him? Wind rushed through his ears. No! She knew him well enough to know he'd never hut her. Didn't she?

His hands clenched. If she knew him well enough, she'd have never raised this issue in the first place.

'We're friends who are having a baby,' she said, her voice low. 'We need certain safeguards in place to ensure—'

'Garbage!' He slashed a hand through the air. 'We can keep going the way we have been—the way we've always done things. When you've had the baby I can come over any time and help, maybe take care of it some days while you're at work, and help you in the evenings with feeding and baths and—'

'So basically we'd live like a married couple but without the benefits?'

Her scorn almost blasted the flesh from his bones.

'No, Ben, that's *not* how it's going to be. Living like that— don't you think it would do our child's head in?' She stabbed a finger at him. 'Besides, I still believe in love and marriage. I am *so* not going to have you cramp my style like that.'

The storm inside him built to fever-pitch. 'You really mean to let another man help raise *my* child?'

'That's something you're going to have to learn to live with. Just like I will if you ever become serious about a woman.'

He went ice-cold then. 'You never wanted me as part of this picture, did you? I've ruined your pretty fantasy of domestic bliss and now you're trying to punish me.' He leaned towards her. 'You're hoping this will drive me away.'

The last of the colour bled from her face. 'That's not true.'

Wasn't it? His harsh laugh told her better than words could what he thought about that.

Her colour didn't return. She gripped her hands together in her lap. 'I want you to decide what you want the custody arrangements to be. Do you want fifty-fifty custody? A night through the week and every second weekend? Or...whatever? This is something we need to settle.'

Custody. The word stabbed through him, leaving a great gaping hole at the centre of his being. He wanted to cover his ears and hide under his bed as he had as a ten-year-old. The sense of helplessness, of his life spinning out of control, made him suddenly ferocious.

'What if I want full custody?' he snarled.

He wanted to frighten her. He wanted her to back down, to admit that this was all a mistake, that she was sorry and she didn't mean it.

He wanted her to acknowledge that he wasn't like his father!

Her chin shot up. 'You wouldn't get it.'

A savage laugh ripped from his throat. He should have known better. Meg would be well versed in her rights. She'd have made sure of them before bringing this subject up.

'I want the custody arrangements settled in black and white before the baby is born.'

That ice-cold remoteness settled over him again. She didn't trust him. 'Do you have to live your entire life by rules?'

Her throat bobbed as she swallowed. 'I'm sorry, Ben, but

in this instance I'm going to choose what's best for the baby, not what's best for you.'

She was choosing what was best for *her*. End of story. Acid burned his throat. Meg didn't even know who he was any more, and he sure as hell didn't know her. The pedestal he'd had her on for all these years had toppled and smashed.

'And as for you living next door in Elsie's house...' She shook her head. 'I think that's a very bad idea.'

He didn't say another word. He just started the dinghy's motor and headed for shore.

'How's Meg?'

Ben scowled as he reached for a beer. With a muttered oath he put it back and chose a can of lemon squash instead. He swung back to Elsie, the habit of a lifetime's loyalty preventing him from saying what he wanted to say—from howling out his rage.

'She's fine.'

Elsie sat at the kitchen table, knitting. It reminded him of Meg's baby shawl, and the almost completed crib he'd been working on in Elsie's garden shed.

'Is she okay with me taking her mother's place?'

Whoa! He reached out a hand to steady himself against the counter. Where on earth had that come from? He shook his head and counted to three. 'Let's get a couple of things straight. First of all, you won't be taking her mother's place. Meg is all grown-up.'

She might be grown-up, but she was also pedantic, anal and cruel.

He hauled in a breath. 'She doesn't need a mother any more. For heaven's sake, she's going to be a mother herself soon.'

He added controlling, jealous and possessive to his list. He adjusted his stance.

'Secondly, she won't be doing anything daft like calling you Mum.'

Elsie stared back at him. 'I meant taking her mother's place in her father's affections,' she finally said.

Oh. He frowned.

'Do you think she minds us marrying?'

Meg might be a lot of things he hadn't counted on, but she wasn't petty. 'She's throwing you a wedding. Doesn't that say it all?'

Elsie paused in her knitting. 'The thing is, she always was the kind of girl to put on a brave front.' She tapped a knitting needle against the table. 'You both were.'

He pulled out a chair and sat before he fell.

'Do *you* mind Laurie and I marrying?'

He shook his head. 'No.' And he realised he meant it.

'Good.' She nodded. 'Yes, that's good.' She stared at him for a bit, and then leaned towards him a fraction. 'Do you think Meg will let the baby call me Grandma?'

He didn't know what to say. 'I expect so. If that's what you want. You'll have to tell her that's what you'd prefer, though, rather than Elsie,' he couldn't resist adding.

Elsie set her knitting down. She took off her glasses and rubbed her eyes. Finally she looked at him again. 'After she left, I never heard from your mother, Ben. Not once.'

Ben's mouth went dry.

Elsie's hands shook. 'I waited and waited.'

Just for a moment the room, the table and Elsie receded. And then they came rushing back. 'But...?' he croaked.

Elsie shook her head, looking suddenly old. 'But...nothing. I can't tell you anything, though I wish to heaven I could. I don't know where she went. I don't know if she's alive or not. All I do know is it's been eighteen years.' A breath shuddered out of her. 'And that she knows how to get in contact with us, but to the best of my knowledge she's never tried to.'

He stared at her, trying to process what she'd said and how he felt about it.

'Your father broke something in her.'

He shook his head at that. 'No. The way they acted—they let hate and bitterness destroy them. She had a chance to pull back. They both did. But they chose not to. She was as much to blame as him.'

Elsie clenched her hand. 'All I know is that she left and I grieved. My only child...'

Ben thought about the child Meg carried and closed his eyes.

'When I came out of that fog I...we...me and you were set in our ways, our routines, our way of dealing with each other.'

Was it that simple? Elsie had been grief-stricken and just hadn't known how to deal with a young boy whose whole world had imploded.

'Your mother always said I suffocated her and that's why she went with your father. I failed her somehow—I still don't know how, can't find any explanation for it—and I just didn't want to go through all that again.'

He pulled in a breath. 'So you kept me at arm's length?'

'It was wrong of me, Ben, and I'm sorry.'

So much pain and misery. If his and Meg's child ever disappeared the way his mother had, could he honestly say he'd deal with it any better than Elsie had? He didn't know.

In the end he swallowed and nodded. 'Thank you for explaining it to me.'

'It was long overdue.'

He didn't know what to do, what to say.

'I'm grateful you had Meg.'

Meg. Her name burned through him. What would Meg want him to do now?

From somewhere he found a smile, and it didn't feel forced. 'I'm sure she'll be happy for the baby to call you Grandma.'

CHAPTER TEN

ON THE MORNING of the wedding Meg woke early. She leapt out of bed, pulled on a robe and raced downstairs, her mind throbbing with the million things that must need doing. And then she pulled to a halt in the kitchen and turned on the spot. Actually, what *was* there to do? Everything was pretty much done. She and Elsie had hair and make-up appointments later in the day, and her father was coming over mid-afternoon to get ready for the wedding, but till then her time was her own.

She made a cup of tea and let herself out through the glass sliding door. The garden looked lovely, and the marquee sat in the midst of it like a joyful jewel.

And then she saw Ben.

He stood a few feet away, a steaming mug of his own in hand, surveying the marquee too. He looked deliciously dishevelled and rumpled, as if he'd only just climbed out of bed. He didn't do designer stubble. Ben didn't do designer anything. There was nothing designed in the way he looked, but...

Her hand tightened about her mug. An ache burned in her abdomen. She'd barely seen him these last two weeks. He'd rung a few times, to check if there was anything she'd needed him to do, but he'd kept the calls brief and businesslike. He'd overseen the assembly of the marquee yesterday afternoon, but he'd disappeared back next door as soon as the workmen had left. He'd avoided her ever since she'd mentioned the C word.

'Morning, Meg.'

He didn't turn his head to look at her now either.

A cold fist closed about her heart. He was her best friend. He'd been an integral part of her life for eighteen years. She couldn't lose him. If she lost his friendship she would lose a part of herself.

The same way her father had lost a part of himself the day her mother had died.

The pressure in her chest grew until she thought it might split her in two.

'Lovely day for a wedding.'

He was talking to her about the weather. Everything in the garden blurred. She lifted her face to the sky and blinked, tried to draw breath into lungs that had cramped.

When she didn't speak, he turned to look at her. His eyes darkened and his face paled at whatever he saw in her face.

He shook his head. 'Don't look at me like that.'

She couldn't help it. 'Do you mean to resent me for ever? Do you mean to keep avoiding me? All because I want to do what's right for our baby?' The words tumbled out, tripping and falling over each other. 'Don't you trust me any more, Ben?'

His head snapped back. 'This is about your trust, not mine!' He stabbed a finger at her. 'You wouldn't need some third party to come in and organise custody arrangements if you trusted me.'

She flinched, but she held her ground. 'Have you considered the fact that it might be myself I don't trust?' She poured the rest of her now tepid tea onto the nearest rosebush. 'I already feel crazily possessive about this baby.'

She rested a hand against her rounded stomach. He followed the movement. She moistened her lips when he met her gaze again. 'I'm going to find it hard to share this child with any-one—even with you, Ben. It wasn't part of my grand plan.' As he well knew. 'I know that's far from noble, but I can't help the way I feel. I also know that you're this baby's father and you have a right to be a part of its life.'

But the first time their baby spent twenty-four full hours with Ben—twenty-four hours away from her—she'd cry her eyes out. She'd wander from room to room in her huge house, lost.

'Having everything down in black and white will protect your rights. Have you not considered that?'

One glance at his face told her he hadn't.

'I don't see why making everything clear—what we expect from each other and what our child can expect from us—is such a bad thing.'

He didn't say anything. He didn't even move.

'I understand that down the track things might change. We can discuss and adapt to those changes as and when we need to. I'm not locking us into a for ever contract. We can include a clause that says we'll renegotiate every two years, if you want.'

But she knew they needed something on paper that would set out their responsibilities and expectations and how they'd move forward.

For the sake of the baby.

And for the sake of their friendship.

'I know you love this baby, Ben.'

Dark eyes surveyed her.

'You wouldn't turn your whole life on its head for no good reason. You want to be a good father.'

He'd stay for the baby in a way he'd never have stayed for her, but she wanted him to stay. She wanted it so badly she could almost taste it.

'And you think agreeing to legalise our custody arrangements will prove I'll be a good father?'

She tried not to flinch at the scorn in his voice. She was asking him to face his greatest fear. Nobody did that without putting up a fight. And when he wanted to Ben could put up a hell of a fight.

She tipped up her chin. 'It'll make us better co-parents. So, yes—I think it *will* make me a better mother and you a better father.'

His jaw slackened.

She stared at him and then shook her head. Her throat tightened. She'd really started to believe that he'd stay, but now...

'I'm sorry,' she whispered. 'If I'd known five months ago what would come of asking you to be my sperm donor I'd never have asked.' She'd have left well alone and not put him through all this.

He stiffened. 'But I want this baby.'

Something inside her snapped then. 'Well, then, suck it up.' She tossed her mug to the soft grass at her feet and planted her hands on her hips. 'If you want this baby then man up to your responsibilities. If you can't do that—if they intimidate you that much—then run off back to Africa and go bungee-jump off a high bridge, or rappel down a cliff, or go deep-sea diving in the Atlantic, or any of those other things that aren't half as scary as fatherhood!'

He folded his arms and nodded. 'That's better. That meek and mild act doesn't suit you.'

Her hand clenched. She stared at her fist and then at his jaw.

'You're right. I do need to man up and face my responsibilities.'

Her hand promptly unclenched.

He ran a hand through his hair. 'Especially when they intimidate me, I expect.'

She stared, and then shook herself. 'Exactly at what point in the conversation did you come to that conclusion?'

'When you said how possessive you feel about the baby.'

Her nose started to curl. 'When you realised a custody agreement would protect your interests?'

'When I realised you weren't my mother.'

Everything inside her stilled.

'When I realised that, regardless of what happens, you will *never* become my mother. I know you will always put the baby's best interests first. That's when I realised I was fighting shadows—because regardless of what differences we might have in the future, Meg, we will never re-enact my parents' drama.'

She folded her arms.

'Are you going to tell me off now, for taking so long to come to that conclusion?'

'I'm going to tell you off for not telling me you'd already come to that conclusion. For letting me rabbit on and...' And abuse him.

'I needed a few moments to process the discovery.' He shifted his weight. 'And I wanted to razz you a bit until you stopped looking so damn fragile and depressed. That's not like you, Meg. What the hell is that all about?'

She glanced away.

'I want the truth.'

That made her smile. 'Have we ever been less than honest with each other?' They knew each other too well to lie effectively to the other. 'I've been feeling sick this past fortnight, worried that I've hurt our friendship. I want to do what's right for the baby. But hurting you kills me.'

He tossed his now-empty mug to the grass, as she had earlier. It rolled towards her mug, the two handles almost touching. At his sides, his hands clenched.

'The thing is, Ben, after this baby your friendship is the most important thing in the world to me. If I lost it...'

With a smothered oath, he closed the distance between them and pulled her in close, hugged her tightly. 'That's not going to happen, Meg. It will never happen.'

He held her tight, and yet she felt as if she was falling and falling without an end in sight. Even first thing in the morning he smelled of leather and whisky. She tried to focus on that instead of falling.

Eventually she disengaged herself. 'There's something else that's been bothering me.'

'What's that?'

'You keep saying you have no intention of forming a serious relationship with any woman.'

'I don't.'

'Well, I think you need to seriously rethink that philosophy of yours, because quite frankly it sucks.'

He gaped at her.

'You think fatherhood will be fulfilling, don't you?'

'Yes, but—'

'So can committing to one person and building a life with them.'

He glared. 'For you, perhaps.'

'And for you too. You're not exempt from the rest of the human race. No matter how much you'd like to think you are.'

He adjusted his stance, slammed his hands to his hips. 'What is it with you? You've never tried to change my mind on this before.'

That was true, but... 'I never thought you'd want fatherhood either, but I was obviously wrong about that. And I think *you're* wrong to discount a long-term romantic relationship.'

He shook his head. 'I'm not risking it.'

'You just admitted I'm not like your mother. There are other women—' the words tasted like acid on her tongue but she forced them out '—who aren't like your mother either.' She'd hate to see him with another woman, which didn't make a whole lot of sense. She closed her mind to the pictures that bombarded her.

'But I know you, Meg. I've known you for most of my life.'

'Then take the time to get to know someone else.'

His face shuttered closed. 'No.'

She refused to give up. 'I think you'll be a brilliant father. I think you deserve to have lots more children. Wouldn't you like that?'

He didn't say anything, and she couldn't read his face.

'I think you'd make a wonderful husband too.' She could

see it more clearly than she'd ever thought possible and it made her heart beat harder and faster. 'I think any woman would be lucky to have you in her life. And, Ben, I think it would make you happy.' And she wanted him happy with every fibre of her being.

He thrust out his jaw. 'I'm perfectly happy as I am.'

She wanted to call him a liar, except...

Except maybe he was right. The beguiling picture of Ben as a loving husband and doting father faded. Maybe the things that would make her happy would only make him miserable. The thought cut at her with a ferocity she couldn't account for.

She swallowed. 'I just want you to be happy,' she whispered.

He blew out a breath. 'I know.'

She wanted Ben to stay in Port Stephens. She *really* wanted that. If he fell in love with some woman...She shied away from the thought.

Her heart burned. She twisted her hands together. This evening Dave meant to offer Ben the chance to fulfil his dream—to offer him a place on that yacht.

'Can I hit you with another scary proposition?'

He squared his shoulders. 'You bet.'

Would it translate into emotional blackmail? Was it an attempt to make sure he did stay?

He leant down to peer into her face. 'Meg?'

She shook herself. It wasn't blackmail. It was her making sure Ben had all the options, knew his choices, that was all.

She swallowed. 'Would you like to be my birth partner? Would you like to be present at the birth of our child?'

He stilled.

'If you want to think about it—'

'I don't need to think about it.' Wonder filled his face. 'Yes, Meg. Yes. A thousand times yes.'

Finally she found she could smile again. What was a round-the-world yacht voyage compared to seeing his own child born? Behind her back, she crossed her fingers.

* * *

'Megan, I'm marrying Elsie because I care about her.' Laurie Parrish lifted his chin. 'Because I love her.'

Meg glanced up from fussing with her dress. In ten minutes he and she would walk out into the garden to meet Elsie and Ben and the ceremony would begin.

'I never doubted it for a moment.' She hesitated, and then leant across and took the liberty of straightening his tie.

He took her hand before she could move away again. 'Before I embark on my new life I want to apologise to you and acknowledge that I haven't been much of a father to you. I can't…' His voice grew gruff. 'I can't tell you how much I regret that.'

She stared at him and finally nodded. It was why he'd given her the house. She'd always sensed that. But it was nice to hear him acknowledge it out loud too. 'Okay, Dad, apology accepted.'

She tried to disengage her hand, but he refused to release it. 'I'm also aware that an apology and an expression of regret doesn't mean that we're suddenly going to have a great relationship.'

She blinked. *Wow!*

'But if it would be okay with you, if it won't make you uncomfortable or unhappy, I would like to try and build a relationship—a good, solid relationship—with you.'

Her initial scepticism turned to all-out shock.

'Would you have a problem with that?'

Slowly, she shook her head. She had absolutely no problem with that. It would be wonderful for her child to have grandparents who loved it, who wanted to be involved. Only…

She straightened. 'I'll need you to be a bit more enthusiastic and engaged. Not just in my life but in your own too.' She would need him to make some of the running instead of leaving it all up to her. But if he truly meant it…

Her heart lifted and the resentment that had built inside her these last few months started to abate. Unlike Ben, bitterness and anger hadn't crippled her during her teenage years. Sadness and yearning had. She couldn't erase that sadness and yearning now, and nor could her father. Nobody could. They would never get back those lost years, but she was willing to put effort into the future.

'Giving me the house was your way of saying sorry and trying to make amends, wasn't it?'

He nodded. 'I wanted your future secure. It seemed the least I could do.'

His admission touched her.

'But moving out of this house brought me to my senses about Elsie too. Missing her made me realise what she'd come to mean to me.'

So that had been the trigger—an illness, a recuperation, and then a change of address. Evidently romance worked in mysterious ways.

'I know this isn't going to change anything, Megan, but when you were growing up I thought you were spending so much time at Elsie's because she'd become a kind of surrogate mother to you. When I was recovering from my illness and Elsie was coming over to sit with me, I found out she'd thought Ben was spending that time here because I was providing the role of surrogate father. With each of us thinking that...' He pressed his fingers to his eyes. 'We just let things slide along the way they were.'

If they'd known differently, would he and Elsie have roused themselves from their depression? It was something they'd never know now.

She squeezed his hand. 'I think it's time to put the past behind us.' And as she said the words she realised she meant them. She had a baby on the way. She wanted to look towards the future, not back to the past.

'C'mon, I think it's time.'

'Is Ben going to do the right thing by you and the baby?'

She and Ben hadn't told a soul that he was the baby's father.

But her father and Elsie weren't stupid or blind. She pulled in a breath. 'Yes, he will. He always does what's best for me.'

She just wished she knew if that meant he was staying or if he was going. 'You have to understand, though, that what you think is best and what Ben and I think is best may be two very different things.' She didn't want the older couple hassling Ben, pressuring him.

'I understand.' Her father nodded heavily. 'I have no right to interfere. I just want to see you happy, Megan.'

'No,' she agreed, 'you're *not* allowed to interfere.' She took his arm and squeezed it. 'But you are allowed to care.'

She smiled up at him. He smiled back. 'C'mon—let's go get you married and then celebrate in style.'

The moment Meg stepped into the rose garden with her father Ben couldn't take his eyes from her.

'Are they there yet?' Elsie asked, her voice fretful, her fingers tapping against the kitchen table. 'They're late.'

He snapped to. 'They're exactly on time.' He kept his eyes on Meg for as long as he could as he backed away from the window. Swallowing, he turned to find Elsie alternately plucking at her skirt, her flowers and her hair. It was good to know she wasn't as cool and calm as she appeared or wanted everyone to think. 'Ready?'

She nodded. She looked lovelier than he'd ever seen her. He thought about what Meg would want him to say at this moment. 'Elsie?'

She glanced up at him.

'Mr Parrish is a very lucky man.'

'Oh!' Her cheeks turned pink.

He suddenly grinned. 'I expect he's going to take one look at you and want to drag you away from the celebrations at an indecently early hour.'

Her cheeks turned even redder and she pressed her hands

to them. The she reached out and swatted him with her bouquet. 'Don't talk such nonsense, Ben!'

He tucked her hand into the crock of his arm and led her through the house and out through the front door. 'It's not nonsense. Just you wait.'

Ben had meant to watch for the expression on Laurie's face the first moment he glimpsed Elsie, but one sidelong glance at Meg and Ben's attention was lost. Perspiration prickled his nape. He couldn't drag his gaze away.

Meg wore a deep purplish-blue dress, and in the sun it gleamed like a jewel. She stood there erect and proud, with her gently rounded stomach, looking out-of-this-world desirable. Like a Grecian goddess. He stared at her bare shoulders and all he could think of was pressing kisses to the beckoning golden skin. He could imagine their satin sun-kissed warmth. He sucked air into oxygen-starved lungs. A raging thirst built inside him.

A diamante brooch gathered the material of the dress between her breasts. Filmy material floated in the breeze and drifted down to her ankles. She'd be wearing sexy sandals and he wanted to look, really he did, but he found it impossible to drag his gaze from the lush curves of her breasts.

He moistened his lips. His heart thumped against his ribcage. His skin started to burn. Meg's dress did nothing to hide her new curves. Curves he could imagine in intimate detail—their softness, their weight in his hands, the way her nipples would peak under his hungry gaze as they were doing now. He imagined how they'd tauten further as he ran a thumb back and forth across them, the taste of them and their texture as he—

For Pete's sake!

He wrenched his gaze away, his mouth dry. A halfway decent guy did *not* turn his best friend into an object of lust. A halfway decent guy would not let her think even for a single second that there could ever be anything more between them than friendship.

He did his best to keep his gaze averted from all her golden promise, tried to focus on the ceremony. He wasn't equal to the task—not even when Elsie and Laurie surprised everyone by revealing they'd written their own vows. He was too busy concentrating on not staring at Meg, on not lusting after her, to catch what those vows were.

A quick glance at Meg—a super-quick glance—told him they'd been touching. Her eyes had grown bright with unshed tears, her smile soft, and her lips—

He dragged his gaze away again, his pulse thundering in his ears.

It seemed to take a hundred years, but finally Elsie and Laurie were pronounced husband and wife. And then Laurie kissed Elsie in a way that didn't help the pressure building in Ben's gut. There were cheers and congratulations all round. Four of Meg's girlfriends threw glittery confetti in the air. Gold and silver spangles settled in Meg's hair, on her cheek and shoulders, and one landed on the skin of her chest just above her—

He jerked his gaze heavenward.

Meg broke away from the group surrounding the newlyweds to slip her arm through his. 'We're going to have a ten-minute photoshoot with the photographer, and then it'll be party time.'

There was a photographer? He glanced around. He hadn't captured the way Ben had been ogling Meg, had he? Please, God.

'You scrub up real nice, Ben Sullivan.' She squeezed his arm. 'I don't think I've seen you in a suit since you stepped in to take me to my high school formal when Jason Prior dumped me to partner Rochelle Collins instead.'

He'd stepped in as a friend back then. He needed to find that same frame of mind, that same outlook, quick-smart.

Minus the kiss that had happened that night!

He dragged in a breath.

Don't think about it.

He'd been a sex-starved teenager back then, that's all.

And Meg had been beautiful.

She's more beautiful now.

'But I don't remember you filling out a suit half so well back then.'

He closed his eyes. Not just at her words, but at the husky tone in which they were uttered. The last thing he needed right now was for Meg to start feeling sexy. At least she had an excuse—pregnancy hormones. Him? He was just low life scum.

If he kissed Meg again it wouldn't stop at kisses. They both knew that. But one night would never be enough for Meg. And two nights was one night too many as far as he was concerned.

It would wreck their friendship. He couldn't risk that—not now they had a child to consider.

'You okay?'

He steeled himself and then glanced down. Her brow had creased, her eyes were wary. He swallowed and nodded.

She gestured towards the newlyweds. 'The service was lovely.'

'Yep.'

His tie tightened about his throat. Please God, don't let her ask him anything specific. He couldn't remember a damn thing about the ceremony.

She smiled, wide and broad. 'I have a good feeling about all of this.'

Just for a moment that made him smile too. 'Pollyanna,' he teased.

Her eyes danced, her lips shone, and hunger stretched through him.

If I lost your friendship, I don't know what I would do.

He swallowed the bile that burned his throat. He couldn't think of anything worse than losing Meg's friendship.

And yet...

He clenched his hands. Yet it wasn't enough to dampen his rising desire to seduce her.

Something in his face must have betrayed him because she

snapped away from him, pulling her arm from his. 'Stop looking at me like that!'

The colour had grown high in her cheeks. Her eyes blazed. Neither of those things dampened his libido. That said, he wasn't sure a slap to the face or a cold shower would have much of an effect either.

'Darn it, Ben. I should have known this was how you'd react to the wedding.'

She kept her voice low—bedroom-low—and—

He cut the thought off and tried to focus on her words. 'What are you talking about?'

'All this hearts and flowers stuff has made you want to beat your chest and revert to your usual caveman tactics just to prove you're not affected. That you're immune.'

'Caveman?' he spluttered. 'I'll have you know I have more finesse than that.'

They glared at each other.

'Besides, you're underestimating yourself.' He scowled. 'You look great in that dress.' With a superhuman effort he managed to maintain eye contact and slowly the tension between them lessened. 'Can we get these photos underway?' he growled.

He needed to be away from Meg asap with an ice-cold beer in his hand.

The reception went without a hitch.

The food was great. The music was great. The company was great. The speech Laurie made thanking Meg and Ben for the wedding and admitting what a lucky man he was, admitting that he'd found a new lease of life, touched even Ben.

The reception went without a hitch except throughout it all Ben was far too aware of Meg. Of the way she moved, the sound of her laughter, the warmth she gave out to all those around her. Of the sultry way she moved on the dance floor. He scowled. She certainly hadn't lacked for dance partners.

He'd made sure that he'd danced too. There were several beautiful women here, and three months ago he'd have done his best to hook up with one of them—go for a drink somewhere and then back to her place afterwards. It seemed like a damn fine plan except...

I don't like the way you treat women.

He'd stopped dancing after that.

His gaze lowered to the rounded curve of Meg's stomach and his throat tightened.

'Hey, buddy!' A clap on the shoulder brought him back.

Ben turned and then stood to shake hands. 'Dave, mate—great to see you here. Meg said you were coming. Have a seat.'

They sat and Dave surveyed him. 'It's been a great night.'

'Yeah.'

'Meg's told me what a help you've been with the wedding prep.'

She had? He shrugged. 'It was nothing.'

Dave glanced at Meg on the dance floor. 'That's not how she sees it.'

He bit back a groan. The last thing he needed was someone admiring Meg when he was doing his damnedest to concentrate on doing anything but.

Dave shifted on his chair to face him more fully. 'Something has popped up in my portfolio that I think will interest you.'

Anything that could keep his mind off Meg for any length of time was a welcome distraction. 'Tell me more.'

'If you want it, I can get you on the crew for a yacht that's setting off around the world. It leaves the week after next and expects to be gone five months.' He shrugged and sat back. 'I know it's something you've always wanted to do.'

Ben stared at the other man and waited for the rush of anticipation to hit him. This was something he'd always wanted—the last challenge on his adventure list. It would kill him to turn it down, but...

He waited and waited.

And kept right on waiting.

The anticipation didn't come. In fact he could barely manage a flicker of interest. He frowned and straightened.

'Mate, I appreciate the offer but...' His eyes sought out Meg on the dance floor, lowered to her baby bump. 'I have bigger fish to fry at the moment.'

Dave shrugged. 'Fair enough. I just wanted to run it by you.'

'And I appreciate it.' But what he wanted and who he was had crystallised in his mind in sharp relief. He was going to be a father and he wanted to be a *good* father—the best.

Dave clapped him on the back. 'I'll catch you later, Ben. It's time to drag that gorgeous wife of mine onto the dance floor.'

Ben waved in absent acknowledgment. A smile grew inside him. He was going to be a father. Nothing could shake him from wanting to be the best one he could be. His new sense of purpose held far more power than his old dreams ever had.

Her father and Elsie left at a relatively early hour, but the party in Meg's garden continued into the night. She danced with her girlfriends and made sure she spoke to everyone.

Everyone, that was, except Ben.

She stayed away from Ben. Tonight he was just too potent. He wore some gorgeous subtle aftershave that made her think of Omar Sharif and harems, but it didn't completely mask the scent of leather and whisky either, and the combination made her head whirl.

Some instinct warned her that if she gave in to the temptation he represented tonight she'd be lost.

'Meg?' Dave touched her arm and she blinked herself back inside the marquee. 'Winnie and I are heading off, but thanks for a great party. We had a ball.'

'I'm glad you enjoyed yourselves. I'll see you out.'

'No need.'

'Believe me, the fresh air will do me good.'

Keeping busy was the answer. Not remembering the way

Ben's eyes had practically devoured her earlier was key too. She swallowed. When he looked at her the way a man looked at a woman he found desirable he skyrocketed her temperature and had her pulse racing off the chart. He made her want to do wild reckless things.

She couldn't do wild and reckless things. She was about to become a mother.

And when he didn't look at her like that, when he gazed at her baby bump with his heart in his eyes—oh, it made her wish for other things. It made her wish they could be a family—a proper family.

But of course that way madness lay. And a broken heart.

She led Dave and Winnie through the rose garden, concentrating on keeping both her temperature and her pulse at even, moderate levels.

Just before they reached the front yard Dave said, 'I made Ben that offer you and I spoke about a while back.'

She stumbled to a halt. Her heart lurched. She had to lock her knees to stop herself from dropping to the ground. 'And…?' Her heart beat against her ribs.

'And I turned it down,' a voice drawled from behind her.

She swung around. *Ben!* And the way his eyes glittered dangerously in the moonlight told her he was less than impressed. She swallowed. In fact he looked downright furious.

'Have I caused any trouble?' Dave murmured.

'Not at all,' she denied, unable to keep the strain from her voice.

Winnie took her husband's arm. 'Thank you both for a lovely evening.' With a quick goodnight, the other couple beat a hasty retreat.

Meg swallowed and turned back to Ben. 'I…'

He raised an eyebrow and folded his arms. 'You can explain, right?'

Could she?

'Another test?' he spat out.

She nodded.

'My word wasn't good enough?'

It should've been, but…' She moistened suddenly parched lips. 'I wanted a guarantee,' she whispered.

He stabbed a finger at her. 'You of all people should know there's no such thing.'

Her heart beat like a panicked animal when he wheeled away from her. 'Please, Ben—'

He swung back. 'What exactly are you most afraid of, Meg? That I'll leave or that I'll stay?'

Then it hit her.

'Oh!'

She took a step away from him. The lock on her knees gave out and she plumped down to the soft grass in a tangle of satin and chiffon. She covered her mouth with one hand as she stared up at him.

Leaving. She was afraid of him leaving. Deathly afraid. Deep-down-in-her-bones afraid.

Break-her-heart afraid.

Because she'd gone and done the unthinkable—she'd fallen in love with Ben.

She'd fallen in love with her best friend. A man who didn't believe in love and marriage or commitment to any woman. She'd fallen in love with him and she didn't want him to leave. And yet by staying he would break her heart afresh every single day of her life to come.

And she would have to bear it.

Because Ben staying was what would be best for their baby.

CHAPTER ELEVEN

WITH HER DRESS mushroomed around her, her hair done up in a pretty knot and her golden shoulders drooping, Meg reminded Ben of a delicate orchid he'd once seen in a rainforest far from civilisation.

He swooped down and drew her back to her feet, his heart clenching at her expression. 'Don't look like that, Meg. We'll sort it out. I didn't mean to yell.'

He'd do anything to stop her from looking like that—as if the world had come to an end, as if there was no joy and laughter, dancing and champagne, warm summer nights and lazy kisses left in the world. As if all those things had been taken away from her.

'Meg?'

Finally she glanced up. He had to suck in a breath. Her pain burned a hole though his chest and thickened his throat. He dragged in a breath and blinked hard.

She lifted her chin and very gently moved out of his grasp. The abyss inside him grew.

'I'm sorry, Ben. What I asked Dave to do was unfair. I thought it would prove one way or the other whether you were ready for fatherhood.'

'I know you're worried. I can repeat over and over that I'm committed to all of this, but I know that won't allay your fears.' And he was sorrier than he could say about that.

'No.' She twisted her hands together. 'You've never lied to

me before. It shows an ungenerosity of spirit to keep testing you as I've done. Your word should be good enough for me. And it is. I do believe you. I do believe you'll stay.'

He eyed her for a moment. He wanted her to stop whipping herself into such a frenzy of guilt. This situation was so new to both of them. 'You don't need to apologise. You're trying to do what's best for the baby. There's no shame in that. Let's forget all about it— move forward and—'

'Forget about it? Ben, I *hurt* you! I can't tell you how sorry I am.'

She didn't have to. He could see it in her face.

'I let you down and I'm sorry.'

And how many times had he let *her* down over the years? Leaving her to deal with Laurie and Elsie on her own, expecting her to drop everything when he came home for a few days here and there, not ringing for her birthday.

'Although I don't think it's necessary, apology accepted.'

'Thank you.'

She smiled, but it didn't dispel the shadows in her eyes or the lines of strain about her mouth. His stomach dropped. *If I ever lost your friendship.* His hands clenched. It wouldn't happen. He wouldn't let it happen.

Music and laughter drifted down to them from the marquee. The lights spilling from it were festive and cheerful. Out here where he and Meg stood cloaked in the shadows of the garden, it was cool and the festivities seemed almost out of reach.

He swallowed and shifted his weight. 'You want to tell me what else is wrong?'

She glanced at him; took a step back. 'There's nothing.'

Acid filled his mouth. 'Don't lie to me, Meg.'

She glanced away. With her face in profile, her loveliness made his jaw ache. He stared at her, willing her to trust him, to share what troubled her so he could make it better. She was so lovely…and hurting so badly. He wanted—*needed*—to make things right for her.

She took another step away from him. 'Some things are better left unspoken.'

He wasn't having that. He took her arm and led her to a garden bench in the front yard. 'No more secrets, Meg. Full disclosure. We need to be completely open about anything that will affect our dealings with each other and the baby.' He leaned towards her. 'We're friends. Best friends. We can sort this out.'

She closed her eyes, her brow wrinkling and her breath catching.

'I promise we can get through anything.' He tried to impart his certainty to her, wanting it to buck her up and bring the colour back to her cheeks, the sparkle to her eyes. 'We really can.'

She opened her eyes and gazed out at the bay spread below them. 'If I share this particular truth with you, Ben, it will freak you out. It will freak you out more than anything I've ever said to you before. If I tell you, you will get up and walk out into the night without letting me finish, and I don't think I could stand that.'

She turned and met his gaze then and his stomach lurched. Some innate sense of self-preservation warned him to get up now and leave. Not just to walk away, but to run. He ignored it. This was Meg. She needed him. He would not let her down.

'I promise you I will not leave until the conversation has run its course.' His voice came out hoarse. 'I promise.'

Her face softened. 'You don't know how hard that promise will be to keep.'

'Another test, Meg?'

'No.'

She shook her head and he believed her.

Her hands twisted together in her lap. She glanced at him, glanced away, glanced down at her hands. 'I love you, Ben.'

'I love you too.' She had to know how much she meant to him.

She closed her eyes briefly before meeting his gaze again. She shook her head gently. 'I mean I've fallen in love with you.'

The words didn't make sense. He stared, unable to move.

'Actually, fallen is a rather apt description, because the sensation is far from comfortable.'

He snapped back, away from her. *I've fallen in love with you.* No! She—

'I didn't mean for it to happen. If I could make it unhappen I would. But I can't.'

'No!' He shot to his feet. He paced away from her, then remembered his promise and strode back. He thrust a finger at her. *'No!'*

She stared back at him with big, wounded eyes. She chafed her arms. He slipped his jacket off and settled it around her shoulders before falling back on the seat beside her.

'Why?' he finally croaked. He'd done his best to maintain a civilised distance ever since that kiss.

'I know.' She sighed. 'It should never have happened.'

Except...that kiss! That damn kiss on the beach. In the moonlight, no less. A moment of magic that neither one of them could forget, but...

'Maybe it's just pregnancy hormones?'

She pulled his jacket about her more tightly. 'That's what I've been telling myself, trying to will myself to believe. But I can't hide behind that as an excuse any longer.'

'Maybe it's just lust?'

She was silent for a long moment. 'Despite what you think, Ben, you have a lot more to offer a woman than just sex. I've been almost the sole focus of your attention this last month and a half and it's been addictive. But it's not just that. You've risen to every challenge I've thrown your way. You've been patient, understanding and kind. You've tried to make things easier for me. And I can see how much you already care for our child. You have amazed me, Ben, and I think you're amazing.'

His heart thumped against his ribs. If this were a movie he'd take her in his arms right now and declare his undying love. But this wasn't a movie. It was him and Meg on a garden bench. It was a nightmare!

His tie tightened about his throat. His mouth dried. He swallowed with difficulty. He might not be able to declare his undying love to her, but he could do the right thing by her.

'Would you like us to get married?'

'No!'

Ordinarily her horror would have made him laugh. He rolled his shoulders and frowned. 'Why not? I thought you said you love me?' Wasn't marriage and babies what women wanted?

'Too much to trap you into marriage! God, Ben, I know how you feel about marriage. The crazy thing is I would turn my nice, safe world upside down if it would make any difference. I'd follow you on your round-the-world yacht voyage, wait in some small village in Bhutan while you scaled a mountain, go with you on safari into deepest darkest Africa. But I know none of those things will make a difference. And, honestly, how happy do you think either one of us would be—you feeling trapped and suffocated and me knowing I'd made you feel that way?' She shook her head. 'A thousand times no.'

He rested his elbows on his knees and his head in his hands. His heart thudded in a sickening slow-quick rhythm in his chest. 'Would you like me to leave town? It'll be easier if you don't have to see me every day.'

'I expect you're right.'

He closed his eyes.

'But while that might be best for me, it's not what's best for the baby. Our baby's life will be significantly richer for having you as its father. So, no, Ben, I don't want you to leave.'

He stared. She'd told him he was amazing, but she was the amazing one. For a moment he couldn't speak. Eventually he managed to clear his throat. 'I don't know how to make things better or easier for you.'

She glanced down at her hands. 'For a start you can promise not to hate me for having made a hash of this, for changing things between us so significantly.'

He thrust his shoulders back. 'I will never hate you.' He and Meg were different from his parents. He lifted his chin. They would get their friendship back on track eventually.

'I expect I'll get over it sooner or later. I mean, people do, don't they?'

It had taken her father twenty years. He swallowed and nodded.

She turned to him. 'It's four months before the baby is due. Can we...? Can we have a time-out till then?'

She wanted him to stop coming round? She didn't want to see him for four months? He swallowed. It would be no different from setting off on one of his adventure tours. So why did darkness descend all around him? He wanted to rail and yell. But not at Meg.

He rose to his feet. 'I'll go play host for the rest of the evening. I'll help with the clean-up tomorrow and then I'll lock Elsie's house up and go.'

'I'm sorry,' she whispered.

'No need.'

'Thank you.'

He tried to say *you're welcome*, but he couldn't push the words out. 'If you want to retire for the night I'll take care of everything out here.'

'I'll take you up on that.'

She handed him back his jacket, not meeting his eyes, and his heart burned. She turned and strode towards the house. He watched her walk away and it felt as if all the lights had gone out in his world.

Ben moved into a unit in Nelson Bay. He should have moved further away—to the metropolis of Newcastle, an hour away and an easy enough commute—but he couldn't stand the thought of being that far from Meg. What if she needed help?

What if she needed something done before the baby came? She knew he was only a phone call or an e-mail away.

When he'd told her as much the day after the wedding she'd nodded and thanked him. And then she'd made him promise neither to ring nor e-mail her—not to contact her at all. He'd barely recognised the woman who'd asked that of him.

'It shouldn't be that hard,' she'd chided at whatever she'd seen in his face. 'In the past you've disappeared for months on end without so much as a phone call between visits.'

It was true.

But this time he didn't have the distraction of the next great adventure between him and home. Was this how Meg had felt when he'd left for each new trip? Worried about his safety and concerned for his health?

Always wondering if he were happy or not?

He threw himself into preparations for the big things he had planned for his future—things he'd only hinted to Meg about. Plans that would cement his financial future, and his child's, and integrate him into the community in Port Stephens.

But somewhere along the way his buzz and excitement had waned. When he couldn't share them with Meg, those plans didn't seem so big, or so bright and shining. He'd never re-alised how much he'd counted on her or how her friendship had kept him anchored.

Damn it all! She'd gone and wrecked everything—changed the rules and ruined a perfectly good friendship for something as stupid and ephemeral as love.

On the weekends he went out to nightclubs. He drank too much and searched for a woman to take his mind off Meg—a temporary respite, an attempt to get some balance back in his life. It didn't work.

I don't like the way you treat women.

Whenever he looked at a woman now, instead of good-time sass all he saw was vulnerability. He left the clubs early and returned home alone.

'Oh, you have it bad all right,' Dave laughed as they shared a beer one afternoon, a month after Ben had moved into his apartment in Nelson Bay.

Ben scowled. 'What are you talking about?' He'd hoped a beer with his friend would drag his mind from its worry about Meg and move it to more sensible and constructive areas, like fishing and boating.

'Mate, you can't be that clueless.'

He took a swig of his beer. 'I have no idea what you're talking about.' Did Dave think he was pining for greener pastures and new adventures? He shook his head. 'You've got it wrong. I'm happy to be back in Port Stephens, and I appreciate all your help over these last couple of months.'

Dave had tipped Ben off about a local eco-tourism adventure company that had come up for tender. There'd been several companies Ben had considered, but this one had ticked all the boxes. Contracts would be exchanged this coming week.

'This new direction I'm moving in is really exciting. I want to expand the range of tours offered, which means hiring new people.' He shrugged. 'But I've a lot of connections in the industry.' He meant to make his company the best. 'These are exciting times.'

Dave leant back. 'Then why aren't you erupting with enthusiasm? Why aren't you detailing every tour you mean to offer in minute detail to me this very minute and telling me how brilliant it's all going to be?'

Ben rolled his shoulders. 'I don't want to bore you.'

'Oh? And sitting there with a scowl on your face barely grunting at anything I say is designed to be entertaining, is it?'

His jaw dropped. 'I…' Was that what he'd been doing?

Dave leaned towards him. 'Listen, ever since you and Meg had that falling-out you've been moping around as if the world has come to an end.'

'I have not.'

Dave raised an eyebrow.

He thrust out his jaw. 'How many times do I have to tell you? We did not have a falling out.'

Dave eyed him over his beer. 'The two of you can't keep going on like this, you know? You have a baby on the way.'

Ben's head snapped back.

'It *is* yours, isn't it?' Dave said, his eyes serious.

Ben hesitated and then nodded.

'You need to sort it out.'

Ben stared down into his beer. The problem was they had sorted it out and this was the solution. He'd do what Meg needed him to do. Even if it killed him.

'Look, why don't you take the lady flowers and chocolates and just tell her you love her?'

Liquid sloshed over the sides of Ben's glass. 'I don't love her!' He slammed his glass to the table.

'Really?' Dave drawled. 'You're doing a damn fine impression of it, moping around like a lovesick idiot.'

'Remind me,' he growled. 'We *are* supposed to be mates, right?'

Dave ignored him. 'I saw the way you looked at her at the wedding. You could barely drag your eyes from her.'

'That's just lust.' Even now her image fevered his dreams, had him waking in tangled sheets with an ache pulsing at his groin. It made him feel guilty, thinking about Meg that way, but it didn't make the ache go away.

Dave sat back. 'If it were any other woman I'd agree with you, but this is Meg we're talking about. Meg has never been just another woman to you.'

Ben slumped back.

'Tell me—when have you ever obsessed about a woman the way you've been obsessing about Meg?'

She was the mother of his child. She was his best friend. Of course he was concerned about her.

'Never, right?'

Bingo. But...

The beer garden spun.

And then everything stilled.

Bingo.

He stared at Dave, unable to utter a word. Dave drained the rest of his beer and clapped him on the shoulder. 'I'm off home to the wife and kiddies. You take care, Ben. We'll catch up again soon.'

Ben lifted a hand in acknowledgement, but all the time his mind whirled.

In love with Meg? *Him?*

It all finally fell into place.

Piece by glorious piece.

Him and Meg.

He shoved away from the table and raced out into the mid-afternoon sunshine. He powered down the arcade and marched into the nearest gourmet food shop.

'Can I help you, sir?'

'I'm after a box of chocolates. Your best chocolates.'

The sales assistant picked up a box. 'One can't go past Belgian, sir.'

He surveyed it. 'Do you have something bigger?'

'We have three sizes and—'

'I'll take the biggest box you have.'

It was huge. Tucking it under his arm, he strode into the florist across the way. He stared in bewilderment at bucket upon bucket of choice. So many different kinds of flowers...

'Good afternoon, son, what can I get for you?'

'Uh...I want some flowers.'

'What kind of flowers, laddie? You'll need to be more specific.'

'Something bright and cheerful. And beautiful.' Just like Meg.

'These gerberas are in their prime.'

The florist pointed to a bucket. The flowers were stunning in their vibrancy. Ben nodded. 'Perfect.'

He frowned, though, when the florist extracted a bunch. They seemed a little paltry. The florist eyed him for a moment. 'Perhaps you'd prefer two bunches?'

Ben's face unclouded. 'I'll take all of them.'

'All six bunches, laddie?'

He nodded and thrust money at the man—impatient to be away, impatient to be with Meg. He caught sight of a purple orchid by the till that brought him up short. A perfectly formed orchid that was beautiful in its fragility—its form, its colour and even its shape. It reminded him vividly of Meg on the night of the wedding.

He'd been such an idiot. He'd offered to marry her when he'd thought marriage was the last thing he wanted. He'd acknowledged that he and she were not his mother and father—their relationship would never descend to that kind of hatred and bitterness. He'd faced two of his biggest demons—for Meg— and still he hadn't made the connection.

Idiot!

Meg brought out the best in him, not the worst. She made him want to be a better man. All he could do was pray he hadn't left it too late.

The florist handed him the orchid, a gentle smile lighting his weathered face. 'On the house, sonny.'

Ben thanked him, collected up the armful of flowers and strode back in the direction of his car. His feet slowed as he passed an ice cream shop. Meg couldn't eat prawns or Camembert or salami, but she could have ice cream.

He strode inside and ordered a family-size tub of their finest. His arms were so full he had to ask the salesgirl to fish the money out of his jacket pocket. She put the tub of ice cream in a carrier bag and carefully hooked it around his free fingers.

She placed his change into his jacket pocket. 'She's a lucky lady.'

He shook his head. 'If I can pull this off, I'll be the lucky one.' He strode to his car, his stomach churning.

If he could pull this off. *If.*

He closed his eyes. *Please, God.*

CHAPTER TWELVE

MEG HEAVED A sigh and pulled yet more lids from the back of her kitchen cupboard. From her spot on the floor she could see there were still more in there. She had an assortment of lids that just didn't seem to belong to anything else she owned. She'd tossed another lid on the 'to-be-identified-and-hopefully-part-nered-up' pile when the doorbell rang.

She considered ignoring it, but with a quick shake of her head she rolled to her knees and lumbered upright. She would not turn into her father. She would not let heartbreak turn her into a hermit.

Pushing her hands into the small of her back, she started for the door. Sorting cupboards hadn't induced an early nesting instinct in her as she'd hoped—hadn't distracted her from the hole that had opened up in her world. A hole once filled by Ben.

Stop it!

Company—perhaps that would do the trick?

She opened the door with a ready smile, more than willing to be distracted by whoever might be on the other side, and then blinked at the blaze of colour that greeted her. Flowers almost completely obscured the person holding them. Flowers in every colour. Beautiful flowers.

Then she recognised the legs beneath all those flowers. And the scent of leather and whisky hit her, playing havoc with her senses.

That was definitely distracting.

Her pulse kicked. Her skin tingled. She swallowed. This kind of distraction had to be bad for her. *Very* bad.

She swallowed again. 'Ben?'

'Hey, Meg.'

And she couldn't help it. Her lips started to twitch. It probably had something to do with the surge of giddy joy the very sight of him sent spinning through her.

'Let me guess—you're opening a florist shop?'

'They're for you.'

For *her*? Her smile faded. An awkward pause opened up between them. Ben shuffled his feet. 'Take pity on a guy, won't you, Meg, and grab an armful?'

It was better than standing there like a landed fish. She moved forward and took several bunches of flowers out of his arms, burying her face in them in an attempt to drown out the much more beguiling scent of her best friend.

She led the way through to the kitchen and set the flowers in the sink, before taking the rest of the flowers from Ben and setting them in the sink too.

'Careful,' she murmured, pointing to the stacks of plastic containers littering the floor.

Every skin cell she possessed ached, screaming for her to throw herself into his arms. Her fingers tingled with the need to touch him. Ben had hugged her more times than she could count. He wouldn't protest if she hugged him now.

Her mouth dried. Her throat ached. The pulse points in her neck, her wrists, her ankles all throbbed.

She couldn't hug him. She wouldn't be hugging him as her best friend. She'd be hugging him as her dearest, darling Ben—the man she was in love with, the man she wanted to get downright dirty and naked with.

And he'd…

She closed her eyes. 'What are you doing here, Ben?'

When she opened them again she found him holding out a box of chocolates. 'For you.'

His voice came out low. The air between them crackled and sparked.

Or was that just her?

She took the chocolates in a daze. 'I...' She moistened her lips. 'Thank you.'

A silence stretched between them. She wanted to stare and stare at him, drink in her fill, but she wouldn't be able to keep the hunger from her eyes if she did. And she didn't want him to witness that. She didn't want his pity.

He started, and then held out a bag. 'I remembered you said you'd had a craving for ice cream.'

She set the chocolates on the bench and reached for the ice cream with both hands, her mouth watering at the label on the carrier bag—it bore the name of her favourite ice cream shop.

'What flavour?'

'Passionfruit ripple.'

He'd remembered.

She seized two spoons from the cutlery drawer, pulled off the lid and tucked straight in. She closed her eyes in bliss at the first mouthful. 'Oh, man, this is good.'

When she opened her eyes again she found him eyeing her hungrily, as if he wanted to devour her in exactly the same way she was devouring the ice cream.

She shook herself and swallowed. Maybe he did, but that didn't change anything between them. Sleeping with Ben wouldn't make him miraculously fall in love with her. Worst luck.

She pushed a spoon towards him. 'Tuck in.'

He didn't move. Standing so close to him was too much torture. She picked up the ice cream tub and moved to the kitchen table.

He'd brought her flowers. He'd brought her chocolates. And he'd brought her ice cream.

She sat. 'So, what's the sting in the tail?'

He started. 'What do you mean?'

She gestured. 'You've brought me the sweeteners, so what is it that needs sweetening?'

Her appetite promptly fled. She laid her spoon down. Was he leaving? Had he come to say goodbye?

She entertained that thought for all of five seconds before dismissing it. Ben wanted to be a part of their baby's life. He had no intention of running away.

She went to pick her spoon up again and then stopped. There was still another three months before the baby was due. Maybe he was leaving Port Stephens until then.

It shouldn't matter. After all, she hadn't clapped eyes on him for almost a month.

She deliberately unclenched her hands. *Get over yourself.* He'd only be a phone call away if she should need him.

Need him? She ached for him with every fibre of her being. And seeing him like this was too hard. She wanted to yell at him to go away, but the shadows beneath his eyes and the gaunt line of his cheeks stopped her.

She picked up her spoon and hoed back into her ice cream. She gestured with what she dearly hoped was a semblance of nonchalance to the chair opposite and drawled, 'Any time you'd like to join the party...'

He sat.

He fidgeted.

He jumped back up and put all the flowers into vases. She doggedly kept eating ice cream. It was delicious. At least she was pretty sure it was delicious. When he came back to the table, though, it was impossible to eat. The tension rose between them with every breath.

She set her spoon down, stared at all the flowers lined up on the kitchen bench, at the enormous box of chocolates—Belgian, no less—and then at the tub of ice cream. Her shoulders slumped. What did he have to tell her that could be so bad he needed to give her all these gifts first?

Flowers and chocolates—gifts for lovers. She brushed a hand across her eyes. Didn't he know what he was doing to her?

'I've missed you, Meg.'

And his voice...

'I needed to see you.'

She shoved her shoulders back. 'I thought we had an agreement?' He was supposed to stay away.

Was this a fight she would ever win? Her fingers shook as she pressed them to her temples. Would she ever stop needing to breathe him in, to feast her eyes on him, to wipe those haunted shadows from his eyes?

I love you!

Why couldn't that be enough?

She dragged her hands down into her lap and clenched them. 'Why?'

She might not be able to harden her heart against him, but she could make sure they didn't draw this interview out any longer than necessary.

'I realised something this afternoon.' The pulse at the base of his jaw pounded. 'And once I did I had to see you as soon as I could.'

Her heart slammed against her ribs. Just looking at him made a pulse start to throb inside her. She folded her arms. 'Are you going to enlighten me?'

He stared at her as if at an utter loss. 'I...uh...' He moistened his lips. 'I realised that I love you. That I'm *in love* with you.'

Three beats passed. Bam. Bam. Bam.

And then what he'd said collided with her grey matter. She shoved her chair back and wheeled away from him.

Typical! Ben had missed her and panicked. She got that. But in love with her? Fat chance!

She spun back and folded her arms. 'The Ben I know wouldn't have stopped to get flowers and chocolates if he'd had an epiphany like that. He'd have raced straight over here and blurted it out on the front doorstep the moment I opened the door.'

'Yeah, well, the guy I thought I was wouldn't have believed any of this possible.' He shot to his feet, his chair crashing to the floor behind him. 'The guy I thought I was didn't believe in love. The guy I thought I was would never have thought he could feel so awkward and at a loss around you, Meg!'

Her jaw dropped. She hitched it back up. 'None of that means you're in love with me. I accept that you miss me, but—'

'Then how about this?'

He strode around the table and shoved a finger under her nose. His scent slugged into her, swirling around her, playing havoc with her senses, playing havoc with her ability to remain upright.

'For the last month all I've been able to think about is you. I'm worried that you're hurting. I'm worried you're not eating properly and that you're working too hard. I'm worried there's no one around to make you laugh and to stop you from taking the world and yourself too seriously. Every waking moment,' he growled.

He planted his hands on his hips and started to pace. 'And then I worry that you might've found someone who makes you laugh and forget your troubles.' He wheeled back to her. 'Are you dating anyone?'

He all but shouted the question at her. For the first time a tiny ray broke through all her doubts. She tried to dispel it. This was about the baby, not her.

'Ben, no other man will ever take your place in our child's affections.'

'This isn't about the baby!' He paced harder. 'Every waking moment,' he growled. He spun and glared at her. 'And then, when I try to go to sleep, you plague my dreams. And, Meg—' He broke off with a low, mirthless laugh. 'The things I dream of doing to you—well, you don't want to know.'

Ooh, yes, she did.

'For these last two and a half months—eleven weeks—however long it's been—I've been feeling like some kind of sick pervert for thinking of you the way I have been. For having you star in my X-rated fantasies. I've struggled against it because you deserve better than that. So much better. It was only today that my brain finally caught up with my body. This is not just a case of out-and-out lust.'

He moved in close, crowding her with his heat and his scent.

'I want to make love to you until you are begging me for release.'

Her knees trembled at his low voice, rich with sin and promise. Heat pooled low in her abdomen. She couldn't have moved away from him if she'd wanted to.

'Because I love you.'

He hooked a hand behind her head and drew her mouth up to his, his lips crashing against hers in a hard kiss, as if trying to burn the truth of his words against her lips.

He broke away before she could respond, before she'd had enough…anywhere near enough.

He grabbed her hand and dragged her towards the back door. 'Where are we going?'

'There's something I want to show you.'

He pulled her all the way across to Elsie's yard, not stopping till they reached the garden shed. Flinging the door open, he bundled her inside.

In the middle of the floor sat a baby's crib. A wooden, hand-turned baby's crib. She sucked in a breath, marvelling at the beauty and craftsmanship in the simple lines. She knelt down to touch it. The wood was smooth against her palm.

'I've been coming here every day to finish it. I wait until you leave for work. I make sure I'm gone again before you get home.'

Her hand stilled. 'You made this?'

Drawing her back to her feet, he led her outside again. He gestured across to her garden. 'Who do you think is taking care of all that?'

For the first time in a month she suddenly realised how well kept the garden looked. She swallowed. It certainly wasn't her doing. She swung to him. 'You?'

'Tending your garden, making that crib for our baby—nothing has filled me with more satisfaction in my life before. Meg, you make me want to be a better man.'

He cradled her face in his hands. She'd never seen him more earnest or more determined.

'I want to build a life with you and our children—marriage, domesticity and a lifetime commitment. That's what I want.' His hands tightened about her face. 'But only with you. It's only ever been you. You're my destiny, Meg. You're the girl I always come home to. I just never saw it till now.'

For a moment everything blurred—Ben, the garden shed, the sky behind it.

'And if you don't believe me I mean to seduce you until you don't have a doubt left. And if you utter any doubts tomorrow I'll seduce you again, until you can't think straight and all you can think about is me. And I'll do that again and again until you do believe me.'

She lifted her hand to his mouth. 'And if I tell you that I *do* believe you?' She smiled. A smile that became a grin. She had to grin or the happiness swelling inside her might make her burst. 'Will you still seduce me?'

That slow, sinfully wicked grin of his hooked up the right side of his mouth. He traced a finger along her jaw and down her neck, making her breath hitch. 'Again and again and again,' he vowed, his fingers trailing a teasing path along the neckline of her shirt back and forth with delicious promise.

'Oh!' She caught his hand before he addled her brain completely.

'*Do* you believe me, Meg?' His lips travelled the same path his finger had, his tongue lapping at her skin and making her tremble.

'Yes.' She breathed the word into his mouth as his lips claimed hers.

The kiss transported her to a place she'd never been before—to a kingdom where all her fairytales had come true. She wrapped her arms about his neck, revelling in the lean hardness of his body, and kissed him back with everything she had.

It was a long time before they surfaced. Eventually they broke off to drag oxygen into starved lungs. She smiled up at him.

He grinned down at her. 'You love me, huh?'

'Yep, and you love me.'

Was it possible to die from happiness? She shifted against him, revelling in the way he sucked in a breath.

'You want to explain about the flowers and the chocolates?'

The fingers of his right hand walked down each vertebra of her spine to rest in the small of her back, raising gooseflesh on her arms. 'Dave said I should woo you with flowers and chocolates. I wanted to woo you right, Meg.'

She moved in closer. That hand splayed against her back. 'And the ice cream?'

'That was my own touch.'

'It was my favourite bit.'

His lips descended. 'Your favourite?'

'Second favourite,' she murmured, falling into his kiss, falling into Ben. *Her* Ben.

When he lifted his head again, many minutes later, she tried to catch her breath. 'Ben?'

'Hmm?'

'Do you think we can make our next baby the regular way?'

He grinned that grin. Her heart throbbed.

'You bet. And the one after that, and the one after that,' he promised.

* * * * *

A CHILD TO
HEAL THEIR HEARTS

BY
DIANNE DRAKE

Now that her children have left home, **Dianne Drake** is finally finding the time to do some of the things she adores—gardening, cooking, reading, shopping for antiques. Her absolute passion in life, however, is adopting abandoned and abused animals. Right now Dianne and her husband Joel have a little menagerie of three dogs and two cats, but that's always subject to change. A former symphony orchestra member, Dianne now attends the symphony as a spectator several times a month and, when time permits, takes in an occasional football, basketball or hockey game.

Dedicated to Ryan McDonald,
who squeezed every last drop out of his young life.

CHAPTER ONE

"Coming!" Keera's sleep-scratchy voice barely cleared the bedroom door and there was no way the person outside on her front porch could hear her. But she didn't really care. This was *her* time. Off work.

She wasn't on call, and after tomorrow she had no hospital obligations for the next week. A few days off after an entire year on. Blessed vacation time for eating, sleeping, reading. Most of all, quiet time to herself. No one to intrude, no one to disturb her. Time alone was all she had on the schedule and she adamantly didn't want to be disturbed before her holiday started. But as chief of cardiac surgery, she didn't always get what she wanted. Case in point, someone was knocking right now, and rather vigorously at that.

"OK, OK. Give me a minute," she grumbled on a weary sigh, the sentiment directed more to the neon green clock light blinking acrimoniously at her from the nightstand than to anything or anyone else.

She blinked back at it, wanted to throw a shoe at it when she saw it was telling her the time was ten after two. And she'd only been in bed since twenty after one. Meaning she'd had fifty full minutes of sleep.

"Figures," she grunted as another knock jolted her out of her blearies. Then another knock, louder this time. Last time this had happened to her, it had been the National Guard come to fetch her in the middle of a torrential storm. *"Hospital's on emergency alert, Dr. Murphy. Don't want you driving in this because of the conditions, so we've come to take you in."* Yep, that had been quite a night, being hefted up into the back of a military helicopter and jostled around fallen trees and power lines.

But tonight there was no rain. No storm or adverse condition of any kind going on. And as Keera's mind started to clear, she began ticking off the various reasons someone might be doing exactly what they were doing. Worst-case scenario—full-out disaster that wasn't weather-related. Best-case scenario—emergency surgery waiting. But why not simply call her, like they always did?

Maybe they had. Maybe she'd slept through it. "I *said* I'm coming," she shouted, cinching her robe as she plodded out to the entry hall. "Identify yourself, please," she shouted, even though a glimpse through the peephole revealed the uniform of a police officer. "And show me some identification."

"Will do, Miss Murphy," the man out there shouted.

Miss Murphy. After fast-tracking her way through medical school and all the other stages that had preceded cardiac surgeon, that's what it all boiled down to, wasn't it? Unmarried doctor, unmarried *miss*... Successful at career, unsuccessful at life. It was pretty much everything that defined her.

Keera pushed her long red hair back from her face, and looked out again. Saw what she required from the first officer.

"Officer Carla James," she said, obliging Keera with a sight of her ID. Short woman, slightly rounded, definitely hiding behind the taller officer.

"And Officer Brian Hutchinson," the taller one added,

bending down to Keera's peephole so she'd get a good wide-angle view of his face then his badge. "Would you please open the door?"

"Is it medical business?" she shouted at them, as she unlatched the first of three safety chains then finally pulled back the dead bolt. A little extra precaution as a result of living alone.

"No, ma'am, it's not," Officer Hutchinson said, stepping forward as soon as the door opened to him. He held out his leather wallet for her to match his photo with his face. Then tucked it away when she'd nodded her satisfaction. "I'm sorry to say it's personal."

That's when the first grain of relief shot through her. Keera Murphy didn't have a personal life. Everything about her was medicine. "How? I mean, what?"

Officer James chose that moment to step out from behind Hutchinson, and the only thing Keera saw was the bundle in her arms. "I'm sorry. I don't understand." Were they bringing her a patient? A child? No. This was a mistake. Didn't make sense. They were at the wrong house, or had the wrong person. That had to be it. They wanted the Keera Murphy who was a pediatrician, if there was such a person, and she was the Keera Murphy who did cardiac surgery.

"I'm sorry to say, there's no easy way to do this," Officer Hutchinson continued. "But earlier this evening your husband and a yet unidentified passenger were killed in a single vehicle crash off Mountain Canyon Road. Your daughter was thrown free, and escaped without injury. We did have her checked at a clinic near there, and except for some scrapes and bruises she's fine. In shock, I think, because she's not talking, maybe a little lethargic due to the trauma. But the doc who looked at her said she was basically good."

"I'm glad, but this is a mistake because I'm not married." Keera took a step backwards, braced herself against the wall. "Divorced. No children."

"Kevin Murphy," Hutchinson continued. "Kevin Joseph Murphy, ma'am. Your husband, according to some legal papers we found at the scene. House deed, this address."

"But we're not… Haven't been…" She shut her eyes, trying to focus. Kevin was dead? Their marriage had been a real stinker and their divorce nasty in epic proportions, but she wouldn't have wished this on him. "You're sure?" she finally managed.

"Yes, ma'am. We have a full identification on your husband but not his passenger. We were hoping…"

Keera glanced at the officer holding the child, wondering why they'd brought her here. Wondering if this was the child who… It had to be. Who else could she be but the child he'd fathered while they had still been married? "Maybe the passenger is his *second* wife. Melanie, Melodie, something like that." Or the one after her, if there'd already been another as Kevin seemed to have his women in fast succession. "Melania, that's her name. Melania." Keera's head was spinning now the information was finally beginning to sink in. Kevin was dead, most likely along with his second wife. And their child… "She's not mine," she said.

"But you were listed as Mr. Murphy's wife and next of kin, so we assumed—"

"Wrong assumption," she said, cutting him off. "Old information. My husband and I divorced a few months ago, the papers you found were probably from part of the agreement." Or, in their case, disagreement. "He called several days ago, said he had some final papers for me to sign, and that child…" She shook her head. "Part of his second marriage." Kevin's secret to keep, along with his mistress.

"Then we have a problem," Carla James said, "because we have nowhere to take the child for the night."

A little girl, she'd been told. Keera had never actually seen her. Hadn't ever wanted to see her. Didn't want to see her now, even though that was about to change. "Surely, there's a foster-home with an opening. Or some kind of contingency in place for situations like this one?"

Both police officers shook their heads.

"Social services?" Hopeful question with an answer she'd already guessed.

"That would be me," a perky young woman said from behind Officer James. "My name is Consuela Martinez, and I'm the temporary case manager assigned to Megan. And right now I don't have a contingency plan that would be in the child's best interests. We were hoping her family—"

"But I'm not her family," Keera interrupted.

Consuela stepped out in plain sight, the yellow of the porch light giving her more of a jaundiced look than it should. And just like that Keera switched to doctor mode, her mind ticking off various conditions that came with a yellow tinge...one of the reasons Kevin had strayed, *he claimed*. Too much doctor too much of the time. Sadly, she hadn't had an argument to counter his because, in the end, she *had* loved her medicine more than she'd loved her husband or their marriage.

"Look, I know there's a contingency plan," Keera said. "When a child is involved there's always a contingency plan." It was said without conviction because she really didn't know that to be the case. But she hoped it was, or else...

"You're right. Usually there is. Except right now. Every spot we have for someone Megan's age and developmental stage is filled," the case worker continued. "But I can have a callout to other agencies in other areas by morning, or we might be able to shift a few children to other situations, and after that—"

"Are you taking flucloxacillin, by any chance, Consuela?" Keera interrupted, so totally *not* wanting to hear that Megan had no place to go tonight.

Consuela looked confused. For that matter, so did both police officers. "Um, yes. I am. For an outer ear infection. Why?"

"You might want to call your doctor first thing in the morning and mention that you're having an adverse reaction to the drug. Nothing serious, so don't be alarmed. But it's worth noting." And that didn't change the problem at hand, as there was still a child bundled in Officer James's arms who needed a place to stay. "Sorry," she said. "Force of habit. Part of my job is paying attention to the details, and I've been told I can go overboard about it."

"It's good to know you're conscientious, Doctor," Officer Hutchinson said, "but it's two-thirty, and we're not getting any closer to figuring out what to do with—"

"With my ex-husband's child." It was an irony coming back to slap her hard. This was his secret child, the one he'd told her he'd fathered but had only told her on the child's first birthday. His first devastating confession, followed by how much he loved the baby's mother, how he wanted a divorce, wanted to keep their house for his new family... But none of that was Megan's fault, was it? "You're sure there's really no place for her to go tonight?"

"The county home," Consuela said, "which I try to avoid when I can, especially for children so young. It's a large facility, too many children. The younger ones get... overlooked."

"It's an—"

"An institution, ma'am," Officer James volunteered. "In

the traditional sense. But if you're rejecting the child, it's our only recourse, because I can't stand on your doorstep all night, holding her."

"No, of course you can't," Keera said, taking a step backwards as she felt her resolve start to melt. Another step, pause…taking a moment to gird her resolve. Then another backwards step, and finally the gesture to enter her home. And as Officer James passed her, Keera took her first good look at Megan, and if it weren't for the fact that the room was filled with people…strangers, she would have fallen to her knees. Would have cried. The lump in her throat started to choke her, and the light feeling in her head caused the room to spin. "Please, lay her on the sofa. I can sit up in here with her, she shouldn't be alone." *Shouldn't be in an institution!* No child should ever be in an institution.

Keera glanced at Consuela, who'd stopped at the mirror in the entry hall and was staring at her yellow-tinted complexion. "But this is only until morning," she warned the social worker. "If you don't have a placement for her before I leave for the hospital, in exactly three hours, you'll find her in the daycare center.

"Oh, and, Consuela, I can't look after her longer than what I've said. I'm not good with children. They don't respond to me, and outside normal medical situations I wouldn't know how to respond if they did. So, come morning, do you understand me? My early surgery will be over by ten, followed by routine rounds, and I don't want to go into my rounds knowing I still have a child to worry about."

It made her sound unpleasant, like a bully or, worse… heartless. Which wasn't at all what she'd intended. But how did a person go about dealing with a situation like this? She'd just taken in the child who had caused the final curtain to drop on her marriage, and she wasn't sure there was a proper way to deal with that.

"So, before you go, do we know if she has any allergies?" Kevin had been allergic to shellfish. "Or medical conditions that require attention...or medication?"

Consuela, who'd finally torn herself away from the mirror, shook her head. "Her doctor is Reid Adams, and his practice is in a little town called Sugar Creek, Tennessee. About an hour or so west of here. But we haven't been able to get in touch with him yet. He's at camp."

"Camp?" Keera asked.

"Youth camp, for kids recovering from leukemia and all the associated conditions. He's the camp physician, I've been told. And I do have a call in for him." Consuela stepped around Keera, who made no move to help Officer James settle Megan on the sofa. "And, Dr. Murphy...she's a good child. Very quiet. She won't cause you any problems."

No, the child wouldn't. Not now, anyway, because Keera's problems were in the past. And while little Megan hadn't caused them, she was a result of them. "Noon at the very latest. Please find your contingency plan by noon."

Ten minutes later, when the house was quiet again, Keera settled into the chair across from the sofa and simply stared at the child. Lovely little girl. Blonde hair, like Kevin's. Probably blue eyes like his, too. Sadly, there was so much turmoil for one little life. Poor thing. Her heart did go out to Megan for so many reasons.

"It's good that you don't have to understand any of this," Keera whispered to the child, while she pulled her feet up under herself, preparing to spend the rest of her night right there, looking after the girl. "But you're going to be fine. You're a beautiful little girl, and everything's going to be fine."

* * *

"I'm sorry, Doctor, but I really don't have anything to tell you." Reid Adams tossed the ball into the grass then stood back to watch the stampede of children go after it. No matter what else was going on in his life, coming to camp was always a highlight. "I'd have to look at her records before I could say anything, but I'm not in my office this week and—"

"Then find someone who can do it for you," Keera snapped, then hastily added, "Look, I'm sorry I sound so grumpy, but…"

"Normally, if someone sounds grumpy, they're grumpy," Reid said, stepping behind the large oak tree as two little girls came running in his direction. Black hair, dark eyes, dark skin. Hispanic beauties, and the lights of his life. His reason for existing wrapped up in a couple of very energetic little girls, aged five and seven. "And I think your situation with Megan would make a lot of people grumpy if it happened to them. No relatives turn up yet?"

"An elderly aunt who refused the child, as well as some male cousins the social worker thought weren't suitable. Apparently there are other family members being contacted, but I may have the child through the afternoon, and I'd feel better knowing about her health situation."

He liked her voice. A little husky, but not so much she sounded like a three-packs-a-day smoker. More like bedroom-sultry husky…an image that caused him to blink hard, clear his throat and, more than anything else, remind him that this was a kids' camp and he was surrounded by a bunch of kids who didn't need a distracted counselor.

"Daddy," five-year-old Allie squealed, as Reid sidled around the tree, only to be waylaid by seven-year-old Emmie, coming at him from the other side.

"I found him first," Emmie shouted.

"Did not," Allie argued, latching onto Reid's leg. "I got him first."

"You both got me first," he declared.

"Excuse me," Keera said. "Dr. Adams?"

"Sorry about that," he said, chuckling. "But my daughters are persistent, and they won't take no for an answer when we're playing. Not that I'd ever want them to. So, getting back to Megan Murphy. I've seen her once, I think, and nothing stands out. But it's a new practice, I'm barely settled in, and I don't know enough about any of my patients yet to even recognize them, or their parents, on the street. Sorry about that, because I'd like to be more help. But let me call either Beau Alexander or his wife, Deanna. They're covering my practice this week and they might know something. Or be able to see what's in the records." Pause.

"Girls, girls! Stay away from that fence! That's the rule. You've been told if you go near the fence, you'll get a time out with your first warning, and broccoli with your dinner with your second warning."

"You punish the children by threatening them with broccoli?" Keera asked. "I'd think that would be a healthy choice. Something you'd encourage them to eat."

"It is, but most kids come naturally equipped hating broccoli, so I use that to my advantage. Then, by the end of the camp session, we'll have introduced them to a couple of ways broccoli can taste really yummy… Excuse me, I have the younger group here this week. When I mention broccoli to older kids, I usually use the term delicious. And the thing is, the majority of these children will leave here and ask their parents for broccoli. Just an FYI—raw with dip works great!"

"Raw or cooked, you're a magician, Dr. Adams, if you get them liking broccoli."

"Nope, just a single dad who's figured it out. If it works with my two, it'll work with anybody's kid. Anyway… Angelica, Rodney! Take off your shoes *and* your socks before you go wading in the creek! Both socks, Rodney."

"Look, I appreciate your time, Dr. Adams, but—"

"Reid. Call me Reid."

"Reid. I'm sorry for sounding so grumpy, or frazzled, or whatever you want to call it, but I'm not good with children, don't know if I even like them so much, and I really don't want to be responsible for one, even if it's only for a few more hours. I was hoping…actually, I don't know what I was hoping for. But you clearly have your hands full with your camp kids, so I'm going let you go. But before I do, could you answer one more question for me?"

"Got time for two, if they're quick." Truth was, he wasn't sure he wanted to hang up. Keera Murphy sounded nice, except for the part where she wasn't fond of children. In his life that was definitely a problem. But she wasn't in his life, so it didn't matter. "So go ahead."

"Megan's two, and she's not… She's still in diapers. I had her in hospital daycare all morning and the ladies working there said she made no attempt to go to the bathroom or even ask someone to take her."

"Does she speak?"

"No, but that could be the trauma."

"She's had a full battery of tests?"

"Everything we could think of."

"Then she's probably just reacting to her circumstances. Once things are normal around her again I'm sure the diapers can come off. And if she's not totally trained, it's perfectly natural for children that age to be a little resistant. But if you have other concerns, please feel free…" He spun around in time to catch Emmie ready to lob him with a big red water balloon. He was fast enough to dodge it, but in trying for the evasive maneuver he dropped his phone. By the time he'd manage to pick it back up, Keera Murphy had hung up.

"Who was that, Daddy?" Allie asked him. Now she was sneaking up, hiding what he guessed was also a filled water balloon behind her back. So, he could take it like a man or, actually, like a daddy, and let his youngest have her turn at dousing Daddy, or he could spin and run like crazy. After all, he was well over six feet tall, considered well muscled by some. Legs that had helped him finish in the pack at a few marathons. So if he couldn't outrun a little girl... "She was a doctor."

"Who takes care of little kids, like you do?" Allie asked. The expression on her face was so determined, he knew what he had to do.

"No, not that kind of doctor, sweetheart." He braced himself for the hit. "Remember when we talked about what having surgery means?" OK, so most parents weren't quite as forthright as he was in his child-rearing ideas, but he didn't believe in lying, not even when it was about something Allie probably wouldn't even understand and definitely didn't need to know.

"Where they have to make a zipper so they can see your insides?"

He chuckled. "Actually, yes." Which meant she did listen to him. Music to the ears of a long-suffering parent. "She's the kind of doctor who makes the zipper."

He thought back to the conversation with Keera. Strained, at best. Maybe more like totally stressed out. Someone he pictured as nervous. Someone he also pictured as... One momentary distraction was all it took, and Reid Adams fell victim to his daughter, who landed the perfectly placed water balloon center chest. "Got me," he shouted, dropping to the ground, where five or six other children converged on him and bombarded him with water balloons the way his own daughters had done.

"No fair," he shouted while laughs and squeals muffled any protest he wanted to make. Not that he really wanted to protest. This was part of his fun. What meant the most to him now was thinking about how his daughters would be exhilarated, and knowing that his two little conspirators had led a group of normally sedentary kids into an adventure was, probably, the most fun of all.

Then he wondered about Dr. Keera Murphy. Would she have seen any of this as fun? Or worthless, as she wasn't a big one for children? More than that, why did it even matter to him? And why did he make a mental note to do a little Internet surfing on her when he had time?

"No more water balloons," he shouted, trying to stand up. But to no avail. As he rose to his knees, a whole new group of water ballooners swarmed him, loaded down with filled balloons of every size, color and shape imaginable. He barely had enough time to cover his face before the fun began.

"I know what I said, Dr. Murphy, and I've got a line on someone who might take her later tonight or some time tomorrow, if there's nobody else available. But Mrs. Blanchard prefers her wards to be toilet trained, and as Megan isn't, I'm not sure she'll get all the attention she needs."

They were sitting in the parents' waiting room across from the hospital daycare center. A very cheerful place. Lots of bright yellows and oranges, like they were tying the conventional child stimuli colors into their parents. This was only the second time Keera had ever been there. The first had been that morning, when she'd left Megan in the able care of Dolores Anderson, the director. "She could be traumatized."

"Maybe, and if that's the case, I'm wondering if a pediatric hospital ward might be the best place for her temporarily."

"Seriously, you want to stick her in a hospital?"

No, that was not acceptable. While she didn't have any strong urges toward the child, she wasn't some cold-hearted dungeon master who wanted to lock all the un-trained kiddies away until they potty trained themselves. This was a child who needed attention, not isolation, and so far all of Consuela's ideas seemed more like isolation.

"Look, just keep trying with Mrs. Blanchard, OK? If she won't take Megan, maybe she'll have a suggestion about who can."

"We'll work it out, Doctor. I promise, that's all I've been doing today."

Consuela was deliberately not making eye contact with Keera, trying to keep her gaze focused on anything else, and Keera accepted that. She'd probably do the same thing if she found herself in that same spot. But what Consuela didn't understand was that so far today childcare had been a breeze because she'd had the help of the whole hospital daycare staff there to get her through it.

Tomorrow was another story. It was her day off—the start of her week off, in fact. And that's when the reading commenced with a whole stack of medical journals she'd had for a year or more. Nowhere in those plans was there room for a toddler.

"I'm not criticizing you, and I hope you don't think that I was. But I grew up in the foster-care system. A lot of it in institutions, and it's horrible. Being passed off from one place to another, never knowing where you might end up next. I never got adopted because I was older when I went into the system, so I was in a grand total of nine different homes and three different institutions, all before the age of eighteen. And, no, I wasn't a good child because of that." She closed her eyes, fighting back those memories.

"This child doesn't need that kind of trauma in her life." As much as she'd disliked Kevin by the end of their marriage, Keera knew he would have been a very good father. A doting daddy. Megan didn't deserve to go from that to cold indifference, which was what would happen if she was sent to an institution. Or even the wrong foster-family.

"It's not always a traumatic situation, Doctor. We have very good caregivers."

"Yes, I'm sure you do, and I admire people who would take on the responsibility. Right now, though, Megan needs more that what you're able to find her, and I know that's not your fault. But it's not her fault either. Yet she's the one who's going to be bounced around or institutionalized."

And she was waging the battle with the wrong person. She knew that. But the right person—the one who should have made arrangements for Megan in the event something like this happened—was dead. True to Kevin's form, he hadn't thought about the practical things. Hadn't when they'd been married, hadn't after they were divorced, and now his daughter was paying the price.

"I'm sorry about your childhood, Doctor, and I understand your frustration but, like I said, I'm doing my best. There aren't any distant relatives suited to take her, or who even want her, for that matter, so I have to come up with another plan. But you've got to understand that in the short term Megan might have to go to a hospital pediatric ward, a group home or even the county home. It's not what I want to do but what I may have to do if you can't or won't keep her for a little while longer."

"In the meantime…" Resignation crept in a little too

quickly, but maybe she saw something of herself in Megan. Abandoned child. It was hard to get past that. "If I keep her a day or two, that doesn't mean I want to be a temporary guardian or any other kind of custodial figure. It simply means I'll feed and clothe her while you continue looking for a better situation."

"Which I'll do," Consuela promised.

"Good. So now I've got to go to the grocery and buy a few things a toddler would eat. Maybe pick up some clothes, toys…" OK, so she was relating to the situation but not to Megan herself. It was the best she could do. Better than most people would do, she thought as she bundled up the child and took her to the car. This was an honest effort, and it kept the child out of all those awful places Keera knew so intimately. Shuddered even thinking about them. Dark places, bad for children…

While having children had never been part of her plan—past, present or future—there'd been a time when she'd needed what Megan needed now, and no one had reached out to her. So how could she refuse?

"Megan, did you have a good day today?" she asked as they wended their way through the hospital corridors on her way to her car. "Play with lots of nice toys? Meet new people? Conquer any toddler nations?"

In response, Megan laid her head against Keera's shoulder and sighed.

"You're congested," Keera said, listening to the slight rattling she could hear coming from the girl's lungs. Immediately in doctor mode, she veered off into one of the pediatric exam cubicles, pulled her stethoscope from her pocket and listened. Nothing sounded serious, but the fact remained that the child had something going on that needed to be attended to…sooner, not later. And every thought in her went to Reid Adams.

CHAPTER TWO

"IT'S OK, MEGAN," she said, barely creeping along the mountain highway. "We'll be there soon, and Dr. Adams will take good care of you." She hoped so, even though she wasn't sure the message had gotten through because he hadn't called her back. Something about mountains and cellphone interference.

"You've seen him before, and he's very good." Not that the sleeping child cared. But Keera did. She wanted some familiarity for Megan, and Reid Adams was the closest thing she could think of. And maybe, just maybe, he'd have a solution for the child's situation. "We're not far away now, so you just sleep there, and when you wake up things will be better. I promise."

What was she promising, though? What, really, could a trip to an isolated camp in the mountains in the middle of the night do for Megan? Nothing. That's what! But it made Keera feel better. Feel like she was doing something rather than simply sitting around waiting for something to happen or, worse, doing the wrong thing. Reid Adams was all about children, he had children. And for some strange reason, he seemed like her best port in the storm. A beacon of light.

"He'll know what to do," she reassured the sleeping child. "Yes, I'm sure of it." Because if he didn't...well,

Keera didn't want to think about the alternative, since it wasn't acceptable. That was something she knew in profound ways no child should ever have to know. Confusion, fear and long, empty days and nights when the futility threatened to eat you alive. "He'll fix you up, and he'll help me help you, too."

Those were mighty big expectations for one pediatrician to fulfill, but it's all Keera had to cling to. Reid Adams had to come through for both their sakes. He just had to!

He wasn't sure who she was, but for some reason he thought he could wager a pretty good guess. Carrying a child in her arms, she was trying to make her way up the dirt path without stumbling, and she was quite obviously not a woman of the woods. Determined, though. With the scowl of a mighty huntress set across one of the softest, prettiest faces he'd ever seen in his life.

Which was what had brought Keera Murphy to mind. She'd tracked him down and she was bringing him the child. He wasn't sure why, wasn't even sure that he liked the idea that the huntress had set her sights on him. But something about a woman who would trudge all the way out here in the middle of the night just to find him did fascinate him.

"You would be Dr. Murphy?" he asked, as she approached the porch of his cabin.

"I would be. And this is Megan Murphy. She's sick. Since nobody knows her, nobody knows a thing about her, well, with you being her physician and all, I thought you'd be the best one to take a look."

"You couldn't find another physician closer to you? Or even track down one of my colleagues?"

"You didn't get my phone call?"

"Mountains and cellphones aren't always a good combination, even in this day and age. Reception out here is spotty, which is why we still rely on the landline."

"Well, I called because I hoped she'd remember you. With everything she's gone through, I thought that would be good. Maybe it doesn't matter, but…" Keera started up the wooden steps and Reid took the child from her arms, immediately seeing how sick she was.

"How long has she been this way?" he asked, turning and nearly running into his cabin.

"Just the last few hours. She'd been getting progressively sicker and I wasn't too worried about it at first, but when I listened to her chest a little while ago, the congestion had more than doubled from earlier and her temperature had elevated two degrees."

He laid Megan carefully on the sofa then dashed into the next room after his medical bag.

"Well, I hope I didn't do the wrong thing bringing her here." She shrugged. "And I'm sorry for the intrusion. Maybe I panicked a little." Panicked because she'd known what would happen if she'd taken Megan to the hospital. The system would have gotten her. As much as she didn't want the child, she also didn't want the child to end up in the system, which was what would have happened because a trip to Emergency tonight would have started that process. "I didn't know what else to do."

"You followed your instinct. Did what you believed was best. It's not a bad thing, Keera." He took a quick blood-pressure reading, followed by the rest of Megan's vitals, then pulled off his stethoscope and laid it aside.

It was a simple action yet so sexy. And she wanted to kick herself for noticing. "I may have overreacted, but—"

"Look, I don't know the dynamics here. Don't know why social services left the child with you when, clearly, she's not your responsibility. Don't know why you avoided a quick trip to an emergency room rather than driving all the way out here. But I'm not going to ask. We all have our reasons for the crazy things we do, and I don't mean crazy in a literal sense but more from a point of observation. Seems crazy to me because I don't know what makes you tick, but obviously it doesn't seem crazy to you because you understand the situation. So as far as I'm concerned, it's all good."

"I appreciate that," she said sincerely. "Thank you."

"Don't thank me yet. I want to keep Megan for a day or so. It's probably a slight upper respiratory infection, although I want to make sure before I let her go as I don't think she's up to another trip back with you so soon. So I'd like to keep her in the infirmary here for a little while, if you don't mind. It's empty and I can quarantine her there just to make sure the other kids don't come in contact with her. Then I'll get her hydrated and start her on some medication to make her feel better." He frowned. "Unless you'd rather admit her to a local hospital because she is a little dehydrated. Your choice."

No choice. This was where Megan had to be, at least for the night. "And the infirmary is…?"

He pointed to a door at the rear of the living room. "Through the kitchen, out the door, first building you see beyond my cabin. The clinic is on the other side of the compound."

"Why do you keep them separated?"

"These kids are very susceptible to illness. Don't want sickness anywhere near regular medical duties."

"Makes sense."

"Also, I bought the camp as is. Didn't have one place large enough to house both the clinic and infirmary. Anyway, there's always someone on duty. Usually me, sometimes Betsy, the camp nurse, who stays in the cabin adjacent to this one. We alternate nights taking call.

"As far as the infirmary, I think you may have to help a bit there because Betsy's pregnant and I don't let her near the sick kids. Which means it's basically you and me, and I do have a volunteer who isn't medical but who had leukemia when she was a kid and enjoys helping out where she can."

"You need to know I'm not good at pediatrics."

"Maybe not, but I don't have a lot of options if we're going to keep Megan here. Like I said, there's always the hospital…"

An unacceptable choice. That was her first thought. Her second was that she could leave Megan here, go home and let Consuela, the social worker, deal with the rest of it. This was certainly her chance to step aside and know Megan was in good hands, but something inside her was stopping her from taking it. "So you want me basically quarantined with her?"

"Not quarantined as in locked up. We have a guest cabin. Nothing fancy, but a place to sleep for the rest of the night, if you want it, while I watch Megan. Then in the morning we can work out the schedule."

"Maybe she'll be ready to travel in the morning." And maybe in the morning Consuela would call her and tell her she'd found a perfect placement. Maybe even a good family who would eventually adopt Megan. One who'd been on the waiting list, praying for a beautiful two-year-old girl. Sure, it was a long shot, she knew that. But it was also a very nice dream—a dream she'd never had for her own.

"That's possible," he said. "But unlikely. In the meantime, you look like you're due for a few hours of sleep."

Yes, she did want that sleep. More now that he'd mentioned it. Hypnotic effect—her eyelids were getting heavy.

"Definitely no hospital, so I guess it looks like I'm staying. I think I'll talk to Megan for a minute then I'll take you up on that cabin. Oh, and, Reid, I really am sorry to put you through this. If there's anything I can do…"

"How about I carry her to the infirmary then you can tuck her in while I run over to the girls' dorm and check on my daughters?" He smiled. "They may think they're getting away from Dad, but it's not happening. Anyway, one last kiss goodnight while you settle Megan in, then I'll point you in the direction of the guest cabin and you're on your own. Oh, and breakfast is at eight. Big white building in the middle of the complex. Meals are prompt, but if you sleep in, I always have cereal and milk in my own kitchen."

He was tall, a bit lanky. Wore wire-rimmed glasses, needed a haircut. She liked his scraggly look, though. Light brown hair, slightly curly, slightly over his collar. Slight dimple in his chin. And, oh, those blue eyes. Wow, they were perceptive. So much so they almost scared her. "I don't sleep much so I'll be good to grab something with everybody else."

"I'm just saying…" he said, scooping Megan into his arms and heading out to the infirmary.

Keera opened the door to the infirmary, saw exactly four beds. It was a tidy space, not large, not lush. Just basic. "Do many of your kids get sick?"

"Not really. By the point in their recovery that they're allowed to come to camp, they're usually pretty far along in the whole process, with all kinds of specialists making the determination whether or not they're ready for the whole camping experience. In other words, barring normal things like colds and flu, they're usually doing pretty well."

"Well, it sounds like you're doing important work. So don't you think the owners would put a little more effort into the medical facility that might have to treat those kids? I mean, this place will suffice, but it could certainly stand some updates and expansion." After Reid laid Megan in the bed, Keera pulled up the blanket to cover her. "Closer to the clinic would be nice, too, to save you some steps."

"Are you always like this?"

"What?"

"Outspoken. Opinionated. Whatever you want to call it." Grabbing a fresh digital thermometer from the drawer in the stand next to the bed, he pulled it from its wrapper, punched the button and waited for it to calibrate. "Something to say pretty much on every subject." The thermometer end went under Megan's tongue the same time his eyes went to Keera's. "I'm right about that, aren't I?"

"It's been said." Amongst a lot worse things. "I'm a cardiac surgeon in a large hospital, and—"

"I know who you are."

"How?"

"Internet search."

"When?"

"Earlier. After you called. You sounded like someone who might come back to haunt me later on, so I decided to read up. Good thing I did, because…"

She smiled, almost apologetically but not quite. "Because I came back to haunt you."

The thermometer beeped and Reid pulled it out and read it. Then shook his head. "One hundred three and a couple of decimal points." Immediately, he pulled up Megan's eyelids, took a look. She responded by whimpering and trying to jerk away from him.

"I talked to Beau a couple hours ago. He'd looked at the records we have for her, saw nothing significant. In fact, the only time she's been to the office was when her parents first moved to Sugar Creek, and they were establishing me as their pediatrician. I gave her a preliminary exam, sort of as a baseline, and there was nothing remarkable. She's developed properly for a child her age, and according to her parents there's no history of any chronic illness or condition.

"But that's me taking their word for it because they never had her medical records transferred to us, and there's no mention of a former pediatrician, so right now we really know very little. Which means we're coming into her care pretty much blind."

"Trust me, blind is bad."

"I get the feeling that has nothing to do with Megan."

"Actually, it has everything to do with her. But not in the medical sense."

Pulling out his stethoscope, Reid listened to the child's chest, her heart, her tummy then pulled out his earpieces. "Didn't hear anything more remarkable than what you probably heard. Bilateral congestion, wheezing." He shrugged. "Indicative of any number of things. Which means I'm going to need lab work that I'm not equipped to do here."

"Did it before I came here. Results should be in by morning. And I have her X-ray in the car."

"You come prepared. Too bad all my patients don't come in with all their tests already done."

"Like I told you, I don't know a thing about children. Don't treat them, don't operate on them, don't want to. But getting everything done beforehand seemed logical."

"Well, even though you've complicated my life by bringing her here, you've made my complication easier."

"You're not supposed to treat anybody who's not at camp? Is that the problem? Because I can talk to the owner or director. Apologize. Make the appropriate donation for her care, if that's what's needed to make this better."

"Actually, I own the camp so I can do what I want. And donations are always welcome. But just so you'll know, she's got the start of a rash on her stomach, so I think she's probably coming down with measles, most likely in the early part of its three or four days of infectivity. Meaning while she's in here I can't have other children anywhere near her. So if somebody else needs the facility…" He shrugged. "I'll treat her here for now, certainly for the night, and we'll do the best we can with what we have. But I can't make any promises beyond that. Fair enough?"

"More than fair," she said, grateful for what he was offering.

"Have you had measles, by the way?"

"Not that I remember. But I don't remember a lot of my childhood, so I don't really know."

"Vaccinated?"

"That, I was. Required in school." When she had gone, which hadn't been too often. "Could this be something else, though? An allergic reaction of some sort?" Reid Adams was an acclaimed pediatrician—she'd done her Internet surfing as well. So it was highly unlikely he'd make a mistake of a pretty basic diagnosis. Still, an allergic reaction resulting in a rash beat measles any day, so she was keeping her fingers crossed.

"If I were a betting man, I'd bet she's going to have a full-blown rash by this time tomorrow."

"And you still want to keep her? Especially with all the other children being so susceptible? I mean, I could take her to a hotel someplace close, so she wouldn't have to suffer that long drive back tonight."

"She's too congested to move her any place, if we don't have to. It would risk complications. And she has to be sick somewhere, doesn't she? Seeing that you're not in favor of taking her to the hospital, which would really be the only place I'd approve sending her…"

"If she absolutely needs to be in a hospital, that's what I'll do. I just have personal preferences about not leaving an already abandoned child in an institution." Keera looked down at the girl, and her heart clutched. Poor thing, she didn't deserve cold detachment, but that's all Keera was capable of giving. She knew her limitations.

"She's not my child, but I want what's best for her, and while I know you're a pediatrician and you'll disagree with me, I don't happen to think it would be in a hospital. And I don't say that lightly as I work in a hospital."

"Couldn't agree with you more about hospitals." He pushed a strand of hair away from Megan's face then stood. "Don't like them myself if they're not necessary. Look, I really do need to go say goodnight to my girls, then I'll be back to put an IV in her and give her some fluids to keep her hydrated. I think that will be easier than trying to get her to drink anything right now. It'll only take me a couple of minutes…"

"I'm really sorry about this," Keera said, feeling the need to apologize over and over because of what she was doing to Reid and his camp. It was an inconvenience at very best and a danger at worst.

"She's sick. Bringing her all the way out here might not have been my first choice, but it's a difficult situation. Can't say I understand your decisions, but I'm not going to argue about them. So why the worried look?"

"I'm still concerned about exposing the other kids. I didn't think about that before I came here, and I feel terrible."

"See, the thing about being a pediatrician is you're always in contact with something that's highly contagious. In my office, I actually have separate waiting areas for kids with something *catchy*, as I like to call it. They never go to the general waiting room, never come near one of the other kids. Bottom line, I'm cautious and it works. So does the fact that we're surrounded by the great outdoors so there aren't any environmental factors that would help promote exposure."

"You sure?"

He nodded, smiled. "Sure."

"Do you have a solution for my fear of children as well?"

"Afraid of children, yet you're a good doctor."

"Definitely afraid of children. Don't know what to do for them, or with them. I was a nervous wreck every time I had to rotate through Pediatrics when I was a resident."

"Somehow I don't picture you being a nervous wreck about anything."

"I appreciate the compliment, but I'm serious about children. They're not my strength. Speaking of which, there's something you should know about Megan. And it's not really her so much as the whole situation. But only because you're her doctor."

He motioned Keera to the door. "Tell me as you walk me out."

She did, then stopped at the door as he stepped out into the night. "Without dragging out all the dirty laundry, what you need to know is that Keera is the child my husband conceived with another woman while he and I were still married, still going through the motions that made it look like a good marriage. We had our share of problems, like all couples do, but I didn't know he was cheating on me. Didn't even know his affair produced a child until she was a year old, and he was wanting out of our marriage so he could invest himself fully in his other family. That was a year ago. Haven't seen him since except across the table at the lawyer's office. And I'd never seen the child until…"

"Yet here you are with her, going above and beyond the call of duty to get her what you think is the care she needs." Reid whistled quietly. "I'd say that's pretty admirable in an uncomfortable situation."

"It is uncomfortable. The authorities brought her to me…well, I'm not really sure how that worked out because once I realized they intended to leave her with me the rest of it turned into a blur. But there were some papers in the car—it was a car crash that killed them—and my name was on the papers. Papers from before we were divorced, I think.

"Anyway, the child was fine, so they brought her to me because they believed she was mine. Then they more or less coerced me into keeping her because they didn't have a place to put her for various reasons, she got sick, here I am…"

Reid laid a steadying hand on her arm. "And here you are, frantic."

"I'm sorry. In surgery I'm in control. But with Megan?" She shrugged. "It's hard, Reid. And I really don't have the right to be burdening you with all this. I wouldn't have, except she got sick and…"

"And you fixated on me as your solution."

"Not my solution. Megan's solution. You're her doctor. Which is a lame reason for me showing up here the way I did, but I panicked because my alternative was to take her to the hospital, and as a place to work it's fine, but for a child…" She stopped explaining. "So, how are we going to deal with all these problems I've created for you?"

He chuckled. "Minor glitches."

"I wouldn't call them minor as it involves more than I

ever expected. I mean, tying up your infirmary, keeping you away from your daughters. And your…wife?"

"No wife. Never married. Adopted daughters. Long story."

"Well, whatever the case, I haven't made things easy for you here, so…"

"So, that donation you mentioned?"

She nodded. "Happy to do it."

"Money's always great, but I'm thinking about some clinic time while you're here. That way I can sneak off and see my girls."

"I'm all for you getting to spend time with your daughters, and I'll do anything I can to help make that happen. But seriously? You want me working with your kids after what I just told you?" It was probably the most uninspired thing he could have suggested.

"Think of them as future adults and you'll be just fine."

"Wouldn't it be better if I simply hired a temp to come help you? Two temps, three. However many you need?"

"But you're going to have to stay here with Megan anyway. Or were you thinking about leaving her here with me and vanishing into thin air?"

She smiled an especially guilty smile, because that thought *had* crossed her mind a time or two. "Not thin air. I'm too easy to track down."

"But she's a ward of the state, and you, apparently, have been given some sort of temporary custody. Which means you can't just walk away from her. At least, I wouldn't think so. And I don't think you'd do that anyway, otherwise you'd have taken her to the hospital in the first place and just left her there." He grinned. "Or left her on my doorstep when you had the chance."

"OK, I'll admit it. Leaving her here might have crossed my mind…"

He chuckled. "You're too transparent, Keera."

"And you're too perceptive, Reid. But I meant what I said about children. So if you still want me to work with your kids here, knowing what you know about me, I'll give you a couple of days as I'm the one who messed you up. You'll have the right to terminate my services, with no notice, though. Just thought I'd throw that in there for your protection."

"What happens if you discover you don't mind working with children? Or, better yet, even like it?"

"I'll return to my blessedly all-adult practice with the memories. But you're not converting me, Doctor. If that happens, I'll concede a slight change of heart after the ordeal is over, if I have to—which I don't expect I will have to do. But that's all you'll get from me."

"OK, then. Now that the ground rules are established…"

"What ground rules?"

"The ones where I'm going to work super-hard to change your mind and you're going to fight me off every step of the way." He smiled, mimicking a gauntlet sliding over his right arm. "You threw down the darned gauntlet, so don't blame me for picking it up and seeing what I can do with it."

She couldn't help it. She liked this pediatrician, in spite of his choice of medical specialties. Liked his humor, liked his rather frazzled look. In fact, while the prospect of children underfoot didn't exactly appeal to her, spending a few days with Reid underfoot suddenly seemed like a nice way to pass time that would have been time lost in books and sleep. He was cute.

"Fine, I'll do what I need to do. But I wouldn't be putting on that other gauntlet just yet." To honor the deal, she extended a hand to him then had to bite her lower lip to keep from gasping when he took it, as the smooth feel of his skin on hers ignited a spark that arced all the way up her arm.

"So, about that IV…" he said, rather reluctantly. "Let me run over to the dorm for a minute then I'll be right back. In the meantime, maybe you could check over supplies. I'll start the IV as you don't do kids and you could get everything ready."

Backing his way down the steps, he only turned round when he'd reached ground. Or maybe he lingered. In her mind, the uncertainty she saw there most certainly had to be over his routine gone horribly wrong, but she wished it could have been more. And while she wasn't open to a relationship of any lasting sort, a nice flirtation from time to time wasn't off her list. Except this man ran a camp for kids, and he had kids of his own—a reality that slammed her back to earth in a fraction of a breath as she went looking for IV supplies.

But a little while later, after his round of goodnights had been said to his daughters, and as she watched him skillfully master the insertion of an IV catheter into such a tiny vein, she was almost changing her mind again. No flirting allowed! Admire the man, admire his skill. Every bit of this was trouble and if she was smart, she'd turn round, go home and hire him some temps.

But she wasn't smart. Not about the kinds of things going through her mind, anyway.

"You don't spend much time away from them, do you?" Keera asked, catching Reid staring out the door at the cabin where the girls were sleeping. Megan was tucked in for the night, resting as comfortably as she could under the circumstances.

"Try not to. I mean, I work, have to take call when it's my turn. But I have fantastic friends who look after them at home, which makes life easier for me. And now, even when they're here at camp, in the dorm, I can visit them when I want."

"If you want to be free to go over there whenever, I can spend the night with Megan."

"That's not it. I know they're safe, and just a few hundred yards away. But I'm over-protective. Can't help it. Emmie had leukemia when I adopted them. She was a little over two and Allie was still a baby. Their mother..." He shrugged.

"I never really knew what happened. Apparently, she brought Allie into the world so her umbilical cord stem cells could be used in treating Emmie. They're only half-sisters, but the match was perfect. Their mother—her name was Maria—stayed around long enough to see that Emmie was responding to treatment, and then one day she didn't come to the hospital. I'd heard she'd come here seeking medical care for Emmie, and once she'd found it she'd gone home to Mexico, but I really don't know.

"Anyway, after that..." He shrugged. "Emmie improved, Allie was placed in foster-care for a while, but there was always a thought that if the stem-cell therapy failed, there was still potential for a bone-marrow transplant, with a sibling donor. So, Allie was brought back to the hospital to stay, and that's where I met the girls, actually. Allie wasn't sick but she was put on my service to care for."

"And you adopted them?"

"It became legal six months ago. But I've had them for nearly four years. Because they had to stay together, and because of Emmie's leukemia, they weren't considered highly adoptable. Then the restrictions for adopting parents were huge because of the medical considerations. One thing led to another and I took them. I don't regret it."

"And Emmie, is she in remission?"

"I like to think of it as full recovery because she's so healthy now. But, yes, she's in remission. We've got one more year left before we can celebrate her *recovery.*"

"Lucky girls," Keera commented.

"Lucky me. They slowed me down, forced me to look at life differently. I was on a pretty self-destructive path, indulging in just about every unhealthy kind of lifestyle habit there was. Smoking, fast foods three times a day, little to no sleep, amphetamines when needed. But when you have kids, you have to be…better." He smiled. "Or else they'll beat you down to a bloody pulp and walk all over you.

"Anyway, we have some choices here. The camp doesn't wake up for several more hours so, like I said earlier, you can go find the guest cabin and take advantage of the time while I stay here. Or you can stay with Megan while I take advantage of the next few hours. Your choice."

"My choice would have to be the noble thing, wouldn't it?" she said as she headed back into the clinic. "So save whatever's left of the night, and I'll be fine in one of the infirmary beds. Besides, I think it would be better if I stay closer to her because if she wakes up there's a chance she'll remember me."

"No arguments here. So, there are clean scrubs in the supply closet. Feel free to use the kitchen in the back of the infirmary and help yourself to tea, coffee, anything you want. And if you need me…" He held up his cellphone. "Or lean out the window and shout. I sleep with my windows open, and I'm a light sleeper."

"Literally?" she said, grabbing a pair of scrubs from the closet then pulling the curtain around the bed next to Megan's to afford herself a little privacy while she changed.

"Dad training is good for a lot of things," he said.

Megan's response was to whimper then turn on her side.

Keera's response to that was to sit down on the edge of the bed next to Megan, lay her hand gently to her cheek to feel for a temperature then go immediately for a cold compress.

Reid, on the other hand, stood back and watched. Then decided that for someone who didn't like children, and who claimed she didn't have a way with them, Keera had a way with them. A very nice way, when her guard wasn't up.

One o'clock, two o'clock, and now it was going on three and he hadn't gone to sleep yet. In fact, he wasn't even sleepy. Which was highly unusual, because most of the time he was worn out by the time his head hit the pillow. His head had hit the pillow at least twenty times in the past three hours, but hadn't stayed there. All because Dr. Keera Murphy, the avowed child-hater, was next door, and she was all he could think about. Pretty, with her coppery long hair and her green eyes. Feisty with her opinions. But compassionate, in spite of her blustery no-kids-allowed attitude.

He'd seen the way she'd held Megan, and protected her. He'd heard the way she comforted her. Nothing about that showed any kind of dislike for the little girl, so he wondered why the attempt at an outward persuasion against children when he didn't believe that was her inner feeling.

We all have our fears, he reminded himself, returning to the bedroom window for at least the tenth time to look over at the infirmary, to the single light shining inside it. *Fear.* Such an immense word. His biggest fears were for his daughters. Always. And specifically for Emmie's health. What were Keera's fears?

He wondered about that as he thought back over the years, back to a time when his own life had been fearless. Or, as some might describe it, stupid. Actually, as he might describe it now that he'd grown up. He'd been typically bachelor-selfish, making his various conquests along the way. Doing nothing so different from the majority of hotshot interns and residents. Bad life, bad attitude, all changed for the love of two little girls.

And out of that love had grown his fears. But he wouldn't trade what he had now for anything from his old life because even now, thinking about the way he'd been made him shudder.

Or was he shuddering because he could see the silhouette of Keera in the infirmary? She was awake, like he was, and standing at the window, too. Looking over at him perhaps?

CHAPTER THREE

"I'VE GOT YOU set up in the guest cottage," Reid said, giving Keera a gentle nudge.

Keera opened her eyes, looked up and there he was, looking down at her, almost as disheveled as she felt. "What time is it?" she mumbled, rubbing her eyes, trying to focus, and hating the fact that the sun was already up to remind her she'd only gone to sleep a little while ago.

"Going on to eight. Did you sleep well?"

"Like a baby. For three hours. Megan had a restless night. She kept waking up, calling for her mommy." She glanced over at the child, who'd finally gone to sleep after several fussy intervals. "And she was spiking a pretty high fever for a while, which finally broke around four. Poor thing was miserable."

"Well, there's a nice shower waiting for you in the guest cabin, if that'll make you feel any better."

"If there's a bed in the shower, that'll be perfect."

"I don't know about you, but I used to have nights when three hours of sleep were a blessing."

"Back in my residency," she said, sitting up and stretching. "Which, thankfully, has been over with for a while. And my hospital had a very strict policy with its surgical residents about taking care of ourselves. If we came in and looked the least bit tired or sluggish, we'd get bumped out of the OR and they'd put us on chart duty and paperwork for the entire shift. Once or twice doing that and you learned to get your sleep."

"You were lucky, then. Where I did my Pediatrics residency, they were so short-staffed we were always tired and sluggish." He smiled. "Makes for a better story than well rested and perky, doesn't it?"

Keera laughed. "Want to hear about all the paper cuts I got the first time I had to spend a day on chart duty?"

"Good try," he said, holding out his hand to pull her out of bed. "But I can top that with the time I worked thirty-six hours straight in the middle of a blizzard, and I was the only pediatrician in the hospital. Didn't even get a nap in."

She swung her legs over the edge of the bed, then stood, and immediately brushed her hair back from her face. "Yes, but did you get physically wounded, the way I did? Paper cuts can get infected, you know."

"Do leg cramps, aching feet and a sore back count?"

"*Six* paper cuts, Reid."

"And the only food available the whole time was from a vending machine." He smiled. "Can't top that, can you?"

"Yuck. Vending machines? Seriously?"

"Nothing but snack cakes and candy bars and potato chips for thirty-six hours."

"Enough!" she said, holding out her hand to stop him. "You win. I can't top that because we had a catering service…even though I was barely able to hold a fork to eat my shrimp Louie salad."

"You just don't give up, do you?" he asked, leading her to the tiny kitchen in the rear where a fresh pot of coffee was awaiting her.

"Where I come from, giving up came with serious side effects," she said, pouring a cup for Reid first then one for herself.

"And where would that be?" he asked lightly.

"The streets," she said, quite surprised how that had slipped out so easily. Normally that was a piece of her life she didn't put out there for other people to know about. Too often they judged or pitied her. Gave her funny looks or were wary. None of which she wanted. "Growing up was rough. My mother and I had a hard time sometimes," she said, then took a sip. "I made it through, though, probably because I'm too stubborn to give up."

"Then I'd say stubborn suits you."

"Most of the time," she conceded. "Look, I need that shower you mentioned."

"Take all the time you need, as long as it's not longer than an hour. I've got clinic this morning after breakfast, and the kids will start lining up in about an hour. So I can watch Megan only until then."

"Clinic?"

"We do basic checks, vital signs, that sort of thing, just to make sure we're not wearing them out. Most of the kids are in early remission or recovery, and they're not always the best judges of how they feel, so we keep a pretty close eye on that."

"I could do that if you want to stay here for a while and rest, because you look about as strung out as I feel. And as that's my fault, the least I could do is some of your work."

"Sounds like an offer I shouldn't refuse," he said. "You take the clinic, and I'll stay here with Megan, get some paperwork done, do a supplies inventory, answer some long-overdue e-mails from parents interested in sending their kids to camp here."

"Do you have more than one session a year?"

"Actually, we run eight, various ages and stages of recovery."

"And you personally oversee them all?"

He shook his head. "I oversee the one Emmie attends. Which will probably change in another year or two when she'll be old enough she doesn't want Dad hanging around her all the time. For the other sessions I have some of the best medical help in the country come in." He smiled with pride. "People are generous."

"I'm impressed."

He shrugged off the compliment. "Kids need to be kids, no matter what their medical condition. Camp Hope simply facilitates that."

"And you're too modest."

"Not modest. Just grateful something like this worked out in my life. Like I told you, I was a real screw-up before the girls."

"Then good for the girls for bringing out all the potential in you. Anyway, let me go grab a quick shower then… what, exactly, will I do in clinic?"

"Vitals, a few meds."

"Anybody on chemo?"

"No, we don't do chemo here. Our kids have, for the most part, already gone through that stage a time or two. Although giving chemo's an option for the future because even kids who are that sick need a diversion, which Camp Hope would give them. Right now we just don't have the facilities for it. Someday, though…maybe a chemotherapy facility. Who knows, maybe even an entire hospital devoted to leukemia.

"Anyway, right now we do follow-up therapy with drugs for nausea, and a couple of our kids are getting prednisone and methotrexate. It's all basic stuff, pretty much. Each kid has a chart. Medicines are stored away according to the child." He handed her the key to the medicine storage. "So check their ID with the chart and, well…you'll figure it out.

"Betsy can come in later and help after her morning

sickness has ended for the day. Just let me know if you need her, and I'll give her a shout."

"Basic stuff," she repeated. "I guess I find it difficult to believe you'd leave me alone with your kids. You don't even know me."

"The Internet's an amazing tool. I know what I need to know. As in do you want me to tell you what color dress you wore when you received your Surgeon of Distinction award last year?"

"I don't like awards and accolades."

"So you said in your acceptance speech. Oh, and it was black—with sequins. Nice look."

"Yeah, well, I prefer scrubs." With that, she turned away and headed for the door. Keera stopped by Megan's bed on the way out though and straightened her blanket. "I'll be back in a little while," she whispered. But the child didn't so much as stir, so Keera tiptoed away.

"Good morning, Doc Keera," the first boy said, as he held up his banded arm for her to read his name.

"Good morning." She looked at the band and smiled. "Gregory Carson. So, you get…" She glanced through his chart to see what was ordered for him.

He gave her a quizzical look. "Weight, temperature, blood pressure, pulse," he said. "And a pill for my nausea. It's what we all get, except the pill. I still need it. Some of the other kids don't."

"Really?" Gregory was astute. Very much on top of his condition. Which impressed her more than she'd been expected to be impressed.

He nodded. "Every day while we're here. Then I go to the doctor once a week when I'm home. Sometimes twice, if I'm not feeling well. I'm in early recovery, so they need to make sure nothing is changing."

The child was so matter-of-fact about his condition and, more than that, his whole life situation, that she wasn't even sure how to respond. "How old are you?" she asked him.

"Seven and a half, but you can consider me eight, if you want to." His broad grin revealed a missing tooth.

"Well, since you're *eight*, I think you're old enough to take some responsibility for yourself, like recording your own pulse, maybe taking your own temperature, and weighing yourself. The more control you take over your physical condition, the better off you'll be." Her check of him revealed his blood pressure, temperature and pulse to be normal. Weight consistent with the past several days. A little under his normal but not losing.

"Does that make sense to you?" she asked, as she recorded the numbers in his chart.

"I—I don't know. Isn't that what a doctor's supposed to do?"

"Or a nurse. Or your parents." She looked up from the chart and smiled at him. "Or, you, if you think you're old enough. I mean, almost eight…that's getting pretty old, you know."

OK, so maybe her doctoring approach was a little beyond his years, but it made sense that gaining more confidence in dealing with his condition would serve him well in the long run. Living with the idea that his cancer might recur had to be frightening, but spending every moment of his life depending on someone else to tell him he was doing fine had to be difficult.

Of course, she'd never had leukemia, never been chronically ill, but she'd spent too many years being dependent on someone else's conclusions about her, and it was such a helpless feeling.

"So, here's what we're going to do as soon as I can get

it squared away on the schedule—and only if you think you're old enough to take on some responsibility. I want you to come back over here to the clinic, and we're going to talk about making your own choices. Then, if we have time, maybe I can show you how to do some medical procedures. But only if you want to."

He frowned, not sure what to say.

"Do you want to do that?" she asked him.

"Yes, I think so," he said, sounding nearly as tentative as she felt taking the initiative. But it was a good idea. She knew it! Would have loved someone teaching her the right initiatives to take when she had been as young as Gregory.

"Good. So, do you have a computer with you?"

He nodded. "It's mostly for games."

"Games, and in a little while we're going to start using it to track what doctors call your vital statistics. Do you know what those are?"

This time Gregory shrugged.

"Don't worry," Keera said, patting him on the shoulder. "It's easy stuff. But it's also very important. So, about your pill…"

After she shooed Gregory out the door, she went through much the same process with the next child, Charlie. Aged seven. And Heather, aged eight.

"So what are you teaching these kids?" she asked Reid an hour later, after all the kids, including Emmie, had gone through their routine morning check-up, and those who needed medication were medicated.

"Yesterday we went over some of the physiology of leukemia. Talked about white blood cells and how they—"

"They're not much more than babies, Reid. They don't need the physiology lectures. What they need are the practical, day-to-day aspects of coping with their condition. They're all in some form of remission or recovery or whatever you want to call it, but they need to know what's normal for where they are in their recovery, and how to take care of some of their basic medical needs. Which I told a few of the older kids I'd teach them, if that's OK with you?

"And while I know you're so close to it, with your daughter in recovery, I think your tendency may be to baby them or protect them more than they should be protected."

"So you're here for one day and you know what's best for them?" It was said not so much in anger as in practiced reserve against the way he might really feel.

"That's not fair. I'm responding to a medical condition, and—"

"And you don't have a clue, Keera. Not a damn clue." Now the anger was peeking through, but only a little. "Last night you were pretty clear about how you don't like kids and now you're changing my program?"

"Not changing it. Just giving some of the kids a different option. You know, more control."

Reid took a deep breath to steady himself, then physically squared his shoulders. "OK, I know you want to help and I appreciate that, but these kids...they put all their trust in us, rely on us, and if you get yourself involved more than I asked you to, somewhere down the line one of these kids is going to put trust in you that won't be fulfilled.

"You can't do that to them, Keera. Medical procedures are one thing, but what you want to do is embark on a course that will change their lives in some way, and while I'm all for that, and would do it myself if I had time, the program this camp follows isn't about giving a few minutes of commitment then moving on. These kids depend on us, and you're about to step into the position of having them depend on you. Which isn't what you want, is it?"

He was right. She'd overstepped without thinking it through. She saw that now, and felt bad, especially as she was the intruder here. But her approach to medicine had never been laid-back. In fact, her approach to life had never been laid-back, and that's all Reid seemed to be—laid-back. Truthfully, her preference in men had always been for someone who was forceful. Of course, look what that had gotten her. Married to a man who had forced himself right out of their marriage and away with his mistress. Still…

"I didn't mean to do something I wasn't supposed to," she said. "And you're right. I don't want these kids relying on me then maybe getting hurt in the process. That's not what I meant to do."

"I know it's not. And to be honest, I'd love to expand my program here. But I don't have the means or the volunteers. Until we're larger, and can support larger programs, we're minimalists, and that's the best we can do."

"Then say the word and I'll tell the kids there's been a change of plans." She drew in a stiff breath as the sinking feeling set in that she was about to bite off way more than she'd ever expected to chew. "But I'd still like to do this, if that's OK with you. Because it is the right thing. Also because I promised and I don't want to let these kids down. So to prove how strongly I believe that empowering them over their conditions is the right thing to do, I'll…" Keera swallowed hard. "I'll stay for the week to follow through with teaching them. Only if you want me to, though."

"*Seriously?* You'd really stay and help?"

"Seriously," she said. Then instantly felt queasy.

"When I called you outspoken and opinionated, I guess I didn't know how much. But go ahead. You promised, and if the kids are expecting it, then we should give them what they're expecting." He grinned. Extended a hand to her. "Welcome to the staff of Camp Hope."

Or, in her case, Camp Hopeless, she thought as she

shook his hand. "So, this is how I'm going to spend my summer vacation." Keera watched Reid's face, couldn't determine what he was feeling. He had an odd expression, and she didn't know him well enough to read it, but she could only guess that he was wishing she'd never come here. "It's the right thing, Reid. I promise, they're old enough."

"As interpreted by the doctor who doesn't like children?" he asked.

"As interpreted by the doctor who was forced to grow up too young and take on responsibilities no child should ever have to face. But it got me through My independence is what saved my life many times over. And while you might not agree with me, I sincerely believe that giving these kids a bit of independence over their situations will save their lives, too.

"Maybe not in dramatic ways. Or maybe it will be in a dramatic way for one of them. Who knows? But, whatever the case, it's going to count for something. And, yes, it's also being interpreted by the doctor who warned you she wasn't good with children. I am good with my patients, though. Damned good, Reid, because I learned my childhood lessons well."

"And never had time to be a child?" he asked, his voice now sympathetic.

"I didn't need to be a child." With that, she moved past him into the infirmary to spend the next shift sitting with Megan and planning her first lesson—*"Taking your temperature."*

Poor Megan looked miserable, lying there in bed, with a rash finally popping out on her. She was awake, though. Looking around. Alert. "Remember me?" Keera asked, keeping a sideways glance on Reid, who was trying very hard to seem busy with a supply inventory when she knew he was really trying to keep an eye on her. She didn't blame him. All things considered, she'd be doing the same if the situation were reversed.

Megan shook her head. "Want my mommy," she whimpered.

Keera didn't know how to respond to that so, instead, she said, "You came to visit me yesterday. Then I took you to play at the hospital, and we came here last night when you weren't feeling so well. My name is Keera. I was a friend of your daddy's."

"She was in a hospital daycare center?" Reid asked from across the room. "Exposing all the other children? Have you notified them yet?"

"You really want to be critical of me, don't you?" she said, smiling for Megan's sake, even though she was gritting her teeth underneath.

"You get high praise for surgery, but this isn't surgery, and I haven't seen enough of your style to know whether or not I'm a fan. But I'm giving you the benefit of the doubt here. You're out of your element, so that does start you off with a few extra points in your favor, since you're trying."

"Well, in or out of my element, I did call the hospital first thing this morning. Talked to the daycare director, let her know. Offered all the apologies I could muster. Unlike you, she wasn't grumpy about it. She said contagion happens all the time with kids and they simply look at it as a way to bolster young immune systems."

"You say that with a lot of indifference."

"No. I said it with a sigh of relief because I really don't like going around spreading infectious conditions everywhere I go. Especially here, where these kids have compromised immunity. But as far as the center goes, I got lucky because the director told me the children are all vaccinated before they're allowed in, that they sanitize the entire area several times a day, so not to worry."

She frowned. "Are you OK, Reid? Yesterday you weren't this...testy. In fact, you weren't even this testy earlier this morning. Is it because I suggested a program?"

"No. I'm just not a big fan of change."

"But I thought that's what you wanted for Camp Hope. Growth. Change."

"It is, but I don't have to adjust to it easily. That's just me. Kicking at progression when I'm the one egging it on."

"We do get used to our ruts, don't we?"

"Sometimes a rut isn't such a bad place to be. When Emmie was sick, she'd have these periods where she wasn't as bad, maybe not even sick at all, and I found myself praying to stay there. I didn't want to move forward, or sideways or backwards, for that matter. That one spot was..."

"Safe?" she asked.

He nodded. "Even though there was always the possibility that tomorrow might be even better, if today wasn't so bad, I didn't want to move away from it."

"Uncertainty can be paralyzing. When I was a child, nothing ever stayed the same in my life, and I think I was like you. If it worked, I didn't want it to change. But life changes every time we blink our eyes, doesn't it? And for Camp Hope, I was that blink."

"You're welcome here, Keera. I'm sorry your little girl is sick, but we'll manage it. It all just disrupted my routine, which..."

"Makes you grumpy."

He smiled. "Welcome to my world."

"We all have our quirks. You're likely to see my grumpiest come out if my surgical instruments aren't lined up a certain way on the tray. Or the wrong music gets played. I have a sequence I follow, never vary it, and if someone changes that, for any reason…" She shrugged. "Let's just say it can get ugly. I'm not mean, mind you, but I'm very demanding."

"I can't picture you any other way. Look, I'm sorry, Keera. Sorry I came at you so abruptly this morning, and I'm mostly sorry about my reaction to what's really a good idea. Because you're right, these kids do have to take responsibility for themselves, but sometimes when I look at them, all I see is…"

"Emmie. Who's spent most of her life being dependent on her daddy. I do understand that, Reid. For me it's a practical matter, and for you it's personal."

"What's personal is she doesn't need me so much any more. Which scares me, because at the end of the day I'm a father before I'm anything else. And it has nothing to do with her leukemia and everything to do with it. Maybe it's also because I don't know what normal's supposed to be. The three of us really don't have that in our family."

"Is being a single dad that difficult?"

"Yes and no. Because there's never been a mommy in the picture, we make it work the way it needs to. As they say, it is what it is. But I'd be lying if I told you that doing this alone is easy, because it's not. When the adoption became final, the judge congratulated me and told me single parenting is the new normal. Not sure what that's supposed to be, though."

"One person's lack of normality is another person's normality." Keera smiled sympathetically at Reid. "And as far as Emmie goes, she's seven. Trust me, what she's going to need from you has only just begun. And that has nothing to do with her medical condition." She turned her attention back to Megan, who'd dozed off again. "But what she's going to need…"

Her voice trailed off because Keera knew. Dear God,

she knew in all the ways no child should ever have to know. Love was the start of it, which Reid had in abundance. And protection. And guidance. None of which she'd ever had given to her.

But Emmie, Allie and Megan would all need room to grow and develop as well, and that was something she'd created for herself because no one else had ever been there to help her. It was something Reid would eventually have to create for his daughters, like it or not, in spite of Emmie's physical condition. And something someone would have to create for Megan.

"Do you suppose if I wandered over to the dining hall, I might be able to beg a scrap of toast or a sandwich? Seems I haven't eaten since…" She thought for a moment. "Lunch yesterday. Except for an apple on my way here last night."

"That's an option. Or there's my kitchen. I wield a pretty mean toaster. And I have jam…"

"Please say strawberry!"

"Allie's favorite. Can't be without it."

"Then, by all means, lead me to Allie's favorite. I need a little fortifying before my first group of kids expect me to teach them the intricacies of taking a temperature. And maybe a couple of scrambled eggs, if you've got them."

"With green peppers and onions?"

"In my fondest dreams!" She smiled. "Oh, and, Reid? Don't worry. As fussy as you are over your daughters, I'm sure your girls will keep you in first place until they meet the boys who will steal their hearts away from you."

"Like I really wanted to hear that," he said, on his way out the door to go and fix Keera's meal.

Fifteen minutes later he returned with a tray complete with eggs, toast, and orange juice. Keera couldn't remember when something had smelled so good. Something about being at camp made her ravenous, and this was a perfect brunch. "You hungry?" she asked Megan, wondering if the child might eat a piece of toast.

Megan shook her head.

"Would you eat a small piece with strawberry jam on it?"

Apparently the bribe of strawberry jam caught her attention, because Megan nodded tentatively, then proceeded to eat an entire half a slice of toast and drink a small glass of apple juice before she slid back down into bed and rolled over on her side.

"You're persuasive," Reid commented.

"Strawberry jam is persuasive. I'm merely the means to that jam." She pulled the blanket back up over Megan and returned to finish her own food.

"So, how did your father manage it when you started to not need him as much?"

"He didn't," she said without a hint of emotion. "In fact, I was the daughter of a single mother. No daddy in my life. Not even in absentia. My mother…she wasn't interested in lasting relationships, I suppose you could say. Men came and went, none ever stayed."

She glanced at her watch. "I promised to squeeze my class in between agility training and lunch, if you could stay here with Megan for about thirty minutes. Or maybe one of the volunteers…"

"Sally Newton said she'd be glad to sit with Megan when we need her. She's a retired schoolteacher, loves the kids with a passion. Had leukemia herself when she was a child. So let me give her a call as I need to go and oversee agility."

"Am I making you late?"

"That's fine. It takes about ten minutes to get the kids settled down anyway, so I'll be just on time." He was finally feeling less stressed than he had all morning. Basically, he liked Keera. Liked her strength. Or, as some might call it, her brute force. And she was a force to be reckoned with, make no mistake about it.

He did have to admit, though, that he wasn't sure about her ideas about the children. On the surface it sounded good, and what she wanted to do with the children seemed reasonable, because he was all for these kids taking responsibility for various aspects of their health, even at their young ages. Keera seemed to have an agenda, though. She'd alluded to a rough childhood and needing her independence to get through it.

Still, there was something bigger. Something deeper. Maybe something to prove? And that's what worried him a little because the only agenda here was giving these kids everything they needed to be a kid in recovery. Simple plan with a single purpose.

He wasn't going to stop her, though, because he did see the value in it. And maybe when he got to know her better, he'd be a little more trusting. *Provided* he got to know her better. Which he hoped he would.

"Well, Dr. Reid, for a pediatrician you're a pretty darned good cook. My full stomach thanks you for the wonderful breakfast, or lunch, or whatever it was."

"My culinary skills thank you for the compliment. And just so you'll know, I can make a pretty good grilled cheese sandwich, if you're hungry later on."

"Good to know, just in case. Anyway, let me go sit with Megan for another ten minutes, then if you could ask Sally to come round?"

He nodded on his way out the door, stopping first at the sink to scrub his hands.

"And, Reid, the class is the right thing. I'm glad you're going to let me try it. I know you're worried, but I really believe these kids should take part in their care, and I want to get started because there's so much to teach them and I've only got a few days."

"I'd be lying if I didn't say I was concerned, because I am. Yes, it's important to empower them, but it could also be said that because their lives are so overwhelmed with their conditions they don't need to do anything more than they already do. You know, give them time to be children."

"How about giving them time to be responsible children? Because they do have to go about their lives differently, and you can't deny that. That's not robbing them of their childhood, though. It's only adding another layer to it."

"You don't ever give in, do you?"

She smiled. "Not unless I'm backed into a corner."

"No corner here. Although I'm going to warn you that for a woman who doesn't like kids, you're waging a mighty tough battle on behalf of these kids. Could it be the facade is cracking a little?"

"I don't have to like kids to want to do the right thing by them."

"You're right, you don't. But battles are waged because of passions, and you're waging a battle for them, Keera. Seems like someone's trying to fool someone, doesn't it?" He gave her a wink then grabbed a paper towel to dry his hands. "Now, let me go find Sally."

"Is her little girl sick like Emmie used to be?" Allie asked. She was sitting on the step outside when Reid left the infirmary.

"Aren't you supposed to be in arts and crafts?"

Allie rolled big, sad eyes up at him. A gesture that always melted him right down to nothing. Even at five, she knew that. "I missed you."

"And I missed you too, Miss Allejandra Lourdes Reid.

But you need to go back to arts and crafts." He scooped the child up into his arms and walked across the compound with her, heading to the building where Allie should be occupied with finger-painting and sculpting with modeling clay, while the older children were involved in basic agility exercises on the obstacle course. "And, no, Dr. Murphy's little girl isn't sick the way Emmie was. Do you remember what I told you about something being contagious? How when some people get sick, other people can get sick from being too close to them? What Emmie had wouldn't make anybody else sick, but what Megan has can make people get sick if they get too close to her, which is why you can't go inside the infirmary. I don't want you getting sick."

"Will you get sick, Daddy?"

"No." And this was where he didn't want to launch into the explanation of vaccinations and how some illnesses, like measles, you'd only catch once. Which he'd had "Doctors have special ways to protect themselves."

"Good," she said earnestly. "Because I don't know how to take care of you yet."

"Yes, you do," he whispered, as he headed down the back steps and handed the child over to Ciera, the arts and crafts volunteer. Hated like hell watching Ciera take Allie away.

Turning away to head off to agility training, he saw Kccra watching him from the infirmary window, and wondered why someone like her didn't like children. What had she missed out on in her life that had scared her off so badly from what he believed to be one of the fundamental joys of life?

"You just don't know you like them," he said to himself. "But you will. Another few days here, and you will."

CHAPTER FOUR

"HOW DID IT GO?" Reid asked, catching up to Keera, who was crossing the compound, her arms loaded with supplies, on her way back to the infirmary.

"Pretty good. We learned all about thermometers, what a body's temperature indicates, and how to take and read temperatures. I had them taking each other's temps, and I think there may be a few budding doctors in the group. Including Emmie. She's quite a little leader."

"As in bossy?" he asked.

"As in taking charge and being helpful. She's a sweet little girl, Reid. You're doing a good job with her. Oh, and she and Allie and I have a date for lunch in a little while. They want to show me something. Sally said she'd sit with Megan, so I hope that's OK? Because I asked the cook to pack us a little picnic. You're invited too. Something about the wading place."

He smiled. "The water's nice there. Not very deep. And so clear you can see the bottom."

"Well, apparently I need to go wading, and as I've never been, I've got able volunteers who want to teach me. All with your permission, of course."

"Something about being around a strong woman seems to be bringing out the best in my girls."

"I'm not overstepping the mark, am I?"

He shook his head. "They asked me first. I said yes."

"And you're coming?"

"I'll try. I need to do a physical on one of the kids, but that shouldn't take too long."

"Something wrong?" she asked.

He shook his head. "Physician request. It happens all the time."

"Good, then I'll see you at the wading place. But be warned, we might be talking *girl* things most of the time."

"See, that's the part of single parenting that's tough. They need a woman's touch, and it's just not there. I don't have a sister near by, and my mother and dad are in South America right now, running a medical clinic in Ecuador. No aunts or female cousins either."

"No girlfriend?"

"Had a fiancée for a while, but she didn't like the idea that I adopted a sick child. She thought it would take too much time away from her. And she was correct about that. It did. So she was right to dump me. Haven't really had time for a social life since then."

"Which leaves two little girls without a female influence in their lives."

"Right. It's amazing what you can pick up in the parenting magazines, though," he said, grinning. "I've got a whole stack of them, if you'd ever care to…"

She shook her head. "I was talking to social services a while ago, and they're going to place Megan with a nice foster-family as soon as she's medically able. And don't even begin to think I can be as generous as you and take her in, because I can't.

"She's the…well, she's not the reason my marriage ended, but she was one of the factors. My husband's secret baby. So while I know it's not her fault what her daddy did, and I totally understand that she's the only true innocent in a very ugly situation, I can't spend the rest of my life looking at her, knowing that…"

"That you failed?"

"Yes, I failed. But that's not even it. I didn't even know how to try. And Megan's that reminder."

"So you'll let her go to some stranger because of something you perceive as a lack in yourself."

"Fostering that little girl has never been an option for me. My lifestyle won't allow it."

"Yet you'll go on a lunch date with my little girls. That seems to conflict with your *no-kids-allowed* rule."

Stepping into the infirmary, Keera dropped her armload of supplies on the nearest desk, then spun to face Reid. "You did a good thing adopting your girls. You're a good man. A generous man. A very caring man. And that's all you.

"But I don't want the responsibility, OK? I feel sorry for Megan. My heart is breaking for her and I want to make sure she gets into a good situation. But that's not me. I work. I sleep. Then I work some more. Nothing there's going to change because I don't want it to change.

"So don't think that because I've agreed to give you one week of service here, and go on a picnic with your girls, that I'm going to come out of it with some big change of heart. My life is fine the way it is. It's not empty. I'm happy."

"And pretty damn defensive about it, too," he added.

"And pretty damn honest about it, Reid. I know what I can and can't have, and what you have…" She shook her head. "I can't have that."

"But can you have dinner? Tonight, after the kiddies are asleep? I've got enough people on call to cover us, I'm sure Sally will be fine spending an extra couple of hours looking after Megan, and there's an amazingly elegant little café about ten miles down the road. It sits on top of a mountain, and they say the sunset is breathtaking."

"In scrubs?" she asked. "Because that's all I have to wear."

"There's a little mercantile on the way. We could stop and do some shopping. Maybe for Megan as well, because she'll be up and out of bed by tomorrow or the day after."

An evening out with a man sounded surprisingly good. So did shopping for Megan. And while she and Reid didn't see eye to eye on a lot of things, she really liked him. Was curious to see him away from his element. "This isn't you asking me out on a date so you can get some personal satisfaction that you broke down my code a little, is it?"

He laughed. "Are you always so ungracious about what's just a simple gesture of friendship?"

"Not ungracious." She tilted her head up to look him straight in the eyes. "Just cautious."

"I don't want anything from you, Keera, except the days you promised me. Because, believe it or not, I'm as *cautious* as you are. Maybe even more, since I've got my daughters to consider."

"Then I suppose it's a date." She smiled. "Cautiously speaking."

"Eat one more bite," Keera encouraged Megan. Who would have guessed one bowl of soup could have taken so long? But Megan was being stubborn, and Sally was standing ready to swoop in and take over as soon as Keera admitted defeat.

"Maybe she's not hungry," the older woman said. "It doesn't always do to force children to eat if they don't want to."

"She's going to get too weak," Keera protested. "And

it's just soup." She felt totally defeated, failing at such a simple task.

"But does she like the soup?" Sally asked.

It had never occurred to her that Megan would have food preferences. Which just went to prove, even more, that she wasn't the one to take care of this child. "Do you like the soup?" she asked Megan.

Megan shook her head, indicating an adamant no.

"Then is there anything you would like to eat?"

"Strawberries," she said. "Want strawberries."

"Which would be toast with strawberry jam." She looked at Sally. "It's what she had for breakfast."

"And it's what she'll have for lunch. Let me run over to the kitchen, and I'll fix some."

"Is that all you want?" Keera asked Megan.

This time Megan nodded in the affirmative.

"They do have their opinions, even at that age," Reid said on his way in, as Sally flew out the door. He pulled out a stethoscope and listened to Megan's chest. "Bet you like peanut butter, too, don't you?" he asked the child, once he pulled the earpieces from his ears.

"Yes," she said. "And bananas."

"Then we'll see if we can find you some peanut butter and bananas for dinner. OK?"

Megan nodded.

"See, it comes naturally to you," Keera said. "And I don't have a clue."

"Well, I have an advantage. Not only am I a father, I work with children every day of my life. Before I went to med school I didn't have a clue, but I've learned. And that's what it's about, Keera. Learning. Trial and error, in my opinion, is the best way to figure it out. Oh, and she's not as congested as she was last night. I think the medicine is working. And as she's eating, it's time to yank the

IV. You want me to get rid of that nasty old tube in your arm, Megan?"

"It itches," she said, nodding.

"Well, we don't want you itching."

Keera stood back and watched the natural interplay between Reid and Megan, and admired the way he was so at ease with the child. It was like he knew exactly what she wanted. In a way, she envied that as it was a rapport she didn't have with her own patients. If ever there was someone who'd been put on this earth to work with children…

"Try," he prompted Keera.

"Try what?"

"To find your way in. One little thing—that's all it will take."

"Except I don't have a clue what that one little thing is."

"There's no specific one little thing. Like I said, trial and error. Think about something children love. Something you loved when you were a child."

She thought for a moment then smiled. "Megan, after you eat your toast and strawberries, would you like…" she glanced over at Reid, then back at Megan "…ice cream?"

Megan's eyes lit up. "Yes," she squealed.

"Then ice cream it is," Keera confirmed, feeling the same sense of accomplishment she usually felt after a long, grueling surgery.

"And you think you don't have a way with kids," Reid said. "One bowl of ice cream is going to go a lot further than you thought. Just wait and see."

"One bowl of ice cream doesn't make me parenting material. And even with that, you had to prompt me."

He laughed. "When Emmie was younger, and on chemo, getting her to eat was maybe the hardest thing I had to do, other than standing around and feeling so helpless. Bribes were good, though. What worked as often as not was a good honest talk with her about the importance of taking a bite or two. Kids her age...even kids Megan's age...do understand, and sometimes we forget that because we're so busy trying to convince them in a child's logic. But they live in an adult world as well, and you have to keep that in mind."

The adult world she'd known as a child had been harsh, cruel. Unfair. "I think it's better to let them live in their childhood world as long as they can, because when the adult world takes over..." She shrugged, then turned to Megan. "I'm going to get your ice cream now. Vanilla or chocolate?"

"'Nilla," she said, then smiled for the first time since Keera had known her.

Beautiful little girl, beautiful smile. She did look like her daddy, though. Especially the depth she saw in Megan's eyes. Kevin had always had that depth, had always seen things so deeply. She thought about their marriage as she dashed to the kitchen to scoop up the ice cream. It had started so well, all the regular hopes and dreams and plans. Then had ended so badly she'd blotted out most of everything past the midway point.

How did something like that happen to two people? It scared her because while on one level she understood how they'd grown apart, on a much deeper level she didn't understand it at all. Which meant she was doomed to repeat her mistakes—the reason why she wasn't going to do that ever again.

"Where'd you go?" Reid asked her, when she returned with the ice cream, only to find Megan munching away quite happily on a piece of toast.

"What do you mean? I'm right here."

"I don't mean in the literal sense," he said. "There was this look in your eyes when you came back in."

"Ex-husband stuff. Megan looks like him."

"And that bothers you?"

"Not really. But I was wondering how a marriage could go as wrong as ours did. There was a time when we were good, but it didn't last very long. And from the point we started losing, there was no way to get any of it back."

"But did you try?"

"Honestly, I don't know. Wouldn't have mattered, because he was already so invested in his other life."

"But you still loved him?"

"I'd like to say yes, or even no. But I don't know if I ever did, at least in the way you're supposed to when you commit your life to someone." She glanced down at the ice cream, and smiled. "But now I have his little girl, and I'm sure she'd prefer her ice cream not melted. So..." She stepped around Reid but stopped. "I'm not an indecisive person, Reid. Most of the time I'm probably more forceful than most people you know. Which is what made the end of my marriage so bitter, because it turned out that's the trait he hated most in me."

"As they say, 'One man's mistake is another man's opportunity,' or something like that."

"Only if she wants to be another man's opportunity. But I don't." And she meant it. Some people were meant to be alone, and she was one of those people. Although there were times she wished that weren't the case. "See you in a little while at the wading place."

The wading place turned out to be a wide spot in the pristine stream that ran serenely through the property. Surrounded by trees and rhododendron bushes, it was very isolated, and so clear and perfect that the pebbles on the bottom glistened like diamonds in the sun. Before they were even settled into a picnic spot, the girls had their shoes off and were wading across the shining pebbles, the water only coming barely above their ankles.

"I think I was just an excuse to come here," Keera said to Reid, who meandered in a few minutes after she was settled on the blanket. "This is...beautiful. It's a shame Megan couldn't have come along, too."

"Another day," Reid said, dropping down beside her. "To be honest, this spot is one of the reasons I bought the whole camp. I was looking at three different places for sale—two were former camps that had closed, and one was an undeveloped piece of property. I'd known for a while this was something I had to do." He smiled as he began to remove his shoes. "It came to me in a dream one night. Inspired, I think, by a picnic I'd taken the girls on earlier that day. Emmie was pretty sick, but she'd really enjoyed her time outside, and I thought about all the other kids with leukemia who barely ever get to see the light of day.

"Then I remembered all the fun times I had as a kid when I'd gone to camp...one thing led to another and I literally had a dream about being a camp leader.

"It stayed with me, so after a while I started looking into what it would take to set up a camp. The answer was, pretty much everything I had. But money's replaceable, you know. Children aren't. So I started looking, took the girls along with me. And when we were walking over this property and stumbled on this spot...well, you see how the girls reacted. What could I do?"

"Other than buy it for them and go broke."

Reid smiled. "So I'm flat broke for a while. No big deal. I have a good medical practice, and I'll earn it all back, and then some, over time. The thing about the camp is this is where I really learned to not think in terms of material possessions so much as value or worth. It changed my whole outlook on life. Allowed me to give something to the girls that goes beyond what money can buy."

"Allows you to give that to other people's girls and boys as well. I like the way you're putting your medical skills to other less traditional applications. I'm basically a traditionalist. I need four walls and surgical instruments, and anything else throws me for a loop. But this is...well, in a sense I suppose you could call it a hospital, because it does tend to the needs of children who need tending."

"A hospital without walls," he said. "I like that. So, are you coming wading, too?"

"Are there things in the stream that can bite me?"

Rather than answering, Reid nearly doubled over laughing. "Maybe tadpoles," he finally managed, "but I don't know if they even have teeth."

"I'm serious. I've never really been a nature girl, and sometimes I'm not so brave in the unknown."

He pointed to his daughters, who were busy splashing each other.

"OK, I get it. If they aren't afraid, I shouldn't be afraid."

"And I won't desert you, Keera. If I see a menacing tadpole swimming in your direction, I'll shoo it away."

"My knight in shining armor," she said, as she slid out of her sandals and rolled up the bottoms of her scrub pants.

"It's hard to believe you've never been wading," he said, extending a hand to help her up off the ground. "Makes me wonder what other kinds of things you've never done that I might be able to show you."

She took his hand and let herself be pulled to her feet. But once she was up he didn't let go of her hand. Instead, he held it as they walked towards the stream. Like lovers, they strolled along the path, hand in hand, shoulder to shoulder, as if they'd done it before. Or should have done it before. "I've lived a sheltered life," she admitted at the stream's edge. "You know, die-hard city girl."

"Well, welcome to the country, city girl." He led her into the water. She clung to him even harder.

"It's not like a wading pool," she said as she relaxed.

"No, it's better."

"Yes," she almost purred. "It's much, much better." But she wasn't sure what, exactly, was better. Was it the water or the fact that she liked holding Reid's hand? Or the fact that he still wasn't letting go? That was the part she liked best, she decided. Definitely the part she liked best.

"It's only for a week," Reid said, laughing as Keera picked out the tenth outfit for Megan. Clothes, plus dolls, accessories, all kinds of little-girl things.

After a little wading and a quick picnic, they'd returned to camp and she'd spent the rest of the afternoon with Megan, reading to her, playing games, even watching her sleep. Something about the child pulled her in. Maybe it was the fear she saw in her eyes, or that look of being a little girl lost. A look she was sure she herself had had most of her childhood.

Her heart did go out to Megan, more and more with every passing minute, because each minute brought the poor child closer to the reality that awaited her. A reality Keera couldn't change. So even after an afternoon spent renouncing the material things in life, Keera was having a good time trying to compensate for Megan's terrible losses by piling new material things on it. And, admittedly, she loved little-girl shopping, and wished desperately Megan could have come along to be part of it.

"I want her to have nice things wherever she goes to. Wherever social services puts her."

"I imagine they'll gather up some of the things she already owns," he said.

"Which will only remind her of what she's lost. No, I'll buy her everything she needs for her new life."

"But what if she has a favorite doll or book? Doesn't she deserve to have those with her?" He liked this fierce attitude she was taking up on Megan's behalf. Whether or not she wanted to admit it, Keera was investing a little of herself in that child, and that was a good thing. Although Reid wasn't about to fool himself into believing that she would keep the child, as she'd been brutally honest about that more than once.

"What she deserves is to move into her new life without sadness left over from the old one," Keera said as she grabbed the cutest little pink, fuzzy pajamas off the shelf, looked them over, then went back for an additional pair in yellow.

"So, what about you? We've been here an hour, our reservations are in twenty minutes, and you're still in your scrubs. Remember how we came here to buy you something respectable to wear to dinner tonight?"

"Twenty minutes?" Keera rolled the shopping cart at Reid, then spun away. "Go ahead and start checking out," she called back to him as she literally ran to the ladies' department. "By the time they get most of it rung up…" The rest of her words were lost as she rounded a corner, while he stood in the middle of the aisle, simply smiling. Losing her had definitely been her ex-husband's mistake. Huge mistake!

It was a thought still on Reid's mind a few minutes later when Keera skidded into the checkout line behind him, her arms loaded with…well, he wasn't sure. Dresses, underwear, shoes? No way she could have done all that shopping in such a short time. But, as it turned out, she had, because as the last of Megan's items were scanned, Keera added her armload to the end of it. After she'd paid, she grabbed one of the bags and headed straight for the ladies' room, from which, a minute or two later, she emerged looking remarkably put together in her little black dress, matching shoes, and…make-up.

"How did you do all of that in…?" He glanced at his watch, exaggerating a shrug.

Laughing, Keera brushed her fingers through her hair. She'd pulled it out of its no-nonsense ponytail a minute earlier, but hadn't had time to run a brush through it, and it looked like the mane of a wild horse. Untamed, a bit flyaway. But she was dressed otherwise, and actually felt pretty good about the way she looked. "Years of practice, street clothes to scrubs in a minute flat. My best record." She grinned. "This took a little longer."

"Longer? I think if you could patent the formula, husbands all over the world would buy it. I know my dad and my brothers-in-law would."

"Just a matter of practice," she said, taking several of the bags from Reid then following him out to the car. "My mother and I had to…let's say we had to be on the move at any given second, so I learned early on that I either had to be fast or things got left behind." Including her, several times.

"Well, you look amazing," he said, eyeing her from head to toe. "Can't imagine how you'd improve on it if you'd had, say, half an hour."

"Primping for half an hour's a waste. In that same thirty minutes I could have a patient totally prepped for an incision. Or have that incision made, and be well on my way to exploring an occluded artery."

"Nice dinner conversation," he said, holding open the car door for her.

"Except we're not at dinner yet." Stepping in, she smoothed her dress and tried to pull it down a little over her legs, but it was a bit short, riding halfway between her knee and thigh when she stood and scooting up even shorter than that when she was seated. A fact she caught Reid checking out. Surprisingly, she liked seeing that he liked what he saw. "And I promise to be on my best behavior as soon as we arrive at the restaurant."

"Coming from you, that almost sounds boring."

"Maybe it will be," she said, as he climbed in next to her. "So, you're sure it's OK, both of us being away for the evening? And your girls?"

"Tonight I'm running second place to cook's basset hound, who's the dorm guest for the evening. Besides, I promised the girls I'd tuck them in later."

"Do you read them bedtime stories?"

"Sometimes. Or we just talk. They tell me about their day, I modify my day for them. We talk about their plans for the future. Those kinds of things."

"Sounds nice."

"Didn't you ever do that with your mother?"

"My mother was…she was usually working when I went to sleep. We didn't have a lot of time for the traditional mother-child kind of thing. Or, in your case, the daddy-daughter thing."

"Too bad, because I enjoy it. Probably more than my girls do. For them it's a bedtime ritual, but for me it's about staying in touch and keeping myself involved in their lives."

"Lucky little girls," she commented, settling in to watch the view.

All those years ago, when she'd moved to Tennessee, it had been to get away from the harsh realities her life had slammed her with. Being the daughter of a prostitute hadn't been easy. Neither was big city life when you were a little girl alone. So she'd promised herself someplace nice when she got away, and that was the first thing she'd done.

She'd loved Tennessee, loved the mountains, the blue skies. Even loved the occasional bear that had come raiding her trash cans at night. For Megan's sake, she hoped the child would have an adoptive family who stayed in Tennessee. A family like Reid's.

Or…would he adopt her? Would he want one more daughter to tuck in at night? Traditional families were good and social services usually held out for those, but untraditional or single-parent families were good, too. Just look at Reid's family. As a child, she'd have loved having a parent like him instead of what she'd had.

So, maybe seeing if Reid would adopt Megan would be worth pursuing. Just not now, though. She'd have to wait until he knew her better and got attached to her. She'd also have to wait until she knew if Reid even wanted more children. Although he certainly seemed like the type who would.

"But overall a situation like yours wouldn't do for me. Like I said, I'm not cut out for it. Half the time I'm not even home at bedtime, and if someone expected me to tuck them in or read to them, they'd be out of luck."

"You really don't want children, do you? I've known a lot of women who say they don't but they eventually change their minds. Especially when their biological clock…" He stopped, exchanged a quick glance with her. "None of my business, right?"

"I don't hide the fact, Reid. Never have. So it doesn't matter whose business it is, because it's simply a statement of fact. And even when my so-called biological clock starts ticking, nothing's going to change."

"Even if you meet the man of your dreams who wants children?"

"*Especially* if I meet the man of my dreams, because he's not going to want children. That's part of my dream."

"You're a hard case, Dr. Murphy. And you'll be quite a challenge for some man someday."

"I take that as a compliment, Dr. Adams." So maybe the harder she pushed the child away, the more he might be inclined to keep her. Because she truly wanted Megan to have a daddy like Reid. All children deserved to have a daddy like Reid.

"The mountain trout is wonderful," she said, taking the last bite of her food. "Everything about this restaurant is wonderful. Do you bring the girls here?"

"No, they prefer pizza. But every now and then I need some adult food, and an evening without the girls, so The Trout is usually my destination. An hour from Sugar Creek gives me a nice drive, time to relax. Nice scenery along the way. Then all the ambiance here."

"I guess I'm surprised you'd leave them."

"Sometimes you have to." He grinned. "Parents have lives too, you know. And Brax—my partner's father— loves taking the girls for pizza, along with his grandkids. They have a pizza night once a week."

"So, how does parenting work with your medical practice?"

"My partners, Deanna and Beau, have a couple of children, and Brax is always ready to babysit. So they were more than happy to throw my girls into the mix when I moved there. Like I said, there's pizza night, and Brax is always willing to stand in if I'm called out."

"Sounds like you got lucky."

"I did. We originally lived in Memphis—it's where I

did my residency, then I stayed. But that's where Emmie was so sick for so long, and I didn't want her to always have the reminders around her. So, when her medical care scaled back to where it is now, we started over. Little town, big life. It's perfect for us. And with the camp being so close..." He shrugged. "It works."

"So, have you ever considered adding a Mrs. Adams to your family? I know you said you're not dating right now, but what about the future?"

"She'd have to be awfully special. Like I said, I'm pretty protective of my girls, and I don't want to upset the balance only to find it doesn't work."

"Like my marriage. Definitely a balance out of whack there."

"But you got out before there were kids." He swallowed hard, looked embarrassed. "Well, except the one."

"Except the one," she repeated.

Keera was so easy to talk to. In fact, Reid had never known someone he'd wanted to open up to the way he did with her. Maybe it was because she was safe. Because she wasn't out to snag a doctor the way so many women in his past had been.

With his past couple of dates, the subject of marriage had come up almost immediately. Marriage, the future as a couple, building a house together...first-date nonsense in which he didn't want to indulge. Besides, if they'd known what they were trying to snag—a doctor whose every last cent went to his camp or to his daughter's medical care, who worked more hours than any one should ever have to, who lived in a rented, cramped cottage rather than owning a sprawling mansion—there wasn't much there to snag.

He chuckled to himself. It wasn't the lifestyle he'd thought he'd have when he'd committed to being a doctor. No, it was a much better one. He wouldn't trade a second of it, hard knocks and all.

"So, have you given any thought about what you're going to do with Megan once she's better? Keep her until social services place her, give her up right away?"

"Hope that social services can find her a good situation as soon as possible. Or maybe that's something I could do. She deserves someone who wants children. Someone who wants to be a mommy or a daddy, together or separately."

"Which is still not you?"

Keera laughed. "Which is *still* not me. Good try, though."

"She's an amazing little girl. Smart. Very pretty."

"And very much the product of an affair that was, in part, responsible for the demise of my marriage."

"Ah, yes. The illegitimate child."

Infuriated, Keera spun to face him. "Don't you dare call her that! Whatever her parents did isn't her fault and she shouldn't have to…" Stopping, she saw the amused look on his face. "OK, I get it. You're testing me. Trying to see if I might have feelings for her. Or if I would come to her defense. Well, yes and yes. I'm not heartless, Reid. I just know who I am."

"You're sure about that?"

She hunkered down into her chair and folded her arms stubbornly across her chest. "Absolutely. I've had a lot of years coming to terms with me, and I know exactly who I am and what I'm about."

Sometimes, though, she did wonder how much she really knew, or didn't know. After all, she was spending a week at a camp for kids, even enjoying it, and nowhere in her knowledge of herself would she have ever thought something like that could happen.

"Look, it wasn't my intention to turn this evening into

a battle. How about we get off the subject and talk about something else? Because the cherry cheesecake here is the best in the whole state, and I don't want you missing out because I've said something to get your gut roiling. So..." He tried coaxing her with a smile, and only succeeded in getting the scowl off her face.

"Maybe the weather? Or the fact that I'm backpedaling on my opinion of what kinds of responsibility I think the children at Camp Hope can handle?"

No luck moving back to neutral territory yet. He tried again. "Medical school? We could talk about that. Like what made you decide you wanted to be a doctor?" He watched, saw her face soften a bit. Let out a sigh of relief. "I'll start off by telling you mine then you can tell me yours."

"Mine isn't much to tell," she said, relaxing a little.

"Neither is mine. I came from a large family, three sisters, two brothers. I was the oldest, always in charge of looking after the younger ones. My parents are both doctors, by the way. Dad's a surgeon, Mom's an anesthesiologist. So I grew up in the life. As it turned out, they produced a family of doctors. I have a brother and two sisters still in med school, one brother in his surgical residency, and a sister who's a full-fledged obstetrician."

"Which means your parents were good role models," Keera commented.

"They were. Still are. But it was a hectic life growing up, never being able to plan anything when they were on call. Never being able to count on them coming to school events."

"Don't tell me. You played clarinet in the band."

"Almost. I was the quarterback on the high-school football team. It got me a scholarship to college, so I played in college, too."

"Sounds like a charmed life," she said.

Her face was so impassive he didn't know what to make of it. "Not charmed. We were like any other family, with our ups and downs."

"Which is why you know how to be a good father now. Because you understand all that."

"Some of it. Although I'll admit my girls present me with challenges I could never anticipate. The thing is, when I ask my mom for advice, she usually smiles and tells me to go with my instincts. Like that helps."

"But she's right. At the end of the day, all the parenting books in the world are only words when you have two little flesh-and-blood human beings to deal with. Children, I might add, who haven't read the parenting books and don't know the proper way you're supposed to be parenting them."

"Good insight for a non-parenting type."

Finally, she smiled. "I grew up poor. Good insight was about all I had to get me through."

"You mentioned that your mother worked a lot?"

"Sometimes days in a row."

"And no father, so what about brothers and sisters?"

She shook her head. "It was only the two of us."

"But you got to medical school. How did that happen?"

"Getting an education wasn't easy because we moved around a lot for my mother's work. Anyway, I liked knowledge, so when I wasn't able to go to school I'd find a library and read. Anything, everything.

"I really liked the sciences and found out, early on, that I loved biological sciences. From there it was reading about human anatomy, and the next logical jump was medical articles and textbooks. I practically memorized *Gray's Anatomy*, and by the time I was fourteen or fifteen there probably wasn't an advanced physiology book

I hadn't devoured. Knowledge was my…everything. And all that reading got me a college scholarship."

"I'll bet you passed your med-school exams without batting an eyelid."

"I did," she admitted. "I was told I was one of the top scorers in the country. And the rest, as they say, is history. I made it through, found my job, secured my future."

"And your mother. Is she proud?"

Keera shrugged as she picked up her coffee cup. "I haven't seen her since I was thirteen. The state took me away from her, put me in foster-care, except I was too old for most foster-homes. I went to a few, but they didn't work out so I spent the remainder of my formative years in the guardian home as a ward of the state."

This wasn't what he'd expected. Not at all. "I…I don't know what to say."

"There really is nothing to say. My mother was a prostitute, and by the time I was thirteen she was expecting the same from me. We lived in cardboard boxes in alleys and in the backseats of abandoned cars. Sometimes we'd find a vacant house, or rent a room where the roaches and bed bugs were thicker than the nicotine stains on the ceilings. Sometimes she'd be gone for days, and I'd have to scrounge for food in garbage cans.

"That was my life, Reid, until the authorities caught up to us and took me away. Something I don't talk about because it's in the past."

"I'm so, so sorry." Now he understood her need for independence. "But you've done an amazing thing. Most people—"

"Most people would have let it beat them down, but I didn't. It's no big deal. In fact, the only big deal I want to talk about now is that cheesecake. And if it's as good as you say, I want two pieces. One for now, one to share with Megan tomorrow."

For once he didn't know what to say, didn't know how to respond to her indifference. But maybe he didn't have to. Keera had given him insight into the strongest woman…no, make that the strongest person…he'd ever known. But she wanted to take cheesecake back to Megan, which meant that maybe he'd be able to help her find an even deeper insight into that same person—the softer side of her. Because whether or not she wanted to admit it, it was there.

And whether or not he wanted to admit this to himself, he thought he might be a little in love. Or at the very least head-over-heels infatuated. "Waiter, seven pieces of cherry cheesecake, please. Two for here, five to go." He glanced over at Keera, who once again wore her typical impassive expression. "One for you and me tomorrow when we give the girls their cheesecake."

"Cheesecake two days in a row. Sounds decadent."

"Decadent but good." He reached across the table and took her hand. "And for what it's worth, I like your strength. But you do have a gentler side, Keera. You just don't let it out."

"Because I don't want it to get out. Softer sides are what get you hurt."

"Or what make you human."

She shrugged. "Softer sides aren't all what they're cracked up to be. Personally, I like being tough around the edges and all the way through."

"But I see you, Keera Murphy. And I know better."

"Then quit looking so close, Reid, because if you think there's anything more there, you're only seeing what you want to see."

"Or what you want to project."

She pulled her hand from his. "What I want to project is who I am. You know, what you see is what you get."

"And what I see is someone who isn't comfortable with her softer, gentler side."

"What you're seeing is someone who doesn't have a softer, gentler side."

"Is that a challenge?" he asked, smiling

"It's a fact."

"We'll see," Reid warned, as the waiter placed the cheesecake on the table. "We'll just see." Truly, he was looking forward to what he would see.

CHAPTER FIVE

"OK, YOU'RE LOOKING at it upside down," Keera said. "Turn it over, take a look at the numbers, then tell me what you're seeing."

Gregory studied the digital thermometer for a moment, frowning at first as he pondered it, then finally smiled and pronounced, "Ninety-eight point six."

"Good! Now, tell me what that means." Megan was inside asleep, within earshot, and Keera was teaching today's class outside, on the infirmary's front steps. Her hospital without walls. Or, in this case, her classroom without walls. When she'd been homeless as a child, she'd loathed being outside. Now she couldn't get enough of it.

"It means perfect," Gregory said, smiling. "I don't have a fever."

"Excellent! So, what do you do next?"

"I write it down in my journal?"

"That's right. But how?" she asked him.

"I write the date first, then the time, then the temperature."

"Very good!" she exclaimed, actually feeling pride in his accomplishment. "I'm proud of you for learning so quickly. So now I think that tomorrow you'll be ready to move on to taking your pulse. Remember what I said about that? That it's the number of times your heart beats per minute."

"And normal is from sixty to one hundred. I read that on the Internet last night." Gregory beamed from ear to ear. "I texted my mom, told her I want to be a doctor like you and Doc Reid. Do you think I can do that, Doc Keera? Do you think I can be a doctor when I grow up?"

"I think you can be anything you want to be, Gregory. And if that's a doctor, you'll be a very good one."

He stood up from the chair he'd brought outside and crossed over to Keera, who was sitting on a step, and gave her a great big hug. "That's from my mom," he said when he backed away. "When she texted me back she said she was happy, and to give you a hug for her."

Surprisingly, Keera was touched by the simple gesture. She'd taught a little boy to take his temperature and it was like she'd taught him a valuable life skill that opened up a whole new world of possibilities for him. Who knew? Maybe it had.

Simple accomplishments and small steps to a child were life-changers, she suddenly realized. Too bad she hadn't had an adult in her life to show her how that was...*how anything* was when she'd been Gregory's age.

Somehow, fighting to survive took precedence over just about everything else because, back in the day, her small step had been a full belly and her simple accomplishment a place where she could take an honest-to-goodness bath. Of course, those life skills had taught her how to survive, hadn't they? And they'd made her as tough as nails. All in all, not bad skills to have in the life she lived now. At least, that's how she chose to look at it. But she was still very proud of Gregory.

"His mom called me a little while ago," she told Reid a couple of hours later. "She was actually crying, she was so elated over a silly little thing like taking a temperature. It was…"

"Gratifying?" Reid asked her.

"I was going more for embarrassing. But I suppose it was gratifying." She was sitting at the front work station in the infirmary. Reid had made coffee and he'd poured two cups for them. Megan was awake, sitting on the side of the bed, playing dolls with Sally and intermittently watching a video cartoon.

"When you wake up in the morning and don't know if your child will survive the day, even the silly little things, like taking a temperature, can make you grateful." Sitting down across from her, he took a sip of his coffee. "I had some pretty rough days one time when Emmie was having a particularly bad crisis. She'd been on chemo for a while, it was her second time, and she'd lost her hair. That, plus she didn't have enough weight on her body to sustain her. She was always so cold. Nothing made her warm up, and she'd lie in bed, under the covers, and shiver so hard…"

He paused and swallowed hard, and Keera reached across to lay a comforting hand on his arm. But said nothing, because her words would only intrude on a moment that required nothing more from her than compassionate support.

Their eyes met for a moment, stayed locked on each other until Reid finally broke the silence. "Do you know how beautiful your eyes are?" he asked, totally out of the blue.

"My eyes?" she asked, keeping her hand in place.

"Beautiful eyes. Like Emmie's are. But when she was sick…the only way I can describe them is hollow," he continued after a moment. "They were hollow and so distant. It was like my little girl was slipping away from me, Keera. She was getting further and further away every time I looked into her eyes, and there was nothing I could do to get her back. I think that was the first time I really, truly thought I m-might lose her." He pulled his arm away from her hand, and reached up and stroked her cheek.

"But I remember sitting there at her bedside one afternoon, watching her look out the window at a little bluebird that had landed on the ledge. It was looking in at her, and she laughed. Her eyes were bright again, so full of life just for that single moment—a moment that froze in time for me. And her laugh—I hadn't heard it in months, but when she laughed, well, I can't begin to describe how grateful I was to hear it. It gave me hope.

"For the first time in I don't know how long I finally let myself think about a future, about how things were going to get better for her. A simple laugh from Emmie or making plans to be a doctor from Gregory, it's the same thing. It's about hope.

"And for a kid like Gregory it's everything because he's never made plans for the future, like most kids do. You know, things like when I grow up I want to be a firefighter or an astronaut. This was the first time his mother has ever heard that from him, and it's because you gave him a different kind of hope for his life. With that one simple accomplishment. You showed him he can have a life."

"I don't know what to say," she murmured, quite touched. "In surgery I know I make a difference, like save a life, but it's never quite so...I guess the word is *profound*. They thank me, I wish them well, and it's all well and good. It's what I'm supposed to do because I'm good at what I do. But it doesn't affect me one way or the other."

"Because you won't let it affect you."

"Because I don't want it to affect me. If I were to get involved on the kind of personal level you seem to be involved with your kids on, I would lose objectivity. Become too vulnerable to things that could, ultimately, diminish my work as a surgeon. And I can't afford to lose that objectivity because, for me, that's what saves the lives of my patients."

"It's not your objectivity that saves lives, Keera. It's you. Who you are."

"Who I am is what I do, and I'm fine with where I am in that equation. You know, one equals the other. It's good. I'm used to it, and it works for me like your life works for you." She smiled as she gripped her cup. It was a sad, reflective smile, though. "But you really don't like the way I live my life, do you?"

"I'm not judging you, Keera. Please don't think I am. But I think the bigger question is: do you like the way you live your life? Because I'm not sure you do."

"What I like is the result I get at the end of the day when my surgeries are over with and my patients are stable."

"But isn't there some loneliness in that result? Because without my girls, no matter what I've done for my patients, that's all I'd have if Emmie and Allie weren't there to remind me that I have a purpose outside being a doctor."

"Being a doctor is my purpose, though. The only one I want. And the result I get doesn't come with loneliness. More like…well, to use your word, I experience gratification because I enjoy my work, and I also enjoy the ability to make things turn out the way they should."

"You're talking about results, though, not people. Do you ever see your work in terms of the people involved? Or having something more than work-related gratification? Maybe being happy? See, for me, being a pediatrician makes me happy. Sure, it's gratifying, but I want more than that. And being a pediatrician, working with kids the way I do, I find it."

"Isn't enjoyment the same as being happy, though?"

He shook his head. "I enjoy a good ice-cream cone, and maybe for the moment or two I'm eating it I feel a certain sense of happiness. But that's not the deep, abiding kind of happiness I want, or need, in my life."

She paused, thought about his question for a moment, then shook her head. "Then if I don't have the same kind of happiness in my life that you have in yours, does that make me shallow? Because in terms of my patients, good results do make me happy. I want all my patients to have a good result.

"But as personal involvements outside my professional life…if I did get involved personally then my objectivity would fly out the window, and I can't afford that in order to go after that elusive happiness you're talking about. People trust me for a certain outcome and it gets right back to how I'm gratified I can make that happen. Like it or not, that's who I am."

Reid reached across the table and laced his fingers through hers. "That's who you *think* you are. But there's more to you, Keera. There's a genuine quality I don't think you recognize, but I can see it and when you're ready to see it, you will."

"Or maybe I won't. You're the real deal, not me, and we can't all be you, Reid." She wanted to be offended by his comments and presumptions and especially by his intrusion, but there was nothing about Reid she could be offended by because she was right. He was the real deal. Genuine, caring. And she liked his touch, liked the way his friendly gestures toward her seemed so natural.

In fact, they seemed so natural she feared they could be become habit-forming. But she wasn't reading anything into them other than friendship because that's the kind of man he was—the kind who made friendly gestures, squeezed an arm, held a hand, without pretense or thought.

"You have a good life. Probably a great life. One most people would want. But that's not me, Reid. If anything, I'm probably the most self-aware person you've ever met, and the one thing I'm most aware of is me. I am who I am, and I accept that, even for the things you see as limitations. Or character flaws."

"Yet you must have had a romantic notion once, because you got married. And marriage is all about seeking happiness. You know, happily-ever-after."

As reality sank in and she realized how much she enjoyed his lingering touch, she unlaced her fingers from his and gripped her coffee cup with both hands.

"Happily-ever-after is a myth, and when I got married I was in love with the idea of being in love. It's everywhere you look, everywhere you go. You know, you have to be in love, or be nothing or no one. Television and movies revolve around it; the advertising world makes billions selling it. Mothers teach their daughters that to be fulfilled you have to grow up and marry a Prince Charming, and the bestselling books on the market are all about finding that one true love.

"So, yes, I bought into it for a little while, but I don't think I ever really loved him. Not in the traditional sense. If I had, I would have been more involved in our marriage, and fought harder to keep it." She shrugged. "But I wasn't involved, although he really should have divorced me rather than cheating. Because I believe in absolutes, and in a marriage that's one of them. If you do the deed, you do it the right way or you don't do it at all."

She pushed back from the table. "Look, I promised Megan we'd play some games, and right now Sally's having all the fun with her. It's my turn. And I was also thinking that now, as she's feeling better, maybe we could expand our horizons a little since she's not too happy about being confined. So, you're the pediatrician. How long before she can go outside?"

"Today, if she's up to it. But as the contagion period is four days before the rash and up to four days after, I still don't want her around the children. So if you could take her out somewhere east of the hospital—we don't have activities out there today, and it's a pretty area. I think she should enjoy it."

"Yes, if she's up to it. Or maybe we could sit out on the porch for a while. Whatever works best for her. And you? What's on your agenda for the rest of the day?"

"Nature hike down to the river, a picnic lunch, then some well-managed, very tame river-rafting. I have a company coming in this afternoon that specializes in river adventures, and the kids are going to have their first outing in a rubber raft. The gentle kind, not the white-water kind that goes over rocks and waterfalls."

"Sounds like fun. They're going to enjoy it. I know I would have when I was their age." She smiled. "You take very good care of these children, Reid. They're fortunate to have you."

He certainly knew how to make a difficult childhood bearable, and while her childhood couldn't compare to what all these kids had gone through, she wondered how she might have benefited from having someone like him in her life when she had been a child. Yes, these children, and especially his daughters, were very, very lucky.

"It's not just me. A lot of people are generous with the kids. Tomorrow we're going on a zip line. You know, when you harness up and zip across a wire from tree to tree?"

"The kids are all up to it?" she asked, genuinely surprised.

"It's the training facility. Very tame, very safe. And like the rafting, I think they'll love it because it's something they haven't been able to do before. Then in a couple of days my medical partner's coming in, bringing in a few of his horses for the kids to ride. Horseback riding is always a highlight around here and we try to get it in once with every camp session."

She laughed. "I'm wondering if you're wasting your time being a doctor when camp counselor is so definitely your calling."

"The way it is now, I've got the best of both worlds," he said, grinning.

"Yes, I think you do."

And he seemed so happy whichever world he was in. That was remarkable, and she wondered how he did it because all his worlds were so vastly different. It spoke of the quality of the man, she supposed. And Reid Adams was quality through and through.

Yes, Reid Adams was definitely the daddy she wanted for Megan. She knew that for certain and now all she had to do was find a way to convince him of it. After all, for a man who loved being in a family, like Reid did, one more child shouldn't matter to him. In fact, he should welcome the opportunity…she hoped.

"He's really a very nice man," Keera explained to Megan as she settled the child into the porch swing. The compound was empty this afternoon, except for a couple of volunteers puttering around in the gardens, and it surprised Keera how much she missed the activity that had surrounded her these past few days, even though she really hadn't been out into it very much. And the children. Yes, she actually did miss them as well.

"And a very good doctor. What I'm hoping is that I can convince him to take you in, then you could come here whenever he does, and you'd also have two sisters."

Of course, at her age Megan didn't understand all this. In fact, she was dozing off, her head resting on Keera's lap, so not only did she not understand, she also wasn't listening.

But for Keera, hearing her plan expressed aloud made it all the more real to her. While she couldn't keep this child, and social services didn't seem to be making any headway in placing her in a suitable situation, Megan was a sweet little girl who deserved better than this limbo she was in right now. Keera wanted the best for her, and every time she thought about that, the only thing that popped into her head was Reid. He *was* the best. But the arrangement had to be by his choice and not her persuasion. That much she was adamant about. Reid had to do the choosing.

Of course, that didn't preclude her from making the right choices for Megan that would help her get chosen for ever.

"So, what I have in mind is that tomorrow I'm going to go into town and ask him to watch you for a little while, so he can get to know you better now that you're not feeling so bad. Then the day after that I'll figure out a way to have him spend even more time with you. I think that, given the way he feels about children, once he gets to know you, he won't want you going into the foster-care system, the way I don't want you there either.

"So when that happens, I'm going to have to rely on you to turn on your girlish charms to help woo him into daddyhood thinking. Think that's a good plan?"

Of course, Megan didn't respond. She was now sound asleep, well past the dozing stage and into a deep slumber, with her breathing heavy and even. Smiling, Keera pushed back the blonde hair from Megan's forehead and lightly stroked her cheek. So much innocence, she thought. At that age, her own innocence had already been taken from her, by the way she'd lived, by the things she'd seen. She didn't remember being two, but life around her must have made its impression on her. Even on someone so young. Even on Megan.

"It's not going to be easy for you," she whispered, "but I'm going to make sure you get what you need. I promise, Megan. I may not be the one to take care of you, but I know who is. And you'll never, ever have to go into the foster-care system." Easy words, tough challenge. But as a child of the system herself, she knew the life she didn't want Megan to have. "I promise," she said again, as Megan curled up in a precious little ball, hugging a teddy bear. It was such a cozy sight, it almost made Keera wish she could be a part of something like it.

A flash of the two of them together crossed her mind… mother and daughter. Nice thought, but not practical for either of them. Especially not for Megan. And Keera knew better, knew and fully realized her potential as well as her limits, and understood that all this domesticity wasn't in her. Maybe in fantasy it might be there, but not in reality.

In some ways, she was her mother's daughter. At least in those aspects. Megan deserved so much better than that. So much better…

"You up to a short walk?" she asked Megan later, after she'd rocked her in the swing for an hour and had caught herself enjoying the relaxation. It wasn't something she did too often—simply sit and do nothing. Admittedly, it had been nice, just existing without an agenda or a to-do list. No patients to take care of, no worries. Just listening to the birds, taking in the magnificent scenery.

"Mommy," Megan whimpered in response. "Want Mommy."

"I know you do, sweetheart. I know you do. But right now you have to stay with me for a little while longer." She didn't know how to tell the child her parents were dead.

Telling anyone a loved one had died was the worst, but in her world she dealt with adults. How to do it with a child, especially one so young, she didn't have a clue. "Let's walk over to the woods…" Instinctively, she felt the girl's forehead, not like a doctor but more like a mom, to see if she had a fever. Which she didn't. "Or we can go back inside. Whichever you want to do."

Megan didn't respond so Keera took her by the hand and led her off the porch and in the direction of the woods. She didn't expect to go very far, and was surprised how Megan resisted when she'd decided it was time to turn back. So they trudged on, only now Keera was carrying the child, pointing out the very few things she knew about nature…birds, flowers, trees, none identified by their proper name. But Megan was two, so Keera wasn't too concerned about that.

"Look at that tree," she said, putting Megan down and pointing to a giant pine. "It grows needles, not leaves. And pine cones." She bent to pick up a fallen pine cone then placed it in Megan's hands. "See how pretty that is? You can keep it if you want to."

Megan did look at the pine cone, clenching it tight in her little hands.

"That's the seed, Megan," she explained. "A whole tree can grow from that." She felt a little silly explaining that to a child too young to understand, but it seemed like the right thing to do. "You plant seeds in the ground, and they grow trees and bushes, even grass and flowers. But this one will grow a tree just like that one." She pointed to the pine. "Isn't it beautiful?"

"I'm surprised she's up to it," Reid called from the trail behind them.

Keera spun, surprised to see him there. "I thought you were rafting with the kids."

"They're rafting, I'm not. Sometimes I can be...over-protective, let's call it. The kids don't need a doctor hovering over them all the time, and that's really who I am to them. So I stayed through the picnic lunch and made sure they all understood what they were supposed to do. Then let some of the camp volunteers take charge. After that I left." He grinned. "And nobody noticed I was gone, they were so excited to get on the water."

"Poor Dr. Adams, feeling so under-appreciated," Keera teased. She glanced down at Megan, who was beginning to look weary, leaning hard against her leg and clinging. "I think you're going to be needed here shortly to carry her back, if that makes you feel any better."

"Needed maybe. But only for my brawn."

And a very nice brawn it was. "I'm surprised she's held up this long. But it's been fun, hasn't it, Megan?"

In response, Megan shrugged, then hugged her teddy bear and her pine cone even tighter. "She's missing...you-know-who."

"I expect she would be. So, what have you told her?"

"Me?" Keera exclaimed. "I can't tell her. I don't know how. I mean, she's too young to really understand, and I expect you've got to use the right words so you don't cause some sort of trauma that would pop up later in her life. So maybe her social worker will have a better idea of how to do it." *Or you,* she wanted to say. But she wouldn't be so presumptuous. Still, if he volunteered, she wouldn't turn him down.

"But she's been asking so she's going to have to know."

"That's one of the reasons I'm not suited to the job. I don't know what to do."

"Child experts say be honest and simple in your explanation."

Keera shook her head. "Not now. Maybe I'm not a child

expert, but I don't think telling her…well, you-know-what is a good idea when she's still not feeling well. There has to be a right time for it, and I suppose you play that by instinct."

"Which in you seems pretty good."

"Or resistant. Because I don't want to." She lowered her voice and whispered, "I don't want to break a little girl's heart."

"Maybe you're right."

"I know I'm right, Reid. Now's not the time."

"Then I bow to your instinct, because it's better than you think. Look, I'm going to run down to the river, it's only a few hundred yards, and wave to the kids as they float by, then we'll go back to the infirmary."

He scooped Megan into his arms, and urged Keera to follow him. "Just because they don't need me hovering doesn't mean I can't hover a little bit. Right, Megan?" he asked the child.

She responded by pressing her head to his chest, and it looked right. Like they were meant to be together. In fact, it looked so right it gave Keera some hope that her plan might just work.

Reid knew exactly what Keera was up to. She wanted him to fall in love with Megan then keep her. It was a good plan, and so far Keera wasn't pursuing it too aggressively, for which he was grateful because while the idea of adopting other children had crossed his mind more than once, he wasn't sure if he was ready for it. But he knew that's what Keera wanted, even though she was about as subtle in her pursuits as anyone he'd ever seen. It was there, though, in her eyes, in the way she looked at him, the way she looked at Megan. Good heart in the right place, but a heart that was a little trussed up.

Whatever the case, he had faith in her maternal instincts—more than she did, apparently. So he'd go along with her plan for a while, let her continue to think she was pursuing him, but take every opportunity that presented itself to turn that around on her without her knowing he was doing it, and pursue her into mommyhood.

Now, that was the perfect plan.

Could he take in Megan, though, if his plan failed? Adopt her, make her his third child? Maybe that was something to consider, a second-best plan. God knew, he knew how to raise a two-year-old. That, and his girls were secure, so in his future he could see fitting one or two, maybe three more children into his family.

In fact, he'd already approached his daughters with the idea, and they'd put in their order for all girls. Dr. Reid Adams and his half-dozen or so daughters. It brought a smile to his face. And since he wasn't rushing toward the altar any time soon, adoption seemed the best way to make that large-family dream happen. Then if, somewhere down the line, some woman wanted him, and his daughters...

But that wouldn't be Keera, by her own admission, so he was steering clear of her in that regard, as much as he didn't want to. Steering clear and hoping to hell he could keep his head, his wits, and even his sanity, because Keera was... He thought about all the things he wanted and she was all of them except for the one thing. *And that one thing was huge.* She didn't want to be a mother. For him a family with lots of kids wasn't negotiable, especially as he had already started on the course and was loving it.

"Here they come," he said to Megan, as three big, yellow rubber rafts came floating gently around the bend in the river. "Can you wave to them, Megan?" To help her, he raised her right hand and waved it for her.

"Looking good!" he shouted, as the first raft of children waved and yelled at him. They were all animated, yelling, clapping, wearing orange life-vests and black helmets, having the time of their lives. Briefly, Reid glanced over at Keera, who stood there unaffected, her arms folded across her chest. Staring at the…well, not at the children. And not at Megan. "Bet I can beat you to the next turn in the river," he shouted.

"Can't," one of the boys shouted back.

"Can too," he shouted in return, then passed Megan back to Keera. "Looks like I've got to take up the challenge. Sorry, but I think you're going to have to carry her back to the clinic. She looks like she could stand a good nap, probably sooner rather than later."

With that, he sprinted off into the trees, leaving Keera standing in the woods holding Megan in her arms. He didn't go too far, though. Just far enough that she couldn't see him duck behind a large tree and watch her turn and hike back to her cabin, toting one very heavy little deadweight.

"I'm on to you, Keera Murphy. And I know I'm right about you. Deny it all you want, but by the end of this week you're going to be that child's mother through and through."

OK, so maybe his talk was more confident than the way he actually felt, but in his heart he knew that if she only let herself go…

The shouts of the kids coming from downriver prised him away from watching her, and Reid turned and ran to his next rendezvous point. *"Yes, Keera,"* he said, as the kids floated into view, *"you're going to discover—"*

"Dr Adams!" came the unanimous shouts from the lead raft. "How'd you get here so fast?"

"Because I know how," he said, but not to the kids, as

his mind was still on Keera. Sure, he might know how with the kids, but did he know how with her?

Hell, he didn't even know why he wanted to know how. But he did. In a big way.

CHAPTER SIX

"I'll bet you'll be glad when life gets back to normal," Keera said, settling onto the porch swing outside the infirmary door, while Reid was seated in the chair across from it. "I really am sorry I'm disrupting you so much. I mean, you're not even getting to see your girls as much as you probably want to."

"Emmie and Allie are having the time of their lives without me hovering over them, which is what I usually do when I have the chance. And it's not like they were staying here with me in the first place."

"Yes, but you snuck in visits in your free time, and now you're barely getting any free time."

"Well, Emmie, I think, is particularly glad to get away from all that togetherness for a while. She's growing up, needs her space, even though I'm not ready to give it to her yet. Here, or back home in Sugar Creek. So you being here is a blessing in disguise for them."

"Knowing when to let go—one of the challenges of being a parent, I suppose."

"One of the many. Lately, though, the big thing has to do with fashion. I'm not good at it, don't have a clue. I remember the way my mom used to dress my sisters, but…"

"Old school," Keera chimed in. "I'll bet she dressed them old school. I mean, we come from a day when colors coordinated and matching patterns with similar patterns made sense. Now anything goes as long as it's fun. Nothing has to coordinate, nothing has to match if you feel good wearing it and it expresses…you."

"Don't I know. And what I'm finding out is that my daughter is hiding her clothes. *'Oh, Daddy, that's so gross,'* she always tells me. Then I never see the outfit again. Did you do that when you were a kid?"

"I never had enough clothes that I could hide something. But I definitely had my preferences." She smiled, remembering how she used to love window shopping.

She and her mom had never gone in to buy, and most of what she'd worn back then had been shoplifted from various thrift stores. It had always been her job to distract the store clerk while her mom had stuffed her coat with whatever she had been able to lift in mere seconds.

Usually it hadn't been pretty. Usually it hadn't even come close to fitting. Sometimes it had been in good shape, though, and she'd pretended it was brand-new. "Want me to take your girls shopping? Let them express themselves to me rather than having Daddy foist his taste on them?"

"I thought you'd never ask. How about after the zip line tomorrow afternoon? I'll sit with Megan then that will free you up to take the clothing nightmare away from me."

If ever a plan had played directly into her hands, this was it. How perfect was that? Leave him alone here, let him bond a little more with Megan…yes, perfect. "Well, I've never been shopping for kids' clothing, except that once for Megan, but it can't be that bad, can it?" she said, laughing.

"Just wait until tomorrow. Then you'll see."

"Well, call me crazy, but I think I might be looking forward to it."

"I know I am," he said, smiling. "And the girls will be excited to have some female input rather than letting dear old Dad horn in on their fashion creativity."

"This is where someone might normally make a profound parenting comment, offer condolences, or say something to the effect that you're better at it than you think, but as I don't have any experience in childhood situations or parenting, I don't think I'm qualified."

"Sounds like a cop-out to me. Especially when I'm clearly drowning and need a lifeline." He faked a pained expression. "Or sympathy."

"How about dinner? I'll cook. Not sure how, or where…"

"How about we spend our separate time with our respective girls then meet up later when they're all tucked in, and have our own meal?" Pausing, he smiled. "I don't know how my parents did it, taking care of so many kids going in so many directions and still finding time for themselves. But they did, and I guess I never even gave it any thought until now. Because the thing I'd like to do most is go for a walk, take you down to the river, have a late-night picnic and spend some time relaxing under the stars. But you have your responsibilities, I have mine, and those responsibilities come first."

"Would have been a nice evening, though," she said, trying not to sound too dreamy, or too disappointed. Because she could picture the evening playing out, and it was so real she almost felt immersed in it. But being immersed in an evening with Reid was a dangerous thing, because she was beginning to like him too much, and like was tantamount to love or other places she couldn't go. "But you're right, work and children come first," she said, shaking herself back into the true Keera Murphy mode.

"Maybe we could have sandwiches on the porch?"

"Or skip the sandwiches, and just spend some quiet time," she suggested.

"Quiet time is good, too. But what just happened here?"

he asked. "How did we go from planning a meal together later on to whatever you just said?"

She laughed. "I was thinking in practical terms."

"And what about eating a meal together isn't practical, as we've already done it before?"

"The timing. After you do this, after I do that. Get the kids settled down, finish the day's worth of charting, plan tomorrow's class. Relaxing without a purpose after all that just seems nice. At home I'd just go straight to bed, but here relaxing seems almost required, doesn't it? You know, sit back, watch the stars, listen to the bullfrogs court their lady loves. Just breathe."

He pushed his glasses back up on his face and grinned. "Then it's a date to relax and breathe."

"You are different, Dr. Adams. Like nobody I've ever met before."

"Because men always want something else from you?"

Most of her life they had. Until she'd perfected her demeanor and polished her defenses. Which had started at a very young age, and had only gotten better over time. "Yes, to a point. I grew up in a situation where there were always men coming and going. So I got my fair share of looks, and I knew what they'd want, given the opportunity."

"Which makes you cautious."

"I try to be."

"Do you assume every man is giving you one of those looks?"

"Not every man. But I don't need to waste my time distinguishing between them because I'm not interested. Been there, failed miserably at it, saw every one of my character flaws exposed, and realized I can't go near it again."

"Said adamantly."

"Adamantly," she agreed. "But breathing is a practical matter and I'm looking forward to breathing with you later on." To show him her practicality in the matter, she leaned forward and extended her hand to shake his. But when his smooth palm glided across hers, it wasn't only his palm she felt. It was also the thousand impractical goose-bumps that were suddenly marching up and down her arms, up her neck, down her back.

His response was simply to arch his eyebrows at her then stand up and walk away.

And her response to that? More goose-bumps.

"She's what?" Keera asked, totally composed.

"Chest pains. Shortness of breath. Rapid pulse, elevated blood pressure. She's in her cabin, sitting on the couch, refusing to budge, and seeing as you're a cardiac specialist…"

"Surgeon," she corrected. "And I can't come because I'm the only one here to sit with Megan."

"And I can't leave Clara alone to trade places with you." So they were in a spot. He in one spot, she in another, and never the twain shall meet. Which also described their lives, it seemed. "Let me call Sally and send her over there."

Keera glanced over at Megan, almost hating to leave her. They'd been reading stories, having a nice evening together. "Then I'll get some supplies ready. You keep her head elevated, give her an aspirin."

"No aspirin. She's allergic."

"Fine, just try and keep her calm. Keep checking her vitals. Are either of your girls with you, by chance?"

"Emmie is. Why?

"Send Emmie over here, and I'll give her an IV set-up, plus whatever drugs I can scrounge for a cardiac episode. Is Clara coherent?" Clara, the camp cook.

"Very."

"That's good. So hang up. Call Sally and I'll—"

"Daddy sent me," Emmie said. She was standing in the doorway, a little out of breath from the hard run across the compound.

"So fast."

Emmie nodded. "Miss Clara is having a heart attack," she said so matter-of-factly it rattled Keera. It also reminded Keera a little of herself at that age—all seriousness, no innocence or typical childishness.

"Look, you go back out on the porch and wait. OK? We don't want to expose you to Megan's measles."

"Measles are a normal childhood disease," Emmie explained, without budging from the infirmary doorway, "but my daddy doesn't want me exposed to anything that will make me sick."

She raised a finger to Emmie to indicate she'd get back to her in a moment, then returned to Reid on the phone. "Look, Emmie's here, so I've got to go. I'll be there as fast as I can."

"Clara's not going to die, is she?" Emmie asked.

"We're going to do everything we can for her. Beginning with this." She grabbed a box of IV tubing and catheter, and a bag of normal saline from the supply closet. "Take this to your daddy."

"Could you talk to him, tell him I'm all better now? That he doesn't have to take care of me so much any more? Or keep worrying. That he needs to have some fun, because he doesn't. Not ever."

"He's asked me to take you and Allie shopping tomorrow. We'll talk about it then, OK?"

Emmie nodded on her way out the door, her arms full of medical supplies, and Keera stood there and watched her run across the compound to the cook's cabin. Only when she was inside did Keera leave the door and return to the locked drug supply to find whatever medication might be necessary to see Clara through her heart attack.

By the time Sally arrived, Keera had a fairly substantial bag packed, but before she left the cabin she took a moment to go over to Megan. "Look, I've got to go away for a little while. Sally's going to stay and read more stories to you, and I'll be back as soon as I can. I promise, Megan. I'll hurry back here as soon as I can."

"No," Megan said very quietly.

"I'm sorry, but I have to."

Big tears welled in Megan's eyes. Tears that surprisingly tore at Keera.

"She's going to be fine, Doctor," Sally said. "I'll get her settled down, and she'll be fine in no time."

"I hope so," Keera said, bending down to give the girl a kiss on the forehead. "But that doesn't make me feel any better."

"They're resilient at this age. Bounce back from disappointment very quickly."

Maybe they bounced back, but did they get over it? That's what worried Keera about Megan, because she had so much to get over in her young life. More than any child her age should have to worry about.

"Oh, and if you don't mind, as soon as Megan dozes off, I'm going to do the same in the bed next to hers. So take the night off if you'd like, because I don't intend to budge from this place until morning."

"Are you sure?"

"It's hard to keep up with these kids. I love them to death, but they're wearing me out. That bed there is looking pretty inviting."

"Call me if you change your mind."

"Not going to happen," she said, sitting down on the

edge of the bed with Megan. "Trust me, five minutes after Megan's having pleasant dreams, I will be too."

Keera gave the older woman a hug then headed to the door. But she took one look back before she left, saw Megan watching her. And she felt...just like a mother for an instant. A mother torn between her child and her duty. Which was why she couldn't be a mother for real, because duty would always have to win.

Sighing, Keera stepped out into the night then flew across the compound and entered Clara's cabin, to be greeted by Reid, who was wearing a troubled expression.

"She's not...?" Keera asked, stepping into the tiny entry hall.

He shook his head. "We've got it sorted out and I'm pretty sure it's indigestion. But I'm going to send her to the hospital to be looked at anyway."

"Then why the grim face?"

"Emmie told me she came into the infirmary and saw Megan."

"Just in the doorway. Which is probably not close enough to have been exposed, especially as she's up to date on her vaccinations."

"How could you have let that happen, Keera? You know I don't want these kids exposed—"

"I didn't *let* it happen," she interrupted, whispering because she could see Emmie and Allie peeking out of the next room at them. "She came in, I gave her the supplies and she left. It took place over the course of about a minute."

"She shouldn't have been in there for a full minute. Don't you understand? She's vulnerable. All the kids are vulnerable, with compromised immune systems in many cases, and I shouldn't have—"

"What? Let me stay? You shouldn't have let me stay?

Because you're right. You shouldn't have, and I shouldn't have accepted when you offered. But you did, and I did, and as a result Emmie was exposed to measles. She's healthy now, though. You're the one who said it."

"Healthy now doesn't mean she still doesn't have immunity problems. She does, and she's very susceptible to colds and flu and...measles."

"And her daddy's phobias. She wants to talk to me about it, Reid. She's pretty upset that you want to keep her so isolated. And I must say I'm impressed at the level on which she communicates. It's very adult. Maybe too adult." She looked past him, saw the girls still peeking out. "Like this. Suppose Clara *was* having a heart attack. They're in there, watching it. Did you know that? Talk about your daughters being exposed to something they shouldn't be."

He spun round in time to see his daughters scamper off into the kitchen. Then he went after them, took them to the rear bedroom in Clara's cottage and shut the door. "So you're giving me parenting advice now?" he said, once he'd returned to the front room.

"Not parenting advice. Just telling you that you can't always predict parenting the way you can't predict life. And also telling you what I think she's afraid to say to you. Emmie wants you to have your own life, Reid. She's worried that you don't because you're so fixated on her. I used to worry about my mother—all the bad things she did, all the bad situations she ended up in.

"I was too young to worry like that and Emmie's too young to worry about you the way she does. But it's up to you, as the parent, to change that for her."

"Easier said than done."

"Maybe so, but I'm right. And this is something I understand better than most. Look, you go wait with your daughters and reassure them about Clara's condition, and

I'll give you a second opinion about her heartburn. Then you can take the girls back to their dorm for the evening, and as Sally's settling in with Megan for the night, I'll fix us a late dinner. If you haven't eaten?"

He smiled. "You're back to cooking for me?"

"You've had a rough evening. It's the least I can do." With that, she pushed past him into the living room, where Clara was sitting up on the couch with her feet propped up and an ice pack on her head. "Dr. Adams said he believes you're suffering from indigestion. Mind if I take a look?"

Clara motioned her over to the couch. "I cook healthy for the kids, but I don't always eat my own cooking. Looks like those burritos got me this time."

Keera sat down next to Clara, took her pulse, blood pressure, listened to her heart. Blood pressure high, heart sounded fine. "The thing about burritos is they're good in moderation. But when your indigestion gets so bad it can be confused with a heart attack, that's when you have to reconsider your eating choices. Otherwise next time it could be a heart attack, which you might ignore because you think it's only indigestion again.

"And I don't want you ending up on my operating table, Clara. The kids here need you, need the way you cook for them and take such good care of them. So you owe it to yourself to take as good of care of yourself as you do them."

"I've never been a skinny person, Doctor," she said, sniffling. "I come from large stock."

"You can be large and still be healthy." She patted the woman's hand. "And I don't think you'd look right being skinny. Look, I don't know if Dr. Adams mentioned this, but we want to admit you to the hospital for the night for some tests. Just to make sure it's not cardiac related. If it is, they'll get you taken care of. If it isn't, and you're up to it, you can come back to camp tomorrow."

"What about breakfast and lunch? Somebody's got to do the cooking."

"Don't worry about the cooking. I know my way around a kitchen, if that's what I have to do."

"But we have different diets for different kids."

"If it's written down, I can read. All I want you to do is rest and let the doctors at the hospital take care of you. We'll figure out everything else tomorrow. OK?"

"You're not cold, like they're saying you are," Clara said, as the ambulance pulled up to the front of the cabin.

"Who says I'm cold?"

"Allie, but it came from Doc Reid. Only Allie interpreted it as meaning you needed a blanket."

"He thinks I'm cold?"

"That's what you want him to think, isn't it? You do kind of put it on, you know."

Maybe it *was* what she wanted him to think. Maybe it was the way she wanted the entire world to see her. Because there was safety in that frostiness. But it hurt, hearing someone say it out loud, because she wasn't cold deep down. She knew that. If only Reid knew that as well.

"So, what's the plan?" Reid asked. She was puttering around Reid's cabin kitchen. Looking pretty good at it. But she looked pretty good at everything she did.

"Looks like I'm going to be the camp cook until Clara gets back," she said, trying to sound as cold as he thought she was. "So I'm going to go over there right now and familiarize myself with the kitchen. Oh, and about that dinner I promised you." She pointed to a sandwich on a plate, sitting there alongside a glass of milk.

"That's it?"

"That's it," she confirmed in her best, and iciest, voice.

"You're angry because you've got to cook?"

"No, I'm angry because you decided it was necessary to discuss my cold demeanor with your daughter, who discussed it with the camp cook." Facing him, she leaned back against the counter and folded her arms across her chest. "Cold! Really? Is that what you think of me?"

"How about cold by design?"

"I'm not a cold person, Reid. Maybe reserved but not—"

"I didn't mean to offend you."

"Because you didn't think it would get back to me."

"There's that. But it was something mentioned the first night you were here."

"So this is where you're going to tell me you've changed your mind?" she asked.

If anything, she was blazing hot tonight, and sexy as hell. "Look, you're not an ice maiden but you do put on this air of chilliness. Which, by the way, I don't think is the real you."

"But why mention it to your daughter?"

"I was irritated that you'd barged in and disrupted my entire life, not to mention my camp. So I may have spoken in haste, called you a cold…"

"A cold what?" she asked.

"It wasn't meant for little ears. She accidentally overhead."

"A cold what?" Keera persisted.

"And I corrected myself, and left her with the impression you were cold, as in temperature-wise."

"A cold what?" she asked again. "Let me hear you say the word."

"OK. I called you a cold bitch, because I knew your intention was to leave Megan here and walk away. And I meant it. For a few minutes. Now I apologize, because I was wrong."

"Because you got caught?" she questioned, fighting

back a smile. He was kind of cute, trying to worm his way out of this one. He definitely looked like the little boy who'd got caught doing something he wasn't supposed to, and she couldn't help but be more endeared than enraged.

"Clara's fine," he said, trying to change the subject.

"She doesn't think I'm cold."

"We're back to that?"

"We never got off it." Walking to the fridge to put away the milk, she brushed past him and paid particular attention to their proximity because she didn't want to touch him, didn't want another epidemic of goose-bumps. But the intensity between them was suddenly making her nervous. She could feel the heat of his stare on the back of her neck, which was where her goose-bumps began again. Oh, to be cold at this precise moment, because she was feeling anything but.

How could any man make her so acutely aware of herself? Make her feel so self-conscious? Make her feel so vulnerable to thoughts she didn't even know he was having? But that she herself definitely was having?

In truth, he was awakening something in her that was a complete and messy surprise. Did she want this man? In the physical sense she was almost willing to admit she might. She was only human and, God knew, she did come with those needs like everybody did. Only she fought harder to keep them under control. So the really messy part here was how he'd got through the barriers.

Thankfully, she still had her controls in place so he'd only get so far. Which was as far as goose-bumps and a few straying thoughts.

"What I think is that you show me exactly what you want me to see, and believe. What I also think is that maybe you kid yourself about what you feel, even about who you are. Don't know why, not going to guess." He grabbed her arm and pulled her back to him. "But I have a confession of my own to make. I'm attracted to you. And when you talked about men looking at you…I looked."

She looked up into his eyes. Swallowed hard. "But we can control the urges, Reid."

"Because we want to or because we have to?"

Nothing in her wanted to because she liked the way he held her—his grip not rough yet not gentle. And she liked his dominance. It was firm but not unrelenting. "Because it's the only practical thing to do."

"Depends on your definition of practical," he said, pulling her up roughly against his chest.

Keera looked up, put her hands on the sides of his face to hold him where she wanted him, which was no place but here, in this moment. Then she wound her fingers up through his hair, tugged it slightly and smiled when he started to breathe faster. Breaths to match hers. The edges of their bodies melted into each other.

Keera's body ached from a terrible emptiness, one never before filled, and she was so acutely aware of Reid, more than she had ever been of anything or anyone else in her life. The way he looked down over the tops of his glasses at her—glasses that she removed and laid on the kitchen countertop. How his light evening stubble felt under her fingertips. But what made her quiver, as she explored his face, was the slight dent in the center of his bottom lip. And that discovery about him, and about herself was where the exploration stopped and the kiss began.

In that instant their mouths pressed together hot and tight as his free hand entwined through her hair. Gasping when he eased her head back and kissed down her chin, down her throat, she responded by putting her palms flat to his chest, as if to push him away. Only she gripped the fabric of his shirt, two hands clinging tight to him, feeling the muscles underneath. Hard, smooth… "We shouldn't," she gasped.

"And we won't," he agreed, without retreating a step. "In a minute."

The growl of his sex-charged voice was heavy and hypnotic to her ears and just the sound of it caused her whole body to ache like she'd never known it could. A betrayal of sense and soul, and she fought to get it back, but as his kisses returned to her mouth, all she could do was kiss him back. And hang on for fear she might drown if she didn't.

But all too soon reality overtook the moment, in the form of a jingling cellphone, the jingle being the specific one he'd assigned Emmie, and Reid stepped back, cleared his throat, and assumed the role of daddy.

"What do you want, sweetheart?" He listened for a moment. "No, like I told you a little while ago, it wasn't a heart attack. She'll be fine. I just talked to them at the hospital and she'll be back tomorrow afternoon. And, yes, I did feed her dog. He's outside right now, and I'll bring him in when I go to bed." Another moment of listening, then, "I love you too, sweetheart. Tell Allie I love her, too. Then turn off the cellphone and go to sleep."

Once he'd clicked off, Reid grinned sheepishly. "So, is this where we ignore what happened and go on like we were?"

"It was a kiss," she said, her voice sounding wobbly. "Just a kiss."

"Just a kiss," he said, picking up his peanut-butter sandwich. "Between colleagues."

Keera nodded, trying to appear practical about the matter. "A kiss between colleagues." And one that had shaken her to the very core. Which meant what?

That was the question she didn't want to answer.

CHAPTER SEVEN

"I DON'T WANT to do this," Keera said, as the instructor secured her into the zip-line harness. "I'm fine keeping my feet on the ground. Never did have a need to simply go flying through the air without an airplane around me. And I don't like all this protective gear..." Harness, pads, goggles. "It pinches, and I especially don't like helmets."

"Necessary for safety and insurance. And it sets a good example for the kids. Especially when you're not fussing and fretting about it," Reid said, then took a picture of her with all her gear.

"But I am fussing and fretting," she said, looking over at Megan, who was sitting under a tree with Sally a good distance away from the rest of the children. "And complaining outright, as it wasn't my idea to do this."

Reid laughed out loud. "Like I said, you have to set a *good* example for the kids. They're watching you, you know."

Yes, they were all watching her, so she pasted a smile on her face and gave them a thumbs-up sign. "It's all a lie," she said under her breath. "I don't like this, don't want to do it."

"Role model," he reminded her, nodding sideways in a gesture toward to the kids. "They have high expectations of you. Even Megan does."

"Megan's too young to understand most of this, and why would the others expect anything from me?" she asked, as the instructor cinched the harness tighter.

"Because they like you, and trust you."

"Then they don't know me," she said, scooting her elbow pads into place then pulling her goggles down over her eyes. "And the last thing I want to be is a role model. Too much responsibility, especially when children are involved. They need someone like you, not like me." And she'd survived perfectly well without a role model in her own life. Or with the worst role model a child could have, depending on how you looked at it.

"Too late for that. You've been thrust into greatness, Keera, as far as these kids are concerned, and there's no turning back. They trust you, respect you and even look up to you. And your confidence in them learning to take responsibility for themselves has made you more of a role model than you can know, because these kids have never had someone who trusts them that much. Not even me."

"It wasn't trust. It was practicality. And you know how that governs my life. It should govern theirs as well, as far as their health issues are concerned."

"But they don't see it that way. To them, it's a very personal thing, making you their—"

"Role model," she said, tightening the chin strap of her helmet then bending over to adjust her knee pads. Taking a quick look at the kids out of the corner of her eye, she saw the way they were watching her, and realized every last word Reid had said was true. Which made her feel uncomfortable for sure, yet strangely moved. "Fine, I'll do this, and I won't make a scene. But I may have to scream, and there's nothing you can do about that."

"I'll bet the kids will love that."

"Yeah, right," she said, turning to the group of kids now

that she was all garbed up and taking a proper bow. Only to be met by applause and shouts of excitement. "And if I die…"

"You're not going to die," he said, walking her over to the platform.

"But if I do…"

"Then I'll be properly put in my place, and you can come back and haunt me, and tell me *you told me so.*"

"And I will," she said, as she began her climb up the wooden ladder nailed onto the post holding up the zip-line platform. "I promise you, Reid Adams, I will haunt you until your dying day."

He'd tossed and turned a bit last night, thanks to the kiss. But somehow he'd finally settled down into a sound sleep and had slept like a cozy baby. In two-hour stretches, as he was up and down, gazing across the compound at Keera's light, wondering if she was sleeping or if the kiss had her tossing and turning as well.

So far that morning they'd been only colleagues and sparring partners. She'd cooked breakfast for the kids while he'd done morning rounds. He'd cleaned up the kitchen while she'd taught her class on taking vital statistics. Then they'd met to collaborate on preparing lunch, and now this. So far there was nothing personal between them. In fact, it was almost like last night hadn't happened. But it had, and there was no denying it. Short, intense and unforgettable. The best kiss he'd ever had.

Looking up, he watched her finally make it to the platform and wave over to Megan, then he pointed his camera up and snapped another picture, and turned it on to video record.

"Seriously, Reid? Do you have to record every aspect of my total, abject humiliation?" she yelled down to him.

Laughing, he stepped back to get a better, wider shot

of the whole event about to take place. "Total and abject is when you get halfway across the line and can't go on, and someone has to come and rescue you."

"You did that?"

"No. But I'm just saying…"

"You're just saying it to put the onus on me."

"But I'll have a video."

She glanced down at all the kids, who were much more eager to do the zip line than she was. "One time, then I'm taking Megan back to camp."

"What if you enjoy it?"

"I won't!"

"That sure of yourself?" he yelled.

"That sure of myself. I *will not* enjoy this."

"Then shall we make a wager? If I win, you take me out to dinner. You win and…well, name your prize. Within reason."

"If I win? I'll have to think about it."

"Don't bother. I'm going to win this bet."

"That sure of yourself, are you?"

He shook his head. "No, but I'm that sure of you."

He watched Keera position herself on the platform and take last-minute instructions. Then he saw her hesitation as the instructor hooked her to the line and she inched towards the edge of the platform. It wasn't such a high wire. In fact, he'd gone zipping on higher, much more extensive wires. Zipped over canopies of trees, skimmed along mountains. Taken an all-day outing once, combining zipping and hiking. All that had been back before he'd become a dad, and had had dad responsibilities.

Sometimes he did miss that freedom. Wondered what it would be like to share his parental responsibility with someone so he could afford a little time away. Mostly, though, he loved the responsibility, loved everything that came with it.

Although, after last night, some of the longing had returned—longing he'd put on hold the day he'd made his decision to adopt the girls. Well, it was good to know it was still there. Unfortunately, it was now dusted off and raring to go, and as long as Keera was here, it wasn't going to go back into storage. The fifty or so photos of her he'd taken already, and now the video, were proof enough of that.

"Do you seriously think I'm going to step off this platform?" she called down to him.

"Want me to come up there and give you a push?"

"What I want is an activity where I can keep both feet planted firmly on the ground. Something sane, like taking a hike. Or jogging."

"One step, Keera. That's the way everything starts in life. With one step." And she needed that step because she did keep everything so locked up.

She looked down at him again then looked over at the kids, and shrugged. Then took that step, to the shouts and screams of the children, who were jumping up and down, applauding her. In a few seconds she was on the opposite platform, raising her arms in the air in victory. Waving at the kids. Shouting her own glee at the task completed.

"I didn't hear you scream," he said, showing her the playback of the video.

"Because it happened so fast. One moment my feet were on solid ground then the next I was flying."

"See, I told you." he said, helping her off with her helmet. "Want to do it again?"

"Think I could?"

"We have two hours here. I'll bet you can do it several more times."

"That was…" She smiled. "Pick your restaurant, Reid.

You win. You were right. So revel in it now, because that's all you're getting from me. One admission and one only. It was fun. I loved it."

"One admission leading to one dinner but an admission with so much significance. Because victory is sweet. Trust me, one is all I need from you." And maybe another kiss at the end of the evening. But he wasn't going to hope too hard for that. Once was pushing it, twice would be... well, very nice, but also a very long long-shot. Still, long-shots were good to bet on because when they won, they paid off big.

"I'll talk to him, but I can't promise he'll like anything we've bought today." They'd been shopping for two hours, and the clothes were cute. Not traditional, not frilly. More like bright, and fun, lots of colors, lots of layers. And accessories. Oh, my heavens, his daughters were starved for accessories. Apparently their daddy was quite practical in some aspects of his personality, and allowing his daughters to express their true creativity was one of those aspects.

When they'd hit the accessories aisle of the little girls' section in the boutique where she'd shopped for Megan, it had been like a whole new world had opened up for Emmie and Allie. Bows and matching socks, purses, belts. And shoes to match specific outfits. These girls lived in basic colors and basic sneakers. Red and pink shoes were entirely new to them, and she couldn't quit buying.

In a way, a whole new world was opening to her, too. Partly because of Megan, and partly because of Emmie and Allie. It was so much unexpected fun, like the zip line. It was also all the things of which she'd been deprived when she'd been a girl that were coming back to remind her now, and she was regaining, vicariously, some of what she'd never had. Even now, her own shopping was practical, quick, and of necessity. And always, always basic.

But this…instead of regretting her past and even parts of her present life, she was enjoying every minute of the outing with Reid's daughters, and being ever mindful that Megan could be part of this in the near future, if all went well.

Also wishing Megan could be part of it now. She truly would have liked to include her.

"Was your daddy like that?" Emmie asked innocently, as she plowed through the section of hair accessories, looking for individual pieces to match each of the six outfits she'd picked out so far. "Like my daddy is?"

"I never got to know my daddy," Keera said. "He went away before I was born."

"He's lost?" Allie asked.

"I suppose you could say he is. But I don't think he wanted any little girls the way your daddy does."

"Would he want you if you were a boy?" Allie asked.

Keera laughed. "No, honey. I don't think he would. Some people don't want to be mommies or daddies."

"Like you?" Emmie asked, picking out a green and yellow hair bow. "I heard you and daddy talking and you said you didn't want children."

"You don't want Megan?" Allie asked.

This really wasn't the conversation she wanted to be having with the girls but apparently it was the conversation they wanted with her. "I like children. I like both of you a lot. Megan, too. But I work almost every day, all day, and I wouldn't have time to be a good mommy, and Megan needs a good…" Well, she was hoping for a daddy, but how could she say that to these two?

"She needs a good home where someone's there to take care of her more than I could. Look, would either of you like ice cream?" That was the way to do it. When the situation got tough, cure it with ice cream. Yet another reason she wasn't cut out for motherhood. Simply put, she was stuck for what to do.

How in the world did Reid do this day in, day out? It was beyond her, and she realized she admired him not only for wanting to do this but for being good at it. And as she ordered two chocolate cones and a dish of strawberry, she realized even more that this was where Megan needed to be.

"They had a great time," Reid said. "I'm not sure about their—or your—fashion choices. But I suppose I'll get used to that, won't I? And I really insist on paying you back for everything you bought."

"Donate the money to the camp. I want this to be my treat."

"Because you're a surgeon who earns more than a county pediatrician?"

"Actually, I'm sure I do. Which isn't the point. We had a nice time and I thoroughly enjoyed the afternoon. So, please, don't spoil it by being…"

"Practical?" he asked, smiling.

"You're using my own life to prove me wrong?"

"You're the one who insists on being practical. So what can I say?"

"I can say that you've done a good job with the girls. I'm impressed you manage it all so well. Your life, your work, your parental responsibilities…"

"I manage it because I want to. It's all about priorities, I suppose. You know, the overall priorities, then the moment-to-moment priorities."

"And I manage my surgical practice the way I want to,

so I guess that pretty much tells you everything there is to know about my priorities."

"Which will never change?" he asked.

"Which I don't anticipate will change. Don't want to change."

"Even if your life situation changes?"

"Another thing I don't anticipate or want." Pulling into the parking spot of The Overlook, she looked at the building and almost wished she'd chosen the restaurant. This place was so romantic. Too romantic maybe? Rustic, and with a view the literature said couldn't be topped anywhere in the vicinity. And in the aftermath of that kiss. What was she thinking?

That she was flirting with things best left alone. That's what she was thinking. But this time she was better prepared. She knew she succumbed too easily to, well, it was either his charm or the clean mountain air, or the moment, or any number of the other reasons two people found that fleeting mutual attraction. And it was only fleeting. Had to be! She was going to make sure of that or she wasn't Keera Murphy, the cold bitch. Make that the *stone*-cold bitch.

But darn it. Once she stepped inside the restaurant, saw the dimmed lights, heard the violin music, her knees nearly buckled. And they really did buckle when she and Reid were shown to the table with the best view in the restaurant, and she had to hold on to that table for support. It was stunning at twilight, with the pinks and grays of the evening sky peeking over the distant mountains. "How did you manage this?" she asked Reid.

"Owners' names are Gwen and Henry Carson."

"As in Gregory Carson?"

He nodded. "They've struggled to hang onto the place, with all their medical expenses. Amazing people, though. They do it all, and take care of a recovering kid, too."

"So this is going to be another exercise in how I could or should be a parent, even with my circumstances, and the Carsons are going to show me the way? Is that why we're here? It's an object lesson?"

"No, but they are going to serve you one of the most amazing meals you've probably ever had."

"Which is meant to prove that I, too, can be a super-mom, like you're a super-dad, and they're super-parents?"

Suddenly, she had no desire to be here, no desire to spend the evening with her face being rubbed in her inadequacies. Sure, she felt guilty about Megan. Her feelings for the little girl were growing. She liked taking care of her, reading her stories, taking walks with her, playing games. But that was largely due to the circumstances—she was out of her element, living a life that wasn't hers. And now, with so many people trying to prove the point, she wasn't comfortable any more. Didn't want to be here, being forced to face the obvious.

So she wasn't going to stay and subject herself to that, no matter how the evening was *intended*. It was as simple as that. Reid could stay, and she'd leave the money to pay for it because nowhere in that bet had there been a mention of dinner for two. Or an object lesson on essential parenting guidelines, which this was all about.

Was she angry? Maybe a little. Or feeling guilty? Probably some of that thrown in there as well. Because she couldn't do it all and she knew it. Knew her inadequacies and didn't have to be reminded of them over the soufflé. But she also knew her strengths, one of which wasn't going to be the commendable kind of parent Reid, or even the Carsons, were. So she pulled her credit card from her purse, slapped it down on the table, and said, "Enjoy yourself. Don't hold back and, please, just slip the card under my cabin door when you return to camp." With that, Keera spun around and marched straight out of the restaurant, quite sure she could hear Reid following her. But she wouldn't turn around to look, not even when she got to the car and had to pause a moment to find the key fob in her purse.

"It was supposed to be a simple dinner," he said. "I'm not sure what you read into it that turned it into something else, but I'm sorry if I said the wrong thing."

"There's not one wrong thing," she said. "Everything's wrong. A week ago I didn't know this camp or you existed, and Megan was only a name and not a child with real-life needs. And this time next week I'll have my real life back and this whole mountain fantasy where I end up being mom of the year will be over and I'll have my elbows up in somebody's rib cage, repairing their heart. It's all I can do, Reid." She looked up at him.

"All I'm supposed to do. It's the reality where I control my life and everything in it. And it's where I don't feel guilty because I can't do the noble thing, the way you can."

"Control is that important you?"

"It has to be. Or else I end up...like this." She spread her arms to take in the whole expanse of town that could be viewed from their vantage point.

"What's so bad about this?"

"For you, nothing. For me, everything. Absolutely everything." She drew in a steadying breath and leaned back against the car. "You were right, you know. I am cold. Because I want to be cold. It keeps the world from intruding, and it keeps me in the place I need to be. Where I belong."

"Which is alone."

"Which is unaffected. I know you want me to be that little girl's mother, or at least her guardian until a permanent home can be found for her."

"That's true."

She laughed, but it was a bitter laugh. Or one filled with regret. "You sound like your daughters. The subject came up when we were shopping and I think they were amazed that I couldn't step in and rescue Megan the way you stepped in and rescued them. But being the good role model that I am, I distracted them with ice cream because I didn't know what to say. So tell me, does the person who takes the low road really sound like the best candidate for motherhood?"

"She sounds like me when I struggle to find the right way to go. There's no book with all the answers you'll ever need to know, Keera. Not about parenting, not about life in general. But it works out, one way or another."

"For me, it works out when I'm scrubbed and ready to step into the OR."

"Having a child doesn't mean you can't do that."

"You don't know me, then. In my life all I can do is one thing. Look, dinner here was a bad idea because this place…you…Gregory's parents…suffocate me with my inadequacies. And I'm really not hungry. So, please, go back, have a nice evening on me. I'm sure you can catch a taxi back to the cabin. Or I can catch a taxi and leave you the car. However you want to work it out."

"Why do I scare you so much?" he asked.

There were so many reasons on so many levels, but most of all he reminded her of the things she'd never be able to have. Reid was everything, he had everything. And she was a shell. She knew that, and was OK with it. "You don't. I'm the one who scares me."

"Because of this?" he asked, tilting her face up to his. "Because you don't want to want it?"

With that, he lowered his lips to hers, but it was not a kiss filled with fire and raw need. It was tender, and gentle. Filled with hope she so desperately wanted to feel. Wanted to hold on to. "We shouldn't do this," she said, hating that she had to pull away from him. But she had to, because she so feared getting lost in the very thing she knew she couldn't have yet was only now beginning to realize she desperately wanted.

"You're right," he said, smiling. "We shouldn't. But once wasn't enough."

"Why do you even want to…well, do anything with me? Nothing can come of it."

"Or everything, depending on your perspective."

She shook her head. "There's only one perspective, and I think maybe the mountain air's gone to your head, Reid. Or perhaps you need more adult companionship. I don't know which. But have you thought this through? If nothing else, think of our proximity. We live more than an hour away from each other."

"Half an hour if we meet in the middle."

"And neither of us have that hour or half-hour to spare. And in the end we're too different."

"And opposites never attract."

"Not in reality," she said.

"So then why do I want to kiss you so badly, and why do you want me to?" he asked, clearly on the verge of their next kiss. "And we're pretty much opposite in everything?"

"Too many children around, and I'm back to believing you're craving some adult companionship."

"So, any adult will do, right? Any set of lips? Any curvy, sexy-as-hell hips…"

"Hmm," she murmured, as his lips met hers, but this time with a hunger that no romantic meal was going to satisfy.

"Wow," she said groggily, rolling over and looking at the naked body stretched out next to her. She certainly hadn't expected what was lurking beneath his clothing. Reid had a magnificent body, lean and well muscled. As a doctor, she knew physical perfection. As a woman, she'd never known she could enjoy it so much. Every inch of it. "Time to get up, leave this hotel and get back to camp, before anybody notices that we're missing."

"What time is it?"

"A little after one. And even though Sally is always happy to watch Megan, I want to spend the rest of the night with her. Which means we've got to go back to camp before it gets any later and people start wondering if we're doing what we just did." She smiled. "And I mean it, Dr. Adams. Appearances are important."

He reached over and twined his fingers through her hair. "I never knew how much I liked red hair before last night. But I definitely like red hair."

"I know," she said, not sure whether to be bold or opt for being demure.

"Nice red hair."

She sighed. "Seriously. We've got to go, Reid. Somebody's going to find out." She sat up and pulled the sheet up to cover her breasts, but he immediately reached over and tugged the sheet back down.

"I like your breasts as much as I like your hair. If you're going to kick me out of your bed, the least you could do is give me one last look."

She liked being admired, liked that it was Reid doing the admiring. "Technically, I'm not kicking. Just urging." And, oh, how she didn't want to. But getting here had been such a fluke, and then discovering how good they were together? Suffice it to say he'd melted the stone-cold bitch into a puddle, and she wasn't ready to have that end. But, practically speaking, it had to. Because they weren't practical together. Neither was this relationship. A few hours together were good, but anything beyond that… "And if you're not going to avail yourself of the shower, I will."

"Please, avail away. But leave the sheet here, because as much as I like your red hair and your breasts, well, all I can say is that watching you walk away from me, naked, is my fondest fantasy. Well, one of them."

His grin was wicked, his demeanor sexy and funny—everything she'd always wanted and had never had. Still couldn't have, and that's the only thing she could think of as she gave him his show on her way into the shower. She couldn't have any of this.

In another few minutes it would be over, and it all would be relegated to the past tense and dreams to be put away on the shelf. But no regrets. She was a modern woman, and modern women had flings. It was accepted. Something totally different from her mother's life and lifestyle. Although this was the first time she'd ever slept with a man outside marriage, which meant…

Actually, she wasn't going to ponder that one. No, she was going to take a shower and go about her plans for the rest of the night, and let Reid worry about what to tell his children, or anybody else for that matter, if he lollygagged too much and they didn't get back to camp at a respectable time.

But a little while longer in bed with him would have been nice. Sighing, Keera turned on the shower full blast and stepped in, and let the water pellets ping her skin a little harder than she usually did because she'd felt alive in his arms these last hours, and now she wanted something else to make her feel alive. Only a few minutes away from Reid and she needed a physical reminder…

"What have I done?" she whispered as she sank back against the shower wall and let the water beat hard against her.

"Room for one more?" he asked, snapping her out of her reverie.

"We shouldn't," she said, desperately wanting to anyway. "Because after tonight…" Keera shrugged.

"What? We're done?"

"We should be."

Reid turned on the grin. "Because we're not practical?"

"Something like that," she said, as he pushed back the shower curtain and entered. "I don't do this. Tonight, you and me. It's not me."

Picking up the bottle of body wash, he raised it and squeezed so that the pink soap inside slithered down between her breasts, all the way to her belly, and below. Then he began to spread the soap, the palms of both his hands making a circular motion on her flesh that left her gasping for breath. "Oh, this is definitely you," he said, taking particular care to tweak her nipples to erection then linger there, stroking, pinching lightly, then returning to his circular motion as his hands continued on their journey, down her belly, and even further down, until one hand forged ahead and the other hand reached around to grab her bottom.

"Reid, no." She gasped, "We shouldn't."

"Go on," he urged. "We shouldn't what?"

"Stop," she choked out, as the paroxysms of his efforts began to overtake her.

"Now? You want me to stop now?"

"No!" she practically screamed. "We shouldn't stop. Not now! Please, don't."

"As if I could," he growled, as she quivered beneath his fingertips. "Or would."

But they would have to at some point. That's what she was thinking when their shower was over, and an hour later when, car lights off, they drove into the camp and parked behind her cabin. Then Reid left her with a quick kiss to her cheek, while she went to the infirmary, tiptoed past a sleeping Sally, and slid into the bed on the other side of the aisle. Still feeling the lingering of that kiss, and everything that had come before it, as she pulled the sheet up over her.

It was dark, and the camp was quiet and asleep. And somewhere out there Reid was sneaking away like a thief in the night. In a sense, though, that's what he was, because he had stolen something from her. Not her virginity, not even her sense of moral purpose. More like her certainty.

With Kevin, there had never been doubts or questions or a roller-coaster of emotion. Their meeting, their dating, their marriage had always been the practical matters she'd wanted them to be.

With Reid there was nothing practical about it. Not one little aspect. That's where her certainty wavered because, for the first time in her life, she wasn't sure she wanted to be all that certain. Wasn't sure she could be any more. And that's what scared her. What truly, honestly scared her.

Raising herself up to peek out the window, Keera saw Reid heading round to the rear side of his cabin and imagined him going in through his kitchen door. An affair with Reid Adams—and, yes, this was an affair of some sort—was like zip lining, where she was flying through the air, tethered to a very small cable. The zip-line cable she trusted because it was proven. Her own private cable wasn't proven, however, which meant disaster could surely be sneaking around in the dark, the way Reid was.

Only this time she wasn't wearing a safety helmet or any of the other protective gear. And she feared that she needed all she could get—to protect her heart.

CHAPTER EIGHT

"IT'S WHERE?" KEERA asked, clearly alarmed by the forest fire that was now engulfing one of the surrounding ridges. She and Reid hadn't had contact for an entire day. In fact, she'd refused to even look at him. But the memories had lingered, made her mellow, caused her to sigh wistfully more times than she wanted to. Nice aftermath with too many warm, leftover sensations. Then this. Life changing too fast, too unpredictably.

"About four miles east of here. I talked to one of the rangers a little while ago, and he wants us to get ready to evacuate. They're hoping that if weather holds, and everything works in their favor, they'll get it contained before it makes it all the way down to this valley. But he also advised that we need to get the kids out of here pretty soon."

"Then that's what we do," she said, seeing the worried look on Reid's face. He had a lot at risk here. Everything he owned, a life's investment in jeopardy. "So, in spite of trying to look calm, I know you're not," she said. "And I think I need to know the worst-case scenario."

"Other than the obvious problems that I may lose my camp, or the smoke that's going to make some of these kids sick, I just went down to the highway, and the roads are already congested. People driving crazy, trying to get out of the valley. I don't want the kids caught up in all that mess."

"Do you have a back-up plan?"

He nodded. "Already implemented. But I'm worried about the time crunch."

However it worked out, it was time to disband camp and in doing that leave all kinds of unresolved feelings behind. Couldn't be helped, though, couldn't be prevented, couldn't even be postponed. Because once she walked away from this place, that's exactly what would happen. Nothing would be resolved, not about her growing feelings for Reid and especially not about what to do with Megan.

"How much time do we have?" she asked.

"Not a lot. Maybe an hour, an hour and a half before it starts getting critical. So let me call a staff meeting, get everybody in on this, because we're going to have some disappointed kids. Today was the day we were going to go horseback riding."

"Have you called your partner and told him not to come?"

Reid nodded. "He's my back-up plan. He's up in the sky right now, looking at the fire, assessing our best options. We do mountain search and rescue, so he's authorized to be overhead. And he's ready to come and grab us, depending on the roads."

"Helicopter?" she asked.

Reid nodded.

"Seriously?" The more she heard about Reid's medical practice, the more impressed she was.

Reid grinned. "Which was why I got my pilot's license recently. The chopper is what we make house calls and hospital runs in. Oh, and we go out on horseback for some of the closer house calls. Personally, I prefer my motorcycle over the horse."

"You're a pilot *and* you have a motorcycle? Let me just say *wow* to your diversity." Keera laughed. "I wouldn't have taken you for a cowboy doctor. But a pilot? I can see that. And I can definitely picture you in leathers. I hope you wear leathers on the motorcycle."

"That would make me some kind of a bad boy, wouldn't it?"

"I saw the bad boy in you last night, Reid. Trust me, the leathers would only enhance what's already there."

Blushing slightly, Reid cleared his throat. "That's me, pilot-cowboy-bad-boy-doctor. But today I'm all camp counselor, who's trying to figure out the most efficient way to get these kids out of here. Which I think will be by air. Also, by taking the kids out in the chopper we can keep them together better until we can make arrangements for their parents to come get them."

"And they'll have a blast doing this, as long as we don't let them know why we're evacuating. You know, turn it into an adventure rather than an emergency." She regarded his brooding expression and her heart went out to him. Sure, she'd spent the night with him. And, sure, she admired him for what he did here. But he was struggling, and so distressed, yet he was trying to hold it all together for everyone else. Who held it together for Reid, though? As far as she knew, nobody.

"The kids are going to be fine, Reid. Trust me, everything's going to turn out OK. They'll be safe, and that's all that matters."

"You're right. That's all that matters." That's what he said, but it's not how he'd sounded when he'd said it.

Keera stepped forward and wrapped her arms around him. "Your camp's going to be safe, isn't it? I mean, it's not in any real danger of..."

She couldn't bring herself to say the words, because she knew how much of Reid's life was tied up in these few wooded acres, and to even think it was at risk made her gut knot.

"The big danger here is the smoke, right? If the wind shifts?" She was saying that to reassure herself, although nothing on Reid's face was reassuring about anything, and she knew what he was thinking, what he was dreading.

"Let's hope so," he said, responding to her embrace by wrapping his arms around her. "But if it burns…well, what I can say?"

"You can say that you took care of the kids first."

"That's right. You're always practical, aren't you?"

"Yep. Always practical." She forced herself out if the embrace. "So now what?"

"Now we get everybody the hell out of Camp Hope."

"Then I'll get the staff together while you figure out what we need to do to get this camp shut down."

"About last night," he started, then stopped when Emmie came running up to him and latched onto his hand.

"When do we get to go riding?" she asked. "Because I told Molly and Nathan I'd show them how because they've never been on a horse before, and I have!"

"Sorry, sweetheart," Reid said. "But we're going to have to save that for another day. Beau can't bring the horses right now."

"But he promised," she whined.

"And we'll do it another time." He looked over at Keera, who was already running in the direction of the dorm. "Today, instead of horseback riding, it's helicopter rides for everyone. So go tell your friends to get ready, that Doc Beau is going to be here with his chopper in a few minutes."

"Really?" Emmie cried. "We're going to fly? You're not going to say *no* when it's my turn? Because you always say *no* when we're home."

"I'm not going to say *no*. Before long you're going to be going up and over that mountain," he said, pointing to a ridge in the opposite direction from the fire.

"Promise?"

"Cross my heart," he said, crossing his heart as she shooed Emmie back to the other children.

"Everybody's alerted, and getting ready to get out," Keera shouted, running up to him minutes later. "And I was thinking, maybe the kids can all come back later this summer and make up their last couple of days. I know if I can get the time off I'd come back and help you."

He glanced up in the sky, looking for Beau, saw the helicopter off in the distance. "Did you say what I thought you said? That you'd come back?"

"If you needed me to. I mean, I did volunteer for a week, and I'm still good for it."

"I appreciate that, Keera. You don't know how much. And I appreciate everything you've done here so far, even if I've given you a hard time about certain things."

"They're your kids, you have the responsibility."

"And I'm stubborn."

"As stubborn as I am?" she teased.

"Is anybody as stubborn as you are?" When he saw Beau's helicopter making its final approach the somberness slid back down over him. "Guess it's time to get this thing started."

"You don't like the idea of these kids flying, do you?"

"I don't like the idea that this might overstress some of the kids, and I won't be on the other end to take care of them. Because they will hear about the fire. Might even see it from the air."

"I called the sheriff in Marston Springs, Reid. He's going to be contacting Beau about where to land then he's going to get the doctor over there ready to look at the kids once they set down."

"That's a good instinct," Reid said appreciatively, as the camp staff began to gather around him. "Remind me to invite you back to camp some time."

A minute later all but a couple of people who were busy attending to the kids were huddled around Reid, who was on the phone to the ranger. "Looks like the wind is shifting, and it's coming this way. Not fast, but we're going to start airlifting out of here immediately." He drew in a deep breath.

"You all know the emergency plan. Beau will take charge of getting you on the chopper, Betsy is gathering up the medicines we need to take with us, and Keera has arranged to have the local doc meet us over in Marston Springs. Other than that…" he shrugged "…have a safe trip, and I'll see you on the other side of the mountain.

"Oh, and anybody who wants to drive out is welcome to try. The highway is congested, but if you know your way through Moores Valley, he suggests using the Moores Valley road and taking the turnoff to Marston Springs from that."

As it turned out, only Clara opted to drive, and that was because of her basset hound. The other six volunteers agreed to go by chopper and take care of the kids when they arrived at the other end.

"And Megan?" Keera asked Reid.

"We'll fly her out with the rest of the kids, put her in a chopper with the volunteers to keep them separated. Or you can drive her out. It's up to you."

"What about you?"

"Hanging in to the bitter end. I can't leave until I know everything here is as protected as it can be. And I'm hoping to rescue all the computers. I've got the data backed up to the cloud, but the equipment is expensive and I'd like to save it."

"But you can't stay here by yourself," Keera protested. "It's not safe. What if something happens to you, and you're the only one here? Who's going to help you?"

"Nothing's going to happen to me," he said, taking hold of Keera's hand and heading towards the clinic. "I'll get everybody out, load up what I can, and hang around a day or two to shut the place down if the fire doesn't get it, maybe let parents back in to pick up their kids' things, and hope nothing happens."

"What about your girls?"

"Beau's going to take them back to Sugar Creek with him, and he and Deanna will look after them."

"Will they look after one more?" she asked.

"What do you mean?"

"Megan. Will they look after Megan while I stay here with you?"

"You can't stay! It's not…"

"Safe?"

"It might not be safe. And you're not experienced."

"Does that mean you're experienced with forest fires?" she asked.

"No. Until a few months ago I was a city boy. Only came to the country to be closer to my camp."

"Then shut up and quit arguing with me. If it's safe enough for you to stay behind, it's safe enough for me. I'm not leaving you here alone, and I'm not going to fight you about it."

"But Megan needs a familiar face. She's already gone through enough, and to be put in the arms of strangers again…."

"And she'll have a familiar face in a day or so. Look, Reid. I've already made up my mind, and there's not a darned thing you can do to stop me, short of tying me up and throwing me on the helicopter." She smiled. "And I'd like to see you try."

"Are you sure about this, Keera? Because if the fire accelerates…"

"Then we'll be in it together." She shrugged. "No big deal. We'll take that back road you suggested."

"It's a very big deal," he said, tilting his head down to give her a gentle but oh-so-brief kiss on the lips. "And I appreciate it. Oh, and so you'll know, you're not the woman I thought you were."

"In a good way or a bad way?"

"Tell you later," he said looking towards the east, as the normal smoke in the mountains, which was actually mist and humidity that lurked just above the treetops, was being engulfed by real and very ominous black smoke. "Because right now I've got to go get the kids ready to ride."

Keera's first instinct was to run to get Megan ready, and when she got to the infirmary Megan was wide awake, looking much better than she had in days. "I don't know what's going to happen after today," she said to Megan as she relieved Sally of duty and helped dress the little girl in street clothes, "but it's not going to be an institution. I can promise you that. Even if you have to come and stay with me for a little while until arrangements can be made."

She glanced wistfully out the window and saw Reid lead a parade of kiddies across the compound. "I'm still not giving up on him, though. I'm just not as optimistic that I have time to convince him to be my solution."

Once Megan was dressed, Keera did a quick exam to make sure she wasn't running a temperature or had some other problem going on, then she bundled her into her arms, carried her outside and fell in line with the rest of the people awaiting their turn for a helicopter ride. The adults were waiting with a sense of trepidation while the kids were anxious and excited. But Reid looked more worried than he had earlier. He kept glancing up at the ridge in the distance, watching the smoke get thicker. And closer.

"Maybe we ought to go, too," she said, sidling up next to him. "Get everybody out of here first then drive out together."

He took Megan from her arms. "It's all I have. All I own. This camp. I've put everything I have into it. And I have to be here, no matter what happens to it."

"But you have your girls, Reid, which makes you a lucky man. The rest…" She looked around, saw the man she assumed to be Beau waving her over. "I think it's time for Megan to fly."

"She'll be fine. Sally's going to hold her, and I'll let Beau know she's to go home with them for the time being."

"By chopper?"

"No. Deanna's driving over to get the girls because Beau's going to hang around and join in rescue efforts."

"But that will expose Emmie to measles."

"Desperate times, desperate measures. If she gets measles, I'll get her through it."

Something about Beau's courage brought tears to her eyes. Or maybe it was the smoke beginning to waft in. She didn't know which it was but she nodded numbly as she watched Reid walk forward to place Megan in Sally's arms. Suddenly a lump the size of her fist formed in her throat and that, added to her already spilling tears, caused her to run forward and take the child from his arms. "I need to do this," she said, sniffling as she carried Megan the rest of the way over. "Look, sweetheart, I'll see you in a little while. I promise. These nice people are going to take you on a ride, and you're going to go stay at a very nice place where they have horses."

"Mommy," she whimpered.

"I know you want her, but Mommy can't be here, sweetheart." Megan hadn't said very much over the past few days—Megan had assumed because of the trauma from her accident combined with being sick—and it was so good to hear her voice. In fact, it caused the lump in her throat to swell a little more. "And we'll talk about that next time I see you. But right now, promise me you'll be good. Can you do that for me?"

Megan nodded, and Keera kissed her on the forehead. Then reluctantly handed her over to Sally, who took her immediately to the helicopter. In another minute they were lifted off the ground and turning away from Camp Hope. And Keera felt so hopeless. Maybe as hopeless as she'd felt all those times when, as a child, her mother had abandoned her. The same way she was sure Megan was feeling right now—abandoned and cast off to strangers.

"They'll be fine," Reid said, as he slipped his arm around her waist. "Deanna's great with kids. So are Brax and Joey…he runs the ranch. They'll take good care of her. And just so you know, I think she was calling *you* Mommy. She's growing attached to you, Keera."

She swiped at her tears. "I hope not, because life's about to jump out and bite her in the ugliest possible way, and…"

"You want to keep her, don't you?"

She shook her head. "I want you to keep her because I can't. She needs a good family now, and you and the girls are the best one I know. You can give her a life that I can't, and she deserves that."

"But it's still not for you—the whole family thing."

"You're right. It's still not for me." For the first time in her life she actually regretted the words. "There are things inside people they can't change, and for me, that's one of them."

"Do you think I ever anticipated being the single father of two little girls?"

"Maybe it's something you didn't anticipate, but you come from a background that doesn't limit you in the capacity it takes to be a father. And not just a father but a good father. I'm limited, Reid. More than you can know. More than I want to know."

"And limits can't be overcome?"

She laughed. "You're always the optimist, aren't you?"

"When it comes to you, yes, I am. Maybe that's because I don't see limits, maybe it's because I see someone fighting hard against so much potential. I still think it's in you, Keera. I'm not sure how to convince you it's there, though."

He couldn't, because it wasn't. But it was so nice to hear him tell her she had potential. No one ever had, not for any reason, and not in any endeavor. Too bad she was hearing about a flat-lined potential that couldn't be shocked back with a defibrillator.

Less than an hour later, after the chopper lifted off for the last time, the camp felt utterly desolate. Reid wasn't sure where Keera was and, right now, standing out here in the compound alone, watching the tail of the helicopter disappear over the ridge, he was spooked. Had to admit it. He was spooked, and it wasn't about being here so much as it was about what he stood to lose if the camp got caught in the fire.

"It's getting closer," Keera called from the porch of the infirmary. She'd been gathering up all the new clothes and toys she'd bought for Megan and packing them into a box to take away with her when she left. "I was looking out the back way, and it's moved down quite a lot. So, what can we do? Should we be hosing down the buildings or something?"

He could feel the grit of the smoke in his lungs now. Or maybe it was his imagination because that's what he expected to feel. Either way, she was right. The fire was marching down the side of the mountain like an invading army, and there wasn't much he could do except put as much gear into the camp van as he could, and keep his fingers crossed.

"If it comes any closer, yes." Who was he kidding? If the fire came any closer it would take the camp with it no matter what they did.

"Is there anything to pack up and take with us?"

"Don't know," he said on a discouraged sigh. "I don't really have much here that's of any value. I've packed all the girls' things, and gone through and gathered everything of value the kids left behind. As far as medical equipment…" He shrugged. "It's insured, and none of it was new to begin with."

"So why stay?"

"Because I'm the captain of this ship. It's all I own. When I decided to do this, I invested everything I had in it. Guess it goes to show you how fragile life is, doesn't it?" He looked up at the fire, which was now visible from their vantage point. A while ago it had only been the smoke threatening Camp Hope, now it was the fire itself.

"But the kids are safe. I talked to Betsy, and they're having fun on their adventure. The Marston Springs sheriff let the kids all ride in his police car, sirens blaring, and now he's treating them to ice cream. The doctor there said every last one of them is fine, and the parents have all been notified and are on their way. Deanna Alexander's already on the way back to Sugar Creek with the girls, so it's a good outcome, Reid. Maybe not the one you wanted, but everybody is safe. So it's time to go."

He looked up into the sky. "Maybe you're right. But damn it all! Why did this have to happen?"

She took hold of Reid's hand and walked with him over to where her car was parked next to the camp van. "Life dealt me a pretty bad hand once so I know what bitterness feels like, and it's not a good feeling because it consumes you, and sucks in everything around you. I understand your bitterness, Reid. But I also understand your strengths, and those strengths will get you through this."

"My girls," he said. "They're my strength."

"The camp is important for them—for Emmie because she's a survivor, and even for Allie because she has a connection to leukemia as a donor that few people ever have. So, if it burns down, you'll build it up again and your girls will be there to help you. It's as simple as that."

"Would that be two or three girls?"

"I shouldn't have said anything. But I thought…"

"You thought one more wouldn't matter."

"That's bad of me, isn't it?"

"Not bad so much as…unfortunate. Because you've got all the qualities. You just don't want to see them."

"My qualities." She laughed bitterly. "Like I told you, my mother was a prostitute, Reid. A prostitute! We lived on the street, half my meals came from whatever I could scrounge from garbage cans, and we were homeless half the time. Or when she did manage a room, she'd put me in the closet while she…she did her thing with the men. Sometimes I lived in cardboard boxes or under bridges, and I hardly ever got to go to school because we never stayed one place long enough.

"Then when I was thirteen, social services finally took me from her, but only because I went to the library every chance I could to read, and confided to my favorite librarian that my mother wanted me to do...do what she did. You know, turn tricks for money because I was developed, and pretty. And young. So I talked to the librarian, who was nice to me, and she helped. If she hadn't, I don't even want to think how it might have turned out.

"But after that, after I was in the system, I was wild, couldn't be controlled, couldn't be kept in a home because I did everything I could to act up. Kind of like my mother was, come to think of it. But I was smart, which is the only saving grace I had in this life because I whizzed through school once I was allowed to go, and even managed to graduate early. Got scholarships, and the rest..." She shrugged.

"The rest isn't fit to be called mother because I'm not going to let anything stand in my way of achieving what I need to achieve. That was the only promise I made to myself through everything, and I've never broken it. I won't let *anything* stand in my way.

"But I know my limitations, and I'm more than ready to admit what I'm not capable of doing. I've been a wife once and failed miserably at that, but Kevin moved on to a life he wanted. A child doesn't have that same option when a parent is bad. I didn't, and I don't want to put another child in the same position I was in. Which is why I'd hoped..."

"Hoped I'd keep Megan."

"So sue me for trying. I don't want bad things for her. In fact, I want only the best."

"Which isn't you?"

"Which isn't me. But I'm good with it."

"I saw how reluctant you were to let Megan go a while ago. That's not being good with it, Keera. If anything, I think you're kidding yourself. And I'm sorry about your childhood. I can't even begin to imagine what it must have been like for you, but you persevered. You got through it and look at you now—what you do, who you are. You're not the little girl who lived in cardboard boxes, and you're not your mother."

"Maybe I'm not but…" Pausing, she smiled. "But I'm me, the person I designed me to be. And I didn't design children into that."

"Then update the design."

"What if I did? What if I *updated* and tried, then somewhere along the way realized that I had been right about it all along? That I wasn't cut out to be a mother? Or, God forbid, that I was like my mother? What would happen to Megan then? I mean, living in a situation where you're not wanted. I don't think you can understand that. It's desolate. There's no hope. And I don't want to do that to her."

"But what if you discovered that you *are* cut out to be a mother? Keera, you're so strong that if you turned out to be like your mother, it would only be by choice. You are who you want to be, and you're completely in control of that, no matter what you might think."

"No matter what I might think? What I think, Reid, is that rolling the dice on who I am is taking a big risk. That's what it would be."

"But if you're capable of designing yourself into the person you want to be, and you want to be a mother, doesn't it stand to reason you can design that into yourself?"

"You've got an argument for everything, don't you?"

"Not everything. But I know I'm right about this. And I do understand how you're afraid you'll turn out to be just like your mother. But, Keera, I can promise you that's never going to happen. You just have to trust yourself more to believe it."

"Most of my life I've tried so hard not to be like her because…"

He took her hand and held it. "Your mother's life was a choice, Keera. Just like your life is a choice. You get to control what you do, what you want, what you want to include. And your mother has no influence in that because you've become your own person.

"I think, though, that you use her as your excuse—to succeed, to excel. You know, be the success you are to prove yourself to the mother who never loved you. The thing is, you can't change what she was. That part of your life is over with, and whatever bad things you were taken away from are in your past.

"Now you don't need to have an excuse to succeed, because all the qualities you'll ever need are in you, totally independent of anything your mother did or was. It's you, Keera. Not her. You can't go back and make her love you, and you're never going to turn into her. So I only hope you'll find a way to trust that and move on. Because until you do, you're depriving yourself of happiness and all the good things you deserve."

"Look, I appreciate what you're trying to do but I really was on the verge of abandoning Megan here a few nights ago and that, if nothing else, should tell you who I am. I didn't want her, and I was angry I had to deal with her. You were her doctor, you ran a camp for kids. I saw you as my solution. And I still do, but differently. And that *is* what my mother would do."

"But it's not what *you* did. That's the difference. She would have, and you didn't. That's all that matters, Keera. You didn't do it."

"That tendency is in me, Reid. Can't you see that? I would have left her here that first night if I'd had the opportunity."

"That tendency is there because you won't let your mother go and, subconsciously, you're sabotaging yourself into thinking you'd be just like her given the opportunity. It's time to quit trying to prove you're not her and start trying to prove you're you. But I can't be the one to convince you of that. It has to be you."

"I appreciate your faith in me, as misplaced as it is."

He'd give her credit for one thing. She was as stubborn as hell, and he didn't know what it was going to take to crack that shell of hers so she could see what was inside. Truth was, she was afraid to look, afraid of what she might find. Even though he understood why, he still couldn't understand why she refused to take that hard, objective look and see all the things he saw. Especially when, just a little while ago, she'd actually gone teary over putting Megan on the helicopter.

Well, at least he saw the conflicts for what they were. What he couldn't see, though, was the reason for his own emotional entanglement. He knew who Keera was and what she resisted, which was essentially everything he wanted in life. Yet he was fascinated. More than fascinated, actually. He was downright captivated, and he didn't know how to undo that. But he had to. That's all there was to it. He had to.

CHAPTER NINE

IT WAS TIME to get out, but Reid was still working methodically, trying to pack away as much as he could in the camp van. Just working. Not talking. And not looking at the fire creeping its way across the valley the way she was drawn to looking. Because he didn't want to see his future. Much the way she didn't want to see various aspects of her own life. Some things were too painful to face—for both of them.

"Anything else I should get?" she asked him. "I've got a little more room for a few small things." Her eyes stung, her throat ached. Her lungs were fighting for every breath now. But she wasn't going to leave him here alone.

Pausing in his frantic efforts, he wiped the sweat from his face with the back of his hand, then shook his head. "I've done all I can. It's time to go. You lead, I'll follow. We'll stick to the highway unless it's too congested, then I'll call you."

"When it's over, Reid, no matter how it goes, maybe I can help you get the camp up and running again. Not so much in the physical sense but I've got some contacts, people who might be able to take on some of the responsibility." She smiled. "I've operated on some people in mighty high places, so all I have to do is call."

"You'd do that?" he asked, walking her to her car. "Stay

involved here past, well…past all this?" For the first time since the kids had all gone he looked across the valley at the fire, saw how close it was to the east end of his acreage.

"I would," she said.

"Why? Why would you be willing to help me when…?"

"When I don't like kids?"

"That's not what I was going to say, but it is a good question as you're not fond of them."

"See, that's the thing. I'm not *not* fond of children. In fact, I've enjoyed my association with Megan, and even with your girls. But I lack that elusive thing some people call the parenting gene, so I'm not a nurturer by nature. Which doesn't mean I'm a kid-hater. More like an avoider.

"But this camp, Reid, it's so important. I know what we did, what we had was only a one-night thing, and I'm not kidding myself about that. It was good. Fantastic. But it was last night, and today I'm extending my hand in friendship because you're going to need help with something that's worthy. Whether or not you accept it is entirely up to you, but the offer stands.

"I'll help do whatever needs to be done when the time comes, if you want me to. Or stay away, if that's what you want. But right now let's just get out of here."

"Agreed," he said, as he opened her door for her. "And I'll see you on the other side of the mountain. Oh, and…" He bent down, gave her a quick kiss on the lips. "Thank you," he whispered. "For everything."

"Be safe, Reid," she said, as she moved her car forward. "Please be safe," she whispered to herself as she looked in her rear-view mirror and saw him climb into his van. "So we can meet on the other side of the mountain."

She wouldn't see what he'd done. And by the time she'd figured out that he'd turned off onto an access road at the edge of the property, she'd be safe in Marston Springs. And he'd be attempting one last-ditch effort, by moving all the volunteers' cars as far away from the camp enclosure as possible then hosing down the buildings. It wouldn't be easy, probably wouldn't even be successful, but he couldn't go down without this fight. And he couldn't have fought knowing someone he loved was in the path of danger.

She wasn't, though. Not now. So parking his van a good distance from the compound, he got out and went, on foot, back to the area, where he started, one by one, to move the cars away. Potential gasoline explosions and all. Although there weren't any good places to stash them, he did take them to a cleared area on the west side of the property—a baseball field. The first car, then second one. Driving frantically, wishing he didn't have to waste the time, wishing he could have had his volunteers do this, but knowing they'd had to take care of the children instead.

Still, getting rid of the explosion hazard made him feel like he was doing something, even if it was futile, and as he ran back that nearly quarter-mile to get the next car, he saw a vehicle approaching him. "What the…?"

"I saw the keys in the cars," she shouted out the window at him. "Figured out you'd want these cars moved at some point if you were going to fight it. Then when I saw you turn off on the access road…"

"You saw that?"

"I'm a surgeon. I observe everything."

"You can't do this. Can't be here."

"But you are."

"Seriously? You're going to get stubborn with me now?"

Rather than answering, she rolled up her car window and continued down the road, while he was left to run back and bring yet another car up. Which was when he met her on the road and stopped. "I'll be fine here. You don't need to do this because…"

"Because I want to? Look, Reid. My life doesn't count for much outside the operating room, but this camp, it adds something and, like you, I'm not going to let it go up in flames without a fight. So…" She gave a shooing gesture then spun away and continued her run down the road to fetch the next car. And so it went until all the cars were cleared away.

"Bet we're not leaving yet, are we?" she asked him when they were both finally back at the compound, running hand in hand.

What they found was not promising. The fire had encroached by jumping the dirt road on the east, and was spreading quickly along the fire trail all the way up to the compound itself—in patchy splotches, though. Thankfully not one great consuming wall of fire. Right now advance small fires were burring rather lazily, like they were waiting for the rest to catch up to them. But they were shooting off blazing embers, one after another. Little bursts of fireworks that would have been lovely in a holiday celebration but so deadly here, and now.

"I'll get the hose," Keera said, as Reid went in the opposite direction to grab a shovel.

When she returned with the hose, she saw him smashing the little blazers down as they hit the dirt, ignited the flower garden and a couple of wooden chair sitting on the edge of the compound. Then the tool shed. That's where Keera went into action, turning on the water and dousing the little wooden structure as best she could.

She had success, initially. The roof suffered damage, but the fire went out without much of a protest and it was a good thing because one of the outlying, unused cabins took an ember to the roof, which quickly had the whole roof flaming, taunting her to come get it, too. Which she did, or tried to. But by the time she dragged the hose over the ground and got it aimed, the roof was already half-gone, which meant the cabin itself wouldn't be long in following.

"Reid," she shouted, looking overhead as another burning ember floated merrily on its way, headed towards her cabin! "I can't contain it here."

"Get back!" he shouted, as his attention caught on the same ember that had caught hers. "Let it burn, and stay away."

Not to be deterred by the embers, she did let that cabin go and immediately ran to her own cabin and started to douse at almost the same time as the roof started to blaze. But her position wasn't good enough and the pine tree that loomed above it caught fire, too, and exploded into flames quicker than anything she'd ever seen burn. Another loss, only this one she fought valiantly, alternately spraying the walls and roof of the cabin as best she could.

The problem was the fiery tree above it had spread the flames to the next tree over, then the one after that, and that's when Keera realized that every last one of the guest cabins in that row would fall victim.

After that she looked around, saw Reid still beating out the small ground fires, which were overtaking him now. Saw that the next structure to go, after the guest cabins, would be the dorm, where the children stayed. And the one after that the dining hall.

"We can't save it," she said, wiping sooty sweat from her brow. It was a realization she hated with everything in her. But it was a fact. The fire had encroached enough that everything on the outer sides of the compound would go up. The dorms, Reid's cabin. Maybe not the clinic, though, which sat in the open and isolated from everything else.

"Reid," she yelled. "All of this." She shook her head. "We can't save it. But your clinic…"

"No! This time we've got to get out of here for real," he shouted back. "It doesn't make a difference now."

"But it does, if we can save that one thing."

"We've got to leave," he said, running up to her. "Before we get trapped."

"But the clinic!"

"Keera, it's only a building. A stupid, damned building." He grabbed the hose away from her, turned off the nozzle, and dropped it to the ground. "It doesn't matter any more. It's all…done."

"But the clinic, that's where you can start over, if we save it. And I want to try, Reid. Please, let me try."

He grabbed hold of her to tug her away from the compound but she resisted and pulled back. "You don't understand," she cried. "You have to fight for the things you love, the things you want in your life. If you don't…"

"I'm fighting for you, Keera, not for the clinic. It's time to go."

She shook her head. Bent down and picked up the hose. "No," she choked, as sooty tears rolled down her cheeks. "We have to try."

"Is this because if I lose everything I won't adopt Megan as I'll be too involved in trying to start over?"

"Wh-what? How could you even think that?"

"What am I supposed to think? That you've had a change of heart, fallen in love with me, even though I have kids? That you want to do this because you want to build a life around me, my children, and even this?"

"Reid, that's not fair!"

"Isn't it? I'm about to lose a large part of my dream, and here you are, fighting harder than I am to hang onto it. Which doesn't make any sense. So why wouldn't I think you're doing this because it's about you? You've never shown me anything that would make me think otherwise!"

This couldn't be happening. He couldn't be saying these things to her. "You don't mean it," she said. "You're talking crazy because the camp is burning down."

"It's not crazy talk, Keera. It's what I think."

"Then you think wrong." She turned and started to walk away. Then spun back to face him. "To hell with you, Reid Adams. To hell with this camp, to hell with your life." They were words that broke her heart because all she'd wanted to do was save a little piece of his dream for him—his starting point for rebuilding that dream.

"Oh, and if you're afraid that now's when I walk away and abandon Megan with you, to hell with you on that one, too."

Keera didn't turn round again. Not to see the expression on his face, not to watch him follow her. No, she went straight to her car, got in and didn't look back. Not when she fetched Megan in Marston Springs and dropped off the camp belongings with Betsy, not when she headed for the highway that took her home. And not even when she had to pull off the highway and have the hardest cry of her life.

"What have I done?" she asked herself in the mirror as muddy tears streaked down her cheek.

The toddler sleeping in her car seat didn't answer. Neither did the reflection in the mirror. Only her heart did, and it wasn't telling her what she wanted to hear.

"OK, let's get you ready to go to daycare," Keera said, as she looked at the mess of toys spread from one wall to the other. Her guest room, now a temporary nursery, looked like a tornado had hit it. So maybe she wasn't the tidiest temporary mom. Her once-weekly housekeeper picked up every Friday, which gave Keera and Megan a fresh start on a new week of messiness. Four weeks in a row now had turned it into a workable routine. Scatter for six days, pick up on the seventh.

And thank heavens for the hospital daycare center. That alleviated her problems in ways she'd never anticipated. They were open seven days, twenty-four hours, and the care was excellent. She knew, because that's where she took her breaks now, instead of hiding away in her office to review a patient history or grab a thirty-minute nap. Now her breaks were spent coloring or finger-painting or sharing graham crackers and milk with Megan. Something she actually enjoyed.

What she didn't enjoy, though, was being alone, having no one there to tell her if she was doing the mothering thing the right or wrong way. She had no instinct for it, but common sense seemed to be working out pretty well. And social services were still looking for an adoptive family. Although Keera wasn't pressing them now.

In fact, she'd told the social worker she'd like to keep Megan for a while longer, and she'd even gone to the effort of starting to legalize her guardianship. Why? For Megan's security, above all. Megan needed this time to adjust. She knew her real mommy and daddy weren't coming back, and she'd become so clingy with Keera that Keera didn't have the heart to send her away until she was more ready than she was now.

But also Reid had been right. She'd thought about his words, over and over, and had eventually come to realize how she'd spent a lifetime trying to prove she wasn't her mother, trying to do exactly the opposite of what her mother had done. Yet in her own heart she'd never truly discovered what she would do without that motivation.

What she would do, though, was love taking care of Megan. Which she did. And which was why, while she still wanted the best adoptive situation for her, there wasn't such an urgency about it now. At some point the time would come to give her up. Keera knew that, rationalized it every single day. Even dreaded it. And when that time came Keera knew her heart would break.

But this was all about Megan now, and what was best for her. Still, for now, every day was a new and better step. And who knew what would happen in the future? For sure, she didn't.

So even though everything was up in the air, Keera was happier than she could remember being. But she missed Reid. Missed him desperately. Unfortunately, that was a bridge that had burned down with his camp.

The newspaper and Internet had carried accounts of the camp's destruction. Nothing specific, only that it was closed down now and that the owner was making no comment about its future. No injuries had been reported from the camp, none from the forest fire either. It had started with a campfire in an unauthorized area. One single, lousy campfire and she'd lost countless hours sleep because she missed Reid, missed the camp, missed his daughters, missed all the things she hadn't known she'd wanted until it was too late.

"After work, we're going to go do some shopping, maybe buy a pizza for dinner," she told Megan. She was surprised a child so young would love pizza the way Megan did, but the child begged for it practically every day. "And tomorrow, when I'm not working—" and blessedly not on call "—we'll go to the zoo. You'll get to see lions and elephants and zebras. Do you know what a zebra is, Megan?"

"No," the girl said.

"Then after you're dressed, how about we find a picture on the Internet?"

"Is it purple?" she asked. Like she'd discovered Megan's

favorite food was pizza, she'd also discovered her favorite color, and had even had a decorator come in and redo the guest room in little-girl decor, predominantly purple.

"No, sweetie. It's black and white, with crazy stripes."

"Crazy stripes," Megan parroted.

"A whole bunch of them." She helped Megan put on her own socks then put on her shoes and tied them. Purple shoes, pink socks. Pink was a definite concession in a purple girl's life. The thing was it was amazing to see how many opinions Megan had. Until she'd brought her home, Keera had had no clue a child so young had preferences and opinions, and, boy, had she been wrong about that.

Little Miss Megan, once she became comfortable in her new surroundings, was all opinion and preference. So much so that in an adult it might have been annoying. But in a two-year-old it was as cute as could be. Which officially put her in the category of moms prejudiced by the cuteness of their children—to the point of near-blindness.

But that was OK. This new life was agreeing with her.

What wasn't agreeing with her, though, were her feelings for Reid. They hadn't talked since that day, which was kind of surprising. In fact, for the first week she'd answered her phone with lightning speed, expecting him to call. The second week—not so much. And now, unless it was work related she didn't bother picking up because another call that wasn't him only punctuated how much she missed him. "I'd have thought he would have called to see if we made it home safely."

The timeline for that call was well past now. And she knew it, felt it in her heart and in the pit of her stomach. She'd made her impression, the one she'd intended to make, and was now suffering the consequences. Her fault entirely, and she didn't blame him for that. Only she wished she'd had time to change his mind.

Now he was back in his practice and picking up what was left over from his dream, and she wasn't part of that. And she couldn't be because he didn't want her. Had declined her phone calls the first few days after their break-up.

Break-up? From what? One night together and a whole bunch of conflicting feelings? How could they have broken up when they'd had nothing to break up from?

"Then after the zoo, maybe we'll go to the bookstore as you don't have enough books, and all little girls need lots and lots of books and bedtime stories." To tell the truth, Keera was looking forward to the bedtime stories maybe even more than Megan was. That's what surprised her. As she settled in with the child, it was like she was experiencing childhood again, a better childhood. The childhood she would have liked for herself.

And somewhere, an hour away, Reid was doing the same with his daughters. In a way it was comforting, knowing they were sharing the same experience under the same sky. But in an even bigger way it was heart-breaking because she'd gone and done the one thing she'd vowed never to do. She'd fallen in love. Only not the way she'd fallen in love the first time. This time it was different. Real. Everything. And everything she couldn't have.

"These are the clothes you're going to have to wear. I'm sorry you lost everything you bought with Keera, but I left them behind and saved the computers instead." He knew, for sure, that he couldn't duplicate Keera's effort, not in clothes, not in the girls' sentiments, and he felt bad about that.

Felt bad about a lot of things, like how Emmie and Allie had begged for weeks to have her take them shopping again. Once he'd almost given in and called her. But one call and he'd lose his resolve. And Keera Murphy wasn't the kind of woman he wanted around his daughters because they got attached, and Keera was incapable of attaching back.

Sadly, he'd gotten himself pretty attached as well. And while there was a part of him that wanted to believe her efforts to save his camp had been genuine, how could he truly believe that when she'd expressed her sentiment clearly, over and over? She didn't want children, and she did want him to adopt the one she had.

"But for now you're going to have to make do."

"But, Daddy," Emmie whined.

He shook his head. "You know what I told you. That for a little while we've got to watch our money. I've got a lot of expenses ahead, and I can't afford..."

Who was he kidding? What he couldn't afford was to have his heart ripped all the way through. It was hanging in tatters as it was. Seeing Keera again would only finish the job. "Work with me here, OK? As soon as I get some of the mess at Camp Hope sorted out, we'll have a shopping day and you can buy whatever you want. But that's going to have to wait for a few weeks." Until he had more time, more energy, more hope.

It was hard hanging on, not just for him but for the girls. Especially when all he owned was some charred acreage and a few remains of buildings. And who would have known there was so much to do in the aftermath of a disaster? Insurance claims, getting the unsafe structures leveled, permits for the work, planners and architects for the camp's future.

During the day, when he was busy, he was optimistic. But the nights were what got to him, when memories of that one perfect night with Keera crept back in spite of his best efforts to keep them out. Then from there, the losses.

Too much, too many. He couldn't sleep. Couldn't let the girls see how much he was struggling because they depended on him to be strong. To be Daddy.

"How about a date tomorrow? We'll have ice cream, maybe go to the park or see a movie? How does that sound?"

"OK," Emmie said, her voice definitely lacking enthusiasm.

"OK," Allie mimicked, in the same voice.

One thing was sure, next time a woman walked into his life he wasn't going to bring her around the girls for any reason until everything in the relationship was sorted out and there was a future involved. Because the girls missed Keera, talked about her every day, begged him to get her back.

Something he couldn't do. But something he would if he could. And wanted to so badly.

CHAPTER TEN

"LAST NIGHT, DADDY," Allie said, her eyes filling with tears. "She didn't want me to tell you. Made me promise, cross my heart."

Reid placed his hand on Emmie's forehead. She was burning up. Practically incoherent. Pale. Sweating. He'd seen this before, last time... Except she was having associated abdominal pain now. So maybe it wasn't another flare-up of leukemia. "That's OK, sweetheart. You're not in trouble."

"Is Emmie sick again?" Allie's bottom lip trembled. "Like last time?"

"She's sick, but not like last time," he said, trying to sound upbeat for both his girls' sakes. Truth was, he didn't know. He hoped, and his objectivity as a doctor told him the symptoms didn't quite match. But as a father, all his worst fears were pummeling him.

"Is it back, Daddy?" Emmie managed to ask. "Did my leukemia come back again?"

"It might be something you ate, as your belly hurts." Or appendicitis. Yes, that's what it was. Appendicitis, which opened up a whole new set of worries, because a quick appendectomy was complicated in the aftermath of leukemia. "I think, though, we're going to have to take you to the hospital and have some tests run to see what it is."

He turned to Beau Alexander, who was already on the phone to the hospital. "If you don't mind, I'd like Joey to fly me. Don't want to waste time in the car."

"He's already fueling up the chopper," Beau said, squeezing his partner on the shoulder.

"Oh, and I have a surgeon on standby, just in case. She's not a general surgeon, but she's agreed to step in and offer an opinion, and she's getting the best general surgeon she knows rounded up, in case we need to go that route."

"Which hospital?"

"Not Mercy. And before you argue with me that you'd feel more comfortable taking Emmie where she's gone before, let me say that you've been moping around here for the past month, and all I've heard is how great Keera is, what a good doctor, good surgeon she is. So I called her, and she's taking care of getting everything ready to receive Emmie at Central Valley. By air, it's only fifteen minutes longer, and I think that right now you're going to need her support."

"And we'll watch Allie, of course. For as long as this takes," Deanna, his wife volunteered.

"I'll step up, too," Brax Alexander, the patriarch of the Alexander family, said. "Can't claim to be a pediatrician but I have my way with the kiddies, so I'll take on your cases until you're ready to get back to work. So there's nothing to worry about here, son. We've got you covered."

Reid let out a huge sigh of relief. He hadn't only become part of a medical practice here in Sugar Creek. He'd become part of a family. "I really appreciate everything."

"You just get that little girl all better and get her back to us as fast as you can," Brax said.

"And patch it up with Keera," Beau said, sliding his arm around his wife's waist. "It's time for you to be happy."

But with Keera? "We'll see," he said as he gave Allie

a kiss, then scooped Emmie into his arms and headed to the front door. Truth was, there wasn't much to be happy about and he wasn't sure he could even fake it, not now that Emmie was sick. If it was leukemia again he'd have to find a way to be strong. If it was appendicitis then maybe having Keera there, making the arrangements, would help. He didn't know. Just didn't know.

The trip was far faster than he'd expected, and he never set Emmie down the whole way. No, he held on to her for dear life, and when Joey landed the helicopter on the hospital's helipad, and when an army of medics rushed and took Emmie away from him, he couldn't think of a time when he'd felt more desolate.

"They'll take good care of her," Keera said, stepping up behind him as the chopper lifted skywards and headed back to Sugar Creek. "I got Wade Andrews, head of oncology and our leukemia specialist, to take charge of her team, and lined up Annabelle Gentry, the best general surgeon I know, in case it's her appendix. Oh, and Brett Hollingsworth, head of Pediatrics, is on his way in to oversee her general care while she's here. I've got her set up in a private room in Pediatrics, and had a bed brought in for you so you can stay."

"I don't know what to say, Keera."

"You don't have to say anything. This is about Emmie, and you know how I feel about her and Allie."

"They've missed you," he said, as she slipped her hand into his and pulled him towards the hospital door.

"I've missed them. You don't know how much I enjoyed our girls' day out. It was a first for me, and it made me realize how much I missed when I was that age. Also how much I like…" she smiled "…being around children."

"See, I told you so."

"Yes, you did, and we'll talk about that later on. Right now, though, tell me about Emmie."

"I didn't know she was sick. Apparently she hasn't felt well for a couple of days—general malaise, vomiting, which she never told me about, achiness, tender belly, feverish. Allie knew, but the girls conspired to keep it a secret because they were afraid if they told me, that would make it be leukemia again."

"We all have ways of deluding ourselves, don't we? Even when we're young, I suppose. Oh, and Allie called me a little while ago."

"Allie?"

"Yep, Allie. She didn't want to talk to you because she was afraid it would make you sad, so she called me. Had Brax dial for her."

"He's a pushover when it comes to kids. Can't ever say no to them."

"Well, he didn't say no to Allie and, Reid, what she said was so sweet. She told me if Emmie is sick like she was before, she wants to be the donor. Actually, she called it a door—near, but I knew what she meant."

"I—I… Twice in a row, I don't know what to say."

"You don't have to. I'll say it for you. You're an amazing father, and you've taught your daughters to be generous." As they stepped into the hospital, they headed straight to Pediatrics, where the team Keera had assembled was fast-working on Emmie. Blood was being drawn, X-rays being taken. Pokes, prods, IV, oxygen, all the usual.

"We're going to get her through this. Whatever it is, I promise, we're going to get her, get both of you, through this."

Reid swallowed hard, looking through the window of the procedure room. "The camp burned to the ground," he said.

"I know. I read the accounts. I'm so sorry."

"Emmie's been helping me with the plans to rebuild. I think I may have a budding architect, because the architect I've hired is actually going to incorporate some of her ideas. He said a kids' camp from a kid's perspective is what I need, and he told her that when she grows up to keep him in mind when she's looking for a..." He slapped a tear from his cheek. "I feel so damned helpless. Done this twice before, I don't know if I can do it again."

Keera stepped up behind him and slid her arm around his waist. "We may not have worked out as a couple, Reid, but I'm your friend, and I'm not going to let you go through this alone. Whatever you and Emmie need, whenever you need it, you don't even have to ask."

"I know," he said. "And I'm sorry. You don't know how much I wanted to answer your calls or call you. Or just come here and see you. Every day, Keera. Every single day of every single week since that day when you walked away from me."

"You were right, though. I didn't give you anything to trust. I was adamant about who I was and what I wanted, and there was no room inside that for us. But it did hurt, Reid, hearing how you believed that my wanting to help you with the camp was me trying to manipulate you. You had a right to that opinion, and everything I'd said or done was responsible for that opinion, and I wasn't even angry at you. It hurt, but I understood."

"Dr. Adams," Dr. Hollingsworth said, stepping out into the hall. "Emmie's pretty sick, but we're not sure yet what's causing it. We've got the first round of tests started, and what I'm proposing, because of her past history, is that we put her in the ICU for close observation until we start getting things sorted out. Might be for a few hours, might be for a few days, until we have everything worked up."

"You don't think she needs her appendix out?"

"There's a possibility but, given her history, we're reluctant to look at that as our first course of action as she's got several swollen lymph glands."

Reid nodded. "I did notice that when I examined her, which is why my first thought was…"

"A recurrence of her leukemia," Dr. Hollingsworth said. "And if Emmie was mine, I'd be thinking the same thing. But Keera said she's been active, not feeling bad."

"I asked Beau when he called me earlier," Keera explained.

"That's right. She was fine. A little tired the past couple of days but before that she was energetic as all get-out."

"In my experience, leukemia doesn't just take you down from being healthy and active one minute to where she is now. So, while we're not going to rule it out, we are looking for other causes. And make no mistake, she's a very sick little girl. But we're optimistic. In the meantime, it's going to take us about an hour to get her transferred to her ICU bed, so the doctors' lounge is available if you'd like to go and wait. And our cafeteria is open around the clock in case you want to grab something to eat. I'll page Keera as soon as we get Emmie situated, then you can come and see her."

"I appreciate it," Reid said, extending his hand to the man.

"Oh, and that camp of yours. I've heard good things. Hope you can get it up and running again because I have a couple of patients who could benefit, and I could be up for a little volunteering myself."

"Working on it," Reid said numbly, because numb was all he felt. Numb, but not alone.

"Are you sure I can't get you something?" Keera asked as they shut the door to the private room that would be Emmie's once she was out of Intensive Care. "Coffee, tea, a soft drink?"

She felt totally helpless because there truly was nothing she could do to help him except stay with him. And that wasn't helping, at least not in the way he needed.

"Thanks, but I'm good."

"You're going to have to keep yourself going for Emmie's sake. You know that, don't you?"

"Is this my pep talk?" he snapped.

"No, it's your reality check. I know you're scared, and I wish I knew what to do to make that better for you but other than being here, trying to take care of you, I can't."

"That's right. Keera the nurturer."

"That's not fair, Reid. And I know you're snapping at me because of Emmie. But I always knew my limitations, and was honest about them. So, please, don't take it out on me now, because I do want to help you."

"I know," he said, sitting down on the side of the guest bed. "And I'm sorry. It's been a horrible few weeks, thinking about everything I did wrong. Then with all the arrangements concerning the camp...now this." He looked up at her. "You didn't deserve what I said about you that day, and you don't deserve it now. I am sorry, Keera. Truly, sorry. Please, believe that."

"I do," she said gently. Then chuckled. "Oil and water. That's us, isn't it?"

He patted the bed, inviting her to sit down next to him. When she did, he pulled her into his arms and simply held her. "Not really. I seem to recall a pretty good mixing."

"We were good, weren't we? And in more ways than *that*."

"In more ways than *that*. But *that* was pretty spectacular."

"Look, Reid. When this is over, when Emmie's back on

her feet and all cured of whatever it is she's caught, and I'm going to believe she caught a bug of some kind until someone tells me otherwise, well, anyway, when it's over, I really do want to help get the camp going again. I've been thinking about it for weeks, wondering what I could do that wouldn't pit us against each other, for starters. So I've decided to rebuild the clinic for you, if you'll let me. Make it a real clinic, though. Not just a make-do cabin. Furnish it with everything you need rather than all the odds and ends, like you had. Will you let me do that for you?"

"Insurance money isn't stretching far enough to get me everything I need. I was on the verge of committing to another make-do clinic simply to get it up and running."

"But I want to do better for the kids." She pulled away from him and looked straight into his eyes. "And I'd like to help with the actual building, as in setting up the interior, if you'll let me. But if you don't think we can work together again, I'll write you a check for whatever you need."

"That's generous. For the third time tonight I don't know what to say."

"Say yes. It's a simple word, and the beginning of something that will be so good."

"The thing is, if Emmie's leukemia has come back, I don't know if I can go through with plans to rebuild. Not now, anyway. Maybe not for a long time to come."

"Then let me take over. You take care of Emmie, and I'll make sure your camp plans go forward."

"Why do you want to do this?" he asked. "Especially after the way I treated you last time you made the offer to help."

"Because I believe now. Believe better, believe differently. And it's also because—" Her cellphone interrupted her, and five seconds later she jumped up from the side of the bed. "Got to leave for a couple of minutes. Be right back."

It was time to visit Megan. She was going through one of her sullen periods, which happened when she missed Keera. And only Keera could take care of fixing it.

"I'm here, sweetheart," she said, picking up the girl, who instantly clung to Keera for dear life.

"She has a real attachment thing going," Dolores, the daycare worker, said. "Kept telling me she wanted her mommy."

"I know she does." But there was no mommy to be had.

"That's you, Doctor. You're mommy to her, no matter what the circumstances. You're the one she wants now."

Keera smiled, not sure what to do. Her initial fears of not being able to manage this were gone. So were her fears about her lack of natural instinct, because she did have her common sense intact. And as far as Megan being Kevin's child, it didn't matter any more. He'd done a good thing bringing this child into the world, and she wasn't a reminder of anything except she was a little girl who needed a real mommy or daddy. "Look, I'm going to keep her with me for a little while. When she gets over this, I may bring her back."

Or she might just beg off the surgical rotation for the morning—she only had one minor procedure scheduled—and ask one of her associates to take it. Then she could stay with Reid and keep Megan comforted as well. For someone who wasn't a nurturer, she seemed to being doing an awful lot of that lately. "I'll call you or whoever's on duty later on and let you know what we're going to do. And in the meantime, I think Miss Megan and I might go down to the cafeteria and find us a banana and yogurt for breakfast. Does that sound yummy to you, Megan?"

With her head tucked as tight as it could be into Keera's

chest, Megan gave her a nod. "Then afterwards we're going to go visit Doc Reid. Do you remember him? He's the nice man who took care of you when you had measles."

She nodded again.

"Oh, by the way," Dolores said as Keera left. "Social services called here yesterday, looking for you. I didn't take the call but I saw the note and wasn't sure if the message got to you or not."

"It didn't," she said, as a lump formed in her stomach, realizing the very best news for Megan could be the very worst news for her.

"Well, you're supposed to call your caseworker as soon as you can. She said it's important but not urgent."

Keera nodded reluctantly, now facing a reality she wasn't sure she wanted to face. "Later. If she calls back, tell her I've got a crisis here at the hospital but I'll get back to her later."

After a quick trip to the cafeteria, then with yogurt, milk, a banana, and a couple of coffees in hand, not to mention a toddler, Keera hurried back up to Reid's room, stopped in her progress by Brett Hollingsworth, who asked her to tell Reid that Emmie was being moved to the ICU right then.

"You've sure turned...well, I guess the only way to describe it is domestic. Just look at you, here in Pediatrics with your child, comforting a worried father, taking on the role of camp counselor."

"Wrong on all counts but one. I am comforting a worried father, because he's my friend. There's nothing domestic involved in that."

"I've heard rumors coming from daycare that you try to get down there to group-sing every day." He grinned. "You know, 'The wheels on the bus go round...'"

"Yeah, yeah," Keera said, shoving past him and hurrying on to the room.

"I'm just saying," Brett called after her.

She ignored him as she pushed open the door, scooted Megan in first, then followed.

"What's this?" Reid asked.

"It's what I do in my spare time now."

"You kept her?"

"Temporarily, which I think may be coming to an end shortly. I mean, when she was sick I promised her I wouldn't let them take her to one of *those* places, and I meant it. I was there, raised in them, and there's no way they're going to do that to her. So I've been managing."

"I'm not surprised," he said, rushing over to take the food and coffee from her. "It's what I saw in you all along."

"No, you didn't. You wanted to, but it wasn't there."

"Yet look at you now."

"Someone else just said that to me," she said, pulling the bedside tray away from the wall and pushing it over to one of the chairs. "And I told him he was wrong." But not as wrong as he once might have been.

"See, there you go again."

She shrugged. "OK, so maybe I'm not as bad at this as I thought I'd be. But I'm still a darned sight further away from parent of the year than you are. Speaking of which, Emmie's being transferred right now, and they should be coming to get you in the next few minutes, once she's settled in."

"You're efficient, Keera."

"Words to turn a girl's heart."

He laughed. "What if I also told you that efficient is sexy?"

"Then I'd nominate you for man of the year." She opened the carton of yogurt and handed a plastic spoon to Megan, who dug right in. "Because most men have other standards for sexy, if you know what I mean. So it's nice to hear that something substantial like being efficient can also be sexy."

"Oh, don't get me wrong. I have the same standards as other men, as far as sexy goes. And you've got all that. But you've got more."

She laughed. "See, now the truth comes out."

A knock on the door startled them both, and a nurse poked her head in the door to tell Reid that he could see Emmie now.

"Give her a hug for me," Keera said, "and tell her I'll come by to see her later on."

"Ten minutes every hour," the nurse warned Reid, as he headed for the door. "Wish we could do better as you're a pediatrician, but I can't. Sorry."

"Then I'll see you back here in twelve minutes," Keera said, and turned her attention to breaking the banana into bite-sized pieces for Megan. Then she dialed the dreaded phone number.

"Hi, Consuela," she said, when the woman on the other end picked up. "It's Keera Murphy, and I understand you've been trying to get a hold of me."

"Hello," Reid said very quietly, as he stood over Emmie's bed and looked down. Even though it was a pediatric ward, she looked so dwarfed—by the bed, by the equipment. It was something he remembered from last time, staring at all the hugeness surrounding his little girl. In ways only a parent could understand, it intimidated him, scared him to death. But he couldn't let on—for Emmie's sake, even for his own.

"Did it come back, Daddy?" she asked weakly.

"We don't know anything yet. But soon, I promise."

"I'm so tired."

"I know you are, which is why you're in here. So you can sleep. That's the only thing you have to do now. Just sleep."

"What about your patients? Who's going to take care of them?"

"That's not for you to worry about," he said, pushing the hair from her eyes. "It's all taken care of. Brax is going to see my patients, and Beau and Deanna are watching Allie, so there's nothing to be concerned about."

"Can I see Keera? I want to tell her how all those clothes we bought got burned up. Do you think she'll take me shopping again?"

"Keera's taking care of Megan right now, but she said she'd come and see you soon. Why don't you ask her yourself if you can go shopping? I think she might…" He didn't finish his sentence. Didn't have to, as Emmie had fallen back to sleep.

"How is she?" Keera asked.

"Worried that all those clothes you bought her got burned up. She wants to go shopping again."

"And I'd love to take her again. Her and Allie, and…" She paused. Frowned.

"What's the matter?"

"I got a call from Megan's social worker," she whispered, so Megan wouldn't hear. "They've found a couple who might want to adopt her. She wants to schedule a first meeting between Megan and them."

"That's good, isn't it?"

She shrugged. "It's what I wanted, initially. No, actually, what I wanted was for you to adopt her. I told you that."

"But it didn't work out."

"And now…" Tears suddenly filled her eyes. "Now it's too late."

"But she'll have a permanent home, Keera. That's what's best for her. And I'm sure the social worker was very choosy in picking out the right parents."

"She does need parents, doesn't she?"

"Or parent. Single parenting has its rewards. If you want to keep her."

"I want to do what's best for her, and I've always known it was a home better than the one I could give her."

"Yet look at her. She's eating, perfectly contented to do it by herself. And she seems to be gaining some independence…some of your independence. That's good mothering, Keera, no matter what you want to call it. You're teaching her what she needs to know, pointing her in the direction she needs to go, and at the end of the day that's all a parent can really do besides love and protect them. So, what else did Consuela have to say?"

"I have to let her know by noon."

"That?"

"That I want to keep her myself—*if* I want to keep her."

"Are you thinking about it?"

"I don't know. Maybe. But I'm so confused. Because getting what I wanted—a home for Megan—doesn't feel as good as it should. It doesn't feel good at all."

"So, let me ask you this. Does Megan make your life better?"

"I know my life is different now, but in a good way. She gives me balance. And a purpose I didn't know I wanted, or could have."

"And you give her balance."

"But it's all a novelty right now, and that's what scares me. You know, it's like when you get a new toy and that's all you want to play with. Then eventually you get tired of it and totally ignore it."

"You think you'd get tired of Megan?" he asked.

"No, not Megan. But of the role of mothering. That's the novelty, and I'm enjoying the challenge and trying hard not to let my mother issues interfere—you know, trying to do the opposite of what my mother would do. You were right about that, Reid.

"I based a life not on what I wanted but on the opposite of what my mother would do. And I'm working hard to stop it. But I'm still at the point where it's a conscious effort."

"That will come naturally in due course, the way your feelings for Megan have come naturally."

"I do love her."

"Then adopt her. Simple as that."

Keera glanced over at the child, who'd managed to smear her strawberry yogurt from ear to ear. It was like she was wearing a pink beard. So cute, so innocent.

"I want to." She swiped at the tears beginning to roll down her cheeks. Great, fat droplets of grief that were ripping through her soul for so many things. "But is love enough?"

"Love's enough, Keera. Trust me, no matter what else happens, love is what gets you through. Loving Megan is enough. It's where it starts, and everything else builds from there. So now it's time to trust yourself. You're not the wounded little girl any more. You're the woman who has the opportunity to care for another wounded little girl. You'll make her life better, the way she'll make your life better. And I'm speaking from experience on that one."

"This isn't easy, Reid," she said, swatting at her tears and sniffling.

"The right decisions seldom are easy." He pulled her into his arms. "Weeks ago I met this stubborn, opinionated woman who didn't like kids. At least, not in the sense that she wanted to deal with them on a day-to-day basis. Now look at her, raising one, loving one, her heart breaking over one. I don't think it's a tough decision. In fact, I think it may be the easiest decision you'll ever make."

He pulled his cellphone from his pocket and handed it to her. "Make the call. You'll never forgive yourself if you don't."

Taking the phone from his hand, she nodded and swallowed hard. "I still think you'd make the better parent," she said, then dialed Consuela.

"Dr. Adams," Brett Hollingsworth said from the door, "could I speak to you privately in the hall?"

Keera reached out and squeezed his hand as she waited for her call to go through. "Want me to come with you?" she asked.

"I'm fine. And I'll feel better after I know you got through to Consuela."

"Thanks, Reid," she said, as he turned and walked away.

His response was a lackluster nod to accompany his slumped shoulders, and she wished to heaven she could make the walk with him, but she couldn't. She knew that. And her heart hurt so badly for him she could barely talk when Consuela came on the line.

"Well, the good news is it's not her appendix. Nothing in her blood work indicates she's having a recurrence of her leukemia either."

Finally, Reid let go of the breath he'd been holding. "Then what is it?"

"We think it's mesenteric adenitis." An inflammatory condition that often resulted from general weakening in cancers associated with the lymph system. "Not sure yet, because we're ruling out other things. But the lymphs in her belly are swollen. Combine that with her nausea and vomiting, her lack of appetite, the malaise, fever, and she's been complaining of a headache—all pretty classic symptoms."

"Could she have picked up a virus that caused it?"

"My best guess right now would be yes. Maybe something as simple as stomach flu. It's all interrelated with her leukemia, and not all that uncommon."

"I—I don't know what to say. I mean, that's good news. No, it's great news!"

"What's great news?" Keera said, walking up behind him.

"Mesenteric adenitis."

"Whoa, that's an offbeat kind of diagnosis." She smiled. "But a good one. And it makes sense."

"Well, I still want to do the imaging," Brett continued, "but we've ruled out appendicitis as well as leukemia."

Keera slipped her hand into Reid's. "So do the imaging. STAT," she said happily.

"Already ordered," he said. "Just wanted Dr. Adams to know what we're thinking right now."

"I'm thinking I was too involved to even consider..." Reid shut his eyes, drew in a deep breath. "Whatever consents you'll need, you know you've got them."

"What I want to do is let her sleep the next few hours then see if we can get the imaging in late afternoon, early evening. In the meantime, get her started on fluid and electrolyte replacement, and an anti-inflammatory. Then treat other symptoms as they arise and keep our fingers crossed that we caught this early enough that no other symptoms will come up. Oh, and I do want to watch her overnight in the ICU, but by morning I think she'll be stable enough to transfer to the floor."

"I don't know what to say," Reid said.

"For, what, the third or fourth time today?" Keera teased.

Brett punched him on the shoulder. "Well, I say go get some sleep. You look like hell and in a few hours I think your little girl's going to feel better than you do."

"Thank you," Reid said, as Brett walked away.

"Don't thank me. Thank Keera. She's the one who dragged us all down here in the middle of the night and kept pushing us to find the problem."

"Thank you," he whispered, bending to kiss her on the lips.

"He's right, you know. You do look worse than Emmie does."

"That's what parenthood does to you sometimes."

"Guess I'm about to find out," she said.

"Really? It going to happen?"

"It's going to happen. I'm going to adopt her."

Suddenly Reid pulled her into his arms and the kiss he gave her was neither circumspect nor proper for a hospital corridor, but he didn't care because everything was right in his world. More than right. Everything was perfect.

"Well, Brax has Megan and Emmie down at the stable looking at the new foal, and Deanna and Beau took Allie, along with their kids, Lucas and Emily, to go get ice cream. So we're finally alone. At long last."

"It's a nice place. I can see why you love raising your girls here. I'm hoping Megan and I get some weekend invitations to come down every once in a while."

"See, that's the thing. I wasn't planning on weekend invitations. They're too disruptive."

She saw the twinkle in his eyes, didn't know what it meant. "So we're not invited?"

"That's the other thing. You are, but not in the way you expected."

"What are you trying to say, Reid? I'm not invited, but I am?"

"I was thinking like more in the permanent sense. And before you shoot me down, I know you vowed never to get married again, never have a serious relationship, whatever that nonsense was you kept dropping on me at camp. But that was then, and you're a mom now who needs a dad for her daughter. And I'm a dad who needs a mom for my daughters."

"What about the other part?"

"Which part?"

"Where you're a man who needs a wife for himself? Because the rest are good reasons, but that's the best one. That, and the one where I love you more than I can even tell you. For me it was love at first sight. Or else I would have shoved Megan in your arms and gotten the heck out of there. But when you opened the door…" She shook her head.

"You had me at the door, Doc Adams, and I really didn't want to be had. Although deep down I knew I did, even though I didn't think I could ever be what you needed."

"You were, Keera. I needed to make you see who you really were, though. Who you really are. Really can be. So, can you do this? Because I don't want you making all the compromises while I sit here and do nothing. You're going to get two other children in the deal, and that's a huge compromise, because they want you to be their real mommy."

"I'm not compromising a thing because I want to be their real mommy. I love those girls, Reid. Yours, mine… *ours*. But you do have to understand that I'm the one who needs to make the biggest change. For the first time in my life, though, I want to. Because I need to. There's nothing else that will ever make me complete the way you and the girls do. And it scares me how much I'll need your help in this. Maybe every day for the rest of my life. But I want to make the change. Walk away from everything I was and walk towards everything I want to be. As long as you know exactly what you're getting."

"Oh, I know. And, seriously, all your aversions to children, family and marriage scared me for a while, or else I would have proposed maybe the day after I met you. Which was when I think I fell in love with you. Or maybe it was at first sight. I'm still a little foggy on that. The thing is, I saw through you pretty quickly. Saw how much you were trying to hide, or hide behind. And always fighting to prove you were tough, and impervious to the world. Except you weren't, and I knew that."

"Your camp changed me, your girls changed me, Megan changed me. Most of all, you changed me. Made me realize I can have the things I thought I never could. The worst thing anyone could ever know about me is what you know, and it doesn't matter to you."

"Because everything you were in the past turned you into the woman I love today."

"My past isn't over, though. You've got to understand that it may rear its ugly head from time to time. And you may see that stubborn streak come back as well. That's part of who I am."

"Only a small part. And we'll face it together if it does peek in every now and then. No big deal."

"Easy for you to say."

"Easy for me to know, because I know you."

"And I know you."

"But can you be a country GP, give up your surgical practice and settle down to the kind of life we have here? Because we're a very family-centered practice, and our families always come first, no matter what. Which might be a little difficult for you—"

"Not difficult," she interrupted. "Although I still want to keep my surgical practice, just limit it to maybe a couple days a week. An easy flight to Central Valley if the man you're married to is a pilot."

"Married sounds good, doesn't it?"

"Very good. Because for once in my life I think I'll be able to relax, breathe, just enjoy life. And with three daughters to raise, and take shopping!"

"About that shopping, and your choice of clothes for them…"

"What's wrong with my choice of clothes?" she asked.

"Not traditional. Just saying."

"Just saying you think I'm not traditional? Hey, Doc! We've got an hour to kill before anybody misses us. What do you say to going over to your place so I can show you exactly how untraditional the rest of your life is going to be?"

He reached for Keera's hand, then when he had it pulled her roughly into his embrace. "What do you say about going over to *our* place so we can do we do just that?"

* * * * *

17/05